PUNK LIKE ME

What Reviewers Say About BOLD STROKES Authors

KIM BALDWIN

"*A riveting novel of suspense* seems to be a very overworked phrase. However, it is extremely apt when discussing Kim Baldwin's [*Hunter's Pursuit*]. An exciting page turner [features] Katarzyna Demetrious, a bounty hunter…with a million dollar price on her head. Look for this excellent novel of suspense…" – **R. Lynne Watson**, *MegaScene*

ROSE BEECHAM

"…her characters seem fully capable of walking away from the particulars of whodunit and engaging the reader in other aspects of their lives." – *Lambda Book Report*

GUN BROOKE

"*Course of Action* is a romance…populated with a host of captivating and amiable characters. The glimpses into the lifestyles of the rich and beautiful people are rather like guilty pleasures.…[A] most satisfying and entertaining reading experience." – **Arlene Germain**, reviewer for the *Lambda Book Report* and the *Midwest Book Review*

JANE FLETCHER

"*The Walls of Westernfort* is not only a highly engaging and fast-paced adventure novel, it provides the reader with an interesting framework for examining the same questions of loyalty, faith, family and love that [the characters] must face." – **M. J. Lowe**, *Midwest Book Review*

RADCLYfFE

"…well-honed storytelling skills…solid prose and sure-handedness of the narrative…" – **Elizabeth Flynn**, *Lambda Book Report*

"…well-plotted…lovely romance...I couldn't turn the pages fast enough!" – **Ann Bannon**, author of *The Beebo Brinker Chronicles*

Visit us at www.boldstrokesbooks.com

PUNK LIKE ME

by

JD GLASS

2006

PUNK LIKE ME
© 2006 By JD Glass. All Rights Reserved.

ISBN 1-933110-40-6

This Trade Paperback Original Is Published By
Bold Strokes Books, Inc.,
New York, USA

First Edition: Justice House Publishing 2004
Second Edition: Bold Strokes Books 2006

Library of Congress Control Number: 2005939244

Credits
Editors: Shelley Thrasher and Stacia Seaman
Production Design: Stacia Seaman
Cover Photo by Emma Sheahan Harmon
Cover Design By Sheri (GRAPHICARTIST2020@HOTMAIL.COM)

Acknowledgments

I want to publicly thank my beautiful Shane for putting up with me and the long hours of "Huh? Oh yeah, I heard you...um...could you repeat that?" and supplying me with tea, chicken soup, and dinner so that I wouldn't have to leave my keyboard. Cousin Heather, I would have never walked this road if it weren't for you—I owe you. Ah, music, and the people who play it...yes. Thanks. For everything I'll ever be. I'd also like to thank Shelley for showing me that editing could be fun and of course Radclyffe, for her enthusiastic support.

Dedication

For all of us who've been there
and keep it going on

Chapter One:
Start It Up!

Yeah, okay, I come off as tough, and I like that. I'm only about five foot seven inches, but I know how to handle myself in just about any situation, and if not, I know where to find backup.

I'm Nina, and I write the lyrics and guitar for Adam's Rib, even though Stephie, my bud, does most of the lead vocals. 'Sokay with me, I don't worry much about it.

Like I told you before, I'm not too tall and I'm not too short. I like to keep in shape, so I dance and do martial arts and stuff—healthy in wind and limb, just like they say about horses.

My hair's black—well, okay, it's really red-brown, but I make it shiny raven black, and I've got a bloodred streak running down the center length of it.

I'm not just any old punk; I've got to be myself. My hair is long, and I mean really long, down the back and top. I've got the sides shaved (to the skin, yeah!) to the top of my ears. Then it's a straight-up tight buzz for about another two inches before we hit the top where it runs down my back. I love the smooth skin, I love the fuzz, and I love the don't-fuck-with-me attitude I give with this mop.

I might sound like an egomaniac and that's okay—I'm not one really. It's just that I really, really like my hair—and I'm not the first to ever feel like that.

My eyes are blue, though they can look a little gray sometimes, and my mom used to tell me that I have a nice smile, but moms are supposed to say things like that, as well as other things such as, "When are you going to settle down?" or "That's not a real job," and "I could introduce you to this nice young man…" Okay, there, time to tune that one out.

Yeah, let me get this over with right now. I'm gay. Not confused, not experimenting, not bi (although I think Keanu Reeves is great), and not a phase. Gay. *Gee-aye-wye*. If that's a problem, get out now, 'cuz I don't deal with 'phobes too well.

In case you were wondering, I don't have a "type." What attracts me to someone is a very individual thing, so I might date a short brunette or a tall blonde or whatever. It's really about personality for me, the tilt of the head, tone of voice, you know, stuff like that. But—and this is a secret between you and me—green eyes kill me.

So help me, I'm fascinated; I just can't help it. Present me with someone with green eyes, and I mean deep, dark forest green, not light new grass, and I can get lost looking at them, looking into them, trying to find, well, I don't know. But it's my fatal flaw.

Good thing they're sort of rare, right?

So here we are, the four of us, hanging out and getting ready to play our first real gig. Stephie looks like she's ready to puke, and I have to stop the Jerkster, also known as Jeremy, also our bassist, from sucking down any more beers before he actually pukes on the stage.

Not that it would hurt the stage, though. There are burn spots, holes, and dried splotches of what could be anything from booze to blood on the nasty green carpet that covers the back half of the stage. My brother and some of our friends are taking bets as to whether or not the wood is stained with blood or dirt, although a faction is guessing roach carcasses.

There's something about being at CBGB's that makes you want to shake your head in wonder—and the rest of you in fear.

Now if you've never heard of CBGB's, which is located at 315 Bowery Place right on the edge of the East Village (and that's New York City, y'all), then you've never heard of rock 'n' roll, at least not here in the good ole US of A.

From Blondie, to Talking Heads, Joan Jett in her Runaways daze and the Police, John Mellencamp when he used to be John Cougar, Tom Petty, *and* the Indigo Girls, everyone has played there, stomped, sweated, dreamed, and poured it all out on that stage.

The scrawl of graffiti's everywhere—on the walls of the stage, the base of it, all along the stairwell, and, of course, every inch of the bathroom that isn't painted black, the rock 'n' roll version of hand- and footprints in cement—everyone leaving their mark.

You might have guessed by now (if you didn't know already) that CBGB's is sort of an icon in and of itself on the rock 'n' roll landscape, and it honestly never occurred to us that it's one hell of an arrogant thing to make this the site for the first infliction of our material on the public.

Tucked up against a wall off to the side of the stage, I finally get a chance to sit back and wait for a while with my friend, Trace—short for "Tracy," of course—who's coming on to me. This is a little unusual— not that she's coming on to someone, she's come on to lots and lots of people—it's just that she's coming on to *me*. Not that I really mind, of course—I know she's just showing off and I'm okay with that.

Trace is absolutely beautiful, tall and slender, almost elfin (but incredibly strong), with long wavy black hair and eyes the color of steel, a shade of gray like I've never seen before or since. I love her as a friend, and I think maybe a little something more, too. She has this incredible appeal for me, but Trace is scary, too, in a lot of ways, to a lot of people. Ask anyone.

When you're with her, Trace leaves you with the feeling that if she were a flame you'd be a suicidal moth, and pretty darn happy to burn, too.

Tonight, during my little break from Jerks—um, Jeremy—Trace is seducing me into one of those moments of torture and righteousness where you kick yourself later, sometimes years later, for being so good and darned noble. She knows, because she's been checking up on me for the last several hours, I've been a little achy and feverish all day (hey—the flu does not stop for gigs, and gigs do not stop for the flu. Them's the rules, and that's the way I play), and she's damned and determined to make me feel better—any way she can. Darn that chivalrous stuff, anyway!

I suppose I forgot to mention, Trace and I live together. No, not in that eternally bonded way, or even as roomies. I live in a three-floor brownstone apartment building, one apartment per floor. Two friends and I share the top floor, Trace lives on the second, and the mom of one of my roomies (a nice guy we call "Cap," short for "Captain," 'cuz he can be a little bossy, ya know?) lives on the first floor.

Since we're all pretty tight with one another, we have an open-door policy between the second and third floors (Cap's mom can't climb stairs very well—lucky for us), and it really is anyone's guess as to who'll stay where—third or second floor—on any given night. Okay, well, maybe that part only applies to me, but you get the idea. We're one big fucked-up family.

So, like I told you before, I'm sitting there, finally able to take a bit of a break before we go on stage for the first time, and Trace has decided to be Florence Nightingale and the Rock of Gibraltar simultaneously, with a very healthy, and I mean *very* healthy Mae West and Tallulah Bankhead thrown in.

Somehow, she has her arms around my shoulders, her legs wrapped over and around mine, and when I lean my head back against her shoulder because she's petting it, she strokes my neck oh so very lightly with her fingertips. "You okay, baby?" she's whispering into my ear, her voice a honeyed whiskey. Then she nuzzles baby-soft lips into my neck. That feels so amazingly good, I just groan in reply.

Suddenly, she grabs my hips with surprising strength of purpose and pulls me tightly against her just as she starts to nip, nibble, and lick the sensitive skin of my neck. I open my eyes in surprise. I'm tired and nervous and feverish, and I know my temperature's running high, because wherever Trace's body meets mine I burn, and everything else is lonely cold.

I close my eyes again. "Oh, what the hell," I think as I stretch my legs out farther along the bench, "might as well enjoy this while it lasts," and I settle my back into her warmth while I enjoy the patterns her lips have begun to leave on my throat.

Trace starts to massage my hip with one hand, while the other dangles between my thighs, sometimes resting on one, perilously close and not close enough to the restless situation she's creating in my already unstable body.

"Damn!" I hear Jerkster say to no one in particular. "We're not even on yet, and she's already got chicks all over her. How the hell does she do it?"

Nicky, I mean Nico (we'd all started calling him that in the last year), my younger and only brother, answers, "She's got some mojo. I don't even have to introduce my girlfriends to her—they all go for her right away."

Trace has got her tongue in my ear so it's kinda hard to think, but I just realized—this is definitely a far ways away from my last visit to CBGB's.

CHAPTER TWO:
YOU SAY IT'S YOUR BIRTHDAY

So the real story starts back when my best friend Kerry and I, and a whole slew of our friends, had gone to the Carter boys' annual "Everyone's Birthday in July" party right off the boardwalk in a place called South Beach, a popular destination for New York City dwellers in the forties and fifties, but now a semi-abandoned beach (except for the occasional National Parks people or whatever they are, who inspected it whenever a bonfire got too out of hand).

Now, at this point in life, I wasn't too tall, being just about five foot three inches as a junior in high school (yep, it's true, I was one of those late bloomers), and Kerry, with her dirty-blond hair and cat green eyes, was even shorter as a sophomore. In grammar school, she'd been Nicky's classmate, and of course I knew who she was and all that, but we weren't what you could call close.

Somewhere, though, between junior high and high school, we'd just started to click, and by freshman year we were an inseparable duo, despite the fact that she went to Tottenville, the local public high school, and I went to a place nicknamed "The Hill"—an all-girls' prep school run by nuns—that was great academically, but sucked socially. Freshmen had to take Latin *and* self-defense/judo, for Chrissakes. Hmm…maybe the judo was because of the uniform? I dunno. Besides, I'd figured out a loophole in the student handbook (yeah, we had one of those—and we had a test in it every year, too, just in case we forgot something or the nuns added something new). Anyway, I changed into jeans or army pants and my favorite pair of boots before I left school every day, so it wasn't really an issue for me anymore.

But still, the fact that I did better in judo than in Latin—not to mention my ability to find loopholes in that dumb rule book—might have been a good indication as to why I was always in trouble—so often, in fact, that I'd met my other best friend, Samantha, on one of the many afternoons when I was on detention that first year of high school. A year ahead of me, she became, among other things, my detention partner.

But I digress. Back to the party in South Beach, which, by the way, if you had good eyes, good binoculars, and an even better imagination you could see Coney Island from. This party was for the forty-some-odd percent of our friends who had July birth dates—it allowed us to have one massive gathering instead of having to coordinate and reschedule fifteen conflicting ones. Everyone, and I do mean everyone, brought something from dips to drinks, and we had plenty of everything. We also experimented making our own drink concoctions. At the annual Halloween party in the fall (and the first one I'd ever been to—Carter boys' party, that is), we'd made something we named the *Thing That Came and Stayed* because no matter how much of that Hi-C orange-colored stuff we drank, spilled, and were afraid to offer to the sea because of toxicity, it never disappeared. We finally used it to put out the bonfire in the backyard.

The beach party was no different. The fire was lit, the *Son of Thing That Came and Stayed* was born (purple Hi-C this time), and we were dancing and laughing 'round the fire to "Planet Claire" and "Rock Lobster" by the B-52s.

Now you might be surprised, all those kids and alcohol (together again, film at eleven!), but ya know, none of us did drugs then (me and Nicky never will, knock wood), and there was only one guy who took it too far. Even though his name was Rob, we called him "Chuck" or "Yack," not only to prevent confusion with Robbie from the comic book store Universe where we all hung out (and they were cousins, by the by) but because it was also the level he drank to. But we were too young to know he had a problem, and our ride home was dryer than twelve days in the Sahara and keeping it that way so he could shove sixteen of us—no joke—into a '76 Dodge Dart.

The weather was warm, the sky was clear, and our blood was filled with wild, wild joy.

I had invited Samantha to the party, along with Nicky, Kerry, and me—people were always inviting fresh faces to the group, which gave it its wildly eclectic nature—and she and I hadn't really seen each other since school had ended for the summer. Samantha had been having a really rough year—her father had passed away that spring—and I guess she wasn't feeling very social.

Not that I blamed her, though. It's just that she was so withdrawn, and after almost a month of "space," I thought that maybe she could have a little fun, hang out a little, get out into the world a bit, and I wanted her to meet my bro and my buds. Besides, she had a July birthday, too, and I had bought her a little present.

Nicky and I had been there a little while, mixing and mingling about, chatting with friends, dancing, drinking a little, and the sun hadn't truly gone down yet. It lay about a third of the way above the horizon, casting gorgeous shadows and reliefs everywhere it chose to, and every now and again, I'd glance back across the beach to the parking lot to see who else was joining our party.

At some point, having taken my socks and shoes off a while before, I walked over to the water's edge just to breathe it all in and enjoy the sun, the sand, and the surf all together and washing over me. Feet sunk into the sand and water bathing my calves, I was peacefully blank, lost in non-thought.

"Knew you'd be near the water, Nina," a low female voice I knew spoke over the crash of the waves. And slightly startled, I turned from my place in the sand with a smile to see Samantha—dark hair loose about her shoulders over a cut-off sleeve, hooded sweatshirt with our school logo on it, a knee-length pair of surf shorts, and bare feet.

"Yeah, well, you know, we start out swimming and we never stop." I grinned at her, referring to our mutual love of water and our membership on the school swim team. "Hey, by the way, I'm really glad you made it!"

Still being respectful of Samantha's need for time, I hadn't called too often, just left a message every now and then. She hadn't really called back, so I didn't know if she was going to show or not. Obviously, though, she had. Glad she got the message.

Samantha crossed the few feet from where she stood to join me in the cooling waves, and we gave each other a hug. When we released each other, she casually draped an arm over my shoulder and I put one lightly around her waist. We watched the sun drop down in companionable silence.

"Had to come," Samantha finally said. "You asked me so nicely." She looked at me and grinned, then tousled my hair. "But I can't stay long," she added, and her expression became a bit rueful. "There's some things I have to do."

Well, I could understand that, and I figured maybe she was feeling a little awkward. It couldn't be very easy to just try to be normal when so much in her life wasn't, and I said as much—at least the first part about understanding, anyway. I didn't want to say the rest 'cause that was sort of obvious.

I pushed the forelock back off my face that her tousling and the wind blew. "And besides," I added, "it *is* 'Everybody's Birthday in July' party, ya know, so you had to be here, even if it's just for a little bit." I smiled back and mock-punched her shoulder, trying to keep things light. My knuckles barely grazed her shoulder.

I remembered the present I'd brought for her, and suddenly, I felt a little shy. I could actually feel my face start to flush. The sun was just about to dip below the horizon, so I hoped Samantha wouldn't notice in the lengthening shadows.

"I, uh, I got you something, nothing big, ya know, just, cool," I managed to say without stammering too much. I don't know why I felt so strange. I mean, we'd spent almost every day of nine months hanging out during the school year, for the past two, going on three, years. Maybe it was because this was the first time we'd actually hooked up outside of the semester? That sure enough sounds right, anyway.

My words seemed to blow away in the light breeze that played off the water as Samantha jammed her hands into the single pocket of her sweatshirt, and she just watched me briefly, an expression in her eyes I didn't understand and a tiny little smile playing on the corner of her mouth.

Finally she pulled a hand out of her pocket and very gently brushed the hair the wind had blown onto my face behind my ear and lightly cupped my cheek. "You shouldn't have. You know," she spoke softly, "it's not necessary."

Her fingertips were cool and soft against my heated cheek, and I felt a weird new little pressure build in my throat. I must have had more purple Hi-C than I'd realized, I thought to myself when I felt that same pressure build in my face, even though Samantha removed her hand.

"Sure I should, sure it was," I struggled to answer, only the words came out in a whisper, and I jammed my hand into the pocket of my shorts, scrabbling with my fingertips to find the little wrapped bit that I'd gotten. Finding it, I jerked it out, practically shoving my hand in her face. "Here, for you," I stated firmly. "Happy birthday," and I opened my fingers to let her see the little blue package.

The sun had sunk even lower, and now the water was grayish blue, the way it looks before a storm.

Samantha simply stared at me, and I was struck by her eyes. They were the same color as the ocean. Very slowly, very carefully, she reached for my hand, and with a touch so gentle that I could barely feel it, she withdrew the tiny little package.

I held my breath as she opened it and simply stared at her gift, and I shifted my weight slightly from one foot to another. I found a balance that suited and dug my toes into the wet sand while I waited and watched for, well, I don't know, something.

"Oh wow…" she breathed out quietly.

"Do you, um, do you like it?"

Samantha finally lifted her eyes to mine, her eyes wide and a soft smile across her lips. "Like it? I love it, Nina." She grinned at me, slid the little bit of wrapping paper into her front pocket, then held the gift out before her. "Help me put it on?"

It was a very simple gift, a perfectly reproduced miniature sword— a claymore—two inches long on a silver rope chain. I had picked that for her because of her nickname, but more on that later, 'kay?

"Yeah, sure, no problem." I smiled back and stepped closer, taking the chain from Samantha's hand. I reached up around her neck, closing the ends of the chain under her hair, brushing it out to make sure it wasn't caught. "There," I said finally as I released the chain, "you're done." I stepped back to critique my handiwork. "It looks great on you," I told her in honest admiration, and watched her fiddle with it.

"It's very cool, Nina," she told me, that same little smile playing about the corner of her lips. "Thank you." Her eyes caught mine and she stepped closer to me.

"This is it," a part of my brain thought. "This is what?" asked another. Suddenly I could feel that pressure again in my face and throat—I could feel my pulse jump in my neck—and it seemed to me that we almost swayed into one another. Her face came closer to mine, and all I could see were her eyes, and then her lips. The pressure was so great my cheeks tingled with it, and I closed my eyes against it as all the sound disappeared except for the waves, which seemed to dominate everything.

"Thank you," whispered Samantha warmly against my face, and the lightest feather of cool heat touched the corner of my lips. It might have only been a moment, but it seemed to last forever. The touch disappeared. "I have to go," she whispered, and I felt her warmth leave.

I've no idea how long I stood there like that, with my eyes closed and the wind off the water making colder the space Samantha had left, but when I finally opened my eyes, she was long gone.

I shook my head to clear it from the strange pressure it had felt without and the fuzziness within. Enough of that. I wasn't drinking anymore *Son of Thing*, and I had to make my way back to the bonfire—there was a party going on, and I was there to party, dammit!

It was funny, though, I thought as I made my way across the sand to the fire, where Nicky and our friends were—I could even just make out Kerry coming across the sand to the fire; she must have just gotten there—I had been absolutely, positively sure that Samantha had been going to kiss me.

I shoved that crazy idea firmly out of my head and chalked it up to the effects of too many clear liquors mixed with purple Hi-C. I put a big smile on my face as I rejoined the party.

"Heya, Hopey," Kerry called, meaning me. We'd taken to calling each other the names of our two favorite characters from the comic book *Love and Rockets*—Hopey and Maggie. Nobody knew for sure whether they were or weren't—lovers, that is—but everyone knew they were close, just like me and Kerry, and somehow we thought it was appropriate. Don't ask me why. I didn't ever really bother to analyze it at the time.

"Wassup, Maggie?" I danced my way a bit closer to her, and she grabbed my hand.

"Hey, don't look now, girl, but I think you've got a fan club—no, don't look now." She grabbed my other hand as I turned toward the area she'd pointed out and steered me away from the fire. "Just keep dancing."

I kept bopping about to "Ballroom Blitz" and tried to casually glance over to where Kerry had indicated. Sure enough, across the fire, two guys who were new to our group were standing around, each with a plastic cup in his hand, trying to seem casual. Then the taller of the two, a six-foot blond, caught me watching him watch me.

His face registered surprise, then he turned to his companion and gestured with him to make like they were in the process of discussing the sand, or the fire, or something really close by to where Kerry and I were, but not us.

Yeah. Right.

Well, whatever. They seemed like nice-enough guys, average everyday sorts, with plain white T-shirts over jeans and bare feet in the sand. I had no idea who they knew in our bunch, and I thought I was pretty much familiar with everyone.

"You know 'em, Kerry?" I asked her, pointing with my now-warm Coke. I'd had enough of *Thing That Came and Stayed* at the Halloween party and after my adventure earlier. Now I was keeping an occasional eye on Nicky to make sure *Son of Thing* didn't turn out to be *why-I-spent-my-summer-in-the-house-when-my-mom-and-dad-yelled-at-me-and-grounded-me-forever-because-my-younger-brother-got-drunk-and-I-didn't-bodily-restrain-him thing*.

"Nah," she said, glancing over her shoulder to give them a fuller look-see. "Where's Nicky?"

I scanned around and felt panic squeeze my heart when I couldn't see him on our side of the flames. I craned my neck a bit and finally, about twenty feet beyond the fire, I saw someone bending over a dark form by the bushes where the sand met the boardwalk. When the figure straightened up, I could see the light glance off something around their neck. I knew it was the lion-head medallion Nicky always wore. "Over there!" I pointed for Kerry and reached for her hand. Together, we walked over to Nicky.

"Nicky, what happened?" I called out as we approached.

"Hey, Nee. Rob here said his stomach was bothering him and he felt sick and all, and I didn't want to leave him alone if he was sick, so I, um, well, here I am..." and Nicky looked at me with troubled eyes.

A side note here: Nicky is definitely one of the good guys. He's going to make someone a great catch someday, and I hope they take good care of him. Or else. Okay, to continue...

Rob was moaning and groaning on the ground, clutching his stomach. "Ah, Nicky, did you stop to ask him why he's wearing a garbage bag as a shirt?" I indicated the shiny brown plastic that covered

Rob from shoulders to hips.

Nicky looked at me like I was losing it. "No, I just thought he was being, you know, silly and all, like everyone. Why else would he do that?"

Suddenly, Rob lurched and grunted; he brought himself onto all fours in the sand. "Oh, God, oh, God, I'm dying…" he groaned.

I grabbed Nicky and Kerry by their sleeves and backed away a good three feet. I knew what was coming, and so did Kerry as she quickly shuffled behind me, but Nicky was confused.

"Whatchya go and do that for?" he asked indignantly, jerking his arm away. "He's gonna die or something and…" He gestured toward Rob, then broke off suddenly to watch the jerky motions Rob was making with his head as he swayed on his knees and elbows.

A soft, wet sound, like a soaked paper being punched, flowed out of Rob's mouth as a pool formed under his head.

"That's why you guys call him Chuck!" exclaimed Nicky in sudden understanding.

A horrible gagging, choking sound followed almost immediately, and Rob raised his head like he was about to howl at the moon. Suddenly, something *flew* out of his mouth and landed on some poor sand rabbits or something with a nasty squelch.

"And that's why we call him Yack," Kerry chimed in from behind me.

I draped my arms over Nicky's and Kerry's shoulders. "C'mon, let's get going," I encouraged now that the show was mostly over. Once Yack, well, yacked, things would be fine, especially after he did his little ritual, which I didn't want to stick around for—I'd already seen it on Halloween. We headed back to the fire.

Nicky hung back a moment and turned around. "But what about—?"

"He'll be fine, give him thirty seconds." I turned and reached an arm around his waist. "C'mon, let's…" Shit. Too late.

I'd had another reason for getting back, besides avoiding the rest of Rob's I'm-drunk-enough-to-puke ritual. I had wanted to get us back over by the fire before anyone, especially the new guys, had noticed we'd gone off. I didn't want to give them ideas, you know what I mean, catch each other's eye over the fire, wander off, hook up in a dark corner, that sort of thing, since it just wasn't a "me" thing to do, but the fire fan club had noticed something was up and had walked over, jostling and shoving each other on the way.

"Hi, um, we were, um, can we help?" the taller one asked me, holding his cup in one hand and rocking back and forth a bit on his heels.

"Uh, yeah, is there sort of a problem?" asked his friend.

"No, just, ah, could you guys step back about, um, three feet?" I asked them, since they were standing right in front of Rob, where he'd huddled himself on the ground again, "and maybe move over here? C'mon, hurry!" I had seen Rob's hand move, and I knew it would be just a matter of minutes before, well, we were between him and the water, while he was between us and the fire.

The guys shuffled over to us, and with a suddenness that would have surprised anyone who had seen Rob in what had seemed to be his final agonies only twenty seconds before, he lurched up to his feet, screaming, "Puke Poncho!" He ripped his plastic shirt off and waved it around like a flag before letting it loose to fly in a graceful (if gross) arc—and it flew over the two new guys.

"Aaaarggghhh!" he continued to scream as he pounded his feet and ran furiously toward the surf. Faintly, we could hear him yell before he dove in, "From the sea ye come, to the sea, return!"

I looked at the guys. The blond had gotten a miserable soaking, and the shorter one had gotten stuck holding the bag, literally. It had landed on his head and slipped down his back. I felt really, really bad for them. Well, bad and revolted.

We all stood there, staring dumbly at each other.

"I'm Nina, this is Nicky, this is Kerry," I finally said. What else was there to do?

"I'm Joey, and this is Jack," the tall one said, and they both appeared as awkward as we felt as everyone thought about shaking hands. Thankfully, everyone settled on just waving.

"Uh, I've got a couple of towels in our bag," I said.

"I've got an extra pair of shorts," Nicky chimed in.

Kerry had been tugging on my shirt since I'd offered the towel, and I finally turned to find out what she wanted. "Dude, what?" I asked, wondering what was up.

Her hand was warm as she placed it on my forearm, and her eyes glittered as she stared at me with a strange intensity, measuring me, like there was something I should have known, but didn't. My own eyes revealed nothing but my own lack of knowledge.

Finally finding what she was searching for (or not, I guess), she dropped her eyes from mine to look at Joey the Vomit Shirt and Jack the Vomit Head.

"Um, well, if you don't mind bike shorts," Kerry said in a tone that sounded very reluctant as she slipped her hand into mine, and while the Vomit Twins made their way to the ocean to wash off, Kerry and I walked over to the promised rescue clothes. On the way, she kept glancing over at me with that same expression and dammit—I had no idea what it was I was supposed to know.

CHAPTER THREE:
THE THING THAT CAME AND STAYED

We had a really good time the rest of that summer, I mean, Nicky and Kerry and me. After the whole thing at the beach, when Joey and Jack bathed themselves in the dubious cleanliness of the ocean and put on borrowed shorts, Joey called me a week later. He wanted to return my towels and Nicky's shorts. Jack called Kerry, and before you knew it, I guess you could say we had "dates" for the rest of the warm weather.

Joey had a boat, and Nicky and I went fishing, swimming, and daydreaming with him for hours at a time off the Jersey shore. Honest and truly, there's nothing like getting out onto the water to forget about everything, even the fact that you live in a "civilized" world. If you're in the right place at the right time, hours can pass without the sight of buildings or people or the sounds of cars and trucks. Complete, blessed silence. I definitely recommend it to everyone.

After one of these day trips toward the end of the summer, Nicky and I took a bike ride out to the end of, well, it's our secret fishing spot, so I can't tell you exactly. There's a little beach over there and when the tide's out, you can walk halfway to what everyone says is New Jersey (but I'm not sure about that) before swimming for another fifty or so feet. We tried it once and almost got stranded, but that's another story that resulted in two days' worth of lectures and a week of hard manual labor. Think flower beds and manure.

Back to the point, though (and free of manual labor), this was one of our favorite spots for fishing, crabbing, and clamming. It was mostly catch-and-release. We never kept the crabs or the clams 'cause they were probably contaminated, but it was fun just the same. Besides, it kept our skills up in case we ever needed them.

"You know," Nicky said, his line in the water, the setting sun glowing in his eyes and making his hair look like molten gold, "Joey thinks he's in love with you." Nicky didn't look at me; he just focused on his line. "Did you know that?"

I sighed to myself. I liked Joey, a lot. I even cared for him, and we'd shared hugs and kisses like many other dating couples, but that's where it stopped for me. In addition to all the forbidding warnings, lectures, after-school television specials, and threats from my parents about the dire consequences of premarital sex, I just didn't feel that something special, that something that I knew would tell me this is the right place, the right time, the right one, and I told Nicky so.

Nicky smiled as he hefted his pole a bit to check the line. "That's good," he said, "because I don't think he's right for you either." His smile turned into a bright grin.

That smile of his looked a little suspicious, and I wanted to know more. "What?" I asked him as I felt what just might have been a tug on my line. I started to take in the slack bit by bit, going very slowly.

"Got something?" Nicky asked in a hush and came closer. He still held on to his pole and divided his attention between his line and mine.

"Yeah, I think I might," I whispered back. "So what's the shit-eating grin for, dude?" I asked him out of the side of my mouth. My eyes were riveted on the water where my line disappeared into it. The sun had sunk even lower, and the backlight made the water look like fire, creating black shadows on the wavelets. It was very hard to see, and I know I must have been frowning in concentration. Nicky focused with me.

"School starts next week," he told me informationally, as if I needed reminding. Of course school started next week. Otherwise why would he and I have spent the last week up late each night cramming in our summer reading instead of fishing like we were at the moment?

"Yeah, so?" I asked a little carelessly. I was really, really focused on the line, and I had the gut feeling it was about to go. My shoulders twitched slightly with the anticipation, and I shifted my grip and my stance for better balance.

"So, are you gonna break it off before school starts or after the first week or so?"

"What?" I asked him, surprised and thrown off track. I wasn't surprised about the breaking-it-off question because I'd made it a rule since I'd started dating that dates were only on weekends and rarely more than two a month. Not because I didn't have a social life, but because I did, with my friends, and I didn't want to be cut off from them. Also, lots of my friends got into trouble with their studies over dating their "true loves," and there was no way I was going to blow my plans for the future for some dumb guy or anyone else.

I was going for a scholarship, dammit. Either ROTC, which stands for Reserve Officer Training Corps, or the United States Naval Academy, otherwise known as Annapolis, and I wanted to fly jets, then become a test pilot, then an astronaut. That's the way you get to space, and that's where I wanted to go.

No, I wasn't surprised by Nicky's subject. I was surprised he asked at all.

"You could always tell him about Hopey and Maggie. He might leave you alone then."

I stood stock-still for a few breaths, then actually took my focus off the line to stare at my brother. He had this silly little grin, and his eyes were open wide, too wide, like when you know something you're not supposed to know, or try to lie. You know, *that* look.

"Dude, Kerry's my friend..." I began patiently, then stopped. I didn't know where to go with this. It's not that the idea of two girls together in that way bothered me. In fact, I thought it was pretty intriguing, except I couldn't figure out how they'd do it, ya know? I just didn't remember ever saying anything that specific about it to Nicky. And I was confused, anyway, about how I felt about Kerry. Yeah, she was my friend, but it was different, too, in ways I had no words for, and I didn't know what exactly that meant.

Oh hell, Nicky and I talked about everything all the time, even the gay thing in general; he knew I couldn't care less which way people went.

"I don't think that would be a good idea," I finally said. "I mean, Joey and Jack are best friends. Kerry might not be too thrilled with the whole thing when it gets back to her." There, that sounded like it covered everything. I was cool and didn't care, at least for myself. I was just considering someone else's feelings, which in reality pretty much did sum it up.

Nicky laughed. "Ya know, man, she probably wouldn't care. It would just add to her reputation or something."

I laughed with him in agreement, then focused back on my line. There—I thought I'd seen a slight movement. "Ya know, Nicky, that might not be a good thing to have on my background check for Annapolis," I mentioned while I shifted my grip a little more. I could feel the play of the line along the rod, the slight pulling stress. There was something there, and that sucker was going to be mine.

"Oh shit, dude! I didn't even think about that. You really think they'll care?" he asked, his voice full of worry. "You think they won't take you just for a rumor of something like that?"

Nicky was totally not fishing anymore, and he gripped my shoulder. "Dude, they can't do that! That would be totally stupid!" he practically shouted in my ear.

I turned my head toward him and tried to give him as reassuring a smile as I could. After all, Nicky and I had the same dream: we were going to go to Annapolis together and graduate one year apart from one another. That was the plan, and that's what it had been for a very long time, since we were small.

If you're wondering what the heck we caught when we went fishing that time, I'll tell you the truth. The more Nicky and I talked about Joey, the worse the fishing got. In the end, while we had gotten one or two "keepers"—porgies—the last thing I caught was a three-foot-long, slightly translucent, mud green, slimy, nasty, ugly eel. The hook had gotten caught between its teeth—the pointy sharp ones, which were an inch and a half long. All of them.

We would have tried, actually, we did try to free it, except it was snapping and spitting, and to be quite honest, neither of us wanted to get bitten by this nasty thing. In the end, we had to cut the line and let it go, hook and all, and it took the opportunity to lunge for Nicky in the waves before it finally, thankfully, disappeared. I guess I somehow took that as an omen of some sort. You'd think that I would have known that it was.

CHAPTER FOUR:
LOVE AND ROCKETS

Well, summer ended, school started, and Kerry and I hung out after school at the Universe comic book store. I'd get off the train, run down the steps from the elevated platform, and there, on Richmond Avenue, across the street from the Eltingville train station, is where I'd go. "Hey, Nina!" yelled Robbie from behind the counter as I walked in that particular Friday. His greetings were always loud enough to rattle the glass, and we all suspected it was because his older brother was in a heavy metal band that practiced in his basement.

Basically, we all figured he was going deaf—but then again, he could hear change falling, and pages turning in the restricted section, and kids sneaking out without paying, so we weren't really sure.

"The new one just came out," he informed me conversationally as I came up to the counter.

"Cool! Where ya got it?" I asked, maybe a little too eagerly. Well, it had been almost eight weeks since the last edition.

Robbie grinned at me, his eyes peeking between the curly strands of brown hair that came down to his chin.

"I kept a mint one for you back here," he told me with satisfaction as he reached down under the counter to retrieve it. He presented it with a little flourish.

I was more than happy to reach for the latest version of *Love and Rockets* by the Hernandez Brothers (and that's Fantagraphics Books, if you don't know, by the way).

"Ah ah," he singsonged, holding the comic just out of my reach and a hand up to forestall me, "first things first."

I groaned inwardly—I had an idea of where this was going. The grin he'd had a scant second before turned just slightly shy, and I was certain that he was trying to hide behind his hair.

"What's the deal with you and Joey?"

Bingo—he went there. My groan moved from the inside out, and I rolled my eyes in irritation. "Damn, Robbie, can't I keep my own business to myself?" I snapped at him.

His face flushed and he lowered his eyes, sliding my now near-mint as opposed to mint copy of *Love and Rockets* to me. Good if he felt a little bad about asking—how nosy!

"It's just that, you know, Joey's been telling everyone that you guys are, like, you know, serious and all, and like, you and him and Kerry and Jack are gonna like, do, like, some double-ceremony wedding thingy after graduation," Robbie stammered out. His face might have been redder than before, and I could tell he was shuffling his feet behind the counter, but obviously he didn't feel too bad if he was going to pursue the subject. Ah well, best to grab the bull by the horns, so to speak.

"Yeah, well, he didn't ask me yet, so you can forget all about it," I abruptly answered, "and as for Kerry, I don't even know if she and Jack have discussed the whole thing." I sifted among some flyers on the counter, trying hard to act normally. "By the way," I asked him casually, "has she come in yet?"

Right on cue, because I swear that girl could read my mind, the glass door swung open with a shake of the bell and a crash on the wall, and there she was—my best friend Kerry.

"Hiya, Magpie!" I waved happily, using her nickname.

"Hey there, Hopeful!" She smiled just as happily back, using mine. We gave each other a fiercely quick hug.

"New one's out, by the way."

"*Love and Rockets*?"

"Yep. Robbie put 'em aside, right?" I asked him with an arched eyebrow as I looked at him, trying to send him the message via mental telepathy that he'd better have laid one aside for Kerry as well as me.

"Um, uh-huh, yeah, uh, sure. I've got one for you, too, Kerr," he stammered, and he shuffled behind and beneath the counter. His face had quickly blossomed to a raspberry pink again, and I suspected he was worried that I might bring up our previous conversation in front of Kerry. He was wrong: I was *definitely* going to bring it up.

"Hey, Kerry. Robbie told me he heard that you and Jack and Joey and I are all going to share a wedding day after graduation. Have you heard anything about that?" I grinned as I asked her and watched the color in Robbie's cheeks deepen.

"Well, you know, rumors," he trailed off into a mumble. "Joey told me that…" more faint mumble, "and I…" Robbie mumbled in conclusion as he dug for Kerry's copy of *L&R*.

I might have been smiling, but I was annoyed. When did Joey speak with Robbie? I mean, I know they went to the same school and all, and also, what the hell was Joey thinking? Why in the world was he going around telling anyone such ridiculous stuff anyway? It would have been nice if he'd at least talked with me first, don't you think? Yeah, me too.

I glanced over at Kerry, who flashed me an evil grin, the one that means, "Play along with me," which I was more than happy to do. Man, I loved this chick!

"Actually, Robbie, Joey's got it all wrong."

"He does?" Robbie blinked at her in confusion and surprise.

"Yeah, he does." She nodded emphatically. "If there's a wedding after graduation, there'll be no Jack or Joey there," she added confidently as she reached for our copies of *L&R* on the countertop and slipped them into a bag.

"Huh?" Robbie's lower lip hung down in shock. He looked completely dumbfounded.

Kerry leaned over the counter and into Robbie's personal space, and intensity burned from her face. Mesmerized, he leaned closer.

"You think I'm just gonna let some jerk marry Nina?"

Poor Robbie just stared and swallowed silently. Finally, he found breath enough to ask, "Well, who's getting married, then?"

Kerry narrowed her eyes, making sure she still had Robbie's attention until the silence grew thick and hard. "No one," her voice cut through the silence. "No one's going to marry Nina. Not unless it's me," she told him in deadly seriousness, thumping her thumb to her chest for emphasis.

Robbie's mouth was an open *O* of astonishment at this point, and though I felt just a little bad for him (but not too much. He was listening to gossip and guy crap and believing it, after all), I couldn't help myself. I started to laugh and forgot all about being mad at Joey.

Kerry grabbed my hand. "C'mon, hon, let's go," she insisted, and very determinedly began to drag me out of the store.

Still somewhat helpless from laughter and with shoulders still shaking, I let her pull me. I managed to fish in my jeans pocket and toss what felt like the right amount of bills toward the register, then carefully scooped up the bag with our comics that Kerry had left on the counter.

"Keep the change, Robbie," I told him as Kerry hustled me out the door.

Kerry kept dragging me behind her as she marched us determinedly down Richmond Avenue toward our homes. Where in the world was she getting all this forcefulness, I wondered. Finally, I collected enough of myself to stop laughing. "Okay, stop a sec," I said. Kerry still held my hand, but at least she halted her forward charge—for the moment, anyway.

"Let me catch a breath here." I took my hand from hers so I could hand over her comic, and I was mentally trying to figure out why she'd said what she had to Robbie. You see, since the summertime I'd had the time to figure out that I kind of *liked* Kerry, more or other or in addition to just as a friend. I was just never going to tell her that part.

I must have looked very serious (I seem to be famous for that), because Kerry searched my face intensely. "I hope you're not sore at me for what I said to Robbie." She seemed a bit anxious.

Gosh no, I wasn't sore. Just, well, a little confused. I mean, she told Robbie she wouldn't let anyone but herself marry me. What the hell did that mean? This was sort of a half-subconscious daydream of mine? Did people joke about stuff like this all the time? Was that normal if they did? If they didn't? And then, there were those weird few seconds at the beach, when she kept looking at me and I didn't know what she wanted, but I had the strange feeling she was, like, jealous or something. No, better let that train of thought go. But did Kerry think stuff about me? Like, maybe, did she think I was, well, maybe was she saying—ah, forget it. I didn't want to prove how stupid I was by opening my mouth, so I said nothing.

Kerry shuffled a bit and glanced down at her scuffed Doc Martens boots. "Yeah well, I, um, know you've got that whole military thing coming up and all, and I wasn't trying to wreck it for you," she said earnestly, gazing back up into my eyes, searching them. "It's just that if people are gonna talk shit, let 'em really have something to talk about. Then they feel stupid when they find out they were wrong."

I gazed at Kerry's Doc Martens, too, and tried to appear very serious and cool as I nodded my head in understanding—an understanding that reached my ears, but not inside them. I couldn't look at her, I couldn't breathe. My God, what was I going to do when she found out they were right—at least about me?

I shoved one hand deep inside my pocket and let the other one swing the bag a bit as I continued walking, my eyes still focused on the ground ahead of me. Kerry trotted a bit, and as she caught up with me, she reached for my shoulder. I jumped, surprised, shocked, scared she could read my mind through my skin.

It was all well and good that we could talk about people being bisexual or gay or whatever, and that we didn't care, 'cuz we were too punk and too cool, and we had heard other people were, but I had the uneasy feeling that it would be different if it was someone we actually knew—if it was, well, me.

"Hey, girl." She bumped her hip against mine. "We still have plans with the guys tomorrow?" she asked me lightly. "We gonna let them in on our fun?"

I stepped out from her reach because I still felt a little uncomfortable, but I smiled anyway because I just couldn't help it as I glanced at her and gave her one of my trademark crooked grins as all those weird thoughts disappeared from my mind.

"Oh, yeah, we did say we were gonna show them what exactly it is we do when we hang."

"Think they're up for it?"

Oh, what a deliciously nasty mind she had with the look she gave me. "Oh baby, they ain't seen nothin' yet!"

CHAPTER FIVE:
FASCINATION STREET

I'm not gonna bore you with all of the details, just entertain you with the most important ones. Here's the deal, see. Nicky and I, or Kerry and I, or the three of us, would go to the Village every Saturday, and I do mean every Saturday—some Fridays, too. We'd take the train to the ferry (yeah, that's the famous one every visitor to New York has to step on at least once—it's kinda cool, actually) and walk up from South Ferry through Tribeca, wander through Chinatown and browse through SoHo, and then finally, the Village.

We'd go to stores like Unique Boutique and buy $2.00 coats, or rummage through stuff at Canal Jean and play with all the guitars in Umanov's, then go over to Googies on MacDougal for a hot chocolate (the best in the world—really—just ignore the roaches) if it was cold, grab pretzels or dirty-water dogs (street-vendor hot dogs—I figured I'd explain just in case that's just a New York thing to call them) and sit in Washington Square Park, avoiding the drug dealers (hey—just say no, right?) and watching the skate punks do their thing.

We'd laugh over the stuff in the window at the Pink Pussycat (um, go look for yourself, okay?) and wander around, just having a great time being, well, us. Sometimes one of us would save for a couple of weeks (Nicky saved for three months to get this cool leather motorcycle jacket), and then we'd make a special trip to pick up that truly necessary item.

Other days, we spent hours in the small record shops, looking for stuff by Sisters of Mercy or Bauhaus or U2—import stuff you couldn't and still can't get here, and especially not in corporate conglomerate chain stores, and the same thing with certain comic books and collectibles. Everything we listened to was underground, and so was everywhere we went.

Occasionally, if it was three or more of us going ('cuz we'd hook up with other friends), the parental units would give us permission to stay out, and we'd swear we were all of age as we went in to see the *The Rocky Horror Picture Show* on Eighth Street, to be thrilled by the sweet transvestite, the virgin, and the asshole—and if you don't know what I'm talking about, you're a virgin, too.

So, this is what we did, no big mystery, and no big whoop either, except that before, Joey and Jack hadn't ever really wanted to go with us, and we'd never really asked them—so this time they asked us, which is kinda weird, thinking back on it.

We all met up at my house and got to the ferry without incident. It was a warm day for November, so we decided to stand outside on the deck, on the "ground" level, where the cars are. We leaned up against the railing on the right, uh, starboard side of the boat, with Joey snugged up against my back and Jack and Kerry holding hands, and it was all nice in its own way, two best friends dating two best friends, and everybody happy just to be alive and hanging out together, with the wind and the salt spray in our faces.

Kerry and I had decided ahead of time that we'd get straight to the heart of it all and take the subway up to the Village instead of walking. We wanted to show off for the guys, since neither one of them had ever ridden on the subway before, while not only had we ridden frequently, we'd actually mastered the art of "subway surfing." Oh, and that's a way of balancing while you're standing on a fast, bumpy ride in such a manner that you're "riding" the train—like a surfboard or a skateboard—without holding on to anything, and then not falling or stumbling when the ride stops. Try it if you get a chance.

So there we were, on the R train and headed uptown, both guys trying to be as casual as could be, sitting there in the muck and mire (not to mention the smell) that's part and parcel of the NYC public transportation experience.

"Hey—there's, like, all sorts of freaks and stuff in the Village," Joey announced authoritatively, like he knew all about it, "and we want to make sure you guys are, you know"—I raised my eyebrow at him—"protected," he finished and put an arm around my waist.

"Yeah," Jack chimed in, nodding his head in agreement. "You two really shouldn't travel here alone all the time. It can be really dangerous," and he reached for Kerry's hand.

I stood up and reached for the center pole, Joey's hand still on my waist, and Kerry stood with me. We looked at each other and rolled our eyes—what a pair of 'burb babies—then I gave Kerry my own version of an evil grin.

"Ya know, guys, there's lots and lots of gay people there," I said with the straightest face I could muster. Truth to tell, the "gayest" thing we'd seen was those pink triangles on certain stores and on bumpers. Contrary to popular belief, the Village is not overrun with gay people doing it in the street and scaring the horses. I don't think we'd even seen two guys or two girls holding hands, never mind anything else, in all our trips there, except for onscreen at *The Rocky Horror Picture Show*. "And I think maybe you'll need our protection. You're both pretty good-looking and all—"

"Oh yeah, chicken hawks are so gonna loooooove them!" Kerry added, and I knew then, no matter what happened, she'd back me up, like always. But something surprised me. I didn't realize she'd even know that the term "chicken hawk" existed, let alone what it meant, and from the way she'd just said it, I knew she wasn't speaking out of ignorance. I wondered how she'd learned it, and I wondered what else she knew.

The boys looked at each other in consternation, then Jack's eyes widened in such a way you could almost actually see a lightbulb flash over his head. "Hey, maybe we should act like we're couples and then we won't get hit on," he suggested very seriously, looking at each of us for approval. All three of us stared at him like he'd grown horns and sprouted wings, or at least I did.

"Uh, Jack?" Joey interjected, "we are couples."

"Oh no, not us," he indicated him and Kerry, and Joey and me, "but us!" And he pointed to himself and Jack, and me and Kerry.

I smiled and was about to laugh it off and protest, but Kerry turned around, grabbed my hand, and said in mock seriousness, "Hey, baby, it's a dream come true." She grinned to let me know she was joking, then slid an arm around my waist.

I loosely hung an arm around her shoulder. "Fine by me," I agreed and grinned back, then angled my gaze and stuck my jaw out a bit at the boys, daring them. Come on, guys, who's cool enough to play? That was my attitude.

Jack twisted in his seat to face Joey. "Oh my love," he declaimed in his stagiest, goofiest tone, and spread his arms for a huge hug, but

Joey put his hands up to ward him off.

"No, that's just silly looking," Joey corrected. "I'm a foot taller than you, anyway. You come over here," and he grabbed Jack in a headlock, then tucked him up under his arm.

Just like that, the game was joined and there we were—two couples, now two different couples, and my God, how different they'd become since we'd left home.

I sat down, and Kerry sat across from me, leaned over, glanced down for a minute, then back up at me, flipping her hair over to reveal a gleam of intent in her eyes and a sarcastic twist to her mouth. "I love you so much, I'd jump off a building into a pile of bricks for you." She smiled.

Jack, picking up on the game, turned to Joey and said, "I love you so much, I'd swim in the Fresh Kill," which, by the way, is this really slimy, disgusting, polluted waterway that runs through part of Staten Island.

"Oh, yeah?" Joey challenged. "I love you so much, I'd drink it!"

"Ewww, gross!" we all chorused, then everyone turned to focus on me. Well, it was apparently my turn, so I guess I had to come up with something good. No pressure, right?

Fine then. I took a second to collect myself and then Kerry's hand in mine. I slowly let out the breath I'd been holding, then stared right into her eyes. "I love you so much," I told her softly, then took a slow breath and let the silence build before I gazed up at her again, "I'd jump off a building, get caught on a nail on the way down, and *then* land on a pile of bricks for you." I delivered that last line with a triumphant big grin.

Kerry ducked her head shyly, letting her hair curtain her face, then peered up at me from behind the long pink strand that fell over her eyes. She'd just put that stripe in the night before, and it fit her perfectly. Her face was so very soft at that very second, and I'd never seen that expression in her eyes before. Then I noticed her lips, and I wondered what it would be like to touch the corner of her mouth.

All of a sudden, I realized the train was screeching into our stop, and I dropped my eyes and Kerry's hand as I stood up to wait for the doors to open.

"Okay, then," Joey announced, clapping his hands together, "let's go with plan gay. C'mon, Jack, you little stud muffin you," and making that classic pincer motion, he chased Jack's butt off the train. They shoved their way past Kerry and me out onto the platform, where our adventure would begin.

Kerry turned to me. "Shall we?" she asked, holding her arm out in invitation.

"Certainly, let's!" I agreed as I placed my arm through hers, and together, we put our noses in the air and marched out of the subway car to join the guys.

This went on for the rest of the day—the joking, the crazy declarations of love-proof, as Kerry and I walked hand in hand and Joey kept his arm around Jack's shoulders. We took those boys everywhere we could, trying to give them culture shock, and we went to all of our favorite hangouts, all the stores and the neat street markets. We fed them bagels and Thai food, hot dogs and gelato, and as the day came drawing to a close, I realized two things: I'd had a great time on this weird double date with the guys, and I really, *really* liked holding Kerry's hand.

At that point, the thought occurred to me that maybe I shouldn't enjoy this so much, that I might be in trouble somehow, but we were having too much fun, and I told that thought to go hide. It did.

On the subway platform on Eighth Street and Broadway, waiting for the train that would take us back to the ferry and then home, Jack and Joey kept up their "couple" façade. "I think," Joey said to Jack, "I've waited long enough to kiss you, and I think you owe me after all those salted pretzels. C'mere, my love pony." And he spread his arms in welcome invitation.

Jack stepped into the space and placed his hands on Joey's waist, but then drew back a second to look at Kerry and me. And I'll be honest, I was absolutely shocked—my eyes were so large, I think I felt my eyebrows touch my brain. Kerry and I were standing next to each other, but not touching, and as I glanced over at her to see what she thought, I saw an expression that matched mine.

She slipped her arm around my waist. "No fucking way!" she exhaled in soft surprise.

"Dudettes, this is a private moment," Jack informed us haughtily, "do you mind?"

"Not at all," I managed to stutter out. I wasn't sure if anyone was still joking anymore, and "plan gay" seemed to be more and more a reality than a game. I was definitely a little confused as I started to turn away and walk to another part of the platform. I think my brain had short-circuited.

But Kerry's brain seemed to be working just fine. "Well, fine then." She pulled me tighter before I could step away—for such a little person she could be very aggressive. "You kiss Joey, and I'll go kiss Nina in decent privacy."

I don't know what I was thinking, but she bumped her hip against my side (you know, the side bump, that hey-we're-a-team gesture thing), and we swaggered off the platform, around the other side of the wall where a tunnel led off to another platform for another train. We must have been amused at some level, because we were both giggling about the whole thing.

"Geez," I heard Jack's voice float out from behind us somewhere in a low tone, "you think they're really gonna do it?"

"They know we're only joking, right?" Joey reasoned with him.

"You sure couldn't tell by *me*!" I called out in answer out over my shoulder.

"Shit, Joey, they're *really* gonna do it!" Jack was starting to freak out.

"Fucker!" exclaimed Joey, and with that, they came running after us.

We both started to laugh at hearing that, but Kerry started moving, too, and stopped for a second to grab my hand. "C'mon!" she earnestly urged, looking up at me, and for whatever reason, I ran with her, the guys' footsteps sounding from not too far behind.

I don't know how we did it, but we flew through that tunnel and took a wrong turn somewhere. We ended up on an abandoned platform and were forced to stop, nowhere to run, the guys coming up our backs, the tracks in front of us, and only God-knew-what in the dark and now-unused rail tunnels that lay to either side.

Still holding hands, Kerry and I faced each other, laughing, breathless, and for the space of a couple of heartbeats, we just simply gazed into one another's eyes. And I knew at the deepest gut level that we were trying to read each other's minds, trying to discern what was real, who was fooling who, if it was safe to just stop playing.

In those moments, it wasn't a game anymore, and I was starting to suspect that maybe, just maybe, it hadn't been for a while, because something was happening. My chest buzzed and my head felt light, and somehow our faces got closer and closer, and she and I both knew, because I could feel it in me and see it in her eyes, that it was going to happen, that in another half second—

"They're over here!" Jack called out, and my head snapped at the sound to see them come charging around the corner. They caught themselves, then sauntered casually the rest of the way toward us.

"I told you they wouldn't," Joey threw over his shoulder in arrogant superiority to Jack. "Hey hey there, I think we've had enough of plan gay for a day," he admonished as he approached. "That's it."

"Yeah, enough for now," Jack agreed, stepping behind Kerry and wrapping his arms around her.

Kerry's eyes caught mine, and I read confusion and maybe even a slight appeal for help in her expression. "I don't know." I cocked an eyebrow at Joey and Jack, viewing them both with obvious doubt. "You guys looked pretty cozy over there." Kerry and I still held hands.

"It was a joke. We planned it when you guys went to the bathroom at Googies," Joey explained as he wrapped his arms around me and lifted me bodily away.

I was stiff but nonresistant as Joey walked us, or carried me really, back to our platform. He'd put me down soon enough. Besides, I wasn't that light.

"Yeah, right, some joke," Kerry muttered angrily as Jack did the same to her. "My *boyfriend*'s gay."

"We just wanted to freak you guys out. It's just a game, dude," Joey explained as he set me down but kept his arms wrapped tightly around me.

I was totally weirded out—I mean, what I had seen looked very, very real—and there were plenty of occasions during the day when it had all seemed so very okay, you know? Like it was supposed to be that way—Jack and Joey, Kerry and I.

Deciding to play a hunch, I reached out from under Joey for Kerry's hand. "Day's not over yet, boy." And I grinned. "Right, Kerry?"

"Hell yeah," she agreed with a sly grin of her own, reaching out for my hand in return, "so Jack, you go back to your boyfriend."

"Uh, no, that's okay," he responded, tightening his hold around her. "I like my girlfriend just fine, how 'bout you, Joey?" And he smiled over Kerry's head.

"Same here," Joey replied, and I could hear the smile in his voice as he pulled me a few feet away.

We stood, the four of us, on the platform, several feet away from each other, Joey wrapped around me, and Kerry with Jack as a barnacle on her back. Silence reigned between us, the boys staring straight ahead while I occasionally looked at the girders that supported the street above us and let out little I'm-bored sighs. Kerry stared at the ground, shuffling from one foot to another, favoring Jack every now and again with a roll of the eyes or a plainly annoyed look.

Finally, the train came roaring and hissing into the station, and as the boys shuffled us in through two different doors, I smiled to myself as I realized something and yelled over the noise to Kerry, "Hey, Maggie, they've got to let go sometime!"

Kerry's head finally came up then, and she gave me a crooked little grin. "Hopey, you are so right…" she cooed, and turned to face Jack as he leaned up against the closed train door, and Joey and I settled ourselves against the opposite doors. "You wouldn't really want to keep me prisoner, would you, honey?" she stage-whispered to him, while running her index finger up and down his chest.

Jack stared down the trail that Kerry's fingers had blazed, and it was with obvious effort that he brought his gaze to Kerry's. His cheeks blazed, and frankly, I was surprised that he had enough blood left to make his face turn that color, most of it having fled immediately, I was sure, to places farther south. "Well, of course not, honey," he finally managed to get out, "it's just that, well, you had us a little worried there, ya know?" and he squirmed beneath her as she leaned into him.

Joey leaned down toward me. "That's true, by the way," he whispered in my ear, then softly kissed my cheek. "Wouldn't want to lose you."

I sighed, because there was something wrong with this whole thing, but I didn't know what to say. I just leaned against him, resting my head on the edge of his arm. His arms lightly encircled me, and he let his hands rest loosely on my waist. We rode as pairs on opposite sides of the train the rest of the way to the ferry terminal, and we were all quiet for a bit.

Did what I think was going to happen actually almost happen back there at the abandoned station? I glanced over at Kerry and Jack, and after watching them make out for a little bit, I wasn't so sure. Maybe the pressure from school was finally getting to me and I was going nuts.

"Hey, I love you so much I'd crawl over broken glass, be sprinkled with salt and rolled in sand for you," Jack announced into the silence, and we were off into another round of "I love you so much I'd jump from a ten-story building and get caught by the eyelid on a nail before falling the rest of the way down," and "I love you so much I'd walk barefoot on slugs."

Yeah, I know, some of the stuff we said was sorta gross (okay, maybe more than sorta), but it was sweet, too, in its own crazy, desperate way.

At some point, the boys gave up playing the I-love-you-so-much game and focused their energies on keeping Kerry and me apart, and okay, I admit that maybe it was just us girls who were still playacting at the lovesick thing. Despite, or maybe even because of, Joey and Jack's enforced physical separation throughout this time, Kerry and I had somehow, silently, telepathically, mutually decided that whenever Jack or Joey would let one of us go, we'd attempt to unite, so we could "pretend" to run off together, like we were crazy in love or something.

As we walked onto the gangway for the ferry that would take us home, Joey grabbed my elbow, tugging me rather sharply off to one side.

"Ow, dude! What the fuck?" I snatched my arm away and rubbed the offended part, and I also favored him with my dirtiest look. Jerk.

Joey at least had the decency to appear embarrassed. "Hey, I'm sorry," he whispered, "it's just that you guys gotta stop playing now. We're going back to Staten Island," he explained, with a pained expression.

"Dude, I know," I answered, glaring up at him, still rubbing the sore spot. I was positive I was going to get a bruise, and really, since when was he the world sophisticate? I wasn't the one who needed geography lessons on where was cool and where wasn't. Double jerk.

Jack and Kerry caught up with us on the gangway to the boat.

"Keep manhandling girls like that, Joey, and it won't matter where they are," Kerry tossed sharply over her shoulder as she passed, shaking her head. She'd seen and heard the whole thing, and her eyes and mouth had the sharp look of anger.

Jack stopped to look Joey up and down, then shook his head. "I don't know about you sometimes, Joey." He continued to shake his head as he walked past us.

Joey's face had been pink from embarrassment before, but with Jack's words, it drained of color. He opened his mouth once, twice, as if he wanted to respond, but he shook his head to the negative, then gave up. He pressed his lips together and swallowed, and his eyes held something new in them—fear? shyness?—when he looked at me again. He held out his hand for me. "C'mon, let's find a seat," he finally croaked.

We settled in our places on the facing wooden benches on the old boat, back to our original configuration: Jack and Kerry on one side, Joey and I on the other. I leaned my back against him, stretched my legs along the bench, and closed my eyes.

The rest of the time passed in a companionable, if slightly stilted, silence, and by the time we got off at our train station, it was very late. Only two places were open in the little town—the local tavern and Universe.

I looked longingly at the entrance of the store as we walked down the stairs, but not only did Kerry and I never hang out there with the guys (well, not both of them—Jack did stop in from time to time, though), I also knew it was time to go home. "Hey, guys, thanks for coming out with us today. I know I had a great time," I said, turning to face Joey with a smile as we reached the sidewalk. "It was really cool."

"Hey, sweetheart." He smiled in return, lightly resting his hands on my shoulders. "It was a lot of fun. Maybe we'll do it again sometime, just us?" He almost whispered that last part and closed the gap between us to lean in for a kiss but, and I freely admit I did this, I accidentally-on-purpose missed his intention and turned my head to rest it on his shoulder, accompanied by a big hug.

I don't know why, but at that moment, I just couldn't do it, just couldn't kiss him again. I felt almost that if I did, I was giving in to him or giving over something that was absolutely mine. I know that might not make sense, but there it is. "Maybe, sometime," I answered noncommittally, snuggling a bit into his jacket.

"Okay, guys, get a room, will ya?" Jack teased us.

"Forget the room," Kerry corrected, "we've got to get home. It's only getting later, and Nina's the one who's going to get grounded."

I rolled my eyes at her reminder, because she was unfortunately right about the grounded thing, and disentangled myself from Joey's arms. "Yeah, let's get this show on the road," I agreed. I held Joey's hand as we started walking past all the sleepy little houses in our sleepy little town, toward the familiar—home—Joey and I in front, hands held and swinging along, Jack and Kerry a step behind us. We passed identical manicured patches of green on the way.

"Yo, Nina," Kerry's voice broke through the suburban silence, "you up for tomorrow at CB's?"

"Yeah, I'm cool," I answered her over my shoulder. "Do you want to catch the afternoon show?" Not that I knew who was playing or anything—I'd never been to CBGB's before—I was just being, well, you know, cool. Besides, I might never have been there before, but I knew where it was, who some of the most famous musicians to come out of there were, and, especially, that they had two shows just about every Sunday, and most of them were "all ages permitted." Even more importantly, I'd been dying to go for the longest time.

"Definitely!" she answered enthusiastically, "if we catch the twelve o'clock boat—"

"Hey there, wait a second!" Joey interrupted and stopped in his tracks to protest. "You already went out to the Village today. I thought *we'd* hang out together tomorrow!" Joey looked perplexed, annoyed, and something else I couldn't define underneath the streetlight. His hair, always so very light colored, shone white, and his face was so very pale, except for his lips, which he held closed tightly, so tightly that they thinned and the very edges of them were almost purple.

"We hung out together today, Joey," I explained. "No more than two dates a month, remember?" He opened his mouth to speak, but I held up a hand to forestall him. "No, really, I meant that when I first told you, and I still mean it. I like to hang out with my friends. I hung out with you today. Tomorrow, I'm hanging out with Kerry. It's *my* time."

Jack and Kerry decided to give us a little space and dropped farther behind us, murmuring to each other, maybe even having the same conversation (I never did ask, and so I never knew). Or they could have been just making out.

As the homeward walk resumed, Joey ran a hand through his hair. "But I just miss you," he tried again. "We don't spend a lot of time together. You really would rather spend time with her than with me? You just spent the whole day with *her*." His mouth twisted with incredulity and something else, and whatever *that* was, I didn't like it. In fact, not only was I starting to get a little annoyed, I remembered the bullshit with Robbie, and I was going from a little annoyed to a little angry. But now wasn't the time to discuss it. I would definitely bring it up in the future though, privately.

I inhaled and exhaled slowly. "Joey, today was our date—a double date, yeah, but a *date*," I explained patiently. "You meet me every other day, if not almost every day, outside of Universe and study with me just as much. You eat dinner at my house so often my parents are starting to think you're one of their kids. I think they're waiting to give me your hand-me-down jeans! I don't get to see my friends a lot, and they're important to me, too."

Joey watched my eyes intently as I spoke, and I touched his arm lightly to reassure him. "Besides, you want me to be a well-rounded, healthy individual, don't you?" I smiled up at him, wanting to take some of the sting out of what I'd said.

Joey dropped his head and sighed. "Okay, you're right, I'm sorry. But…" and he raised his head to look into my eyes, "you'll call me tomorrow, when you get home, I mean?"

"Sure." I grinned up at him, all annoyance temporarily gone. "And I'll actually have stuff to tell you about."

We stopped walking; we'd finally arrived at the corner of the block I lived on, right in front of my house. I looked up at the light that shone out from the second-floor window, the windows of my parents' room. This meant they were waiting for me, probably watching the clock.

Well, another end to another day, I thought as I climbed the three steps of the front stoop, then turned to face Joey, who had stayed on the sidewalk. Ironically, this was one of the few times we were ever actually physically eye to eye. "Hey, have a good night!" I smiled and leaned in to give him a quick kiss, but Joey had slightly different plans. The kiss he gave me almost swallowed me whole, and I could barely breathe, not out of desire, but out of sheer suffocation. How could such a small, delicate face have such a large mouth? I asked myself as I desperately tried to not smother.

"Yo, Joey, you trying to eat her face? I think your girl is turning blue!" joked Kerry from the street corner where she and Jack stood.

"Yeah, dude, it's like watching the Holland Tunnel come to life!" Jack added.

Joey broke off his devouring kiss. "You'll call me tomorrow?" he asked a bit anxiously, searching my face.

"As soon as I get in."

"Okay then." Joey smiled at me and gave me a kiss on the cheek. He was happy, so very happy, that I was going to call. I felt a little bad about being angry with him before. He was just so, so kidlike, I guess. In fact, I felt like I was watching a kid who'd been promised ice cream as he bounced down the walk to the sidewalk where Kerry and Jack waited.

"G'night guys!" I called over to them and waved. "Magpie, whoever gets up first calls, 'kay?"

"Hey, *no problema*, Hopeful!" she called back, "g'night!"

"Night, Jack, Joey!" I called out again, and waved some more.

"G'night, Nina!" they both called back, and with that, I opened the door and went inside.

What happened after this point isn't too important, except maybe this. I went up to my parents' room where they watched television and waited for me, and a quick glance at the cable clock told me I was home with a whole half an hour to spare. Not bad, really. I wasn't in trouble, and since I was early, there'd be a good chance I'd be able to go out the next time I asked to—like tomorrow.

My parents did the normal mom-and-dad thing and asked me all about my day, so I truthfully told them everything—well, except for the part about the date switching and especially not about that weird "this-is-gonna-happen" thing that didn't by the train tracks. I had the funny feeling that they wouldn't have been very happy with that. It wouldn't be too long before I learned how right that suspicion was.

I kissed them each good night, and as I went through the door, I stopped. It was time for the big question. "Hey, Mom?" I turned and asked her, "I um, I was kinda hoping to go to CBGB's tomorrow with Kerry. Is that okay?"

"Kerry again?" my father grunted from his side of the bed. "I don't like that kid. She's a lowlife punk," and he picked up a book off his nightstand to read.

"Honey," my mother murmured chastisingly to him and laid a calming hand on his forearm. "Sure, baby, if you're going to be home before six." She turned away from my father to face me. "Are you meeting or going with anyone else—Joey or Jack or anyone?"

"No, Mom, just us," I answered, shifting my weight from one foot to the other.

"Harrumph," grunted my father, never taking his eyes off his page, "Joey's a Nazi, Jack's a flake, probably a fag, probably both fags. Both useless. Should've been drowned at birth…" He trailed off, immersed in the depths of his book.

It was uncanny. It was almost like he knew about the game we'd all played and freaked me out a little, well, maybe more than a little. But still, Joey and Jack had been very clear. It was just a game, a little make-believe, a little horsing around among friends. Which meant my dad was wrong.

With that in mind, my mom and I shared a look; then, taking a deep breath and squaring myself in the door frame, I asked, "Why, Dad? For being useless or for being"—my mouth went dry and I swallowed—"faggots?"

Dad snapped his head up from the book with a shocked look on his face, either surprised that he'd spoken aloud or, more likely, that I'd questioned him. "What?" he asked sharply.

Now, maybe a smarter person would've said nothing, and maybe a better person would have let it go, but to be *truly* punk is to stand up for your ideals and do the right thing, no matter what. In other words, open your mouth, question authority, and take the consequences that come your way, no matter what they are. "Should they have been drowned at birth for being useless, for being faggots"—I took a breath and folded my arms over my chest to pretend a calm I didn't feel—"or both?" I watched him stonily.

Did he know how close he was to maybe talking about me? If that was me, would he have wished me drowned at birth, too? I had to know.

My father put his book down and sat up straight. For maybe half a second, I thought he'd get up and maybe actually come over and, well, let's not get into that. My body tensed just in case, but he simply readjusted his blankets and took his glasses off.

"Oh, I don't care if they're faggots," he dismissed, "so long as I don't have to watch 'em. What I do care about," he said, punctuating his words with his glasses, "is that they're useless know-it-alls." He slipped his glasses back on, then picked his book up again and found his place. "Same as that good-for-nothing Kerry." And with that he buried himself back in his reading, signaling that this friendly interpersonal exchange was over.

My mom looked at me, sympathy and concern in her eyes, and I'm sure she would have come over to hug me, but I just shook my head as noncommittally as possible and shrugged.

"Whatever," I responded as my cheeks began to burn with the unfairness of it, "but they're not Nazis, and they're not useless. They're nice people—they're my friends."

Why was it that he just never got it? My father, I mean. He used to be my friend, he used to listen, really listen, and talk and share, and now, well, I don't know, it was just different, and not in a good way. I mean, it seemed everything he said was "faggot this" and "fags that," with the Nazi thing thrown in here and there for good measure. And he just kept picking on me, just a constant criticism of everything I did—like nothing I could do was ever right. I tried not to let it bother me, but it hurt, and I didn't understand it. Well, whatever. It would probably work itself out eventually, I thought to myself. It was probably some weird midlife phase or something he was going through.

I turned back to my mother again and asked, "So, is it okay, Mom? Tomorrow, I mean?"

"Sure, honey, just be back by six, okay?" She smiled at me, a little sadly, I thought. It seemed she'd been doing a lot of that lately.

Yes! This was great. Houston, we're a go for countdown! "Thanks, Mom, Dad," I said. "Good night." I went over and gave my mom a big hug, which she returned, then made my way to my room.

"How do you expect her to find a real boyfriend if you keep talking about them like that? How is she supposed to have friends?" I heard my mom ask my dad as I walked down the hallway.

"Damn kid has got to learn, hon, there are idiots in this world. Don't want her to become a lowlife street punk faggot," he answered decisively.

"Don't you dare say those things about my daughter," I heard her respond heatedly. I could just imagine her expression, the hand up in the air demanding silence, the tight twist to her lips. Dad must have wisely decided to drop it at that point, because the rest of their conversation faded to soft murmuring. Me, though, I stood stock-still, perhaps even a bit frozen at the door to my bedroom, the happy feeling I'd had momentarily before completely gone. Instead, my stomach clenched and a sour taste built in my mouth. I thought of going back to their room and almost turned around. But I'd already said what was on my mind earlier. What would be the point if I went back now? He wouldn't listen, anyway.

Fuck it. I went to sleep.

CHAPTER SIX:
WEIRD SCIENCE

The morning dawned as another unusually warm November day, and Kerry called me first thing in the A.M., just as I was stepping out of the shower.

"It's your punk friend!" my father called in a teasing tone from his room where he'd answered the phone.

"Which one?" I yelled back as I toweled my head. Hey, if he wanted to play, I could play, too. Sometimes it was funny and we'd even laugh.

"Smart-ass kid—don't be a punk with me," he grumbled, but I could tell it was a relatively good-natured grumble. "It's that *girl*." He emphasized the word to make sure I understood full well that even if he was in a good mood, he still disapproved of her.

"Yeah, tell her I'll be right there," I called back to him as I jumped into a towel, then grabbed my clothes and ran on tiptoe feet across the hall to my parents' room. Why does everyone do that when their feet are wet? It all drips on the floor anyway, and your feet still get dirty.

"Yo," I greeted as I grabbed the phone from the pillow where my father had left it. "You 'bout ready?" I was pulling on my favorite black jeans and struggling to keep the phone line out of my shirt as I pulled it over my head.

"Yeah, just gotta do the hair—wanna meet at your place or the station?" Kerry asked, referring to the train station that would take us to the boat, then on to freedom and adventure.

"Um," I breathed as I struggled with my "bondage" boot—so called because it had to be zipped, laced up, then buckled, seven times—"let's meet at Universe, since it's right there and you're closer to the station anyway. Sound good?" I got the last buckle in place.

"*No problema*, you wanna get the 10:40 train?" she asked me. I could hear the hair dryer going in the background, and I envied her the fact that as an only child, she had her own phone in her own room, unlike me, who had to share the phone with everyone and my room with my younger sister.

Yeah, I have one of those, too. My baby sister, Nancy, who we called Nanny (and I know, I know, we all have the same first initial— we all have the same middle one, too, but I'm not telling just yet), two years younger than Nicky and almost four years younger than I, shared a room with me. She, being the baby of our little bunch, had a saying: "You're the culprit, I'm the victim," whenever anything happened— anywhere—that any of us could get in trouble for. Come to think of it, Nanny said that a lot.

It's not that she was terrible or evil (well, maybe sometimes) or anything like that. It's just that she was younger enough than me for us to not have too much in common until she hit high school. She was just starting to be cool, and I was just starting to relate to her, but she still had the reputation in our family of being a tattletale, and she thought I was "weird." She hated all of my friends, and she was way too young to hang out with Nicky and me. Well, that's all you need to know for now. Back to the phone call.

"Yup, 10:40, be at Universe by 10:20?"

"Uh-huh, see ya there, 'kay?"

"Okay, then. Later," and we hung up.

I looked over at the clock on my dad's nightstand—it was nine thirty—and I bolted for the bathroom. I still had to do my hair! No luck for me, though, the door was closed, so I did the obvious, I knocked.

"Who is it?" Nanny sang out as sweetly as she could.

"Nanny, you gonna be out of there soon? I've got to get in there and—" I stopped abruptly when I heard the toilet flush. I heard the water start to run in the sink as Nanny washed her hands, and I was getting later and later, so I knocked again.

"C'mon, Nanny, hurry it up!" I said importantly. "I've got things to see and people to do!"

There was silence for a moment. Nanny had turned off the water, and I could hear her rummaging through the cabinets. Suddenly the door opened and she shoved a hair dryer, gel, and hair spray into my surprised hands, then slammed the door shut again.

"Go do your hair in Mommy's room," Nanny told me through the door. "You're not the only one who has a life, you know. My Menudo club is coming over today."

I started to laugh and I couldn't help it, I had to, just absolutely had to tease. "Menudo, oh, Ricky, Ricky, you're so cuuuuute, I luu-uu-uuv youuuuu!" in the highest, drippiest falsetto I could manage.

Menudo was a boy band created somewhere in Mexico, I think, and the members kept rotating—I think the rule was when the pubes come in, the boy goes out, and all these teeny little girls loved them and the stuff they sang. I thought they were all airheads, both the fans and the boys, and I knew for sure that if her club was coming over, I was glad I was going out. Nicky had stayed overnight at a friend's house, so I knew he was clear, or he'd be coming out with me and Kerry, and for once, I didn't want him along.

"You're such a jerk!" Nanny yelled at me from behind the door. "You think you're so big just because your friends are weird and you all read stupid comic books and listen to weirdo radio stations with weirdo music no one ever heard of, and you talk about stupid things and watch stupid movies that don't make any sense!"

I stared in shock for a few seconds, caught between amusement and irritation.

"Yeah, well, at least my friends know how to think for themselves," I finally shot back as I turned away from the door to stalk back to my parents' room with my precious hair supplies.

Something slammed against the door in the bathroom; Nanny must have thrown a brush. "Go do your hair upside down, weirdo!"

I continued down the hallway; it would be undignified of me to explain what I was actually doing. Besides, I had to get going! Kerry and I were going to CBGB's, the mecca of all meccas for us, for the first time, well, for me anyway. This was going to be so cool…

I had my hair done, got some money from my mom, and with a quick kiss to her and Dad, I made it to Universe and the train station in record time, where Kerry waited for me.

We didn't say much to each other waiting for the train or on it; a companionable silence reigned between us. We'd just grin at each other happily from time to time, but once we got on the boat, things started to change.

We were sitting across from each other on the benches in the bottom level, and as the engines roared to life with a thrum that moved through our bodies, I kept thinking about the day before and all the outrageous things we'd done and said. I began to feel a bit awkward. I mean, what if I'd gone too far, what if Kerry was thinking about it, too, and realizing that she didn't want to hang out with a, well, I don't know what. I frowned at Kerry's plaid pant leg that she'd been repeatedly smoothing.

Kerry stopped playing with her pant leg—I guess they were as smooth as they could get—looked up, and smiled at me. "Ya know, Hopey, I love you so much, I'd suffer a thousand paper cuts all over my body and roll myself in salt for you."

I smiled back, glad to be on familiar territory, happy to know that everything between us was still okay. I let out a breath I hadn't realized I'd been holding. "Yeah, well, I love you so much I'd suffer a thousand paper cuts, roll myself in salt, and dry myself with sandpaper," I returned, and we just grinned at each other like idiots for a bit.

"Ah, Hopey," Kerry addressed me softly, leaning over from her side, "do you know what?" She hesitated while I waited for the rest of it. When she started to examine her fingernails, which she'd painted alternately in bright neon yellow and bubble gum pink, I decided to help the conversation along with my brilliant discussion skills.

"What, Maggie?" I lowered my voice to match hers and leaned to meet her halfway across the gap between us, so I could hear whatever she said next.

She fiddled some more. "Do you..." She paused, as if to think about her next words. "Do you..." and she swallowed and stared down again. The silence grew until it felt like a heavy cloud between us—oppressive, dark, and frightening. The intensity was almost too much to bear, and I decided it was time to examine my hands and the red and black nails I'd painted the day before, while I wondered what sort of question was coming my way or if I'd survive this day.

Kerry sat back and so did I. Her brow furrowed as she dug into her bag, but when she finally fished out her glasses and put them on, she looked relieved and happy, or at least happier. "Do you know where we're going?" she asked me with a smirk.

Huh? I was expecting something along the lines of, "Do you know what you're saying?" or "Do you mean what you're saying?" or "Okay, Nina, are you a dyke?" not this question, this loaded question that could be either about my street credibility as a punk or anything else.

Kerry was smiling wickedly at me, and I narrowed my eyes at her a bit. Now, I'm naive sometimes, and I'm not as quick on the uptake as I should be for a self-confessed smart-ass, but as fucked-up and self-conscious as I can be, I can on occasion read between the lines, and from the glasses Kerry hid behind, to the half-hidden smirk on those soft, full, lips, I knew I was being dared into something, and I had the feeling it was one of those you-tell-me-and-I'll-tell-you sort of things. The problem I had, though, was what if it turned out to be an I-tell-you-and-you-tell-me-how-fucked-up-I-am sort of thing? That's what I was afraid of, and no way was I going to fall for it.

I eased myself back on my bench, then stretched my arms out on either side across it, slid down a bit, crossed my legs, and put on the coolest, toughest mask I had, the one that says, "Yeah, baby, I know it all," to all and sundry who cared to look, and oh-so-casually inspected the nails of my left hand before I looked up at her, mask on, smirk in place, and with the full illusion of control.

"You know I do," I answered with a lift of my chin and a smirk of my own. "What about you?" I challenged. "Do you know where we're going?" I held on to my expression for dear life and tossed that hot potato back. Her turn to kick or receive, baby, kick or receive.

Kerry's mouth twisted expressively, and she nodded her head in silent acknowledgment of the new game. She twisted on the bench, leaning her back against the wall and bringing her legs up in front of her, to face the window across from us and hugged her knees. She stared out at the passing bay, the deep throb of the boat engines the only sound around us.

"Yeah, I know where we're going," she answered finally, solemnly, "but you can lead if you want to. You know I'll always follow." She turned to consider my face, then went back to contemplating the water. Well well well, she'd gone for the kick and now it was my play.

I contemplated the buckles on my boots for a minute. Seven on each one, and with a black rope lace underneath and a zipper below the whole thing. Beautiful black leather, and the buckles weren't too shiny. They had a sort of dull gleam, more like pewter, and provided a great contrast. Done with the artistic inspection of my boot, I tried to respond.

"Why don't we just do what we always do, and go together? No one has to lead, no one has to follow, and we just, you know, get there?"

I suggested. I decided it was time to study the other boot while I waited for her response.

Kerry chuckled lightly. "Yeah, we'll just get there. Together, right?"

I looked up at her with a slight grin. "Yeah...together."

A new tension developed between us as the eye contact lingered, but I was definitely not going to suffer another round if I could help it. There'd been enough of that for one day.

"Hey, who do you think is playing today?" I asked, maybe a bit too enthusiastically, but who cared; it was taking us away from some very new and strange territory.

Kerry gave a soft half laugh as we broke eye contact, and I think she was as relieved as I was—at least for the moment. "Would you believe it's Dayglo Abortions, and I think they're opening for Soldiers of Death?"

"Dayglo Abortions? What time do Soldiers of Death go on? You think they'll do 'The Ballad of Jimi Hendrix'?" I asked excitedly, and together we started singing the opening riff, which is just like Hendrix's "Purple Haze." "Duh *nah*, duh *nah*, duh *nah*—He's *dead*!" we shouted joyfully, and laughed.

We spent the rest of the ride quoting and singing lyrics from our favorite songs, but for those of you who want to know, not a one of them was by Dayglo Abortions, since we'd never heard of them before, and by the time we got to Bowling Green Station and the train that would take us to the East Village, neither of us could hardly breathe from laughing so much.

The fare paid, our tokens slid into the turnstiles, we went through, barely making it onto the cars that had just pulled up. We quickly found our seats, across from one another in the empty car, and settled in for the ride. Kerry stretched out on her side, and I did the same on mine.

"Ya know, Hopey," Kerry started, swinging her legs down off the seat to look at me with a smile, "I love you so much, I'd give up hair spray for you."

I was startled, but recovered quickly enough. "Yeah, well, I love you so much," I paused for dramatic effect, "I'd drink it!" I grinned triumphantly. Actually, that wasn't such a big deal, considering how much hair spray got accidentally swallowed during most applications, but still, it was gross.

"You'd drink it, huh?" she asked. "Well, I love you so much I'd spray it in my face while I'm smoking!"

"Nah, don't do that," I admonished, still smiling and swinging my legs down to the floor to face her. "You'd ruin your hair," I joked. "And besides, I love you so much, I wouldn't let you."

Kerry's focus seemed to gather inward, and she looked down pensively. Ooh, too far, I thought, maybe I shouldn't have said that. It's not that I really thought I'd said anything out of line. It was just, anyway, well, I don't know. Too much, too far, and maybe, scarily, too real.

She stared at the ground a while more and I examined my boots again. They really, truly were such a great pair of boots, maybe I should have gotten two pairs if I was going to wear them so often. I'd heard that this pop-star icon had, like, five pairs of the same boots for that reason, and if someone, like, that thought it was a good idea, then maybe it really was and—

"Hey, Nina," Kerry interrupted my important boot reverie, "the guys aren't here. What's our excuse today?" and she gave me her best wide-eyed and innocent look, which didn't fool me at all, but did leave me in the position of having to come up with both an intelligent and nonincriminating answer.

Great. Just great. I figured at this point she had enough on me to say whatever she wanted to whomever she wanted, and there'd be more than a little truth to it, and then people would start to say shit and—fuck it.

I was punk, I was cool, and I never did like bullshit, not then, not ever. I might have been crazy, or stupid, or brave, but I did my best to be as honest as I could despite the trampoline dancers in my gut with what I said and did next.

Leaning back on the bench in my oh-so-casual manner, I stretched my legs and crossed those beautiful boots. Then I lit a cigarette (which, by the way, boyz 'n' gurlz, was and still is illegal now on any and all forms of NYC public transportation, so don't try it!) and dragged on it. Cool, calm, and totally collected, I looked up and arched an eyebrow in self-deprecating mockery at my best friend. "I'd say it's a case of PLT." I exhaled at her, and let my hand dangle along the orange plastic bench backs. I let the smoke rise between us.

"What the fuck is PLT?" Kerry asked with a cocked brow of her own.

"C'mon, Kerry, you know, PLT—Pre-Lesbian Tension." I took a drag on my cigarette and smirked like I knew all about it. Actually, I really did think I knew at least something, though not all, about it. I'd read a lot about "the gay thing" in some books, I watched PBS and stole my mom's *Cosmo* magazines from time to time. That had to give me some handle on the psychology of this thing. Besides, one thing I knew and understood instinctively so far was where there was smoke, there was fire, one way or another.

"I know you have to be covering this stuff in your health class, Kerry. For Chrissakes, you guys study birth control." I continued to smoke while I watched Kerry's reactions, now that I'd basically told her that I knew, really knew, what she, what I, what *we* were really doing here and that I, at least, wasn't going to lie about it and, on the other hand, I was just so cool, I could dismiss this as just a "sophisticated conversation about normal teenage yearnings," or some such shit.

"Pre-Lesbian Tension," Kerry practically muttered under her breath. "Give me a drag of that thing, will you?" and she reached across for my cigarette, which I handed to her. She dragged on it like it held the secret of immortality, her eyes focused or, rather, unfocused, on some point midway between me and the floor. She twisted her mouth into a grim smile and exhaled smoke through gritted teeth.

Hmm...PLT. I didn't know where in my brain that had come from, but it seemed pretty accurate to me at that time. Now too, come to think of it.

"I guess...I think I could do the uptown thing, ya know?"

Huh? I changed the smirk on my face to a quizzical look. As far as I knew, we hadn't changed plans to go up farther than Prince Street.

Kerry looked back at me as if I'd just dropped my mind on the floor, then realized that I had misunderstood her. "No, doofus, no, not that," and she rolled her eyes and stood up. "I mean, you know, uptown!" and she gestured to herself, from the shoulders up.

Oh, okay, I got it, I could go with that, I understood. "Oh, okay, I get it. Yeah, me too, I think," I responded. I figured it was fair, she admitted something, I would too. "Kissing's, like, no big deal—people get accidentally kissed all the time, right?" I thought for a second, and, my mind having just translated from "bases"—you know, kissing is first base, bras and beyond second, that stuff—to city zones, I brought that to its next logical step.

"Well, actually," I reflected, "I think maybe I could do the midtown thing, too," and I gestured between my navel and shoulder blades. "I mean, I don't know, but, like, it's just, you know, skin, like an arm, right? So that wouldn't be too big of a deal, right?"

"Right!" she hurriedly agreed, "yeah, that would be so not a problem, because, well, everyone does it sort of anyway, 'cuz I mean, look at straws and stuff, and that's just sort of a nip—um, anyway, every girl touches her own boobs every day"—and here she blushed crimson—"I mean, putting her bra on."

I laughed for about a second, maybe because of Kerry's discomfort, but then I got what she meant about straws and stuff. My ears grew warm and I stopped laughing. I hadn't ever really thought that far about it. I mean, I guess, maybe I had, but not really, not so, uh, specifically.

"But I don't think I could do the downtown thing. I mean, there's just no way," she continued emphatically, shaking her head from side to side and crossing and uncrossing her hands in a warding gesture. I began to nod my head in agreement, I think I might have even been about to agree, but as I looked at her face and actually started to think about what she was implying, my brain suddenly locked like a camera set on "blur," and I had no idea how or what I really felt or thought. I wasn't sure whether or not I was lying, and I wasn't proud of it if I was.

Then again, I was also feeling a little foolish. I mean, here Kerry had obviously thought about the "whole thing," whatever that was, and me, what had I been thinking about? Skin? Arms? Kissing? That's it? So now, I was not only weird and maybe a fag, I was a stupid fag, too. It occurred to me that maybe I had better think about this a whole lot more, and I wasn't sure what any of this meant for me, my personal future, or my friendship with Kerry, never mind anyone else.

I scowled in concentration at my cigarette, as if answers would be written in the falling ash. In fact, I was a little numb—I'd been shocked into thinking about what all of this might mean. It was fine to talk and think in intellectual abstractions, but to feel, I mean really feel, these different things and attempt to actually define them and then to really, truly think about what the logical end of the road was to acting on all of that, well, those things were worlds apart, and I had the less-than-comfortable suspicion that I had a foot on each one as they drifted farther and farther away from each other.

"Hey, we're here!" Kerry jumped up and announced as the train screeched and slowed into the station. "Dump the frown and let's get slammin'!" And she grabbed my hand to pull me out through the doors and onto the platform.

As we walked east toward the Bowery (CBGB's is 315 Bowery, for those of you who haven't been paying attention), I was overwhelmed with excitement—I was actually going to CB's for the first time in my life! It was all I could do to keep myself from practically skipping the rest of the way and dragging Kerry behind me for once.

The streets were filled with interestingly dressed people of all kinds, and art littered every stationary space, from graffiti to ornate spray-paint murals. I felt like one of those orphaned animals that's saved and then has to be gently reintroduced back to its natural environment. If this was supposed to be home, I was going to like it.

When we finally crossed the street in front of CB's, a huge crowd overflowed the sidewalk, and as we made our way through the throng, I was floored.

Punks, punks of all kinds—Mohawks, skinheads, helicopter haircuts (back and sides gone, top left to grow wild as weeds), boys and girls, boys and boys, girls and girls, punk boys and punk girls with punk babies (and I mean toddlers) dressed up in little combat boots—my eyes drank it all in and thirsted for more. All the different types of people that could possibly be represented, and everyone just hanging and waiting to have a good time. A general friendliness pervaded the crowd. Until this very moment, I had never felt so comfortable surrounded by a tremendous group of strangers. This, this was the world I'd been looking for, a world where differences were not only accepted, but also encouraged.

The smile I felt grow on my face actually hurt, but I couldn't have held it back no matter how hard I tried, because the rest of me felt so full of warmth, awe, and some unnamed, undefined joy that I felt ready to burst.

How long I remained like that, eyes wide-open and face ready to split, I don't know. I was so caught up in everything I'd even forgotten I was holding Kerry's hand.

I settled back to earth quickly enough, though, when I saw everyone start to gather in tight clusters by the entrance. I saw a few guys walk away from the door, shaking their heads in obvious disgust. "Damn ID card!" I heard one of them exclaim to a friend.

A discontented murmur seeped back through the crowd, so I, still holding Kerry's hand, started to work my way forward. Kerry pulled me back.

"Hey, Kerr, c'mon and let's go see what's up," I called out to her halfway over my shoulder and continued my forward motion, but her insistent pull on my hand stopped me. I turned around through the press of bodies to look at her and was surprised—Kerry suddenly looked very uncertain, and I interpreted it as her being shy. Which shocked me.

"Um, let's just wait back here. We'll find out what's going on soon enough," she stammered out and cast her eyes down to wherever the sidewalk was. Her cheeks were flushed, and I thought maybe she was tired out from that brisk walk from the subway.

"Nah, Kerr, I want to see what's going on."

People had started to disperse a bit and regather into scattered clusters. Some were shaking their heads or shrugging their shoulders at one another in the universal "I dunno" gesture. A couple of groups settled in peaceful rings on the sidewalk, pulling out sodas and chips from army bags and knapsacks, and passing around packs of cigarettes in impromptu picnics.

I looked at Kerry again. "You stay here a sec. I'll go talk to the door and see what's up."

She glanced quickly over to the large group still in the general area of the entrance, then turned back to me and nodded.

I made my way through the crowd, excusing myself when I could, challenge-glaring when I couldn't (no, I wasn't trying to cut the line— just needed to get information, thanks) until finally I stood in a small semicircular clearing in front of the entrance of CBGB's, which was half a door.

The bricks on the wall, where they weren't covered with layers of stickers and flyers of glory days gone by, were silver, and the same for what could be seen of the door or, rather, half door. That half was topped with a shelf that held a stamp pad, a stamper, wristbands, what looked like raffle tickets, and the beefy forearms of the door guy. His head was shaved completely bald, and he had a row of small silver hoop earrings running up the edge of his left ear, forming a seam around its edge. Although his head and cheeks were completely hair-free, he had a beard that hung down to his rather prominent chest.

Thickset and well muscled, like a lot of bouncers, he was wearing a white, ribbed, sleeveless T-shirt (which is a guido or a guinea-T to New Yorkers, but if you can't say "howyoodoowin" right, don't call it that—you'll get hurt) that showed off the massive black cross he had tattooed on his left deltoid and a rose and dagger design inside his right forearm.

Arranging my face into a careless but tough smile, I took a breath. "Hey there," I called out casually to Bouncer Boy with a nod of my head.

His eyes slid over to me and ran a quick appraisal. Apparently deciding I was "safe," he nodded in return. "Hey."

"Long day?" I asked him. I figured it couldn't hurt to be polite, and after all, it was up to this guy whether or not Kerry and I got in at all.

Bouncer Boy rolled his eyes skyward and gave me a real grin. "You know it. Everyone here to see SOD. Lot of twelve-year-olds trying to get in." He looked me up and down and grinned some more. "Now, I know you're not twelve."

I snorted and smirked back. "Yeah, you're right—I'm not. But ya know, even kids want to come out and play sometimes, right?"

Bouncer Boy laughed outright. "Too true," he agreed, "just too true. So," he drawled out, shifting positions to prop his head up on a meaty fist, "I'm Ronnie, by the way. What can I do for you?" and he looked at me through his lashes, which, I have to say, were actually pretty for a guy.

What was it with all these guys named Robbie or Ronnie? I wondered. Was there a sale that year on *R* names? I stifled the laugh making its way out and flashed him a quick grin, reaching out to shake his hand. "Nina. I was wondering…" I leaned in conspiratorially and lowered my voice a bit, "what the source of discontent was. I saw people seeming a bit, well, discouraged."

"Oh…that," Ronnie Bouncer Boy straightened a bit uncomfortably, "we um, we oversold the show, so we had to add a second at four o'clock. Dayglo Abortions will go on at two, and SOD at four—and it won't be all ages." Ronnie leaned both hands on the shelf to lean over and practically whisper, "But don't worry, put your money away. I'll make sure you get in."

Shit. I had to be on my way home at four or I'd never make it on time. Yeah, so what, I had to get home, big deal. I was only allowed out in the first place because I always made it back on time. The one time I was twenty minutes late (and that was because a bus didn't show up when it was supposed to), I was grounded for weeks! When you're in school, with no job, no car, and no legal rights, you don't have a lot of choices if you want to live to the age of emancipation. Fucker, this sounded so good, getting comped (complimentary entrance—remember this—it'll come in handy when you hang out) to see SOD…

This was the sort of thing Kerry talked about all the time, 'cuz she hung out here on a regular basis. She always told me and Nicky, or the gang at Universe, all about it whenever she stayed out later than we did—and that was at least half the time.

Fuck. Fuck. Fuck. This was a golden opportunity to be cool, too. I'd have bragging rights forever—I mean, no one I knew, not even Kerry, got comped to CB's, especially not to see a popular band. But if I stayed for the show and got grounded later, forget about hanging out at Universe after school or any new comic books. Forget about hunting around for records in the Village and holiday shopping with Nicky next weekend, forget about everything, because I'd be stuck in the house through the New Year, and that was never cool—ever. Not to mention boring.

All this ran through my head while I flashed a smile back at Ronnie. Suddenly, it hit me. I knew what I had to do. "That is truly cool of you, thanks." I smiled in appreciation.

Ronnie ducked his head and gave me a bit of an "aw, shucks" grin. Not that I believed it. I mean, whoever heard of a shy bouncer?

"I have to go tell my bud what's up. I left her back there, hangin' with some people."

"I'll bet she doesn't have your beautiful eyes," Ronnie said, "but tell her, I'll do it for both of you, since she's your friend and all." He stood up very straight, then crossed his arms over his massive chest, looking very pleased and proud.

I thanked him again and turned on my heel to go find Kerry.

"Hey, Nina?" Ronnie called out and I turned back.

"Yeah?"

"Is it your girl friend or your girlfriend?"

Flustered, I just stared for a few seconds, then recovered myself. "She's my friend. Why?" I felt my ears getting warm again. Maybe I was coming down with the flu or something.

"Really pretty girls like you usually have both, couple of boyfriends, too. Need one or the other? I could be one, and I know plenty of girls that would luuuv to be the other. I'm not a jealous kinda guy." His smile turned sly and smirky.

"Uh, I'm good for now, thanks."

"Oh, I am so very sure you are."

"I've got to get back," and I recovered enough of my composure to smirk, "before the search party comes out," and I turned to make my way back through the crowd.

"I'd be looking for you too, if I was with you!"

Without bothering to turn around, I answered, "Later, Ronnie Bouncer!" and made my way back through the crowd.

Kerry was not where I'd left her, and after a few seconds of looking around in circles, I finally found her standing behind a parked car and off by herself, which was a surprise in and of itself, and a puzzle to boot. Kerry had been here before, hung out with all these different kinds of people. She was the wild woman in our group and even among others. I had figured I'd spend half the time here being introduced to old, new, or even just-made friends.

Either way, I'd never expected to find her by herself, away from the crowd, instead of being in the middle of one, peaceful or otherwise. It's true, the otherwise part, I mean. Kerry seemed to form some sort of vortex around her that sometimes resulted in all-out bitch-slap-fests or slug-away-drunkard contests, but somehow, she was never directly involved, just sort of there, and usually leaving at that point.

Hmm...maybe that's why she'd decided to stay off by herself for a bit, avoid bad karma or something along those lines. She looked a bit, well, withdrawn, maybe even a little sad.

Well, I didn't have time to figure it out right then; I had a situation on hand and a decision in mind that was probably not going to be popular.

"Hey, Hopey!" Kerry exclaimed loudly when she saw me. Like the flip of a switch, her expression changed, and suddenly she was her cool and cocky self again. She sauntered over and ran her finger across my left shoulder. "You find out anything," and she paused to rub her hand up flat against my chest, "interesting?" The look she was giving me was definitely coy, to say the least.

Huh? What the fuck? Two seconds ago she looked like a kid who was told she couldn't have ice cream while everyone else ate their cones in her face. Now she was talking to me like um, like, geez, she was talking to me like I was a guy—like I was Jack.

My back stiffened and my eyes narrowed a bit when I looked down into her batting eyelashes and pouty grin. I had no clue what in the world she was up to. Maybe she had just decided to show off for the crowd. I mean, she was the wild woman, after all. But it was because of this that I was certain she wouldn't be too thrilled about my proposal.

Kerry ran her fingers across my shoulder and up and down my neck repeatedly while I recounted the situation, my conversation with Ronnie Bouncer Boy, and the options as far as I could see them. "What?" she exclaimed. "Ronnie came on to you? I'm gonna go punch his fuckin' lights out, c'mon!" and she grabbed my hand and turned to march through the crowd to the door, but this time, I held back.

"Hey, Kerry, we have to make a decision, dude. It's already after two, almost three, and I have to know: do you wanna watch Dayglo and just walk with me to the train at four, 'cuz Ronnie will let you back in to see SOD, or do you just want to walk with me over to Ronnie, so he knows your face to comp you, and I'll go home now?"

Kerry dropped my hand and her expression became a little more normal—girl-to-girl normal, I mean, not that weird, flirty girl-guy thing. Her usual warmth flooded back into her eyes and tone as she spoke. "Nina, you really want to see Dayglo and miss SOD?"

"Well, of course not, but it's not like I can stay—you know my mom," I reminded her.

Kerry shook her head ruefully in agreement with me, because she did know my mom or, at least, how she was. Grounding, for me, wasn't just not being able to go out. I couldn't have friends over, couldn't talk on the phone, and I pretty much had to stay where I could be seen unless I was working out with my brother in the basement or reading a book in my room, so you see, deviation from the already-filed "flight plan" was not a good, healthy, or sane idea. At all. Ever.

Kerry stared at the ground as she thought. She reached for my hand. "C'mon," she urged softly, "let's go home."

"Are you sure?" I asked her, just letting her hold my hand but not moving from where we stood. "I know you wanted to hang out, see some people you know and all that. It's okay, I mean, you know?"

Kerry stepped in closer to my personal space (and yeah, I have a zone, and it's mine all mine, thankyouverymuch) and lightly combed the hair that curled forward on my forehead with her fingertips. "I came here to hang out with," she lightly stroked my nose, "you. So how can I hang out with you if you have to go home? Come on, let's go," she said softly, and together, we started to make our way back.

"Hey, Nina, we're gonna take a different train downtown, okay?" she asked, as we turned in a different direction from the way I thought we had to go. "Besides, there's a deli"—that's short for delicatessen, by the way, otherwise known as a corner store, in case you were wondering—"on the way, and I need new smokes."

I knew Kerry was much more familiar with this part of town than I was, so I trusted her completely. And I knew she really did need a new pack of cigarettes—she'd been smoking mine all this time, not that I minded. "Hey, no problem, I need a pack myself."

We walked on, and about two blocks later we were somewhere in Alphabet City, deep in the East Side (and by the way, it's not called Alphabet City because it's filled with preschools or anything like that, though I'm sure there are a few—it's because the streets are named after consecutive letters of the alphabet, starting with the letter *A*, brought to you by the Big Apple, for all you *Sesame Street* fans) and in front of one of many typical delis—flowers and bouquets on the outside, junk food, condoms, cigarettes, and beer on the inside, with food staples and specialties from whatever country the owner came from. This deli setup is pretty much a New York City universal thing—think of it as a tradition.

Just before we walked in, I spotted a bucketful of unusual flowers— sunflowers with pink petals and raspberry red centers. I called Kerry's attention to them. "Hey, Kerr, check that out—that's different—pretty too, huh?" I made my way to the entrance.

She stopped and looked. "Yeah, that is different. It's cool." She took the time to light a cigarette, just as I put my hand on the door.

"Shit, I just lit this. Here," she dug into her jeans, "pick up a pack for me? I don't want to put this out yet," and she held out a green bill.

"Get yours, too."

I reached out uncertainly. "You sure? I've got it."

She tucked the bill into my hand and folded my fingers over it with her own. "Yeah, I'm sure. You would've got us off at the door, and I've been smoking yours, anyway." She took a step back and waved at me. "Go on, shoo!" She smiled, so into the store I went.

As I made my way to the counter toward the left of the entrance, a low shelf to my right was filled with even more flowers, and here I found sunflowers with deep purple petals and velvety black centers. Purple was Kerry's favorite color, so I didn't think twice. I grabbed a cellophane-wrapped bunch and took them to the counter. "Two packs of Marlboro and these." I shoved the flowers over to the diffident clerk.

"You want paper for those?" He pointed to the flowers.

"Yeah, sure. Thanks," I responded. I realized then that I was actually going to give these flowers to a girl, and not just any girl, but Kerry. My head started to feel a little tight, and I glanced through the glass of the door to see where Kerry was. I saw a flash of her leather-jacketed arm as she dragged on her cigarette. She seemed to be in conversation with someone, and from the expression on her face, she seemed a little frustrated. Maybe someone was hassling her about her hair or something.

I must have drifted off, because the clerk was annoyed with me. "You pay cash now?" he was asking in an annoyed voice, and I shook myself out of my, well, I guess it was a daze.

I smiled ruefully to myself, I'd just caught myself acting like a loon, then looked at the clerk. "Yeah, man. Here," and I pocketed Kerry's money and handed him my own.

He slid the cigarettes and flowers back over to me, and as I put the packs in an outside pocket of my coat, I wondered how I'd give Kerry the flowers.

Now, a quick word about my coat. It was an oversized, single-breasted, wool men's coat that I'd picked up for a whole two bucks at the Antique Boutique (on Broadway, not too far from Canal Jean—and two bucks, my friends, yo! Good deal!), and it had a pattern of teeny-tiny black and hunter green squares all over. A small rip had opened on one side, under the outside pocket, so I patched it up with a bright red flannel square. Since in my high school, regulations required us to wear either a black or navy blue overcoat, I wore my coat openly and notoriously with pride and not a little touch of defiance. I loved that coat; it fit great, it looked cool, it had a million inside pockets, and it was very warm. It also, for some reason, pissed the gr'ups (grownups, that is) off—I don't know why. I think my mom threw it out when I was really sick and stuck in bed for a few weeks, but that's another story for another time.

I took the paper-wrapped bunch of flowers in hand and a deep breath, squared my shoulders, and walked to the door. I couldn't see Kerry through the glass as I tried to work out in my head what I'd say, and how I'd say it. Would I just hand the flowers over to her with a shrug, like "no big deal," or would I try to hide 'em behind my back and do some courtly type little flourish? Yeesh. That sounded really stupid. No, wait, maybe that was sweet. Wait, no, hell no, that was fucking corny as all hell, forget that.

How to do this and still be cool, not cross too many lines, not lose face and still make it look good, still be sincere—that's what I had to figure out. I slid those purple flowers into an inside pocket of that best buddy of a coat.

I made it to the door and swung it open. My eyes found Kerry leaning against the lamppost, one leg on the ground, one on the base, one hand jammed into a pocket of her leather, the other dangling on her thigh, cig hanging out of her mouth at that perfect angle. She'd taken her glasses off and put them away somewhere, and she watched me with wide, glowing eyes.

Standing in that universal tuff rebel slouch, in the gathering twilight under the glow of the streetlight, with the light catching and throwing shadows on and around her, she was the very picture of everything I thought cool and tuff and sweetly vulnerable could and should be, and I knew the way I should play this, while those cat green eyes of hers pulled me in. She tossed the butt she was smoking to the ground with negligent ease.

"Yo, Maggie!" I called out as I walked over, caught in that pull and taking one of the cigarette packs out of my pocket. I felt that familiar wiseass grin ease along my face and attitude come up and envelop me like a safe and warm cloak. "Catch!" and I tossed the cigarettes toward her.

The hand left her pocket to reach up and neatly pluck the box out of the air as I closed the distance between us. "Hey, Hopey, thanks." She waved the pack at me, then slid them and her hand back into her pocket.

"*No problema*, girl," I answered, and reached into my coat. "These looked like they were yours, so I couldn't just leave them, could I?" and I grinned, holding the flowers before me.

Kerry gasped softly as she looked at them and just as softly put her hand over mine, fingertips warm from having been in her pocket and barely touching the back of my hand.

"They're beautiful. Thanks, Hopey," she barely whispered. "Um, I've got something for you, too," and she slid her free hand behind her back, where she'd been carefully hiding and balancing a bunch of the pink and raspberry flowers I'd admired when we first got here.

We smiled at each other, surprise, shyness, warmth, and wonder all mixed in our expressions, and as we stood there, under the streetlight, we leaned in toward one another until our foreheads touched, and we gave each other a one-armed hug. I closed my eyes and enjoyed the warmth of our bodies together and the texture of her skin against mine on my face. She felt so small against me and yet so solid and strong. Why hadn't I noticed that before?

After some unknown amount of time, I opened my eyes and found Kerry had opened hers, too. It was too close to maintain focus, though we tried for a moment or two. Then we burst out laughing and separated a bit, an arm still around one another's waist, but no longer hugging. "Oh, wait a sec..." I said, digging into my coat pocket with my free hand, "this is yours, too," and I slid my arm around her again and put her money in her back pocket.

"Dude, is that the money I gave you?" She reached over to check. "Man, Hopey, what the fuck? Just let me do something nice, ya know?"

"Hey, it wasn't much, ya know?" I replied, "but if you really, really want to, you can get pizza when we get back to town, 'kay?"

"Fine," she huffed at me, and turned away to put her nose in the air, but she didn't really mean it and turned around to smile at me again. "You really are something, you know?" She squeezed my waist tightly and tucked her head into my shoulder.

"Yeah." I squeezed back. "That's what my mom keeps telling me."

"Oh my God! Your mom!" she exclaimed. "We've got to go now! We're gonna be late!"

Holy shit! She was right. No wonder it was so dark out; it was four fucking thirty, and almost no way we would make it to the boat on time.

"C'mon, this way," and when Kerry grabbed my hand, we started running to the train station, one of the letter trains (the A, the C, there's a whole slew of the them, not including the N and R, which are just different lines altogether and ones I was already very familiar with), and to this day, I don't know where we were or what train we took, but we managed to get one just before it pulled out of the station.

This time, instead of sitting across from each other and talking, we sat next to one another, and we nodded off, her head on my shoulder, my head cushioned on her hair. An announcement came over what passes for the public address system on the subway, a system that manages to take any language and make it sound like it was spoken by a stroke victim, and woke us up. We couldn't make out too much except that the train wouldn't be making any stops below Fulton Street, which was a bit far from where we had to go. If we made the boat, it would be by the skin of our teeth.

"Okay, I know where we are—we get off at the next stop," Kerry announced with confidence, "and then I know a bit of a shortcut."

"Lead on, MacDuff," I responded, and we stood up to stretch out the kinks and get ready to go. Kerry picked my flowers up off the seat. "For you, madam." She presented and bowed with a little flourish, and I returned the favor with hers. "And these are for you, m'lady."

We shared a smile. Then I put the flowers into a huge inside pocket, and she slipped hers into her jacket, and with that, our stop came up.

As we walked up the steps and came out of the station, I looked up at the street signs and realized where we were. Then I noticed a couple of shady-looking guys wearing scruffy jackets and attitudes loitering around the entrance. Two of them had bicycles, and they all wore bike chains crossed over their chests and shoulders like bandoliers, but we ignored them and just kept talking and joking.

We crossed the street and stopped briefly to look at the time. What a break. We had fifteen minutes to make the boat, and it was only a ten-minute walk, maybe less, since there were no people downtown. The area was completely abandoned because this was the heart of the business district and the stock market wasn't in session.

"Hey, dyke!" one of the guys from across the street yelled. Kerry and I looked at each other, like "who the fuck is he talking to?" and kept walking.

"Yo, bo dagger! I mean you!" the voice continued. I stopped and turned around with a raised eyebrow. What the fuck was this guy talking about? Who the fuck did he think he was talking to?

He was starting to make his way across the street, and the guys he'd been with had grouped together to watch him and us. "Not you, gorgeous." The creep nodded at me with his chin. "I mean her," and he pointed at Kerry. He started to hurry his steps. "We'll fix her so she's fit to be a friend for a pretty girl," he continued, and waved his friends over. He picked up his pace, and his friends started jogging across.

Kerry was frozen in shock and fear, but I whirled and grabbed her hand. "Run, Kerry! Come on!" And I dragged her with me, hardly feeling a thing as we went flying down a side street to Nassau Street. I could hear the feet pounding behind us and the sounds of chains slamming into light poles as they chased us. At one point, I heard the sound of smashing glass. I didn't look back to see if it was one of the rare parked cars or a storefront. Now that I really knew where I was, I ducked up past the Federal Reserve Building (it's a landmark— you'll find that on most maps), and then I cut across a building plaza. Still leading Kerry by the hand, I zipped down an alley and up another side street to Broadway, only two blocks away from the ferry.

I don't know when exactly we stopped hearing the pounding, the yelling, and the chains behind us, but honestly, between the fear and the fact that I ran on the varsity cross-country team (and I was on the swim team, and I smoke, so there), I wasn't too surprised that we'd been able to lose them.

We stopped to catch our breath, and Kerry pulled out her new cigarette pack, took one for herself, then handed it to me. "Take one," she panted at me, so I did, and lit it.

We each took a deep drag of our respective butts, looked at each other, then stared at the ferry terminal. I suspect for all the cool that Kerry could be, she was no less relieved than I was to see it.

"I'm gonna get us some dogs and some Cokes, 'kay?" Kerry asked as we walked toward the vendor by the ferry entrance.

I slowly exhaled my cigarette and nodded a bit absently in agreement. "That'd be great, thanks."

She got the hot dogs, two each, and made sure I had one plain and one with mustard and sauerkraut, and a bottle of Coke to share.

We sat down on the curb where the cars load and unload from the boat, not saying much to one another, just eating our hot dogs and gathering our wits, I guess. It wasn't long before the boat arrived, and we ambled on with the other dozen or so passengers that had also been waiting outside. In no time at all, we found a bench to share and quickly claimed our territory, stretching our legs out on the bench across from us. As we settled in, Kerry cracked open the cap on the plastic soda bottle, took a long pull on the neck, and mutely held it out to me in invitation.

Now here's a funny thing. Neither Kerry nor I ever shared drinks with anyone (well, I shared with my siblings or parents, but that's different), not even with each other, really. It seemed everyone in our neighborhood we'd ever known had had it pounded into our collective consciousness about germs and the backwash thing.

Backwash, you ask? Whatinthehell is backwash?

Backwash is gross. It's when you release the suction on your drink and it flows back down, taking some saliva with it. By the time you get to the very end of a drink, unless you're a one-gulper, a "woofer" (you "woof" the drink down—usually milk or chocolate milk) or a "chugger" ("chug" beer—and end up like Yack), it's pretty much a fifty-fifty drink and saliva mix down there at the bottom.

This is totally beyond yuck when you think about it. This is what was taught in every single junior high school health class on Staten Island, along with very vague venereal disease warnings (something to do with the teacher's dog when she was in heat—I didn't get it) and different classifications of neurosis/psychosis (I love you, I hate you, I want to be you, I am you, you are me—what's my name again?).

But, as it turned out, there was and is a completely different way of looking at the whole "shared drinks" issue.

I stared at Kerry for a moment, visually inspected the bottle with its red and white wave, looked back at Kerry, and took the plastic into my hands. As I angled my head back and tossed some of the sweet bubbly brown stuff down, I eased the mental squick factor down a few notches by telling myself that even though the sugar in the soda was enough to keep a continent-sized colony of germies very fat and happy, the whatever-it-is acid in the soda itself could peel paint off a car, so it would probably kill all of those microcrawlers. Probably. I swallowed and handed the drink back, and we stared at each other for several long seconds.

"You know, Nina, we're sort of blood sisters now," Kerry informed me with a small grin.

I raised a brow in her direction. "Oh, really?" I drawled, playing along.

"Yeah, 'cuz now, you know, we've, like, shared bodily fluids," and she dangled the bottle in front of me, swirling the fizzy liquid. "Actually, this bottle could be said to represent the chemical equivalent of many different types of human interaction, you know. It's a concrete metaphor."

I eyed the bottle cynically, then realized what had been tickling the back of my brain. "You know what you have in your hands, Kerry?" I asked her, and reached to take it from her, studied it critically, then held it up for her inspection. "This is no longer soda. This, if we ignore the actual ratios of soda to saliva and enzymes and all that, this has an actual chemical equivalent," and I waved the ratio-challenged item. "This is what you get when you swap spit after drinking soda," I continued. "This," and I swirled it a little more, "is a kiss!" I concluded with a triumphant smile.

"Geez, thanks for putting it that way," Kerry responded sarcastically. "Now pass that damn kiss over here because the kraut is really sour, this mustard is really spicy hot, and," she scooted closer to me, "I'm really," she dropped her voice, "really," and she pushed her face bare inches from mine, "thirsty," she growled, and wrapped her hands around mine where they still held the bottle over my head. She held on to my eyes with hers a moment; then my gaze dropped to her lips with the soft half smile on them and the line that marked the challenging thrust of her jaw, and finally back up to the bottle in my hands.

"Well now, far be it for me to refuse you," I murmured and ran my tongue along the edge of my teeth, "anything." I released my grip.

Kerry fumbled a bit, and as I looked down into her face again, I realized she'd focused on my mouth. Before that strange tension could develop between us again, I nudged her with my shoulder, almost knocking her over.

She recovered quickly enough, gave me one of her evil grins, and, making a game out of it, very slowly and deliberately prepared to drink. "So, if I drink this," she stated, with the rim poised to drink, "now, after you have," and she rolled the bottle against the edge of her mouth, "you're saying it would be chemically similar to kissing you?" and she brought the rim to her lip.

I stared, then stared some more as she licked her lips, then smiled, startling me into recovering myself. "Oh, yeah," I stuttered. "Chemically, maybe, in a purely focused sort of technical sense, but," and I gave her a lazy grin of my own, "mechanically, now, that's a whole 'nother story."

"Well then," she smiled back, "bottoms up, baby!" She licked the rim and proceeded to chug half the soda down.

Wow. I couldn't chug soda like that—it would come out my nose—so I watched in wide-eyed amazement, truly impressed.

"Whew!" She pulled the bottle away and made big gestures of wiping her mouth with the back of her hand. "That was amazing. Your turn," and she shoved the poor misused plastic in my face.

Well, hey, no problem. I'm always up for a challenge. Grinning wickedly back, I took it from her, circled the rim with my tongue, and started to chug. I was watching Kerry watch me out of the corner of my eye, when all of a sudden, she clapped her hands over her face, her eyes watered, and she began to cough and splutter—the carbon gas was making the return trip back through her sinuses.

I couldn't help it. I started to laugh before I could even stop drinking long enough to swallow, and I began to choke. Cough. Splutter. Urgh.

"Oh my God, Nina!" Kerff. "You okay?"

Cough. Wheeze. Distance spit.

"Oh shit," kerff, spit, "shit!" And she started to pound my back.

Slap, cough, hooie, spit. I tried to reach into a pocket for a napkin or a tissue for me and for her, but I wasn't doing too well between the slapping, the laughing, and the choking. "Ha, ha, gurf!" I held a napkin out.

"Shit—Nina!" She just kept slapping my back.

"Erruf, 'keg?" I spluttered and, finally, cleared my throat. "Enough. I'm okay, really. Here," and I finally handed her a napkin, "use this."

Soda must have gotten into her hair, and she must have stuck her head against my back or something, because it was sticking out at odd angles, and not the ones she'd chosen, either. I'm sure I didn't look much better.

Our faces red from choking and laughing, our hair soda-sprayed and reconfigured, and noses burning from the acid, we sat and stared at each other. Then, of course, we burst out laughing again.

"Dude, you should have seen your face!"

"No way, man, how about you making like a fountain? I'm surprised no one threw coins at us," she teased in return.

"Yah, that's 'cuz you were in the way, acting like a rabid squirrel!" I laughed back. "I think the flowers are all crushed now. We should smell nice at least."

"Just shut up," she ordered, exasperated, "just shut up, sit with me, and let's sleep till we get there," and she readjusted herself on the bench and patted the space next to her.

I laughed quietly to myself this time. "Yeah, sure, Maggie, sure," and that's exactly what I did—lean against her, stretch my legs out on the bench, and fall asleep, very comfortably, too, I might add. Girls are nice that way.

We arrived back on "the Rock," as we sometimes called the borough, without further incident, and I grabbed my bag, what remained of the bottle of soda, and what little was left of my dignity, not that I really cared too much one way or another, and got ready to get off the boat.

"Wait a second!" Kerry called out. "I've got to do something!" And quick as a wink, she pulled out a small penknife, traced out a valentine, and cut "Hopey 'n' Maggie" and "11/16" under it into the wooden bench. "There," she said, "what do you think?"

"Beautiful." I smiled and held out my hand for the penknife, which Kerry handed over. I added "4-E" and then next to it traced out the symbol for "New York—Hard Core."

"Now that's perfect!" Kerry said, and rubbed my shoulder. I closed and returned her penknife, and we walked off the boat.

Oh, and by the way, I'm not condoning random acts of vandalism, but if you're ever downstairs on one of the really old boats, somewhere near the front, you can still find the "New York—Hard Core" symbol I traced and, faintly, to the left of it, "11/16."

We silently walked over to the train station that would take us back home, paid our fare, and found ourselves a couple of seats. We didn't actually sit next to each other this time. We sat in the L-shaped seats instead, so we could look at each other and talk without yelling across the car, but not be too close. It was a little weird, because I could tell we both wanted to be near each other, but we also needed just that tiny bit of space.

"Got any more of that kiss left?" Kerry asked me about three-quarters of the way into our trip, getting me out of the blank daze I had been in as I stared at the scenery passing by.

"Yeah, sure." I straightened myself up and dug into my bag. "Here," and I uncapped it and passed over the magic bottle.

She took a quick swig and held her hand out for the cap. "You've been holding it for a while, I'll carry it," she offered, and I passed it over. "Thanks," she said quietly.

"Don't mention it." I was just as quiet.

Silence reigned for the next few stops until the train pulled into good old sleepy Eltingville, and we walked down the stairs from the platform to the sidewalk.

"Got any more of that kiss?"

She smiled up at me. "Yeah, I've got some just for you," and she took the soda from her bag and passed it to me.

I smiled vaguely at the streetlight on the corner and took a sip, then passed it back, and that's how we walked back to my house, quietly sipping and passing that bottle back and forth until we got there.

We stood in front of my door for a minute. Does it seem like a lot of things happen at that door, or is it just me?

"I should go home, I think," Kerry told me uncertainly, biting her lip, and as we looked at each other, that pressure between us started to build, more quickly and heavily than it had before. I reached out and put a hand on her shoulder.

"No, it's early. Come on in, hang out with me a bit, and I'll walk you home," and I lightly tugged her toward me. Not releasing her, I pushed open the door to my parents' home and walked in, Kerry faintly asking, "Are you sure?" behind me.

"Yeah, of course." I turned my head to reassure her. "It's okay. Hi, Mom!" I called into the house and made my way to the kitchen, taking Kerry's leather coat from her while she held her disheveled flowers, taking mine out of my pocket, shedding my coat as well as Kerry's onto the sofa as we passed, with Kerry trailing behind me.

Ringo, the family dog, came over to greet us enthusiastically, and I rubbed his head as I walked.

My mom was downstairs in the kitchen by herself, making a cup of coffee. "Nina!" she exclaimed, and gave me a hug and a kiss, which I returned. "Hi, Kerry," she greeted my friend. My mom put her arm around my shoulder and held me in a loose hug. "You're home a little early. You girls have a good time? Those are very pretty," she added, looking at the flowers, then us, with a pleased and expectant look on her face.

Kerry and I looked at each other and burst out laughing. My mom smiled indulgently at us, then let me go, pulled out two plates from a cabinet, and handed them to me. Kerry and I placed our flowers on the counter.

"Dinner's on the stove. Why don't you serve the two of you and come sit at the table? Everyone ate already. Daddy's upstairs, he's not feeling well. Nanny's watching TV with him, and Nicky's friend's mother is bringing him home now. You can sit with me and tell me all about it." And she finished fixing her coffee and made her way to the table.

I dished out the food, sautéed chicken in some great sauce, which is my mother's own invention, and rice, and carried both plates to the table. We sat down and ate and gave my mom the edited version of the day's events, skipping Ronnie Bouncer Boy's commentary, the near mugging, and the chemical experiments.

"I'm sorry you guys didn't get to see Dayglo Contortions and Soldiers In Debt," my mom sympathized as we came to the end of our escapades. "And that was so very irresponsible of Heebie Geebies, not to mention disappointing. The two of you should do something else next Sunday to make up for it," she added.

I looked at my mom with gratitude and surprise. "Thanks!"

"Don't mention it, sweetheart." She smiled at me. "So what are you doing now?"

"Um, just gonna go outside and have a smoke, and then I'll walk Kerry home. Okay, Mom?" I got up with my empty plate, and Kerry grabbed hers as well.

"That's fine, sweetheart," and Mom got up from the table herself, taking her coffee with her. "I'm going upstairs to sit with Daddy and Nanny." She walked to the stairs. "Tell Nicky to walk Ringo when he gets home?" she asked, pausing at the first step to see my response.

"Okay." I nodded in agreement. "No problem."

Well, you're probably wondering why parents that were so strict with a curfew would let their kid smoke. It's pretty simple, actually. When I was about twelve, a neighbor caught me and a friend "experimenting" with some of her mom's cigarettes and, of course, told my parents.

After the required lecture, my parents told me that if I really wanted to smoke, I'd be allowed to when I was sixteen—but no sneaking, and not before. So, I kept my part of the bargain—no butts and no sneaking—and well, now I was sixteen, so I was allowed. Easy, right?

Kerry and I dropped our plates off into the kitchen sink, then I slid open the glass doors to the yard, and we stepped outside. We could have sat on the porch, but there was a bench along the side of the house that received most of the sun in the day and was the quietest, darkest, and, most importantly, least observable spot in the yard. Of course we sat there.

I pulled out my cigarette, lit it, and sat back to inhale with a contented sigh, sprawling my limbs about in my usual fashion, legs stretched in front and arms across the back.

Kerry lit her own and settled in next to me, and we smoked in contented silence for a while.

"Hey," Kerry broke into the quiet, "give me your cigarette." Kerry twisted to face me and neatly took it from my mouth.

I sat up. "Dude?"

"Mine tasted funny," she said, waving the offending cancer stick in the air. "I wanted to see if yours was better."

An idea hit me, similar to the Coke bottle. "Oh yeah? Pass that over here," I told her and took it from her hand. We were now both sitting sidewise and facing one another.

"Okay, Nina," Kerry said. "We know for sure that neither one of us will die exchanging lip cells, either," and she looked at me archly.

Caught, I shrugged and grinned. "Okay, so we've established that the body is covered with skin, and we're always touching. We've technically already swapped spit, and now we've exchanged lip cells. How hard can this be to do?"

"Since we've already technically done it, you mean," she drawled out, "except without the doing-it part?"

"Right," I agreed. "It's just a matter of degree, in a way."

Kerry pursed her lips and scrunched her brow in thought for a few seconds. "Okay, then, let's just do it. We're both grown-ups here, right?"

I shrugged casually. "Yeah, we are."

Kerry put her hands on my waist, and I did the same. Slowly, she leaned in and kissed my cheek, and I in return kissed hers. "We've done that before, right?" she murmured softly, "so that wasn't a big deal, right?"

"Oh, no, not so big at all," I replied just as softly. With my fingertips I gently brushed away the hair that drifted on to her face and tenderly kissed the very outside corner of her mouth.

Kerry reached for my face and did the same in return. We sat there for a bit simply tracing each other's face, until the sound of a window being opened shocked us apart.

"Nina!" my mom called out, "it's seven thirty."

"Okay, Mom. Going now," I called back up, and I heard the window slide shut again.

"Where were we?" I asked Kerry, as we put our hands on each other's waists again.

"You were almost, but not quite, kissing me," she answered with an impish grin.

"Right. Okay. Well, here we go," I answered, and we leaned in closer to each other, only to stop, less than an inch away. "I can't do this," I said, shaking my head. "I want to, but I can't." My voice shook, my hands shook, my heart felt like it was about to fly free from its bony cage and fall to its doom. It didn't matter how logically, technically, we'd done it. Mechanically, it really was a whole 'nother thing.

Kerry reached up to touch my face. "It's okay, Nina, really. Me too, baby," she said in a shaking voice. "Me, too."

I caught her hands in my own and kissed them, then stood, pulling her up with me, and released one of her hands to dust off my back. "Let's get going?"

"Yeah, let's," she replied, dusting herself off, and we went out through the gate in the yard.

As we walked to her house, we linked our pinky fingers and kept bumping our hips into one another, jostling each other a bit, and just smiling, and finally, as we turned off onto the side street she lived on, walking in the middle of it as was our habit (and I don't know why, but everyone I know does that on quiet streets), I stopped underneath a street lamp to speak.

"Kerry, I don't know, this is like one of those stories people tell you about, where, like, the character tries pot for the first time and then becomes like that book *Go Ask Alice* or something, you know? There are some things that once you start, you know?" I poured out, confused and scared.

Kerry turned to face me and put her hands on my shoulders. "There are some things that once you start, Hopey," and she came in a little closer to me, "you just can't stop."

Her eyes glowed underneath that light, and as her face came closer to mine, they seemed to explode into a million green and blue crystals as a tightness built around my chest with want and my head with dread, and the next thing I knew, the softest skin I'd never felt until that moment touched my lips, and I closed my eyes to revel in the sensation. Somehow, I'd always known that it would feel like this, that it felt just like I'd always imagined I'd felt like to someone else.

I had a brief mental flash of the ocean, of storm-tossed eyes, but that disappeared quickly as I realized, *Oh my God I'm kissing a girl!* and I froze for a moment, but Kerry's hands tightened on my shoulders, and my brain yelled, "Hey there, idiot, *do* something!" and I put my arms around her waist.

The kiss deepened, and as her mouth began to move under mine, I was right there with her, my mouth full with this soft, sweet sensation, and over and over again I kept thinking that this was the kiss I'd always dreamed of, that I'd never had (and I'd kissed a *lot* of boys by then)— just so juicy and sensual and arousing, with all the overflowing promise of a ripe peach. At one point, the thought flashed through my head, "she kisses like me," and then the thought was drowned in this overpowering flow.

We broke breathlessly apart after some unknown length of time, and I had one hand tangled in her hair, the other across her back, while both her hands had a firm grip on my ass. We rested forehead to forehead, panting, easing down.

"Jesus, Nina." Kerry looked into my eyes, with an amazed look on her face. "You kiss just like me!"

"Funny," I said with a little growl, "I was thinking you kiss just like me," and I drew her in again to repeat the experience. Lost in her lips again, I eased under her jacket and traced the curves of her ribs, her spine, the solidness of her hips, while she found her way along my ribs and back, then rested along my sides, thumbs gently easing along the lower curve of my breasts. My lips started making their way down her neck to that beautiful hollow I wanted to taste.

Hrrrooonnnkkk!

That fucking car had to decide to come down in our direction on its way to wherever. Granted, we were standing in the middle of the street, lit up like a stage, but still, there was plenty of room, and the driver could've gone around us, right? Yeah, I thought so, too. Jealous bastard.

Still wrapped up in each other's jackets, we snuggled into one another and Kerry tucked her head into my shoulder, lips barely brushing my neck.

"I love you, Hopeful," she whispered with a kiss.

"Love you too, Magpie," I whispered back, kissing her head.

By unspoken agreement, we separated and straightened ourselves up, linked hands and began to walk, or rather stumble, the remaining three blocks to her house.

Why stumble? Because you know we just had to keep stopping every couple of steps to make out again, and I was in such a daze, I couldn't even tell you my name if you had asked it (which is probably the original reason why people need ID cards, to remind themselves, or at least, I'd like to think so), and I couldn't even tell I was walking because I wasn't aware that I had legs. You hear people tell you, and you read and see it everywhere all the time, "Oh, it was like floating on cloud nine," and "It was the most romantic thing in the world," and I always wanted to know what in the many levels of hell they were talking about.

I found out—they were wrong. This wasn't like floating. This was gliding, whirling—this was being the magic center of the kaleidoscope, the stars, the wind, her mouth, her hands, all melting together into one gorgeously intricate whole.

We finally got to her front gate—a low, whitewashed, ranch rail type thing—and Kerry pulled and I pushed until we were both halfway over that damn railing and we could hear it groan, whether in protest or encouragement, we never stopped to find out—we were way too busy.

A light snapped on in the neighbor's front yard, and we froze in position.

My mouth, having finally tasted that lovely little hollow, had been trailing down the path her open shirt provided (when, no, wait, how did that happen?), and under my hand was the incredibly resilient softness of her very female curve, with that wonderful hard little bud between my fingertips.

Kerry had one leg wrapped over mine as I stood between hers, and had our hips been any closer, the fabric from our pants would have melded, and as it was, I'm sure they almost did. It was getting pretty damn hot down there. One of her hands had found its way down under my waistband and was squeezing its way along my butt—I guess she must have really liked my ass, and it's not too bad of one if I do say so myself. The other seemed to have discovered the same thing mine had, and for the first time in my life, I actually felt something other than chafing or discomfort, and that something felt really good.

I lifted my head and Kerry looked me in the eye for a second, then down at her chest. "Your hand is on my boob, Hopeful," she informed me with a sly grin.

I looked at my hand and its placement, down at myself, and back at Kerry. "Yours, too," I informed her with a smile of my own. I stroked once gently, then removed my hand and straightened up, a little painfully, I might add. Bending over for so long is not comfortable. Kerry stood with me and wiggled to stretch her back a bit. It had been her shoulders against the railing.

She grabbed my hand and put it back. "I didn't say I didn't like it." Kerry smiled and held her hand over mine. "I just wanted to make sure you noticed."

"Trust me, I noticed," I said, and caught her around with one arm. "One more kiss, and I've got to get home," I said, and bent my head again, but she put both hands on my chest and stopped me.

"Baby, how are you going to get home?" she asked distressfully.

"I'm just gonna walk, Kerry. It's only a few blocks away."

Kerry shook her head. "No way. I don't want you to walk alone, I'll walk with you," she insisted, and at that moment, her watch beeped.

"Fuck! Eight thirty!" she exclaimed. That had been the time she'd been asked to get home by. Not that it really mattered much to Kerry. She knew no one was home because there were no lights on and no car in the driveway, and she said as much.

I looked around to verify for myself and nodded in agreement. Then it hit me. Fuck! Eight thirty! We'd been making out for almost an hour. I'm sure my parents knew it didn't take that long to walk four or five blocks. "Yeah, okay, I've got to run," I agreed in a bit of a panic. I was in deep, I mean very deep shit, and I had no idea what to tell my parents if they decided to ask me where I'd been and what I'd been doing for the past hour.

"Well, you see, Mom and Dad, um, Kerry and I were, um, performing some technical experiments, oh, in the middle of the street, and then we performed a few more in front of her house." Or how about "Mom, Dad, I'm going through some sort of identity crisis, and Kerry here was trying to help me out." Or even better, "Ah, Mom? Dad? I think I'm a *homosexual*, so tomorrow, after you kick me out of the house, I'm going to join the local devil-worshipping cult, shave my head, join a rock band, and then get lost in a drug-induced, alcoholic haze, 'kay?"

"Grounded, grounded, *grounded*!" singsonged through my head in Nanny's voice at higher and higher volumes, and I started picturing what my dad might do. He'd really been going after me lately—insults early in the morning as he passed my bedroom on his way into the bathroom, more criticism, more than the usual threat of the occasional swat. If he decided that this was an opportunity to really teach me a lesson, you know, show me exactly who was boss, he wouldn't just hit me. He'd start screaming at my mom, going on and on and get her all crazy until they were both screaming and yelling and flailing for what would seem like hours. Trust me, my mom did *not* hit like a girl, and she had deadly accuracy with a tossed shoe if one of us couldn't find "the belt" quickly enough. After the first "corrective action," miniature repeats would follow for days until they forgot about it or I or one of my siblings did something else to distract them.

I wasn't just in trouble—I was gonna be fucking dead. God, I wished graduation was tomorrow, but it was over a year and almost a half away—if I lived that long.

I know I must have paled and the panic shown on my face. Kerry reached both hands up to stroke my cheeks with her fingertips. I instantly felt a bit calmer. But only a bit. "Nina baby, it's okay," she reassured me. "Don't be scared. Just tell them, um, tell them I dropped my key and you were helping me find it—in the leaves," she continued.

Good idea. I nodded in agreement. No, wait, bad idea. I'm a terrible liar. No way could I get away with it.

Kerry let go of my face and took my hand, and we started walking back to my parents' home. Of course, we walked back the same way we walked to Kerry's, stopping to make out every few steps, and there wasn't a parked car, telephone pole, streetlight, or quiet wooded spot where we didn't take a little time to perform a few more technical experiments, or maybe mechanical experiments.

We got to my front door and started to kiss good-bye—I think I pointed out earlier how that door sees a lot of action—when it struck me. How was Kerry going to get home? I didn't want her to walk by herself; that had been the whole point in the first place, and I said so.

"Nina, we can't keep walking each other back and forth all night," Kerry said, "although it's definitely worth doing." She grinned.

All the lights downstairs were off, and the TV light was the only thing that glowed out the window from my parents' room. My father always fell asleep with the TV on. Maybe I'd gotten lucky, maybe this could work, maybe...

"Wait a second," I told her. "I've got an idea." I stuck my head inside and called up, "Mom?"

No one answered, except for Ringo, who came rushing over in a scatter of nails and fuzz to jump all over me. He gave little whines to let me know he still wanted to go out in between licks. This was so much the better for what I had in mind.

"Nicky?" I called as I scruffled Ringo's head and ears.

"He's not home yet," my mom answered in a sleepy voice. "His friend's mom got sick, and I'm too tired to drive. He's staying over there."

"All right, um, I'm going to walk Ringo, then, okay?"

"Thanks, honey," my mother answered back in that I'm-not-really-hearing-you-because-dreams-are-calling-me voice.

I stepped in quickly, grabbed the leash that was always by the door, and Ringo did a little jig on his hind legs at the sound. I rubbed his head some more and scratched his ears for good measure, then snapped the leash onto his collar. I stepped outside with my dog.

Kerry looked at me then backed up a step as Ringo launched himself at her in a frenzy of doggie-style greeting, hauling me behind him. And Kerry laughed while she tussled with him, bumping heads and wrestling on the lawn a bit.

Greeting formalities over, Ringo came back over to me and sat pressed into my leg. Kerry stood and brushed the grass from her back and legs. She came over to me and laid a hand between Ringo's ears. "So? How're you getting home?"

"Ringo," I answered a bit smugly. "I'll walk with you, and then Ringo will walk back with me, and that way you won't have to worry about my continued health and safety, see?" I smiled—at my luck for having avoided death and at my own cleverness.

"Mmm, Hopey, you inspire me," Kerry drawled out in an undertone and closed in to kiss me, but this time, I stopped her. Something had been kicking around in my head, and I needed to know something very important, well, important to me, at least.

"Hey, I want to ask you something," I said softly, as she put her arms around my neck. "I want to know who you're kissing," she kissed my neck, "when you kiss me." She kissed my throat.

"Who do you think I'm kissing, silly?" And she kissed my lips. I lost myself for whatever length of time, but I stopped her again. Kerry had put her glasses on again while I'd been in the house, and now I couldn't read the expression in her eyes.

"No, really, I'm serious," I said in a low voice. "Are you kissing Hopey? Or are you kissing me? Or are you Maggie kissing Hopey or me?"

Kerry wouldn't look at me as she silently played with the collar of my coat. "Aw, Hopey, you always ask the hard questions," she sighed into my throat, and I smiled grimly to myself. Fine. I'd been afraid of that and expecting it all along. So this was my little red wagon to play with, all alone, and not hers, then.

Kerry looked up into my stony expression and stroked my cheek again. "Oh, Nina, does it matter really? If you're Hopey and I'm Maggie, or whatever? All that matters is these lips," and she kissed me, "on those." She inched back and smiled. "Technically, that is."

"I guess," I got out through a forced smile. I was feeling pretty stupid, or actually s-t-u-p-i-d, nice and big and spelled out in capital block letters.

Ringo whined and his tail beat against my leg.

"We should get going," I said shortly, and Ringo jumped up to drag me forward.

Neither one of us was really in the mood to talk much on the way back to her house that second time, although we did hold hands all the way to her front gate. We faced each other and stood there silently. "Hey, have a good night, Maggie, okay?" I finally asked softly and gave her a lopsided grin. This weight was growing in my chest, almost painful in its intensity. I felt my eyes get large and round, like I was going to cry but wouldn't.

"You too, Hopey," she answered me, and we leaned into one another for a kiss on the cheek. Suddenly, Kerry threw her arms around me and hugged me tightly. "Nina," she whispered in my ear, "my best friend, Nina," and she kissed my lips with a ferocity I didn't know she possessed, and I responded in kind, that weight in my chest let loose into a bursting, searing pain, like burning arrows flying through me and into her, anchoring us, sealing us together.

Finally we broke apart, but the pain didn't stop. It felt worse, like I'd taken my skin off and my rib cage was open, my beating heart steaming in the November air for all to see.

"Go," Kerry said brokenly. She was at the point of tears. "Go before I don't let you," and she kissed me breathless again. "Go." She was crying and I could taste the salt of it. "Go," she ordered between kisses and tears and finally, finally, I drew breath enough to say, "I can't. I just can't."

The wind was cold on my face before I burrowed it into her hair, and I realized I'd been crying all this time, too.

We held and looked at each other wordlessly, helplessly. Don't ask me where this sudden sorrow came from. I didn't know then, and I still don't know now. Maybe we'd been really scared by those guys that chased us down from the subway, or maybe we both knew that we'd crossed a line and couldn't go back, no matter what we did, and that nothing would or could ever be the same again. Maybe we were both really disappointed that we didn't get to see Dayglo Abortions after all. Maybe.

Ringo just settled himself quietly underneath the bottom railing of the fence and lay on the grass, alternately observing and drowsing. Lucky dog, with no decisions to make, no people to answer to, no expectations on him. He didn't care if people said he sniffed butts or licked his fun parts—it was all part of being a dog. Feed him, pet him, play with him, and walk him, and he was pretty darn happy. I wished I could be Ringo.

Somehow, we finally said our good nights and good-byes, and exchanged a flurry of hugs and kisses and soft promises, and eventually, I got home. I remember being about two blocks away from home and just staring at the sky, then finally getting back to my front door in a daze. Bet you thought I'd never get there, hmm? Me either. I looked up at the house, now all dark and silent, and up and down the street where I lived, the very occasional car going by at high speed.

Sighing, I led Ringo inside, snapped off the leash, and took off my coat. I hung both up by the door and quietly made my way up the stairs, my doggie friend behind me the whole way. He let himself into the room I shared with Nanny, and I went to the bathroom. I brushed my teeth, washed my hands and face, and stared at myself in the mirror. I didn't look any different, really. My eyes were a little red around the edges, my nose too. But it was still my face, the one everyone else would see. I just didn't recognize it, from the inside.

I made my way to my room, undressed in the darkness, and slid beneath the blankets on my bed. As I settled in, I lay on my back, head on one hand. I brought the other to my lips, and I touched them. They were so very soft, I just couldn't believe that I'd actually kissed Kerry, that we'd been making out, that, oohmuhgosh, it was a girl. I didn't know who I was anymore. Was I Hopey or Maggie? Was I still Nina? Was I still even a girl? Still human? Maybe it would all be obvious to me in the morning, I thought, but as I drifted off, I kept wondering, why had those guys called Kerry a dyke? It made me feel guilty.

It should have been me.

Chapter Seven:
Oscillate Wildly

Thump. Thump. Thump. Crash. Rustle, rustle. Crash.
"Good-for-fuckin'-nothing kid, out with that punk-ass-faggot dyke friend to all hours. Piece of shit'll probably die of AIDS," drifted into my ears and woke me in the morning as my father got ready for work at five o'clock.

This was how I had been woken up every day for the last few months. I didn't have to get up until six, but my dad, who had to leave by six, was up and at 'em or, rather, me early every day.

Some days I was "good-for-nothing," some days I was a "fuckin' bitch," and others I was a "fuckin' monster piece of shit" and a "fuckin' loser," and he couldn't wait until I was old enough so I could "move the fuck out," and he made damn sure (hmm...bitter...do I sound bitter? Sorry. Not bitter, still a bit pissed, though) he was loud enough so I could hear him, since my room and the bathroom shared a wall.

I lifted my head and opened my eyes to see Nanny sprawled and still deeply wedged in dreamland. I squirmed and tried to settle myself back in and struggled to fall back to sleep for another half an hour, but then I realized, there was that "dyke" word again, and about Kerry, too.

God, that girl had so many guys after her, it could make you dizzy. And she didn't look anything at all like whatever it was a dyke was supposed to, not that I knew what that was, really, just some vague notion of gym whistles and sweatpants. And if those guys thought she was a dyke, and my dad thought she was a dyke, what in the world was I going to do when people like my dad realized it wasn't Kerry but me? And what was a dyke supposed to look like, anyway? And why "dyke"? What the fuck did that mean, anyway?

"Homosexual," I knew. "Gay," I understood. "Lesbian," well, it just sounded too damned strange, like either an appliance (like a refrigerator or a lawn mower) or a job title, you know, "I got my degree, and now I'm a practicing lesbian, got my own office and everything." I know, I know, Sappho, Isle of Lesbos, yes, I know, but still, it sure as hell didn't sound like it had anything to do with women loving other women, and "dyke," well, yeah, dikes hold back water in Holland, and there was a Greek goddess or something like that named "Dyké" (she had something to do with revenge, opposite her sister, "Até," who had something to do with altruistic/universal love), but beyond that, it didn't make any sense to me.

Oh my God. I opened my eyes into the darkness while my father continued his monologue in the shower. I had better get some damn understanding double damn quick. I spent over an hour yesterday making out with my best friend, who was a girl like me, and I was pretty sure that it would make me at least one of those words, if not all of them.

At that realization, I got so cold I started to shiver, and I huddled myself into a little miserable ball with my legs pulled into my chest and my arms wrapped around my legs for warmth. I shook so hard my teeth rattled in my head and made even my eyes hurt.

By the time my father finished his morning ablutions, left for work, and my mom came in to the bedroom to give Nanny and me good-morning kisses, my bone shaking and teeth rattling had made me sweat, even though I was freezing under the bedclothes.

Nanny's bed was closer to the door, so that's where my mom went first. "Good morning, good morning, good morning to you," my mom sang to Nanny, who grunted and rolled as close to the wall as possible.

I heard the kiss my mom placed on Nanny's cheek.

"Nooooo, leave me aloooooone," groaned Nanny. She was always a big grump in the morning.

"Rise and shine, sweetheart," my mom answered gently. "The sun is shining, the birds are singing, and the school bus is here in forty-five minutes."

Nanny groaned and flopped about again, and finally got to her feet. "I'm not feeling shiny," she grumbled as she made her way out of the bedroom, "and there's no sun, and I hate birds," she continued as she stumbled into the bathroom.

I stayed huddled in my little miserable self as my mom came closer and closer and finally sat on the edge of my bed. "Hey, morning bird, you're not singing today," my mom said gently as she leaned down to kiss me and lay a hand on my face.

Her fingers felt nice on my cheek, cool and soft.

"Nina!" she exclaimed in dismay, "you're burning up! How do you feel? Does your stomach hurt? Is your throat scratchy? Is your head okay?" she asked me, all concern as she laid her hands all over my face and neck to see if I was warm everywhere.

"Head hurts a little, Mom," I croaked out. "Little nauseous, too," which was true, because thinking about what those words meant was giving me a headache, and knowing how my father would use them for me with such anger made the bile come up in my throat.

God, I wondered if Kerry was still my friend. Maybe last night didn't mean anything, she was just being cool and punk; maybe it was supposed to just be a game, you know, playacting Hopey and Maggie, nothing to get hung about; maybe she didn't want to hang out with me anymore because I wasn't normal. Maybe she'd tell everyone and I'd lose all my friends, and it would eventually get back to my parents so they could hate me. Maybe she hated me, too. The wondering made me hurt everywhere, and I hugged my knees closer for comfort.

"Nanny!" my mom called, "bring me the Tylenol and a cup of water, please!"

I heard the cabinet doors slide open and Nanny rustle around in them as she followed Mom's request.

"Oh, and the thermometer, too!" Mom added, her hand holding one of mine. She reached up to brush the hair off my brow, and I flinched, imagining how quickly that caress could become a blow if she knew who her daughter really was. Don't get me wrong. I know my mom loved me, but my dad could get her crazy, just wind her up like a top and watch her spin on whatever it was he was mad at, and he'd just watch. And it wouldn't matter who was on the side of the angels, once Mom got going. She was hard, no, make that impossible, to stop.

I remember one time when my mom went to work on a Saturday, my dad had set us to do chores. He went after Nicky in the yard—poor Nicky had forgotten to clean something, most likely, since he'd only been eight or so at the time—and before you could say "oh shit!" the big

JD Glass

guy had lifted Nicky by his striped T-shirt and bent him backward over the porch railing. As he started to rain punches on my brother's ribs, I panicked and jumped on my dad, hanging from his neck, screaming how I hated him. Well, he stopped hitting Nicky and chased me for a little while until I got out of the yard and hid in the woods down the block.

I finally got home just a little bit before my mom did, and when she walked through the door, late in the afternoon and tired from her sixth day of work that week, my dad jumped in her face and started ranting and raving at her about how terrible me and Nicky were, how he had no control over us, and how she'd better do something and do it right damn now because he'd had it and blah blah blah. All this, and she hadn't even taken off her jacket or put her bag down. In fact, she wasn't even fully in the house yet. Three guesses what would happen next. She'd try to say hello, she'd try to talk over him, then she'd be, well, just broken, I guess, and start screaming too, and then, time to get "Suzy," which is what we called the belt. Or if she was just too upset, it was time for the shoe toss. Ow, dammit.

Mom misread my flinching for pain. "Poor baby," she murmured and kissed my hand instead. "You stay home today and feel better, okay, little bird?"

"Okay, Mom," I agreed and smiled weakly, because I really did feel like hell. I snuggled farther into my pillow.

Nanny came in at this and stood there in wide-eyed amazement. "Hey, I don't feel good"—cough, cough—"my head hurts," she protested. "I should stay home, too."

For all that Nanny drove me crazy sometimes, she just looked adorable standing there all indignant, cup of water in one hand, thermometer and Tylenol in the other, making herself red in the face trying to cough. I hid the smile she brought to my lips—Nanny didn't ever want to get caught being cute. She hated being "the baby" because she was almost as tall as I was and a shade taller than Nicky. *She'd hate me, too.* I winced at the thought, knowing how deeply uncomfortable Nanny was with people and things that were outside her idea of "normal." They made her angry, and it was easier for her to hate them all. The smile died.

I was so very much wrapped up in my thoughts, I lay unresisting as Mom slipped the thermometer into my mouth and argued with Nanny over her "cough."

"It's not fair—Nina gets to stay home whenever she wants. Daddy always says you should never miss work or school on a Friday or a Monday."

"Unless you're sick, honey," Mom explained patiently, and held her hand out to me for the thermometer. I handed it over to her, and she studied it. "Hmm…one hundred." She took the pills and the cup from Nanny, who stuck her tongue out at me (I just gave her as much of the evil eye as I could from my half-buried position) and handed them to me.

"Drink all of the water, Nina, the whole thing, so you'll feel better."

I sat up to comply and took the pills and water down in a few gulps. It hurt going down, like it was traveling past a golf ball or something. I settled back into my cocoon.

"She's not sick, Mom. She's just sitting there looking all white and pinky. I can make my eyes and cheeks pinky, too, you know. You just have to pinch them, like this," and Nanny demonstrated her new blush technique.

"Nanny, your sister isn't feeling well. And when you bring home the grades Nina does, you can stay home and pinch your cheeks all day long, if you'd like." Mom tucked me in and stroked my hair. "You okay?" she asked me. "Do you want me to stay home with you?"

"Aw, Mom," Nanny protested, grabbed her clothes, and stomped out of the room.

I turned to look at my mom in amazement. She couldn't stay home from work, we all knew that. I wasn't *that* sick. "No, Mom, I'll probably be fine in a few hours. Please, don't forget to call the school before you leave and then after, when you get to work, okay? You know how they get," I asked her in my scratchy voice.

Here's the deal: at my high school, there was no real cutting. Your parents had to call either the principal or the school secretary before homeroom started, and then again, before the end of first period. If you didn't show up for school and had no verifiable parental phone call, you were up shit creek without a paddle, my friend. You had a detention, even if your parents just forgot to call. Let me repeat that: you had detention, not demerits, and detention consisted of either polishing the endless banisters and trophy cabinets, cleaning the school library, the principal's office, or, and this was my personal favorite, complex math equations with Attila the Nun herself—all of this, after school, for at least an hour. Sounds like a joy, doesn't it?

How did I know this, you ask? Easy. I'd been on detention—a lot—and at least once a year because my parents forgot to call the school.

"I'll go call right now, sweetheart, don't worry," my mom assured me. She got up off the bed and stood to leave, but I caught her hand.

"Mom?" I looked up at her.

"Yes, baby? What's the matter?" She looked at me with concern.

I just looked up at her and stared for a long second, the warmth in her face, the love and worry and tenderness in her eyes. I wanted to etch that image into my memory forever, to never forget it, so that in the days that I was afraid would come, I would remember that once I had been treasured and precious. I had been loved.

"Nothing. I love you," I told her, and I squeezed her hand.

"I love you, too, little bird," and she bent to kiss my forehead. I smiled and then shut my eyes to snuggle back in as Mom shut the door and left the room.

Nanny made some sort of protest to her in the hallway. Faintly, I heard my mom say, "Nina's sick. Leave her alone and don't tease her, Nanny."

I tried to shut out the normal noises of people getting ready in the morning, but in the end, I couldn't and I just lay there, mentally blank, miserable, and still cold, although it wasn't the same bone-deep chill I'd felt before. Maybe taking those Tylenol was a good thing after all.

I heard the sound of feet running across the house downstairs and the front door opening, which signaled Nanny's leaving for school.

"Bye, Mom! I love you! Bye, Nina! Read your comic books and feel better!" Nanny called as she left, and she slammed the door behind her, shaking the house.

By this time things had finally quieted down, and I actually closed my eyes to get some real sleep, but just as I drifted off, my mom opened the door and came back in. "Are you going to be okay by yourself, Nina? Are you feeling any better?" she asked me with the same soft concern she'd shown as she came over to sit on the edge of my bed again. She felt my face the same way she did before. "You seem a little cooler, thank God. Do you feel any better?" she repeated.

"I'm not so cold now," I sat up and answered truthfully, "still kind of yucko feeling, though," and I rubbed my head where it hurt the most.

"My precious, feel better," and she kissed near the spot I rubbed.

"Not there," I smiled, "here," and I put my fingers on the spot. It was an old joke between us—I'd show Mom where it hurt and she'd kiss a different spot, and I'd show her where it really was, and she'd go to kiss it and miss again, and this would go on for a bit until Mom got the boo-boo.

When I was really small, she'd cover me in kisses and tickle me until I was shrieking with laughter and had forgotten where it had hurt in the first place, while in the interim she'd gotten me disinfected and bandaged without my ever even noticing, and there was nothing left but the smile I felt from the inside out and the Band-Aid on an elbow or a knee.

I was too big for tickles now, though, and I didn't know of any antiseptic or Band-Aids that could fix me.

Mom kissed the spot I'd indicated and stood. "There's cold cuts in the fridge, there's eggs, orange juice, bread, and milk. I left you some money on the counter in case you need anything later—food or if you want to rent a movie. You can ask Nicky or Nanny to go to town and pick it up, and tell them to give me change. If you feel better, later, when Daddy gets home, we'll order in pizza or Chinese or something, okay?" she informed and asked me in the same breath.

"Food in the fridge, money's on the counter," I repeated dutifully. "Chinese food later?" I asked hopefully, because that was definitely on my list of favorite things.

Mom laughed as she put her hand on the door. "We'll see how you feel. Okay, sweetheart, I'll call you later, all right?" she asked me from the doorway.

"Okay, Mom. I love you. Have a good day," I wished her from my blanket nest.

A clock beeped somewhere in the house, signaling the hour. "Oh! My bus!" My mom whirled around, then back again to look at me. "Okay, I love you, Nina. Be good and feel better." She closed my door and hurried down the stairs. "I can't miss the bus again!" I heard her call out as the front door opened and closed again.

It was fully light out now, and as I looked past my feet over the end of the bed to the window, I could see a few perfectly white clouds scud across the otherwise clear blue sky.

I was completely awake now and no longer that cold. I rolled onto my back and stared blankly up at the ceiling. "Be good and feel better,"

Mom had said. That was so much easier said than done, I thought rather grimly, easier said than done. I grimaced to myself.

My mind drifted, and I started to review the experiences of the previous day. I'd never been in the East Village before yesterday, and I was surprised at how different it was from the West Village. It was grittier, dirtier, more colorful and freakier, somehow. The vibe was wilder, more creative, freer somehow, and I liked it. A lot. I definitely had to make a return trip there sometime. Maybe Nicky and I would go this coming Saturday afternoon, after our various practices (swim team for me, wrestling for Nicky), if we didn't have other things to do in the time allotted us. He needed to loosen up a bit. He'd like it, too.

Let's see, what else…

I'd never seen so many punks in one place at the same time, not even at the parties I went to, and that's saying something, because we were definitely an eclectic bunch. That was incredible—I didn't know so many people were out there trying to live out the everyone's-an-individual-and-that's-cool ideal.

I'm sure that some of them were just poseurs (and that's pronounced *poe-zer*, just in case you were wondering), and being a poseur is just so not a cool thing. That's someone who talks the talk but doesn't really walk the walk. You know, someone who just misses the point and tries too hard to be cool, instead of not caring and thereby actually being cool. True cool doesn't care if it's "in" or not. Poseurs care—so they're not in. Ever. You can always tell who they are, too; there's just something about them.

Okay, so I missed SOD. Still, though, I got to see and be a part of that crowd, and that was a very good thing—because now I knew for sure I wasn't the only one, that my friends and associations weren't an isolated bunch of crazy people fed up with greed and false middle-class values and hypocrisy, glitter and perfume covering rot and corruption. There were lots and lots of us, trying to tell the truth—that food lay wasting and rotting in storehouses in the richest countries of the world, yet men, women, and children starved in Africa, in Asia, in Central and South America. And hungry and homeless and sick people lived in the most privileged of cities while our governments spent monies for food and medical research on arms development.

And what the fuck was a "Cold War" anyway, dammit? The rhetoric was pretty damn heated, the people in charge were crazy, and the people paying in blood, sweat, and tears to fund the arms race, and that's you and me, baby, would end up dust particles glowing in the dark, the only consolation being that our constituent molecules and particles might glow on in an our-side-won desolation.

The world was run by a bunch of callous, power-hungry, greedy, war-mongering bullies, making rules they didn't follow, writing laws they broke, and happy enough to have us all fighting each other so we wouldn't notice the theft of our lives. You didn't have to be over twenty-one years old to understand that, and who knew if you'd live long enough, anyway. Hello, mushroom cloud.

And we weren't gonna be all "peace and love" about fixing it either, like the hippies had been. You couldn't hug missiles or drop flowers into silos. Yeah, the hippies got some stuff done, but after a while, all the tuning in, turning off, and dropping out left them stoned and disconnected. And they'd come down from their collective high to become the establishment, the law, the middle class and rich hypocrites who ignored hunger and poverty and bigotry and crime.

Now *this* was "Anarchy in the UK," baby, and the U.S., and everywhere else, too, and that's the fuckin' truth. We were betrayed, we were angry, we weren't fooled by the bullshit, and we didn't want to die in this stupid international "King of the Mountain" pissing contest.

But still, I reflected, I felt better knowing that the Punk Army really did exist, that there were lots and lots of people agitating to make things better, even the poseurs. And it didn't matter that I didn't get to see a band. What mattered, what really mattered, was that the message was out there and calling people, even if sometimes all the music said was the irreverent and/or the obvious. That was part of the point, too.

There was other stuff, too, on a more surface level.

Ronnie the Bouncer Boy thought I was pretty. And I wasn't hallucinating; he'd been coming on to me. What the hell was up with that? I never thought I was pretty. I mean, I knew I wasn't hideous. It's just that it seemed wrong somehow to think that I was, or that I could be, like too much ego or something when there were so many other important things to worry about, like becoming nuclear dust (see above rant) or failing the SAT (Scholastic Aptitude Test—important to get a good grade on if you'd like to overpay or attempt for a scholarship to get a higher education at the college of your choice).

Besides, everywhere I went, most guys went for Kerry. In fact, all of them did. If she'd come up to the door with me, I'm sure that wouldn't have happened. Ronnie would never have even seen me. I wasn't sure how I felt about that.

Then there was that girlfriends and boyfriends thing he'd said, about having both at the same time, I mean. That was a new concept, but it did sound like sooner or later someone would get hurt—feelings or otherwise. What did you do, go out on three-way dates? So, if you asked someone out, did they ask someone along? Did you ask them both out? What if you got asked out, then did you bring someone along? Or did the two of them (whoever they might be) ask you out? And what if you didn't like one of the people? Or they didn't like you? What if they didn't like each other? And then, who paid for the whole thing? Especially if you had a first asker and then a second one?

Forget that. It sounded way too confusing. Besides, you'd go crazy trying to share popcorn or a soda, never mind finding someone willing to deal with that whole sort of mess in the first place. Figuring out the logistics for that was really messing with my already fucked mind.

Then what happened? Oh yeah, we got chased by those guys. I could still very clearly hear the way the guy had yelled "dyke," with the same tone of disgust my father had when he said it. I shuddered when I remembered the sound of those footsteps pounding behind us and the glass smashing. Scary. That had sucked big-time.

And what brought that on? Forget about the obvious ignorance and aggression combination for the time being. That was just revolting. The whole dyke thing, though. Was there a sign painted somewhere? And how come Kerry got pegged for that when she was sort of giving me the idea that this wasn't really her thing, and I didn't get tagged like that and I was starting to think it might be mine? Is it a vibe you give out? Would I start giving out that vibe? Did I already? Was Kerry just reflecting mine? Would I recognize it in someone else? Okay, I'd had enough of that for one twenty-four-hour period. I was nauseous now and my head was really starting to hurt, and I wasn't going to think about that anymore for a while.

Okay, then, that left the kiss. Oh boy. That kiss. And other things, that reminded me. I lifted my T-shirt and looked at the breasts that had just suddenly appeared, really, in the last year. I had them before, the breasts, I mean. They just hadn't been, weren't so, well, there, you know? I inspected them with a critical eye. They were okay, I guess, not too big, not too small, although my uniform shirts from last year were tight, but that had happened to everyone else in my class, it seemed.

Everyone was wearing white T-shirts or the regulation sweater or vest to cover the gap that existed between the second and third buttons, all of us waiting for our new uniforms to arrive in the spring. So that wasn't too unusual, I guessed, maybe even normal, and it was a relief to feel even a little normal about something for a minute.

Curiously, I decided to touch one, the one Kerry had. It didn't feel any different than touching my arm or my stomach—maybe a slight bit more ticklish, but that was it. Not a bad feeling, but nothing fantastic, either. This was absolutely not a big deal and definitely not paroxysms of ecstasy waiting to happen. I didn't get it. Why did those girls in those porno videos Nicky and I had snuck from my dad's workshop always grab themselves there or moan when someone else did? Maybe it was just for the viewers. Actors…

I touched the nipple experimentally. The skin was really soft, not just a different color, but a different texture altogether from the rest. But it didn't really seem to be anything special, at least not in terms of any extra-special feeling. I gently squeezed. Nope, nothing. Pressing harder was definitely not nicer, either.

Maybe, if I just concentrated on the tip itself, since that was supposed to be full of nerve endings. Using a fingertip, I did just that, lightly touching the very very end, where I assumed all the nerve endings actually, well, ended.

Okay, that wasn't too bad, maybe even a little nice. It hardened itself into a tiny, circular point, about the diameter of the tip of my pinky. I'd seen them harder than this just running cross-country track, but that was way different—that had hurt—and chafed. They'd been tender and sore for days, even though I'd used the cream that one of my teammates had recommended to ease the sting. Actually, nothing had really helped until I'd picked up True Girl–jock (and that's a bra that slams your boobs so tight into your chest you need to relearn how to breathe. I shared just in case you want or need one, or you just like that sort of thing).

At least this felt somewhat pleasant. Still, though, it was nothing compared to the way Kerry's had reacted. Hers had become larger, definitely much more discernable than mine, soft and solid at the same time, like, I didn't know. I had no real basis for comparison, except those videotapes. Kerry's certainly felt like they looked like that. Mine sure didn't. And she'd reacted a bit more, too.

Maybe my body was retarded.

But still, not bad though, I mused to myself, not bad, as my other hand slid down along my stomach and I felt the muscles under my hand, hard and strong underneath a very thin, soft layer. And then my hand went farther down, under my sleep shorts, to a spot where I knew all the nerve endings were working just fine, thank you, and things that were supposed to get hard did so, without any problem or coaxing, either, and size didn't matter one way or another at all, just the sensation.

And in case you were wondering, and before you get the wrong idea (or the right one, depending on your point of view), this was all strictly magic-button time. A few times, either washing or exploring, I'd slipped and touched lower, you know, "there," but that had stung pretty nastily, actually, so I pretty much left that strictly alone, and no one else was allowed there, either. For the time being, anyway.

Okay, this is a little embarrassing, but by now, I'm sure you might have noticed, and yes, it's true. I jerk off, jack off, jill off, and masturbate. I have made close personal friends with Rosy Palm and all of her sisters, and her cousins on the other side, too. I diddle, fiddle, fuck myself, and fool around. I did it then, I do it now, I've done it in between, and I'll do it till I die. I have formed an intense bond with my friend, my pal, my girl. I know where her loyalties are, and she never, ever, lets me down. It's my buddy and me, all the way.

The infamous "they" say it's the first pleasure we experience as babies and the last we experience as senior adults. I say, why leave it to the beginning and then wait till the end?

A healthy sex life is up to every individual, and this is the best way of finding out what you like, what you don't like, and what you might like to try out. You can trust yourself not to bring home any unwanted diseases, get you (or someone else) pregnant, go too fast or too slow, do it wrong, have a headache, get tired, or keep going when you want a break. And it's always, always, sex with someone you love. Hopefully, anyway. And by the way, it's a great way to break a fever and keep your legs in shape. Trust me on this.

Oh, and if you're someone who swears up and down they've never done it, either stop lying, because I don't believe you either, or please, get help, get a room, get a magazine or a good book (or try the Internet), relax and let it go, man. You'll be much nicer, trust me. Or more succinctly: fuck yourself and feel better. You may find your technique with a partner improves as well. Okay, off the soapbox for now and back down my pants.

My fingers unerringly found the spot that wanted attention easily enough, and as I slowly began stroking my fingertips across my absolutely favorite body part, I thought of Kerry's mouth on mine and of the sweet wetness that was our kiss. On impulse, I licked the fingertip that had been on my boob moments before and put it back there. Maybe this would do something.

Oh, hey now, that felt really, really nice, and as it got harder, it actually got bigger, and I experimentally rolled it between my thumb and forefinger. This was definitely an improvement. Maybe my body wasn't really retarded after all, just a little slow. Then again, I'd thought it was a pretty neato thing when Kerry had done it, so maybe it was a technique thing. Or personality. Maybe my boob just liked Kerry better than me.

Points farther south, I stroked a bit harder, and in my mind, I could feel Kerry's body pressing up against mine, the leg that had wrapped around me and almost thrown me on top of her bringing our bodies into tight contact.

I felt her lips against my neck and collarbone, the light butterfly kisses I'd forgotten she'd laid down from my throat to my partially exposed chest, and the constant, unrelenting pressure of her hips against mine, her hands moving my ass so that we were grinding against each other in a sensual dance.

I remembered the taste and feel of her skin against my lips, how she'd moaned into my mouth when I'd cupped her breast, and that she'd shaken and pushed into me when I'd painted a line with my tongue along the top. One of her hands came off my ass to squeeze one of my breasts in return, but the other gripped harder around, pulling me farther into her and pressing me in the most interesting, not to mention stimulating, way.

I stayed in that moment, my hands making their own rhythm, Kerry and I in that frantic push-pull, until I felt my own pressure build up within. I saw Kerry's face as we kissed for the first time, and the look in her eyes, heard her say, "Hopey, you always ask the hard questions," felt her lips against my face as she whispered I was her best friend and kissed me like she was dying but trying so hard to live. I came and I tasted her tears. No, not hers, mine. I was crying, I was weeping, like a baby, like a lost child, and I was so cold again, so very damn cold. I curled up into a ball and fell asleep and let the tears just fall down my face and soak my pillow.

I must have really slept, because suddenly I opened my eyes to find the light had shifted and was shining way too brightly on my head. A glance over at my dresser where I had my clock said it was about eleven in the morning, which meant it was definitely time for me to get out of bed. I couldn't take lying there anymore anyway. The blankets suddenly felt too heavy, and the weight in my head was oppressive. I threw the blankets off me and hopped out.

Standing finally, I stretched thoroughly, raising my arms above my head, twisting from side to side, and then settled on the floor to do a ballet, otherwise known as a floor, stretch. Satisfied only when I felt the gratifying pull and burn in my legs, I did a few sit-ups, a couple of push-ups, and then ambled out of my room to take a shower and brush my teeth, along with all the other morning routine stuff—relieve the bladder, dry my hair, that sort of thing, and not necessarily in that order.

When I was done, I walked downstairs to the kitchen and made myself something to eat, and Ringo watched me from his spot by the back door. Mom must have had Nanny walk him, because he wasn't jumping around doing the pee-pee dance.

Rooting about in the refrigerator and the cabinets, I got the supplies and tools I needed to put together the start of a healthy day—eggs, juice, and toast—scrambled, no pulp, and buttered, with a glass of chocolate milk, and that was extra chocolate until it looked like mud but tasted really good. Preparations complete, I placed the frying pan in the sink and washed it, then put all my stuff on a tray on the counter.

I looked up and noticed the phone. I walked over, picked it up, and was about to dial, then thought better of it. Nah, I figured, she wouldn't be home; she'd be at school. I put the phone back on its cradle. Besides, she probably didn't want to talk to me just yet.

I wandered into the living room with my tray, sat it on the coffee table, and clicked the TV on straight to the music videos channel. I sat cross-legged on the sofa, and Ringo settled in under my feet. I watched and munched with only half of my attention focused on the TV. I was taking physical stock of myself.

I was feeling quite a bit better, though maybe just a tad shaky. Probably from being out all that time in November, for Chrissakes, with my coat and my shirt half-open, I concluded, and shut the rest of the thoughts that went with that out of my head for a while. I raised the glass of chocolate milk to my mouth so I could wash the toast down.

At that second the phone rang, and I choked, spewing the remains of my bite of toast and chocolate milk on my white T-shirt. Dammit—I had just showered, and that shirt was clean! I put the glass down on the coffee table next to my plate and tried to stand to run and get the phone, but Ringo stood with me and I stumbled, knocking into the coffee table and sending the remains of my tray along with my chocolate milk to the floor. Double dammit!

Ringo went after the spilled and dropped goodies, and I paused to stop him because he was certainly not supposed to eat people food, plus I was sure chocolate milk could not be wonderful for doggie innards, but the phone rang again and I had to get it. It could be Mom or, even worse, my school, checking up on me. I rolled my eyes in resignation and ran to the kitchen, removing my now-dirty shirt on the way.

I managed to get there without further harm to myself, my clothes, or the house in any way, and I skidded to a stop in my socks. "Hello?" I quietly tried to catch my breath.

"Yo, Nina, this is Sister Pernicious from Our Lady of Eternal Discipline. Don't you have classes and exams? What are you doing home right now? Get on the bus or the train and get your pretty, precious, firm, rounded as—ahem," a mock throat clearing, "ah, I meant, sinful, yes, sinful ass to school!"

Holy shit—it was Kerry! Well, that was pleasantly unexpected. I cracked up at her words and the image they created in my head. "Dude! Where are you? How'd you know I was home, um, Sister Perdition?" I asked her, still laughing.

"That's 'Pernicious' to you, sweet cheeks, I mean, young lady!" Kerry told me in mock sternness. "Tell me…what are you doing right now?" she asked in a silky phone-sex voice.

Hmm. I bit my lip. Play? Or don't play? I wasn't too sure where we stood with one another yet, and I wasn't ready to deal with it yet if the news wasn't good. I decided discretion was the better part of valor. Play my way.

"Talking to you, Sister, oh, and by the way? Nuns don't say 'yo,' it's part of their contract with God. I've read it. So, how'd you know I was home?" I asked her again. I felt the smile that grew on my face threaten to take my cheeks off. I couldn't help it, couldn't help myself. She made me feel good.

I was just so very glad to hear her voice, and happier even that she called at all. I realized that I'd been subconsciously convinced for some unknown reason that she wouldn't, that we'd never speak again. I was suddenly feeling pretty damn good about things, and I had this warm glow in my chest, even though there was a strange little tickle I'd never ever felt before in my stomach. Well, I was home sick, after all.

"What do I know about nuns, Nina? My parents are Jewish, remember? Anyhow, I didn't see you at the bus stop, I didn't see you at the train station, so I went into the comic book store and no one had seen you go by. I hung out there a little bit, watched from the storefront as Nanny went by on her bus, and knew there was no way that Nanny would leave before you did, so you had to be home. So, I decided to cut school, hung out longer at Universe, and now I'm across the street from the store, calling you from a pay phone. Good enough? Is this working for you?" she asked teasingly. "Because it's really working for me."

Wow. It was working for me, too. So she'd decided to look for me this morning. I didn't think she'd do that. We never traveled in together—our schools were in completely opposite directions, which is why we always met up afterward, at the store, since it was next to our train station. What I understood underneath all of this working explanation was that she'd missed me, she wanted to see me. She'd looked for me, asked for me, waited for me, and now she was calling me. That glow just kept on growing, and that tickle in my stomach was getting stronger. It wasn't an unpleasant feeling either, just very unfamiliar.

"Nina? You there?"

Oh, yeah, we were talking on the phone, right! "Yeah, dude. I wasn't feeling too good this morning, so my mom let me stay home. No big thing," I hastily replied, "you know."

An uncomfortable quiet stretched out between us.

"You sick from, um," she hesitated, "from being out last night?" Her voice strangled on the last word.

I knew where she was going with this because I'd just been there, and I wasn't going to let her stay on that road. One of us upset was enough, I figured. It touched me to know she cared, and I hurt to hear her sound like that. I didn't want to hear her cry again.

"No, no, it wasn't that, though running around with my, um"—I didn't really want to allude to last night too much, it was still way too raw—"my coat open probably wasn't the healthiest thing I've ever done," I hurriedly reassured her. "Nah, my dad, you know?" Kerry was my best friend. Of course she knew, because I'd told her about my dad's daily wake-Nina-up ritual. "This morning? His usual thing, and I don't know, Kerry, I just started to feel sick—fever, headache, you know, the works. I feel a lot better now, though. I'm glad you called," I added softly. "I wanted to call you, but I thought you'd be in school."

Kerry chuckled under her breath a bit at that, and I could practically hear the gears turning as she digested what I told her, both said and unsaid. Through the phone, I could hear the traffic passing on the street, a bus stopping, and the sound of the train roaring past the station.

"You sure you're feeling better?" she asked, finally, in a doubtful voice.

"Yeah, much," I told her. The silence stretched, then I caught a clue right in the eye. "Hey, you want to come over? I'm just hangin', watching TV and all. I don't think I'm contagious or anything."

Kerry answered so quickly and with such relief, I knew I'd been right in thinking she'd been worried like I was, that maybe I was just being polite, didn't really want to see her. Besides, it's rude to kiss a girl and then not see her the next day, right? Right. Even if you're not sure it will ever happen again. Or even if you're still really friends.

"Dude! I'll be there in a few minutes! I've got a movie on me and I'm bringing junk food! Chips and soda and a surprise! Don't fall asleep—bye!" and she hung up in a rush.

I put the phone down slowly. Kerry had looked for me this morning, she had a movie on her, she was bringing food and a surprise. Weirdly enough, it sounded like she had a plan, sort of. I shook my head in bemusement as I made my way out of the kitchen and tossed my shirt, which I'd had in my hands the whole time, onto the laundry basket by the basement door.

Hmm, I was getting a little cold again. Oh yeah, a shirt, I needed a shirt. I went up to my room and rummaged through my drawer. Maybe I should dress, if I was going to have company and all, not that I wasn't dressed already, just that I should look somewhat presentable, right? Right. Not a big deal.

I found my favorite long-sleeve T-shirt—it was huge, it was soft, it was black where it wasn't covered with different-colored paint splatters. I paint every now and again, and that was my most favorite, extra-special painting shirt. My mother hated it—the shirt, not the painting, I mean—and truth to tell, I still have it..

Anyhow, that's the shirt I slipped on. Then I grabbed my army pants, also nice and baggy and soft, but not for painting (I have a favorite pair of shorts for that), compliments of a weekend shopping expedition in a Village thrift store. I pulled on my boots, made my bed, and figured I was done. I walked over to the bathroom again, for a quick inspection. Okay, I thought. Hey, wait. What about my hair? Should I do my hair? I grabbed the brush and looked at the mirror. Since my hair was still damp from my shower, the ends curled over my shoulders. Aw fuck it, I thought. I'm supposed to be home sick, don't want to look like I'm trying or something. Besides, Kerry had seen me in my school uniform, after track meets, after basketball games, after swim meets, and I usually had a ponytail before and a sweaty mess after.

This was no big deal. Nothing to read into. No reason to go nuts. This was a movie and food. We were just hanging out, like we'd done a million times before. Okay, she was bringing a surprise. I hesitated, then decided to just brush my hair straight through again. I left it at that.

I looked down at my hands as I washed them again. Oh yeah. I had to remove the red and black nail polish from the weekend. Nail polish was forbidden to all but the upperclassmen in my high school and then, only in "natural" colors. While as a junior, I certainly qualified as an upperclassman, this particular shade of red, and certainly the black, would not be considered permissible colors.

My nails now clean, I had to wash them again so I wouldn't reek of acetone. The fumes from the remover made my eyes smart. I cracked the bathroom window open and hoped the smell would dissipate.

Okay, now I was ready, and I wiped my still-stinging eyes and made my way to the stairwell. I hesitated. I knew there was something I couldn't remember. I was positive I was forgetting something.

Sick! I was supposed to be home sick! Me, fever, stomach weirdness, headache, sore throat, remember? Sick people don't lounge at home all day fully dressed and waiting to hang out! Now wouldn't that look like I was trying way too hard, right? Yeah, I thought so, too.

I walked back to my room, ripped the pillow off my bed, and grabbed one of the blankets I'd folded. Now fully prepared, I went down to the living room, set my pillow up, kicked the blanket around a bit so it didn't look like I'd just brought it down, and took off my boots, placing them neatly by the head of my makeshift bed. Sick people don't wear shoes, and shoes aren't allowed on sofas, anyway.

I was just about to sit back down when I remembered the coffee table and the mess Ringo and I had made. I hurriedly put my boots back on (I hate cleaning without shoes on, just a thing with me), picked up my glass, plate, and tray, and ran them to the kitchen sink. I returned with the broom, the dustpan, and the mop.

Now for a quick round of Betty Homemaker, and I returned everything to its place in the kitchen. Okay. That was done. I was getting a little breathless now, from all the running back and forth.

I sat down again, twisted and threw one leg over the sofa back, and I rubbed Ringo's back with my other foot. Poor puppy had run all over the house with me—he was tired now. Plus, he was full. Doggie chow and toast and chocolate milk. He needed a nap. I think I did, too.

I wiggled my back into the pillow and was just about to get really comfortable when the doorbell rang. Ringo jumped up and started barking at me maniacally, his way of telling me to do something about it, and I tangled myself in the blanket as I tried to get to my feet. Fuck it, I was too tangled. I wrapped it around my shoulders and took the damn thing with me.

I finally managed to get myself, the blanket, and dancing Ringo to the door to open it when, of course, the phone rang. Fuck!

Okay, first things first. I checked the peephole (safety first, boyz 'n' gurlz, even when freaking out), and it was Kerry, so I opened the door and let her in.

She stepped through the door into the entryway. "Hey, hi!" she greeted me warmly and opened her arms for a hug. I gave her a quick but strong squeeze and started shuffling as fast as I could in my blanket to the phone in the kitchen.

"Hey, I'm sorry," I apologized, looking at her startled face over my shoulder. "That could be my mom, and I have to get it." I shuffled to answer the phone as quickly as I could.

Ringo kept jumping up and down, first on Kerry, then on me, circling and barking the whole way. I finally made it to the phone, with the two of them accompanying me.

"Hello!" My temper was getting a little frayed as my nerves got played upon.

"May I speak to the person in charge of ordering the *TV Guide*?" the voice on the other end asked.

For this I'd risked hurting Kerry's feelings and breaking my neck? I don't think so. "I'm sorry, we don't believe in TV," I answered and hung up the phone with a bang. Sheesh!

Ringo had finally quieted down and was letting Kerry scratch his favorite pet-me spot. You know the one, right between his ears.

Kerry looked up at me as I turned away from the phone. "Everything okay?" she asked with a cocked brow.

"Fine, totally. Just a marketing thing." I breathed deeply, collecting my wits. "Could we try that again?" and, complete with ghostly draped blanket, I held my arms open for a hug.

Kerry grinned at me. "Sure, I think we can manage that."

She moved into the space, and we held each other for a long moment, then gave each other an awkward kiss on the cheek.

Kerry backed up a step. "So," she drawled out, "whatchya got under that blanket? Anything," she bit her lip, "good?" she asked teasingly and reached out to tweak a fold.

"Birthday suit," I answered smugly. "Come see for yourself," and I threw the blanket open.

Kerry shielded her eyes like she was about to be blinded by the sun. Her hand was enough to cast a shadow if she'd needed one, but definitely not enough to not see anything. "Nice, really nice suit there, Hopey." She smirked at me, her face very bright red. She had the same look on her face Nicky got when he tried to lie. Scared? Hopeful? Relieved? Disappointed? I was going for choice *e*, all of the above. I filed that away into the back of my mind.

I laughed. "Come on," and I led the way back to the living room.

"Um, I left a few things outside when you dragged me in," Kerry said archly. "Mind if I get them?"

"Oh, sorry, no. Go right ahead. Need a hand?"

"No, no, just grab the remotes for everything and settle yourself in. I've got this all handled," and she went to the door and stepped through it.

I found the remotes and seated myself. Then Kerry came back, with a take-out Chinese food shopping bag in one hand, and in the other a plastic grocery bag that I could see had the promised chips and soda as well as a few other sundries within it. She walked over and placed them on the coffee table, and I rose to go to the kitchen to get stuff—plates, cups, you know, stuff—but Kerry reached out to stop me.

"No, no, no need. I told you I've got everything covered. You're supposed to be sick, so you take a break, and I hope this helps you feel better." And with that, she kneeled on the floor and pulled out the soda—Coca-Cola, what else is there?—two plastic cups, two paper plates, plastic cutlery, several different take-out cartons, and one plastic soup container.

She reached into the grocery bag again. "Now this," she told me, standing up, "is Haagen-Dazs, Vanilla Swiss Almond, your favorite." She displayed it for me. "So, I'm going to go put this in your freezer, and it's for later, 'kay?" and she made her way to the kitchen.

I sat down on the floor with my back against the couch, and Ringo settled himself into a little dog-ball on my left. I was more than a little surprised by it all. This was just so not what I expected, but it was definitely more than pleasant. In case you didn't catch the hint when I was talking with my mom before, Chinese food was my favorite, as well as the aforementioned Haagen-Dazs, and well, none of this stuff was cheap, you know. Kerry and I both worked occasional odd jobs like babysitting, raking leaves, and mowing lawns, stuff like that, to have more than transportation money for school and to save for college. And important things like music and *Love and Rockets* comic books.

Kerry walked back into the living room and rummaged through the grocery bag again, and I noticed that the tickle in my stomach had grown more insistent.

"Oh, and I got you a pack of cigarettes, too." She tossed them at me.

Now I was completely overwhelmed.

"Wow, that's just, I can't believe, you're, just, thank you, really," I stammered out. I shyly leaned over to kiss her cheek. "Thanks."

Kerry hugged me and returned the kiss. "You're very, very welcome," she told me, and we just stared at each other again with strange intensity.

"Wow! Let's eat! I'm starved!" She turned away, breaking the eye contact and the tension that had started to build.

We busied ourselves opening the cartons and spooning the contents onto the plates, then inspiration hit me. "Hey, this is, like, a picnic, right?" I asked her while she was pouring soda.

"Absolutely," she agreed, "only no dirt, no grass, no ants, and no bees." She smiled up at me.

"Okay then, wait here a second," and I stood up and ran lightly over to the stairs.

"Where you going?" Kerry looked puzzled.

"I'll be right back, just a sec," and I raced up the steps. I went into my room and grabbed another pillow, then back out to the hallway and into the linen closet, looking for a specific blanket. I heard something move across the floor downstairs, footsteps, the kitchen door slide open, and then Ringo run across the floor. The back door closed. Maybe Ringo had to go. That was nice of Kerry to let him out, I mused, and kept looking.

Aha! Found it! This blanket was one that had seen better days but was still very serviceable, and I figured if we were going to picnic in the living room, we might as well go all the way and have a picnic blanket. The extra pillow was just for more comfort. We were indoors, after all. We had Chinese food, ice cream, a movie, blankets, pillows; what could be better? Supplied and satisfied, my arms filled with the pillow and blanket, I made my way down the stairs and stopped, halfway down. I was frozen in place and stared at the scene before me in open-mouthed surprise.

Kerry had drawn all the blinds and the curtains, darkening the room considerably. She had also moved the sofa back and the coffee table over so that an L-shaped enclave was formed, with the sofa making the long arm of the L, and the coffee table set up in such a way that we could still reach for things if either of us wanted something, but we could sit on the floor with our legs stretched out and the couch at our backs while we watched the movie.

In the cleared-out center, she'd laid out the blanket that I'd left on the sofa, arranged our plates and drinks, and all around the perimeter, she'd lit about a half dozen small candles, with one large one near the food. Next to it on one side was a brand-spankin'-new, not-available-in-the-States imported U2 video collection (and if you don't know, U2 is, like, the super-band of almost all time. Really). On the other side lay a brand-new hard copy of a *Love and Rockets* graphic novel I'd been saving forever for.

It was beautiful.

"Careful." Kerry laughed softly. "You'll catch flies like that." She hesitated before she spoke again. "Surprise. Do you like it?" she asked softly and watched my face.

"It's beautiful," I whispered as I finished the stairway. "I…I don't know what to say." I walked the blanket and pillow over to the sofa and put them down. That ticklish stomach had become a pounding kick, and it made my body thrum with an unrecognized need.

"I would have sent you to get another pillow or something or aspirins or something if you hadn't volunteered already," Kerry explained in a rush. "Do you really like it?" She bit her lip and watched my face.

I looked back at her and just couldn't resist. I reached up and gently touched her face.

"Thank you," I whispered, stroking the silky skin, while she just looked at me with big eyes. "Thank you." I reached up with my other hand to comb her hair behind her ear. "Thank you." And gently cradling her face, I drew her to me.

This kiss was not like the first one, so tentative, so unsure, and not like the last one, so desperate and tearing and painful. This kiss was just as sensual, although it had started out simply enough. Kerry wrapped her arms around me, and I did the same. Our hands began to roam, and as the kiss deepened and our lips and tongues quested, our bodies pressed together, instinctively knowing things we did not consciously. Okay, maybe *I* didn't know consciously.

"Whoa there, hold up a second." Kerry, breathing hard, stopped us. "Before we burn your parents' house down." She smirked at me and I smirked back. "Let's eat, okay?"

I took a shaky breath. That kick was now a roaring in my head, and my entire body buzzed and tingled like a live wire. I shook my head to clear it.

"Hey, if the food gets cold, your parents are, like, the only people in the world that don't have a microwave," Kerry joked lightly.

Somehow the light tone lifted the fog from my head, and the buzzing throughout my body reduced to an inside shaking of my heart. I was okay for the moment. "Hey, we're lucky we have cable TV here. You've no idea how Nicky and I begged," I joked back. "Oh, and speaking of burning my parents' house down, what say we move some of these candles?" and I pointed to the ones on the floor. "We can put them on the coffee table. Besides, we need to put the other blanket down somewhere for our picnic." I smiled to take any possible sting out of that.

Kerry put her hands on her hips and surveyed the lit square of floor. "Okay, good idea," she agreed, and we moved the candles until they were all on the coffee table except for four small ones and the big one from the center; those we placed on top of the TV. Don't worry, they were in containers.

We put the videotape and the graphic novel (and again, that's a collection of comics, or a complete comic story in book format, if you're not taking notes) on the sofa cushion.

"I let Ringo out because I figured he needed to go soon, and also, I figured you didn't want to find out whether or not he liked Chinese. Plus, his tail is really flammable," she informed me conversationally as we smoothed the blanket on the floor. "That's, I mean, that was okay?" she asked a bit uncertainly, and there was a bit of discomfort.

"Oh yeah, good idea," I assured her. "Ringo likes Chinese. Ringo likes Italian. Ringo likes anything he's not supposed to eat. He thinks he's a fuzzy people," I told her with a grin, and the discomfort vanished when she smiled back at me.

I settled the pillows on the floor against the base of the sofa and brought the other blanket down between them, conveniently there if it was needed (hey, I was sick! Fever, remember?), out of the way if it wasn't. "Okay." I straightened up and dusted off my hands. "I think we're all set here. You?" I placed my hands on my hips and surveyed the picnic area with a concentrated furrow of my brow.

"Houston, we have liftoff," Kerry said, and handed me my plate.

"Cool," I said, and settled down cross-legged, back against the pillow and sofa. The coffee table, with all those candles on it and the soda cups and the remotes, was to my left. Kerry, plate in hand, took her boots off by shoving them with her toes and nudged them off to the side. She settled in next to me on the right, and I reached up behind me to feel around for the U2 music video collection she'd brought.

"Forgot something," I told her as my fingers searched. I felt the cellophane and tugged. "The visual entertainment," I explained as I held the recording before her.

"Oh yeah! Wait a sec!" Kerry put her plate down and stood up. "I brought a movie!" And she moved lightly across the floor back to the door where she'd left her army bag.

I grabbed the remotes from the coffee table and popped the TV on to—what else?—music videos. "Please tell me it's not Disney and it's not a slasher flick," I asked as I heard her looking through her bag. Disney isn't bad, I just wasn't in the mood at all, and I really, truly hate gory things. It's just not necessary; there's already too much of that in reality.

"Got it!" I heard her mutter to herself. "You mean you don't want to watch *Bambi and the Chainsaw Dude*? Damn—that's what I got!" She chuckled at her own joke and made her way back over with the movie. "Actually, it's a bootleg of something you really like." She sat down on my right again. "Here…" And she held it out for me.

I took it from her and looked at the slip case, but that was blank. I shook the case and let it slide out into my hand.

"Holy shit! *The Rocky Horror Picture Show!*" I was excited. This wasn't just hard to get, it was almost impossible. Nicky and I had been looking for over a year everywhere we went. "Too cool!" I exclaimed, and leaned over to put it in the machine. "That is just way, way too cool! How did you find this?" I had a smile that reached ear to ear. I impulsively leaned over to hug her. "Hey, maybe I should get sick more often!" I grinned, letting her go.

Kerry smiled back at me and bit her lip. "Maybe you'll ditch with me sometime," she suggested in a half-joking tone. She pursed her lips and looked at me slyly.

I settled back into my spot and looked at her with a raised brow. "Yeah, right," I answered sarcastically, still smiling, though. This was an old, but good-natured, argument between us. Kerry really didn't understand how hard, no, nearly impossible, it was to do that in my school.

We both looked at the screen as white noise filtered across before the start of the movie.

"I knew you'd like that," Kerry told me, indicating the machine with a nod of her chin, then turned back toward the set. She was quiet as she considered for a moment. "Hey, you sure you're not contagious? My stomach feels really weird."

"Shh…movie's starting!" I made an exaggerated shushing gesture with my finger as a pair of giant lipstick-red lips appeared on the now-black screen.

"Oh yeah!" Kerry wiggled in place to settle herself more comfortably, and I did notice that her movement brought her a bit closer to me.

We silently ate our food through the opening credits, interrupting only to pass soda to one another or to sing out the required responses to the lyrics. Eventually, the food was done, the plates and cups were empty and put on the coffee table. I waved out a few of the candles as the "Time Warp" started on screen and sat back down, and I noticed Kerry had put her hand on the floor, not far from where I was sitting. I casually put mine down as well, close, but not too close, pretending not to notice.

Kerry turned her head to look at me. "Enjoying this?" she asked, leaning in a bit and bringing our hands closer together.

"Oh yeah," I responded, leaning closer in turn. Our pinkies touched. I felt that damn tension grow, and now my stomach was playing games with me again.

Oh, this was bullshit. We'd been all over each other just a little bit ago. We couldn't be all that insecure; I couldn't be all that insecure. This couldn't go on, not without someone spontaneously combusting, anyway, and then where would my parents' house be? Burnt, that's what. We were trying to avoid that.

Abruptly, I shifted position and twisted to pull out the second blanket that was behind us and began to spread it out over me. "Dude, I'm a little cold," I explained, and that was true, really, I was, a little. Fever! I had a fever! I was home sick, remember? Verified by Mom with a thermometer and everything, too. Blanket draped over me as before (minus fighting with Ringo and shuffling) I held my arms out. "Want to share and help keep me warm?" I grinned.

"Yeah, sure." Kerry smiled at me and moved in.

Adjusting myself and the pillows a bit, because I'd reached over and stolen Kerry's, I sat with my back now wedged between the arm of the sofa and the coffee table so I could turn my head to the left and watch the movie, with one leg stretched out along the length of the sofa, the other bent up a bit, which formed an armrest for Kerry, who had snuggled up the center and was somewhat on her side, head up on my shoulder. I settled the blanket around us, and with a few more wiggles from both parties, we were settled, comfortable, and warm.

Frank-N-furter was building a man (and I told you before, I'm not telling you more. Go see it for yourself if you really, truly want to know, and take a friend with you) and somehow, that led me to an insight I had to share with Kerry. I don't know how or why I made this connection;

my brain just works in weird ways.

"Hey, Kerr?"

"Yeah, Nina?" She looked up at me.

"Did you know everyone is naked under all of their clothes?"

"Duh!" She sat up to push me playfully, then settled in again. A few more seconds passed.

"Kerry?"

"Nina?" She looked up at me.

"Do you remember, when we were talking yesterday? About the whole, you know, uptown midtown downtown thing, I mean?"

She waited, drew in a breath, then answered slowly, "Yes?"

"Well, it just hit me, like, now. You know how, like, all healthy adults, um," and my face got a little warmer, but we had discussed this before, so I went on, "they, um, do the masturbation thing?"

Kerry pulled away a bit, probably for a better angle to give me the "uh-huh, now what?" look I was getting. "Yeah?" she drawled, eyebrow lifted. I wasn't too sure, but I think she did blush a little.

"Well, if you can masturbate, then it wouldn't be really such a hard thing to, like, touch another guy if you're a guy, or another girl if you're a girl, right? 'Cuz you'd already done it before, touch a guy or a girl," I explained. "Technically, I mean."

Kerry sat up and looked at me wide-eyed. "Hey, you're right! I never thought of it like that before!" She focused on the blanket beneath us, brow knit in concentration. "So, what you're saying is that, in effect," she paused, "that makes it totally…" She trailed off and idly traced her finger along the blanket on the ground. "…like, normal or…" Her voice faded.

"Natural," I finished and nodded my head in agreement. "Yeah. If you do one, you can do the other, and since the first is, like, a healthy thing to do anyway, then it's just a matter of whether or not you want to, I mean, I guess…"

Kerry was still sitting a bit away, and I started to feel uneasy. Maybe I'd said too much, pushed too far. I mean, Kerry did stop our kiss earlier. Maybe she thought I was nuts. Of course, that possibility had always existed. Not that I meant that I wanted to do anything, really (hey—I mean that!). It's just that I was being honest. I'd said yesterday that I wouldn't, you know, do the downtown thing, and now I knew that I already had, sort of, in a way, so downtown with someone else, well, so what? It wasn't like I didn't know the territory well. And

Kerry deserved to know that she was snuggling with someone who was possibly capable of doing that. In case she wanted to move or do something. Like run away screaming.

Kerry surprised me by looking up at me with a knowing grin. "Hey there, Hopeful, you're fucking brilliant!" She moved in closer to me and snuggled back in, so I put my arms around her again and resettled the blanket.

"That's my Hopey," she said, "solving the important mysteries of life, and the most important mysteries of all—the ones about sex." And she settled her head back under my chin.

We both turned our attention back to the TV where the "ingénue" was singing "Touch Me" (no, dammit! I'm telling you enough about the movie as is!), and Kerry, who had started to paint little circles on my arm with her fingertips, was now massaging my arm, while I drew my own little circles on her back. My stomach was kicking me again.

Kerry shifted again and now lay with her back against my chest, still drawing circles on my arms, and my hands naturally fell to her waist and loosely held her.

I decided to lightly massage her ribs, I don't know why. It just seemed like a good idea, and Kerry didn't seem to mind, so I continued to lightly press my fingertips down and up. Suddenly, I realized where I'd been headed; I was right below her bra strap.

Kerry shifted, then sat up. She reached behind her, under the plain black T-shirt she'd been wearing. "You know, this thing is really bugging me," she said in an annoyed tone, shrugging one arm into a sleeve and back out of her shirt and then the other, which reappeared with something in her hand that she tossed onto the sofa.

Hard to tell in the light, but it might have been pale blue or even white, and it was a lacy little thing. I knew what it was, but for some reason I wasn't making the connection—I think my brain might have been oxygen starved. I reached over to push it farther in so it wouldn't fall down. Suddenly, my brain made the connection, then short-circuited. It was her bra.

"That's so much better, don't you think?" and she settled back in place and looked up to smile at my very large eyes. I shut my mouth with an audible click before she had to remind me about catching flies again and swallowed nervously.

"Oh, um, uh, yeah," I stuttered, "pain in the neck." I started to massage her again.

Kerry pushed her shoulders flat into me and leaned her head over a little to the right.

Look, Lord knows, and I know, I know, I'm naive, I'm slow, my body's retarded, and I had never done this before, but that does not mean I'm completely stupid. I watched movies, read a lot, went on dates, and I've got a pretty good imagination under this hair. Besides, even if I can't catch a hint sometimes, I do recognize an invitation when I get one.

I decided then and there, this was one party I was definitely going to, and besides, I had a pretty good idea of how to do the dancing. I'd been practicing the steps for a long, long time.

Her neck was irresistible, and I bent my head to lay soft kisses against it. Kerry sighed like she was contented and reached her arms back over my head. She turned her head and lifted her mouth, and we were kissing—her lips on mine, her mouth warm and sweet, her tongue electric, my hands on the soft weight of her breasts, now filled with the soft curve of them, now feeling the hard tips against my palms.

Her body shifted a bit, and now I was biting, licking, softly sucking on her neck. I slid my tongue into the curves of her ear, then nipped her earlobe. I still held her breast in one of my hands, and my other hand traveled down to massage the top of her leg, right in the crease where it meets the body and all sorts of wonderful things wait.

Kerry's lips turned back up to mine again, and she bit and sucked on my lip before allowing me to slide my tongue into the joy that was her mouth. Momentarily, I removed the hand that was on her breast and broke off the kiss to bring my fingers to my mouth. Kerry gave a little whimper of protest.

"Shh, baby, it's okay," I murmured, and watched Kerry's eyes grow hooded as she watched me slip my fingertip into my mouth. I enjoyed her reaction to watching me, and I withdrew slowly.

"Hmm, mine," she exhaled and reached up to claim my mouth again.

I brought my wet fingertips back to the breast that awaited me and slid them over her beautifully turgid nipple, pinched it lightly, then rolled it a bit like I had done to my own, earlier.

She moaned into my mouth, and that sent such a jolt through to my own body that I jumped, dislodging the other hand from the warm place it had been to a warmer one. It was a happy little accident. I cupped her and she pushed her hips into my hand, so I pressed harder and massaged with my palm.

I brought that hand back under her shirt to her stomach, feeling the soft skin and the muscles underneath, and stroking, gripping, tickling, I came to her waistband. "This okay?" I interrupted our furious kiss to whisper.

"Oh, yeah, Nina," she kissed me in open-mouthed need, "more than okay." She released my head from one arm and brought her hand down near mine. I heard the zip of her jeans, which sent another burst of fire through me, and I slid my hand the rest of the way down.

I was surprised—Kerry wasn't wearing any underwear, but the shock of that pleasant realization came and went in the wonder that surged through me as I felt the soft hairs under my fingertips. Gently I brushed through the light fuzz to reach for the narrow cleft that I knew I'd find, and I found Kerry, hard and waiting.

I slid my fingers through that fold, wanting to feel everything, and Kerry took her mouth away from mine to groan throatily. Her eyes were closed, she rolled her head against my shoulder, and the look on her face was arousing me more, if that was at all possible.

God, I'd never been this turned on before, ever, not even in my own best fantasies. I watched her face, I watched her body, I watched my hands moving on her body in rapt fascination. Have I said yet how incredible this was? Everybody, and I mean everybody, wanted Kerry, and though I knew that she had fooled around a little bit, just like I had, I also knew she'd never done this before, well, not with another person, anyway. Definitely not with another girl. This was a first, for both of us, and I was awed, humbled, and yes, proud that she wanted to share that, to do this, with me, she wanted me…

One finger reached a bit farther down, and I was again happily surprised. She was wet, really wet, like I'd never known anyone could be. And what would I have known about it, anyway. I mean, I'd read about it, but I'd never gotten any more than this thinner-than-water sort of fluid in my own private experimentation, and as far as I knew, neither had she, since this was one of those many things we'd discussed.

Oh my God! This was thick, but not really, and slippery. This was like honey, but not as sticky, like finger painting with the most expensive and luxurious of paints; this was like water but better, smooth and hot; this was wonderful, and this was for me.

Kerry parted her legs, and I was moved on every level. "I ain't spreading these babies for just anybody," she'd say to anyone who asked her the "big sex" question. "You're talking engraved-in-gold invitation here. Better be a damn good kisser, too."

I already knew I wasn't just anybody. I was her best friend, so I guess I was a damn good kisser—I'd just been invited.

I lightly touched the source of that glorious wetness, but Kerry jumped. "Baby, that stings a bit," she whispered, "but don't stop the other thing, okay?" she asked, "because it feels like," and she caught her breath, "like I'm on fire."

"I won't stop," I promised. Oh, the other thing?

Kerry's clit was so hard and swollen that I had it between my thumb and middle finger and was stroking it up and down, and every exposing downstroke brought the tip against my index finger, the one that had been exploring. I loved the way she felt, soft and hard at the same time.

Wait a second, though, my brain caught up with the situation…that spot stung for me, too. Maybe, maybe it was too close to the bottom, just, like, a bad angle or something. What if I brought my finger up to the top of that opening? Would that feel better?

But first, I brought that finger and the glorious wetness on it back over the head of her clit and rubbed it everywhere, then went back to the other thing (see above explanation, okay?) and brought the explorer back to the very top of her entrance.

"Oh yeah, Nina," she choked out, "that's just, huh, really good." Her body leaned back hard into mine.

I pressed that tip a little harder against her and kept up the motion that I'd started before. Kerry's hips started to move, and she pulled my head down for a ragged kiss. I attacked her mouth, and as her body moved faster, so did my hand, matching her.

I felt such tenderness, such overwhelming warmth, that my body felt like it would burst. This was the most incredible thing that had ever happened in my life, and it was the most wondrous, Kerry was wondrous. Her pleasure was an incredible turn-on to me, and every shake, moan, and movement she made, every grab at my shoulders and arms, just made the fire within me burn hotter. It also made her that much more precious to me.

Suddenly, Kerry grabbed the hand that was still on her breast. Crushing it to her, she pulled on my shoulder with the other, and her head tossed and pressed into my chest. Her hips jumped, and I watched this gorgeous flush of color rush up her neck to her face. Her hips jumped again and came up off the floor, and suddenly, I slid inside her. Kerry let go of the hand on her breast to squeeze and press the one inside. She groaned loudly.

My body jolted with her and my mouth was an open *O* of astonishment. Jesus Christ. I hadn't meant to do that, I wasn't going to, was planning on not, but I had, and I think, I hope, she wanted me to. Now I was in her, inside Kerry, and it was soft and hot, and it was pulling, holding, sliding on me, and it was the most erotic sensation I'd had yet, gliding inside of her.

Instinctively I pressed up and the rhythm between us increased in speed, and I was moving within her, smooth and slick, more of an up-down thing than a direct thrusting. I didn't want to hurt her; I wanted her body to tell me what it wanted. I wanted her to feel good.

I finally let go of that luscious breast and wrapped my now-free arm under hers to anchor her to me, holding her tightly. Kerry strained against me as we moved together, and I lavished hot open-mouthed kisses on her neck.

God, how I wanted Kerry to come, here, now, with me, in my arms and with her wet heat wrapped around me. "Come, baby, let go," I whispered in her ear, and kissed her some more. "God, I want you to come."

Once more she brought her mouth back to mine, and we kissed frenziedly while her body and my fingers moved within and without her. Kerry's back arched, then relaxed, arched again and held, the tendons in her neck standing out in sharp relief while the soft heat inside her gripped me with such incredible strength I could feel my own clit throb harder than ever. I was higher than I'd ever been before, and I could have sworn I was going with her to whatever place she was flying to, and Kerry was heartbreakingly, painfully, excruciatingly beautiful.

"God, Nina," she gritted out through her teeth, one last flick of her tongue between my lips, one last push against my hand, sliding me deep within her. Kerry held that tension a bit longer, then released it. Her hips stilled and her body relaxed.

I stilled my fingers, her hand now lax on mine, and cuddled her tighter to me with the other, planting little kisses on her head. "God, Kerry, you are so damn beautiful," I murmured into her hair, "just so very fucking beautiful." I held her tight and drew up my legs to hug her closer. I was going to remove my hand, but she stopped me.

"No, stay please," Kerry requested in a little voice. "I just want to stay like this a little while." She placed her hand firmly over mine. "I want to remember this."

"Okay, sweetheart, okay," I reassured her, and wrapped her up as securely as I could with my free arm and my legs. She was so small, she seemed so very fragile, so vulnerable, and I just wanted to wrap myself around her, not let anything hurt her, ever. "Are you all right?" I asked her in soft concern.

"I feel great," she breathed out huskily, rolling her head back and forth a bit on my shoulder, eyes closed. "Just great." She resettled the blanket we were wrapped in and tucked her head under my chin. She curled her legs up, folded her body into mine as much as possible, and patted my hand to remind me not to remove it.

I started to rock a bit and began to murmur soft little endearments and reassurances, stroking her hair, her face, or just cuddling her and giving her small kisses. I have no idea how long we sat like that, just peacefully mentally blank, rocking and murmuring, still inside her. The movie had ended some unknown time ago; even the hum of white noise had ended when the machine and TV automatically turned off. The room was very dark. The only light left was from the candles flickering on the silent TV set. Even the cable clock had shut off.

The phone rang, startling us both.

"Hmm, I need my hand back, baby. I've got to go get that."

She snuggled more and tightened her grip. "Nope. You have to stay here."

I remained in place, but the phone rang again. "Really, baby, I've got to get that. What if it's my mom?"

"Let the answering machine get it," she mumbled from my chest.

"We don't have one of those, my dad hates them, he thinks they're rude," I reminded her, as the ringing went on insistently. Actually, I think my parents didn't have one so they'd know whether or not someone was home when they were supposed to be, but I kept that theory to myself.

"Oh, okay," she flipped over with a dramatic sigh, "can't have you grounded again," and she took her hand away and removed the blanket.

As gently as possible, I withdrew, hugged her tightly, kissed her cheek, and stood up, then walked to the kitchen on shaky legs. I was a little stiff and a little dizzy. Well, *that* was really unexpected.

I snapped on the light and got the phone, leaning on the wall a bit for support. "Hello?" I greeted in my most bland voice. I was suddenly a little drowsy, too.

"Nina? How are you feeling?" It was my mom, after all, and she was using her "business" voice.

My eyes snapped open. I was now wide awake, standing without any help at all, and I looked at the clock on the wall, where an unpleasant surprise awaited me. Holy mother of fuckin' pearl—it was fuckin' four o'clock! And where the fuck was Nanny? She was supposed to have been home half an hour ago! And Nicky, he should've been home too, or walk in any minute! Jesus H. Christ, where were they?

Mom was using her business voice, my sibs weren't home yet—my eyes opened wider with the realization of a new possibility: either one of them could have, should have, maybe even did, walk in on us. That should have been some scene, Christ almighty.

Holy fuckin' shit. What if I hadn't noticed that one or both of them had already come home, seen us, and gone back out, maybe to a neighbor's or—worse, just so much worse—my grandparents', and called my mom? Where the fuck was my head? What the fuck was I thinking? Don't answer that, I know what I was thinking and where all the blood from my brain went. Shit, shit, shit!

Now seemed like it would be a good time to review my life, before it ended. Well, at least it would end on a high note, right? Okay, take a moment, I told myself. Think, girl, think! Ringo would have noticed if someone had come home. He would have let me know; he would have barked his head off and jumped around, but he would have let me know. No, dammit, Ringo was outside.

So maybe Nanny went to a friend's and I didn't know, and maybe Nicky was at Universe. I took a deep breath and decided to be as casual as possible. Calm, calm, calm.

"Um, I'm feeling, ah, better, Mom. I was just, um, sort of sleeping," I said. I watched Kerry come in from the living room. "Ah, where's Nanny and Nicky? Nanny's not home yet, and I don't remember if—" I was going to say "if she was going to a friend's after school," but Mom interrupted me.

"That's what I was calling for, so you wouldn't worry about them. I had Nanny go to your grandparents' so you could rest and someone could watch her do her homework. You know the problems she's been having with math lately."

I silently let out the breath I was holding. I wasn't dead, neither was my sister, and as far as I could tell, all was fine in the world.

Mom continued. "Nicky is going to Jimmy Doling's after school again, and he's going to stay over again, too. Mrs. Doling asked me today if Nicky could stay. She says it's really helping Jimmy feel better, and Nicky is helping him study." Mom's tone went from business to sympathetic. "Poor Jimmy, he's having a really hard time, with his parents getting divorced and all."

"Uh-huh," I answered her. I'd forgotten about Jimmy; he was a good friend to me and Nicky both. Well, I was glad that Nicky could help him out in some way, though gladder still that he hadn't walked in on me, um, us. Not that he would have told on me, I don't think. I was glad that today wasn't the day I'd find out.

I had been amazingly lucky.

Kerry walked over and, planting herself behind me, wrapped her arms around my waist and whispered in my free ear, "I owe you one, Hopey." She pressed herself into my back.

"What was that?"

"Oh nothing, Mom, just the TV." I tried to look over my shoulder at Kerry with mock sternness. "Oh, Mom, is it okay if I have Kerry over? She could keep me company," I suggested. "I mean, since, you know, no one's home and all."

"Nina, you're supposed to be home sick and resting, not running out to the Universe to read comics."

Kerry's hands slid down into my front pockets, and she was sliding them in such a stimulating manner, I could hardly stand upright, never mind still.

"Oh, geez," broke out of my mouth before I could stop it.

"Excuse me?"

"Oh, no, not you, Mom, um, Ringo! I just watched him try to, um, open the fence with his head again," I answered hastily. "Oh, and I wasn't going to go out. I figured Kerry and I could do homework or study, you know? Maybe watch a movie, and then, could she stay for dinner?"

"Plenty of homework I can do with you right now," Kerry whispered wickedly. "I have a biology exam coming up eventually, couldn't hurt to get"—and she brought her hand to my breast—"started. Might be something to all that reading and studying you do." She tweaked the nipple.

I almost dropped the phone and missed the first part of what my mother was saying, but I did notice that I could actually see the hard little prominence through my shirt. Finally! It was acting normal, thank God!

"...so you won't eat dinner by yourself."

I bit my lip. "I'm sorry, Mom, brain fart. I missed that. What did you say?"

Kerry popped her head over my shoulder and I tried to give her my darkest glare, but it wasn't working. Failing that, I stuck my tongue out at her.

"Ooh," she cooed, "promises, promises." Kerry slid around to the front and started to lay light little kisses along my neck.

I rolled my eyes to heaven, because this was surely some clever devil's idea of hell.

"Dad and I are going to be very late, about nine thirty or so, so if you promise not to go outside, use the money on the counter and order dinner for you and Kerry, so you don't have to eat by yourself, okay?"

"Thanks, Mom, I, um, ah!" Kerry bit me, so I tried to cough. "Um, kerf, kerf, thanks."

"Nina, are you sure you feel better? Maybe I should tell Mrs. Dolings to send Nicky home, and I'll keep you home tomorrow. Maybe you shouldn't have anyone over tonight."

"No, no, I'm fine, really, Mom. I feel A-OK," I reassured her, while Kerry licked my neck. Actually, I felt like I was going to vibrate into pieces. Kerry was driving me crazy, and it wasn't easy trying to act like a normal person on one hand and being mercilessly teased on the other.

"If I'm asleep before you get home, I'll see you in the morning. Love you, Mom, thanks, bye," and I hung up in a rush on my mother. Eesh. I hoped she'd scratch it up to being in a rush to call Kerry.

"Well?" Kerry asked me, arms now around my neck, "what did she say?"

I was actually a little excited, because I'd not only so lucked out this afternoon (and boy, had I), I'd lucked out for the whole evening. I'd get to spend more time with Kerry.

I put my arms around her waist and made my most solemn face. "She said I can't go to Universe with you today, sorry." I tried to look very sad, but Kerry saw through me and tugged a little on my ear.

"Hopey," she said, stretching the last syllable out, "come on, what did she say?"

I let the smile I couldn't hide anymore grow, and I swayed Kerry a bit in my arms. "Well, it seems that Nanny is at my grandparents' and probably staying over, Nicky is staying at Jimmy Doling's because his parents are getting divorced, and," I smiled even wider, "my parents won't be home till nine o'clock so..." I paused again for further dramatic effect and smiled. "You're invited over to study and order dinner with me so I don't have to eat by myself. How's that?"

Kerry looked at me in amazement.

"Oh, and Mom didn't tell me what time you had to go by so, if we just happen to, oh I don't know, say, fall asleep while we're studying, then I guess you could just, well, stay over then, right?" I just kept grinning away. "So is this working for you? It's working for me."

Kerry smiled up at me. "Your mom is being very cool. So what are we having for dinner? I'm starved!" And she bit my neck. "You're looking tasty, Hopey."

I raised her face to mine and kissed her, and again, we were lost, we were being swept into a storm, whirling and falling, and...I put out my hand and found myself pressed up on the wall. "Okay, okay," I breathed heavily. I needed some focus here. "I have to let the dog in," and we separated slightly, though her hands were on my waist. "I have to feed him." I stood up straight. "You have to call your parents," I ran my hand through my hair distractedly, "let them know you're alive." Focus, yes, and a sense of balance. There was an order to things, somewhere.

Kerry looked at me blankly.

I walked past her and over to the back door. I let Ringo in, and he snuffled my knees. I scratched his head, then grabbed his bowls, one food, one water. Finding the dog food, overprocessed dry nuggets made by some famous multinational conglomerate, I poured it out and put the bowl on the floor. I washed the other in the sink, and I focused on getting it sparkling clean before I filled it and set it before Ringo.

I was feeling very edgy, and I had no idea why. Maybe it was because I was too wound up, maybe I felt guilty for not even caring for such a long while about my brother and sister and ignoring my poor dog, and maybe I felt even guiltier about Kerry, not for what we'd done, but for what I'd done.

I didn't ask, and I wasn't told, and I did it anyway. I was a fucking jerk. I was no better and no different than any of the guys we knew. I stared at my hands and there, right on the edge around the nail bed, was the tiniest bit of blood. I let the cold water run over my shaking hands. I don't know how long I stood there, leaning over the sink, water running over my hands until they felt as icy as the rest of me.

"Hopey, you okay?" Kerry softly laid a hand on my back.

"Yeah," I answered shortly. I filled Ringo's bowl and, straightening, I turned and forced a smile. "I'm fine. Just getting Ringo's water. You call your parents?" I waved to the phone and put the bowl down for Ringo.

"They're not home. They're away again, so it doesn't matter," she answered, giving me a look. "What's wrong?"

Kerry eyed me warily, and I stared down at my hands. The silence stretched, while I considered how I felt and what to say. Nothing seemed right. Finally, I decided to just be as up-front as I could possibly be, take this on the chin, so to speak. I leaned back against the counter and looked back at her. "I, um, I think, ah, I think that I owe you an apology," I said. Damn, that sounded so weak to my ears, as if an apology could change anything or really make it better. I was so fucking stupid. I stared at my feet. Kerry shook her head in puzzlement and came closer to me, taking my hands.

"Nina, what are you talking about?" she asked, trying to look into my face, "an apology for what? Are you sorry we, um, that you," her voice trembled a bit, "that you touched me?"

"God, no, no, that's not what I meant." I lifted my eyes to hers and immediately tried to reassure her. Trust me to make something go from bad to worse. Stupid, stupid, stupid. On top of being a fucking jerk. There was no end to my talent. "I was, I mean, it sort of, I didn't mean to…" I stopped and looked at our joined hands.

"Hey, Nina, hey," Kerry lifted my chin so I could meet her eyes, "it's okay." She left her hand on my face and stroked the hair off my temples. "Really." Kerry kissed the corner of my mouth very tenderly.

I looked at her with anguish. "Are you sure? I mean, I know, you were waiting for, you know, someone and…"

Kerry cocked her head to consider my words, then made an *O* of understanding. She placed her fingers on my lips to shush me. "Yeah, yeah, engraved invitation and all that. You got it, baby." She smirked at me and enclosed the fingers that had touched her within her own. "You're wearing the brass ring." She squeezed and I winced, not in pain, but in guilt.

"Really?" I looked at her searchingly.

"Really." She nodded emphatically. "I wanted you, wanted you to do that." She looked down at my chest and began to make little circles on it with her fingertip. "I wanted to know how you'd feel, like that, inside me."

More than any movie or comic book or graphic novel (no matter how desired), this was a gift beyond compare, this basic, primal sharing of the self. It couldn't be returned, exchanged, or taken back. And this time, this very first time, Kerry had allowed me, had asked me, to leave a permanent mark on her body, something she would always, always bear, just like she had left one on my heart and mind. I was humbled and awed by its profundity.

"Oh," was all I could whisper in my rush of comprehension of this basic concept and consummate brilliance. "Thank you." I hugged her tightly. "Thank you."

We stayed like that, closely entwined, and I listened to her breathe against my heart.

Finally, Kerry stirred and looked up at me. "Hey, now I can tell everyone Hopey popped my cherry!" She grinned impishly at me, and I rolled my eyes.

This was the third time or so she'd called me "Hopey" after we, after I, well, you know, we did the overwhelming thing. "God, Kerry, I'm not wearing a costume, physically or mentally, and I wasn't then," I burst out, and looked at her very seriously. I realized this was part of what was bothering me, that her still using those nicknames now, after everything that had just happened between us, was actually hurting my feelings, making me feel disconnected somehow. "Please, tell me you're not, you weren't, either," I asked her. I watched her face for a long moment.

Kerry looked down, then back up at me. I could see her mentally weighing her words. "I was only playing, Nina, not trying to hurt you," she said softly, tracing my cheek with a fingertip. "It's just, well, it's easier if we're them, and not us, living here, in this place, with these people. It would be so much easier if we were where they are, living like they do. Believe me, I know who was touching me, loving me," she cupped my face, "inside of me. That's why," and she kissed my lips softly, "you're Nina, Nina Cherry," she kissed me again, "because you have mine," and I let her kisses sweep me away.

Somehow, we managed to clean up the living room, and we actually did study a bit, up in my room, and I left a note on the table downstairs telling my parents that Kerry was going to stay over because her parents were out and she couldn't find her key.

Normally, they, meaning my parents, would never allow anyone to stay over, and twice never on a school night, but I figured that if we were already, um, sleeping, yeah, sleeping when they got home, well, they wouldn't want to wake up a kid, especially one who couldn't get home anyway, right? And so what if she stayed in my room? It's not like it was a boy or something like that. Yeah. Maybe Kerry was rubbing off on me.

Anyway, somewhere after algebra and trigonometry and before history, with my bedroom door safely locked and Ringo keeping guard in the hallway, we were rolling around on the carpet in my room, making out again. Big surprise, right? I'll bet you can't believe we actually did anything else. Me either.

I was on my back and Kerry was straddling my hips, rubbing against me in an agonizingly delightful way. My mouth was full with hers and my hands were filled with her ass. God, it felt great—soft and firm at the same time. I can honestly say I really had a lot better understanding now of the overeager, overanxious boys I'd dated.

"Nina," Kerry growled at me, "take," and she plucked at my shirt, "this," she had it up past my midriff, "off!" and she had it up above my bra.

I lifted myself onto my elbows to comply, ripped that fucker off, and tossed it somewhere behind my head.

Kerry dived onto my chest, and she was licking, biting, squeezing my breasts, and I could hardly breathe.

"Your turn," I growled and gasped, but Kerry ignored me. She removed my bra and had a firm grip on my tit; then she replaced her hands with her mouth. I gasped at the sensation.

"Beautiful," Kerry told me from the corner of her mouth, "just fuckin' beautiful," and sucked harder.

I went with it, because I couldn't do anything else. The fire I'd felt before was nothing compared to this, this heart-stopping, head-pounding, clit-thumping feeling. I got a sudden surge of strength, and I sat up and gasped for air. I wanted to touch Kerry the same way as she was touching me, and more. "Your, huh, turn," I gasped out, and bringing my hands to the neck of her T-shirt, I ripped it straight down the center. I helped her wiggle out of the remains, and to this day I still don't know where it went. I assume it's resting in happy peace somewhere.

Kerry shuddered, whether in excitement or at the sudden coolness, I wasn't sure. We both watched her nipples tighten even harder, then I was all over her, painting lines with my tongue, feeling those hard little spots with my fingers, and she shook again as my mouth came closer.

When I finally drew that first lazy circle with my tongue on that delicious little nub, I realized that it reminded me a bit of raisins— small, sweet, compact—and as I nipped and sucked, Kerry pressed my head to her.

"Stop!" she ordered huskily, taking my head away, and I looked at her in a daze. She raised herself to her knees over me and inched back. Stretching her back so that her knees were by mine, she traced a line of fire with her tongue down my stomach to my waistband. I groaned.

"These," she looked up at me, placing her hands on my pants, "are coming off, now," and she proceeded to undo each and every button of my army pants with her teeth and tongue. Oh, and by the way, since then I've made it a rule, if I'm out on a date that I'm seriously into, I wear button flies, and they only come off if my date can do it with her mouth. Think of it as an entry examination, with only a pass or fail option.

My pants now open and my undies exposed (light blue, bikini brief, you might as well know, since I'm telling you everything else), Kerry reached up to tug them off, and I lifted my hips to help her. They also flew off to parts unknown.

She stood and I sat up to help her remove hers, and we sent them flying, too, and I kicked off my socks—I hate being naked with socks on; that's just ridiculous, and it's not truly naked, either. A sexy, musky scent filled the room, and I loved it.

Kerry and I just looked at each other, she standing, and me still on my spot on the floor. Then Kerry sat down again, over my legs.

We ran our hands over each other's bodies, enjoying the sensations we gave each other and the feel under our fingertips. Kerry's body was compact and not as muscled as mine; she was a little delicate and very slightly, very femininely rounded in the most delicious way, with hints of muscle underneath, except for her stomach, which was a nice, lightly padded quad, and her legs, which were as defined as mine. That made sense to me, since we both danced.

Me, on the other hand, I didn't have quads. I had a straight split that would never six-pack, though it might quad during the height of the swim and basketball seasons, which happened to overlap a bit. It didn't bother me then and it doesn't now; lots of people are built like that too. It's a genetic thing.

"Nina, you're bald."

"Huh?" I didn't know what she was talking about.

"Here," and Kerry trailed her fingers down and past my navel, resting on the very top of the place that was doing its own little dance.

"Your pussy is bald, well, almost. Why?"

I looked down to where her fingertips were lightly scratching against the very top of my mound and at hers just a few inches away from mine. She had a mix of blond and darker hairs, and I thought it was very pretty, actually. Oh, and she was right. I was practically bald by comparison.

"Swim team." I looked back up and answered succinctly. "We all do it. It reduces weight and drag. Some of the teams get together and have shaving parties, I've heard. Not that I've ever been," I added hastily, "and they shave everything, even their arms and eyebrows." I made a face. Oh, and that's the truth, by the way. When you race, you do anything you can to reduce drag, and while I wasn't fanatic enough to do my arms and eyebrows, and I didn't shave my buddy (I tried that and was rewarded with a couple of painful ingrown hairs, ain't doing that again), I did what I could and just trimmed it as close to the skin as I could.

Kerry nodded as she absorbed the information. "I'll bet that makes you more sensitive, though," she responded thoughtfully. "You probably walk around horny all day."

I shrugged my shoulders and made some noncommittal sound. It was true. I mean, I did walk around horny all day and still do, but I really doubt it had anything to do with that, all things considered, I mean.

Kerry put her arms around my neck and scooted closer. "Poor baby, you're probably dying right now," she said in a low voice, "and we can't have that," and she traced the tip of her tongue up my neck and nipped my ear, "can we?" And just like that, we were off again, burning like a house on fire.

I brought my knees out to the side and drew my feet in together. I wanted Kerry to have a little more room and to sit lower on me, and I guided her hips with my hands. I could feel her—her softness, her wetness—and it sent chills through me.

We made out and moved like that for a bit. "Baby, I want to try something with you," Kerry whispered to me, "here…just," and she moved down a bit and put her hands on either side of my pussy. From my sitting position, I could see that my buddy was so swollen, it actually poked up. I'd never seen it like that before, but for once, I wasn't worried about normal.

"Poor baby," Kerry murmured, parted me gently with her hands, and bent her head. Very softly, she kissed it, and I thought—well, I don't know what I thought. I don't think I could think anymore, 'cuz every nerve ending I had seemed to be concentrated in that one spot.

"So sweet, Nina, so very sweet," Kerry murmured, then straightened back up, and I groaned, whether in disappointment or anticipation, I'm not sure. Probably both.

Kerry took my hands off her hips and placed them on me, to hold myself the way she just had, and still kneeling over me, parted her own lips. She was beautiful to look at, and as her body moved closer and closer to mine, I could see her turgid clit peeking out from its hood and the moisture glistening from her opening. Suddenly she was on me, and I watched my clit disappear into her. The sensation was so intense, I gasped with the shock and could hardly hold myself up. Kerry put an arm around my back to steady me.

It felt like my tongue did when she sucked on it, combined with the kiss she had given my clit before, only magnified, intense, and constant. Forget about that "little death" thing. This was being fully alive, so alive that it's beyond explanation, more than I think I'd ever been before.

Kerry swayed, then shifted her legs so that her knees were also to the side and her heels were against my ass, as mine were to hers. Arms around each other for balance, we shuddered together, and we discovered that Kerry could move in any way she wanted and not break this exquisite contact, but I was a bit more limited, though if I arched my chest, we could still kiss, which was what we wanted to do.

"I figured," Kerry breathed out, "that since you're bald," and she grinned briefly, then breathed again, "if you were, well, you know, that I could feel you, inside me, like, and my clit would rub against the top," she rested her head on my shoulder, "you know?" We continued to move together.

"Good thought," I breathed back. "I like it." My breath was catching, and my body was burning with liquid fire that started at my clit and raced outward. I could feel it. "Think...there's a name for this?" I puffed out, and then there was no time to wait for an answer as the burning finished its way through to every part of my body, and I clutched at Kerry's hips grinding into me.

"God, Kerry," I breathed, and she grabbed my face to kiss me fiercely as I ground myself in and against her. My body felt like it was no longer earthbound—I was floating, I was flying, I was soaring at incredible speed, and lights burst in beautiful hues behind eyes I wasn't even aware that I'd closed. Gradually I became aware of Kerry's arms around me, stroking my head, bringing it to her shoulder, and she was whispering, "It's okay, baby, you're okay. I've got you, shh." I put my arms around her and softly kissed her neck, then just gave soft kisses to her chest, where my head lay, and we sat like that for a bit, Kerry stroking my back and my head.

And that, people, is the butterfly, girly style. Field-tested, lesbian-approved. Feel free to experiment amongst yourselves. Don't do it on a rug, though—your ass will not like that. You can take my word for it.

Eventually, I loaned Kerry a sleep shirt and bottom, and we actually made it into my bed and fell asleep. You're probably wondering why not sleep in the nude, and here's the deal. Let's just say my dad decided to unlock the door. Well, okay, a girl sleeping in my bed with me would be no big deal; a naked girl in my bed, well, we've got problems, see?

Chapter Eight:
Rock 'n' Roll High School

To this day, I've no real idea what time my parents came home. I'm sure they found the note, and my mom must have given my father a good talking to, because what woke us up that morning was my mom's knock and voice at the door, telling me it was time to get up, I'd find the bus fare she'd left me on the counter in the kitchen, and to have a nice day.

That was a little strange, actually, but then I thought about it and figured maybe my mom didn't want to embarrass me by being too "mom-like" in front of my friend. I gratefully left it at that.

I stretched a bit, nudged Kerry up, and after indulging in a quick, very touchy-feely, hungry morning kiss (okay, well, it was sort of quick anyway), I jumped out of the warm bed, grabbed my school uniform from the closet, and headed for the shower.

Kerry took her turn in the shower while I was dressing and borrowed my clothes from the day before.

A fast breakfast (I was starving! But then again, I was always hungry), and we were both running off to school, she on one side of the train tracks and me on the other, wearing my non-school-legal favorite coat.

We entertained ourselves by yelling back and forth in tremendously exaggerated voices all sorts of "I love you so much I'd [insert ridiculous assertion]" across the platform, much to the great annoyance of the commuters, and we promised we'd meet each other later at Universe, of course.

Her train pulled in about two seconds before mine did, and over the sound of the squealing rails, I heard her yell, "Love you, Hopey."

I paused before getting onto my own train and yelled back, "Love you, Maggie," and boarded, not sure if Kerry had actually heard me or not.

I found a window seat, since this far back along the route there were still plenty of spaces, and settled in, watching Kerry's train pull out, and then mine, gazing out at the view as it sped along.

It was funny, I thought, that between us, privately, the whole "Hopey-Maggie" thing had lost some of its appeal for me, but on the crowded platform, it seemed like a good idea, like it was funny, like we were having one over on people or something. I guess looking back on it now, it certainly was, or at least felt that it was, safer, to pretend that we were pretending. Silly, maybe, I know, but there it is.

I pulled out a pen and a notebook and wrote "Hopey 'n' Maggie 4E 11/16" and drew a valentine around it, then "New York City—Hard Core" for good measure. Inspecting it with a critical eye, I added an anarchy symbol. More commuters and schoolmates jumped on the train as we progressed, but I focused either on the various notebooks that I was busily decorating or the changing scenes outside of the Plexiglas window.

I pulled out one of my house keys, looked at the teen-scarred window, looked back at my key. Fuck it. I carefully and surreptitiously, with very small wrist movements, etched "Hopey loves Maggie," adding my own small bit of immortality to the "school sux," and "Tina luvs Bobby" milieu, all the while remembering Kerry's kiss and hands, the feel of her body, and how warm it had been all tucked up in my bed.

I had a moment to admire my handiwork, then my stop came into view, and grabbing my bag, I was up and shoving my way off with the rest. This train station, known as Grasmere, was located under the road instead of over it, unlike the one at home in Eltingville, so the long platform led to a stairway up to the street, where my schoolmates and I had to decide to walk or wait for the overcrowded bus filled with our neighboring school rivals.

As I made the slow and crowded way to the steps, someone came up behind me and clapped me on the shoulder with a friendly hand. "Hey, Nina, ready for tonight?"

I stopped in my tracks and turned to look up into a pair of smiling brown eyes and wavy honey blond hair, cut to the chin, all perched over the collar of a black wool overcoat. A full navy blue and white striped gym bag and an even fuller book bag were slung carelessly over one broad shoulder, and a perfect smile with even more perfect teeth completed the picture.

It was Fran DiTomassa, a top regional finalist and co-captain of the swim team. The whisper was she was going to qualify for nationals this year, and we all had every confidence she'd sweep 'em—she was that good. We had a good solid team, but with Fran, otherwise known as "Kitt" ('cuz she'd been a tiger in the water since she was "a cub") on it, we were a great team, a winning team.

She was a great captain as well, having been in that position since she was a sophomore and I'd started the team as a freshman, with a smile and an encouraging word for the younger or weaker members of the team and good coaching tips as well. Kitt took the time to work with anyone who either asked or was struggling, and all of us had benefited at one time or another from her attitude and her individual coaching. She and the other co-captain gave everyone on their team nicknames as well.

We were going to really miss her when she graduated in June; no one could come close to replacing her abilities in and out of the water. I just tried to follow her example and hoped she got a great full scholarship to wherever she decided to go.

"Tonight?" I repeated, trying not to stare at her too blankly.

"Yeah, tonight," she said, and we started making our way up the stairs. "Instead of practice, we have a meet in Brooklyn College, against…"

The rest faded out to my hearing as we got to the top, and when we reached the sidewalk, I turned to stare at Kitt in shock. Holy fuckin' shit! I'd forgotten I had a meet! Kerry wouldn't know and would be waiting for me at the store; what the fuck would she think? Goddamn! And to top it off, I'd forgotten my equipment, all my stuff—my racing swimsuit, my swim goggles and cap, my towel and spare clothes were sitting in a bag identical to Fran's right by the door of my room.

Where the fuck was my head? What the fuck was I thinking about? Never mind. I knew what I was thinking about. I was remembering, how at some point during the night, warm, sleepy hugs had become caresses, and then heated kisses, and somehow we'd both lost our sleep shorts, and I was again lost in the warmth of her mouth and the tight, wet heat of her body. Only this time when my fingertips were poised at her entrance, it was by very definite request and not by accident that I slid inside of her.

"Are you sure?" I had whispered in her ear.

"Please," she'd answered me and placed her hand on mine, "please," and it was with her hand urging mine that it was done.

She moaned softly in my ear and nipped the lobe. She turned on her side. "Baby, I want to touch you," she growled into my ear. She let go of my hand and brought her fingertip up to my mouth. In the light provided by the streetlight outside my window, I could see it glisten.

"That's me, baby, and what you do to me," she whispered, and she brought her hand down.

"Now, I want to know what it's like," she continued, "to touch your pussy," and her hand went farther down. Her voice, soft and insistent in my ear, and her words were tuning me up to a fever pitch, and I was almost dizzy with anticipation and crazy with want "to know that your wetness is mixed with mine." And as her lips found mine, her fingers slid through my folds.

The sensation was incredible, and I groaned as quietly as I could. I thought I knew right then that nothing in the world could possibly be better than this, and not stopping my own movements on and within her, I parted my legs slightly.

She stroked, rubbed, and tweaked my clit, and I could feel how turned on I really was. Then suddenly, the tip of one of her fingers was at the edge of my untried entrance.

"Kerry," I said. I wasn't too sure about this, I wasn't feeling any overwhelming need to try that.

"Shh, baby, it's okay," she whispered and tenderly kissed my cheek. "I'm not going to hurt you."

She stroked me, she kissed me, and I lost myself in our movement, my hips starting to move, when suddenly I could feel her, feel Kerry start to slide inside me. I gasped with a little more than just the shock.

Don't let anybody fool you. You know how they say jock girls break their own cherries all the time? Not true. The week before I'd been doing racing sprints in school because it was raining, and going up the steps two, then three, then four, finally, five at a time. At the top of the stretch, I received a sharp pain in my "genital area" that I'd never felt before, and when I went to the bathroom, there was approximately a two-inch diameter bloodstain in my underwear, and it wasn't my period, because that had been over the week before. Besides, this blood was different—bright red, a little jellylike, actually, and it was, well, the color of a maraschino cherry.

"Oh," I thought, "that's why they call it that," and figuring I'd done the jock girl thing, I shrugged it off.

Because of that, I was surprised that this hurt, and I placed my hand over Kerry's to stop her. "Please don't," I asked her. "That actually hurts."

"Baby, it won't hurt for long. It'll feel so good you won't even remember your name," she whispered. "I promise." She gave a small wiggle, and I jumped. Nope, that certainly did not feel any better.

I laughed quietly, a little nervously. "I'm sure you're right, but not…just not now, okay?"

"Okay, for now," she agreed and kissed me, and I felt her finger move away. I was tremendously relieved, but I couldn't have told you why—then, anyway.

We kissed more, and we continued the way it had been—Kerry focused on my clit and me on her clit and inside of her.

"Baby," Kerry asked between kisses, "you can use another if you want," and I brought another fingertip by her opening.

"I don't want to hurt you."

"You won't baby, you won't," she assured me, and after a few seconds of gently teasing, I slid in. Her body was tight and pulled me within. Kerry groaned into my mouth, and I groaned with her. It felt amazing.

"Nina, you feel so good inside of me."

"It feels good to be inside you."

Kissing deeply, tongues reaching, we groaned into each other's lips, our rhythm picking up speed and intensity.

"Nina, baby," Kerry breathed into my ear, "I want you deep inside of me," her breath hitched, "when you come."

"'Kay."

We were building to a crescendo—flying, pushing, pulling, straining against each other. I could feel her pussy tighten and her clit throb; I could feel the pulse of my clit under her thumb. Arms, legs, lips entwined, breast against breast and heart to heart, sliding and pushing deep within each other, holding each other closely, we came together in a gorgeous, furious rush, and we held each other tightly as the aftershocks became little tremors and then eased to a steady pulsing.

Softly kissing, we snuggled and I held Kerry on my shoulder as we finally fell asleep, for real this time.

And that's where I was, not here on this cold, gray November street, talking to one of the swim team captains, but I wasn't about to tell Kitt that; and in that second, Kitt noticed I was missing a bag.

"Shit, Razor, you forgot your stuff?" Razor was one of my nicknames on the team and the one Kitt and the principal preferred (unless I was being called to the carpet; then I was just "Boyd," in the absolutely most chilling tones. Hey, now you know my last name! Took long enough, right?).

"Hey, Razor, Kitt! Wait up!" came calling out behind us.

I was saved from having to think of an answer right then by the appearance of a small girl, about four foot five, with fiery red hair pulled into a thick braid.

"Hey, Betta." I turned and greeted her with a smile. Laura was a freshman and, as such, a new member of the swim team and one of the smallest. She was a nice kid, and I'd worked with her in the weight room and on her stroke in the pool after practice. She had a nice form, and after a few of our sessions, she was definitely a stronger swimmer; she'd already been a fierce one, hence her nickname, "Betta." You know, after the Siamese fighting fish, Bettas, which are small, brightly colorful—and ferocious.

"You ready for the meet tonight? Gonna anchor the relay?" she asked me excitedly.

"It depends on Coach Robbins," I answered, "and at this rate, if I can get my stuff in time."

Kitt interrupted and explained for me. "Razor," and she paused to give me an arch look, "left her things at home. C'mon, let's walk to school, see if we can figure something out," and leading the way, Kitt started down the block, and we came after her.

"You know, I'm only about ten minutes away from your house, Nina," Kitt mused as we walked along, kicking at the fallen leaves. "I get out one period early today. I could rush home, get my car, and…"

Hroonkk! Hroonkk! a car screamed by.

"Nina, babe!" called out into the air.

A black '74 Nova, shiny like oil with even brighter chrome that scared away the gray November light, pulled up in front of us, half on and half off the sidewalk. The license plate said "Blade." The driver's side door opened, and the sound of the Doors' "Break on Through" poured into the chilly wind. A figure with a black coat whipping out and tangling around her black-denimed legs, and long dark hair spilling around her shoulders, stepped out. In that moment, I could swear I smelled the ocean.

You met her before—Samantha Cray. Co-captain of the swim team, also a senior, and the coolest, toughest girl in school, and for the first time, I could actually see it, see her, like it seemed everyone else did. I don't know how I could have missed it. Maybe I'd ignored it. Or maybe more than just parts of my body were retarded.

When we had initially met on detention I was a freshman and she was a sophomore. We had to polish the trophy case together, sweep rugs, shine banisters, and occasionally diagram sentences or do complex math equations. Afterward, we'd grab a cigarette together on the way out of school. Samantha had convinced me to try out for the swim team in the first place. She was my friend, my teammate, and my swim buddy since we swam the same events and, more often than not, my detention partner.

While everyone really admired Kitt (and I wasn't completely immune to her either), they sort of hero-worshipped Samantha. I guess I'd just ignored it, because when we hung out and we were on our own, we were just, you know, us, and when we were with the team, well, Samantha was also known as "Sammy Blade" or simply "Blade," just like the one she always wore, since the past summer, hanging from her throat. Sammy cut through the water like a hot knife through butter, like a sword. She made mincemeat of our opponents, and when Samantha and I competed in the same events (we usually ended up in the same race or "heat"), it was called a "Slice and Dice," because we both did our best to win and usually did, getting points for the team.

Samantha didn't act like she cared too much about it one way or another, though. She always shrugged off all the congratulations with an "I was just fuckin' swimming, not curing cancer," unless, of course, it was a teacher or a parent, in which case it was "Just swimming." But modesty aside, she was focused and determined, a force to be reckoned with in the water, and everyone knew it.

Oh, and before you get the wrong idea, Samantha, like me, wasn't a rich kid like so many of the girls in school. The car she drove had been a gift from her firefighter dad, two years before, and it had been car-primer gray, dented, wheel-less and up on blocks.

He'd told her it was for graduation and was fixing it up for that day, until he'd gotten killed last year in the line of duty. I spent most of my free time last spring with Samantha, at the wakes and funeral, just being there if she needed someone, ya know? When school ended, Samantha immersed herself in fixing that car (except for that one time I convinced her to come out and play) until it was perfect, until it was the thing of beauty and babe magnet it was. It was the only thing Samantha showed pride over.

"Come on, get in," Samantha said, then noticed my companions.

"Hi, Betta," she greeted the freshman. "Kitt." She nodded coolly.

"Hi, Blade!" greeted Betta breathlessly, staring at the car with big eyes.

"Blade." Kitt nodded just as coolly, and a silence stretched on as the two of them watched each other guardedly.

Samantha nodded her head once and jerked her head in the direction of the car. "Pile in," she invited everyone with a jerk of her thumb, and slid back into the driver's seat.

Kitt opened the door and sat in the back behind Samantha, and Betta scrambled in from the other side; and putting my books on the seat, I climbed into the front passenger side, tumbling my bag beside me in the seat. I fumbled around with my seat belt, and I wondered when in the hell I'd noticed that car was so fucking cool.

"All in?" Samantha asked, checking the rearview. "Okay, then." She turned to me for a second and patted my leg. I jumped at that, but Samantha didn't notice. She just grinned. "Hang on," she told me in an undertone, and turning her attention back to the road, she slammed on the gas.

Betta shrieked as we tore off the sidewalk with a roar, and I'm sure we must have laid a half-inch-thick stripe of black rubber on the asphalt. Half a block down, Samantha looked at her through the rearview.

"You okay back there?" she asked with a smile.

"Yeah, fine," Kitt answered shortly.

"You've got a great car!" Betta yelled over the music.

"What was that?" Samantha asked with a grin.

"You've got a great—car," she finished as Samantha turned the music down.

"Thanks, kiddo. That ain't nothin'," Samantha answered with a satisfied grin. "Everybody ready for tonight?"

Kitt stirred in the back. "Blade, we have a problem. Seems Razor left her stuff at home today…" I could feel her eyes staring at the back of my head, so I twisted in my seat to face her, "and since we have to be in Brooklyn by five, I'm thinking I get out early, I'll grab my car, pick her up here, run by her house, and then zoom into Brooklyn. Could you tell Coach Robbins? We'll probably be a little late for roll." She meant roll call—when the coach went through the heads to see if we were all there, to sort and slot us for events if we didn't already know our roles, or if there were new ones due to people shortage.

"Hey, Razor, you were out yesterday, right? I thought I saw your name on the attendance sheet. You must have thought it was Monday," Betta chirped.

"Uh, sort of," I answered weakly. That sounded good enough.

By this time, we were pulling in around the school and about to enter the grounds.

"No," Samantha answered Kitt finally, as we entered the drive. "I've already got my car. I'll do it."

"Look, I don't mind, just tell Coach," Kitt responded, her voice slightly irritated. We pulled into the parking lot.

"How come you're parking your car on campus?" Betta leaned forward to ask.

All three of us turned to her in unison and answered, "Senior privilege."

"Oh…" she said quietly, and sat back shyly, as if suddenly aware that she was a freshman in the presence of the vaunted upperclassmen. Poor kid. It had to suck to feel like that. Oh well, I was sure by the time she got to homeroom, she'd be happy enough to have gotten a ride with both co-captains, and that by the time first period started, there'd be a ton of freshmen who decided they wanted to see Kitt and Blade in action later that evening.

Samantha looked over at me and gave me a quick once-over. "You okay to race? You're anchoring with me today," she said and narrowed her gaze.

Her eyes were a steely blue as she searched my face, and I tried not to squirm, but I dived into one of my books for something, anything, to break the gaze. I felt more than a little uncomfortable.

"Yeah, I'm fine," I answered shortly, and found a book that looked like it might be important enough to flip through.

Samantha parked the car and cut the engine, then twisted in her seat to look into the backseat. "Kitt, I've got my car—and I drive faster than you. You go home and," Samantha's mouth quirked slightly, "get ready for the race. We need to win."

Kitt considered for a moment, then nodded. "All right, fine. But be careful, Blade. We don't want to lose both anchors or our top freestylers." She grabbed her book and gym bags off the floor. "Cool, we're set, then. C'mon," and she opened the door to step out, and Betta, silent this whole time, did the same.

Samantha put a hand on my arm to restrain me when I went for the door handle. "Wait," she said quietly. I dropped the handle and simply stared at the hand on my sleeved arm.

Both rear doors slammed shut, and Kitt walked around to my side of the car. Betta had already started running toward the school building, calling out "see you in the water" behind her. I watched her catch up with a knot of freshmen that had just climbed off the bus and come in the gates, talking and waving her hands in the midst of the group as they walked on.

"You guys coming or what?" Kitt asked by my window.

"In a minute," Samantha answered. "Just got some strategy to discuss, you know, for the hundred." She was referring to a specific race event, which was the baby endurance swim, of one hundred yards or meters or whatever it was the pool was measured in. All I know was that it was four long, very long laps.

"Cool. Later, then. See you in the water."

Kitt started off, then stopped and turned. "Oh, Blade? Thanks," and she walked away.

Alone in Samantha's car, we sat in silence. As I fiddled with the strap of my book bag, I heard her scramble around in a pocket and pull something out. "Here," a red cigarette box landed on my bag, "have one," she invited as she took a pull on her own freshly lit one.

"Thanks." Samantha and I smoked the same brand—well, I did mention we were on detention together, a lot.

I pulled one out, then reached over to the dashboard to use the car lighter, focusing on the red glow before me, and when the cigarette finally lit, I took a grateful drag. I shifted and twisted to face Samantha.

A few books slid halfway out of my bag onto the seat between us.

"So," I exhaled, "what's up?" I suppose, no, I know, I was a little leery, wary even, in my approach. It was like I had this new sense, this new awareness, of myself, of my body, of Samantha's proximity, and I didn't know what to do with it, like I was a blind person given sight for the first time and trying to make sense of the shapes. No, actually it was more like always knowing what the shapes meant, but only now being able to see their true colors.

Samantha shifted to look at me and leaned an arm across her door. "You sure you're up for racing today? You look a little pale." She took a drag and blew it back out toward the windshield.

"Nah, I'm fine, Blade, just fine," I drawled out casually, and I stared out the front windshield. "I'll be okay to race. And thanks, for the ride, I mean." I continued to stare out the window. I couldn't, just couldn't, look at her, my pal and partner in crime against stupidity, as we referred to the student handbook. Out of the corner of my eye, I saw her raise her eyebrows when I called her "Blade," which was something I really never did outside of practice or meets. I guess I figured it would be better for both of us, it wouldn't hurt so much later, if and when she found out, about me, I mean. I was reaching for safe distance.

"Okay, just checking," Samantha said in a tone that told me she didn't quite believe me. She pursed her lips in thought and looked down at my books. "Oh, and no problem about the ride. We're buds, teammates, right?" She grinned at me. Unconsciously she reached for the charm hanging from her neck.

I met her eyes with a smile that quickly died and watched her fingers play with the miniature blade that was her namesake between her fingers, glad she hadn't reached out to touch my shoulder or play with my hair, because I felt just so damned raw, so fucking naked. I was afraid that if she did, touch me at all that is, that it would hurt, that I would explode from some unknowable depth of pain.

"Yeah, we are," I finally answered in a soft voice, my mind full of a tangle of images from the beach this past summer, when I had thought Samantha and I were going to kiss or something, and the way Kerry's eyes appeared before she and I did for the first time.

Damn, though. Who knew how long the friendship Samantha and I had would last once she knew. Did she know what I'd thought then? Or would she be relieved that it had been someone else? I seriously doubted she had felt the same way. Why would she? Why should she?

I looked out the windshield again.

Boy, that was an interesting tree there, outside the window. Gray, lifeless, waiting for spring. Those branches reached up for the sky, though, and never stopped. Just held still and held on, knowing spring had to show up sooner or later. But in November, it was definitely later.

In the silence, Samantha had picked up one of my notebooks and flipped through it. She was about to close it, but something caught her eye—she opened it again. She stared for a long, long while and I sat very still, staring at that frozen, reaching tree. I think it was a maple. "Friends of yours?" she asked finally, and I saw what she was pointing at—the "Hopey 'n' Maggie" written inside the back cover.

I swallowed—hard—and almost choked on my cigarette. Samantha pounded on my back a few times. Well, there went no touching each other out the door. At least there were no explosions, either. "Dude, you okay? You sure?" she asked in between poundings. That for sure was going to hurt later.

"Oh, fine, just—gak—fine."

I finally answered her earlier question, now that I was able to breathe again. "Um, no, they're not friends of mine," I told her, taking my notebook from her hands and sliding it and the rest firmly back into my bag. "It's a comic book thing. They're characters in a story line I'm following."

"It's that one you're always reading, right, *Love and Rockets*?" she asked me, nodding her head in understanding. "So, it's good, then?"

"Oh yeah," I answered enthusiastically, self-consciousness momentarily forgotten. "It's not like superpowers save the world from aliens or that sort of bullshit. It's got, like, real people, like, all kinds, you know—black, white, Asian, Hispanic." I turned my head back to the window and took a drag on my cigarette. "Some different religions, and the people are gay, straight, whatever. You know, real-world stuff." I glanced at her as I said it, trying not to put any special emphasis on it, just, you know, it was no big deal. "Cool music stuff that the characters are into, the punk scene."

Samantha looked down at my bag and twisted her lips again in thought. "I'll have to check it out sometime," she said finally, and took another drag.

The silence hung on and on. Honestly, if I had to confide in someone, besides Nicky that is, it would have been Samantha. While

Kitt passed around the shaving tip, or other swim-related esoterica, Samantha pulled me aside to tell me to just trim and avoid side effects, or how to do other things Kitt suggested without doing permanent damage to my skeletal system.

"Let her shave it, she's not gonna use it for anything else, anyway," Samantha had said, her eyes dark and stormy, her mouth a hard line. She'd been silent, considering an answer, I guess, then smiled, and it was like the sun had come out. "Other people like to be comfortable the rest of the time. Besides, who wants to be that fuckin' crazy about it?"

When looking for loopholes or inconsistencies in the student handbook, she laughed with me and found some more, or pointed out others; she snuck out with me from school, from practice, and from meets for cigarettes, or we'd find the most obscure places to hang out on the grounds and just shoot the shit, bitching about parents, school, life, school, death, school, you get the picture. She was one person I wanted to talk with, who'd help me get my head on straight, so to speak. The one real friend I had outside of Nicky and Kerry, and I wasn't sure I could call what Kerry and I were friends either.

And we looked a lot alike too, Samantha and I, same sort of blue eyes and same color hair, same way of standing, walking, even talking. Except for the height difference, everyone joked we could be twins, we'd been mistaken for one another so often. I didn't want her to regret our resemblance or come to despise it.

We smoked on until Samantha broke the silence. "Nina, we haven't really hung out this year, have we," she stated more than asked.

"No, not really," I answered her, and it was true. After the party, we hadn't really spoken much, and during the year so far, I'd been too busy studying to get into much trouble. Mostly we'd been together at practice, and while we spent less time together than usual, when we did it had seemed more intense, more connected somehow. But still, it seemed like we were avoiding each other, too.

"I really wanted to hang out with you this summer, you know, but things were crazy, with, like, all this insurance crap from my dad and all..."

"Yeah, I remember," I said, "and it's totally cool, you know. I understand that." Please, I thought, please don't talk about the beach. I peeked at her finally, and Samantha was staring down at the space between us on the seat. "I'm really, really sorry about your dad," I added sincerely, from the heart. Samantha was officially an orphan now that her father had died, her mother having died before she was two years old, and she had no brothers or sisters. Apparently, neither did her parents, and her grandparents were very, very old and living somewhere in Arizona or someplace.

There had been a lot of concern as to what would happen to her, where she'd live, go to school, all of that, and I knew, because Samantha had told me, that the school had gotten directly involved in trying to make sure she could stay, both in her home and in her classes.

"Me too." She sighed. "I spent all my free time working on this car, trying to finish what he started, I guess, just be near him, somehow, you know?" And she looked up at me for a second with full eyes and a lopsided grin, then dropped her gaze. "Your birthday present was the nicest thing that happened all summer, and I should have called you more—I'm sorry."

"'S all right, Sam," I said. "I figured you needed the space, you know? Room in your head, like." Ohplease ohplease ohplease let's not talk any more about the beach, I mentally begged, because as much as I was really listening to Samantha and sincerely cared about what she felt, I was feeling *very* uncomfortable and a little embarrassed, too.

Samantha sighed again. "I guess I did, maybe. Hey." She looked up with a forced bright smile. "I got a legal guardian over the summer."

ESP worked! Thank you! "Yeah?" I asked with interest. This had been a crucial part of Samantha's continued attendance and ability to live in the house her father had helped build.

"Yeah, turns out, he's, like, an old friend of my dad's, or a really distant relative, or something like that. Anyhow, legally, he's my uncle Cort, or some such thing—the uncle part, not the name, I mean," she added hastily.

"Hey, cool!" I was enthusiastic, then sobered instantly. "Do you like him? Is he, like, decent?"

"He's, um, actually he's pretty okay," Samantha answered, considering. "I don't know him that well yet, but we'll see. I think I do remember him from when I was really small, I'm not sure. He calls me 'Sammy Blade.'" She smiled a little shyly, but at least a real smile this time. "And he registered the car and got the custom plate for me, in August, when I was finally done with the chrome work."

"Cool." I nodded. "Very cool."

"So, how about you? Anything interesting going on, besides Joey, I mean?" she asked.

I almost choked again. I'd forgotten all about Joey. Jerk. Him, not me. I mean, sometimes he could really get on my nerves. What the hell was I going to do about him? I had to end that—soon, really really soon. It had already gone on longer than I would have normally allowed it.

"Remember how I told you about my brother Nicky's former classmate, how we'd become buds, you know, Kerry?" I asked, and Samantha nodded. "Well, we've just been getting closer, hanging out and stuff, you know, that's all," I answered as blandly as I could. "Nothing, really."

It stuck in my throat, and I hated myself for saying it. It most certainly wasn't nothing; it was something, really, truly something, and I crossed my fingers as I'd said it, hoping to somehow negate it. I just didn't know what else to do or say—I mean, I wasn't going to tell her exactly just how close we'd been in the last twenty-four hours. I mean, it was still so fresh and new and still mine somehow, well, mine and Kerry's—ours alone. At least, though, if Samantha heard me talk about Kerry, she'd know it was because we were close.

Maybe someday I could ease it into conversation, feel Samantha out about the whole thing, and tell her. Someday, but definitely not today. God, if Samantha had stayed at the party, I would have introduced them…

Samantha digested my words in silence, and I was now distinctly uncomfortable again, because I didn't want to talk about how close Kerry and I had become so very recently, and that made me think of her mouth, which made me think about her body and how it felt to touch her, and the incredible feeling of being so close and, gosh, it was getting warm in that car.

I had to get air. "Hey, what time is it? We have to get in before—" I'd just started to speak when the school bell rang out, letting us know we were now officially late for homeroom, and my heart sank a notch.

"Fuck. Well, that's that," Samantha said matter-of-factly. "Shall we?" She opened her door.

"Surely. Let's," I replied with a smile, opening my own, grabbing my books, and getting out. Samantha snatched her books and gym bag out of the trunk, slammed it shut, and we started to make our way to the building.

"Hey, Sam?" I asked as we walked, "where's your uniform?"

"Oh, heh." She laughed lowly. "Um, one of those loopholes you found, actually. You know, the one that says you have to wear the uniform in school unless you have exception days, but it doesn't really say anything about outside the building, except for the sweater versus the blazer thing, especially if it's cold out. You just have to have it on by the time you walk into homeroom, or a classroom, if you're late. So…it's in my locker." She paused. "I did it yesterday, too."

She grinned at me slyly, and I grinned back. Another stupidity smashed, courtesy of Samantha and Nina. Very cool, very cool. We kept walking.

"By the way, Nina, you still playing guitar?"

I'd picked it up, guitar I mean, the year before, and it had taken me the better part of a year to find and buy the one I was learning on. It was challenging, but I really loved it (and obviously still do), and I had finally started to progress beyond "Mary Had A Little Lamb."

"Oh yeah, I'm still playing. Still learning, though," I cautioned, "so it's nothing great."

"Yeah, right." Samantha smiled at me. "Like I'd ever believe that. We should jam sometime, you know?"

"Hey, that would be cool. Yeah, sure." I grinned back.

We both reached the door, but Samantha grabbed it and held it for me. "No, go ahead. You were sick, so you need all the rest you can get," she teased.

"Hey, you're right!" I smilingly agreed and went through.

We got in the building, and I led the way up the landing to the first floor where all the upperclassmen homerooms were. As I pulled open that door, I ran straight into Attila the Nun herself. Shit, I groaned inside, and my heart stopped dead, then fell another notch. Samantha was just a step or two behind me and coming up fast.

"Well, well, well, Boyd. Absent yesterday, late today, I see," and she peeked over my shoulder at Samantha as she walked right behind me. "Oh, and who is this? Cray? What a surprise to see the two of you, late, together. Come in, girls, please, by all means, come in. Welcome to school," and she held the door wide open so we could fully enter the hallway. We stood side by side before the good sister.

"Would you like breakfast? Slippers? Clean blankie?" she asked caustically. "Are we sleepies this morning, girls? Should I send you poor dears home to bed, tuck you in? It seems Razor and Blade aren't particularly sharp this morning, seeing as Boyd can't tell solid black or navy from green and black checks, and Cray here forgot to wear her uniform!" She was almost yelling by the time she got to the last part, and I can't speak for Samantha, but I could feel myself shrink in my coat.

Soon, I'd be so small I'd be invisible, and all my stuff would fall to the floor, and I could run away unnoticed by all except quantum physicists. I wished. Boy, did I wish. I wished so hard I'm surprised I didn't rupture something. Instead of shrinking, though, I stood up straight. If I was going to be in trouble, I'd take it head up and on the chin at least.

"So how about it, Blade?" Sister stretched the word out to sound like a curse. "Where's your uniform? Co-captain of the swim team," she added, twisting her mouth in scorn. It was amazing to me that someone as small as Attila the Nun could radiate such malice.

"It's in my locker, Sister," Samantha answered evenly, though out of the corner of my eye, I could see the stress on her face. "I was going to get it and put it on now."

"You'll be doing some gardening after swim practice this Saturday here at the convent, it would seem," Sister informed her silkily, watching for her reaction.

I set my shoulders straight. "In the handbook, Sister," I quickly interrupted, "it says that the student must appear in homeroom in full uniform or their class instead, if they're late. I believe that specificity is to give us leeway in wearing such things as leg warmers or even pants should the weather require it, in the same way that we're permitted to wear boots and change into our shoes once we arrive," I concluded hastily. Samantha shot me the merest flash of a grin and a look of gratitude.

Sister turned on me like lightning. Samantha rolled her eyes behind her back. "Shut up, Boyd. I haven't even started with you yet." Sister came and sneered up into my face, finger in my chest. "I'll be seeing you after school today."

Fuck. The meet! Kerry! My parents! I was fuckin' dead all around. Why Sister didn't just kill me and get it over with, I didn't know. It seemed that she absolutely delighted in torturing and terrifying us. If they had at least brought back corporal punishment, the pain would end eventually, I think, but this, the viciousness of it, it lasted forever, and it's not something I've ever really gotten over. I don't think anyone who has dealt with something like it has, either.

"Excuse me, Sister." Samantha stood very straight and squared her shoulders smartly. "I'm sure as moderator of the swim team, you are aware that we have a major meet tonight, one that requires a win. Nina is the anchor on the relays, and one of our best freestylers, and as such, she cannot be absent from the roster tonight."

"I don't care if she's the King of Prussia and tonight she has to disarm all the nuclear bombs and bring down heaven on earth—" Sister said, but Samantha interrupted her again.

"Tonight, she does her first endurance race, Sister, and I offered her a ride to school this morning. As co-captain of the team, I asked her to review some strategies with me that would help her performance. It's my fault she's late, Sister," Samantha continued. "She shouldn't be punished for following the direct request of a team captain."

"Sam, don't..." I said. I was going to open my mouth to say something, and I tried, but the flash in Samantha's eyes and the quick negative shake of her head stopped me.

"No, no, Boyd, don't interrupt. I want to hear what else Cray has to say."

"Succinctly, Sister, I am both a senior within the school and a team leader. 'Behavior of any classmen under any upperclassmen is the upperclassman's responsibility, for sophomores and above,'" Samantha quoted to her straight from the handbook. "Therefore, a junior is a senior's responsibility, and as both an upperclassman and Nina's captain, I requested that she speak with me, and I should have paid attention to the time. This is very obviously my responsibility, and neither Nina nor the team should suffer for it." Samantha concluded and stood stock-still, her eyes steady on Sister Attila's.

I never respected Kitt as much as I respected Samantha at that moment.

Sister took a step back, crossed one arm across her chest, and leaned the other elbow on it, resting her chin on her palm, as if logically figuring out astronomy equations. Of course, that was very possible—

she was the math teacher, after all.

"Okay, then." Sister straightened and placed her hands on her hips. "You," and she pointed at Samantha, "have Saturday detention after swim practice as we have already discussed, and you," she pointed to me, "will help with the garden on Saturday as well, instead of staying after today. Since the two of you insist on sticking together and being a team, then as a team you'll work on Saturday, and as team captain, Ms. Cray, you will spend the rest of the week as of tomorrow instructing Ms. Boyd as well as yourself in the lovely intricacies of differential equations and artificial division, since I am *lucky* enough to have you both on the math team as well."

She observed us, making sure the impact of her words had sunk in, then glanced at her watch. "Cray, you have four minutes before homeroom is over. I suggest you put your uniform on," and her gaze ripped across Samantha with venom, "so that you may be within handbook guidelines," she grimaced, "and attempt to be both not late for first period and enter the classroom in appropriate attire. I shall inform your homeroom teacher as to your whereabouts. And you, Boyd," she focused on me next, "have assignments to make up. I suggest you spend the next four minutes discovering what they are. Dismissed, girls," and she turned on her heel to stalk down the corridor, hands now clasped behind her back, and Samantha and I started to relax.

"Oh, and one last thing?" Sister turned back, and Samantha and I both straightened up. Sister gave us a hard, evaluating glance, then nodded with a satisfied expression on her face, as if we had passed some sort of inspection or test. "I'll see you in the water, Razor, Captain." She nodded at us each and turned again to stride off—probably to not only speak with Samantha's homeroom teacher, but also to commune with God or something.

Maybe we had passed something important, after all. I don't know and Sister never told.

"Can you fuckin' believe it?" I turned to Samantha and asked, rolling my eyes. "The day hasn't even fuckin' started yet!"

"Tell me about it!" Samantha had a frustrated look on her face that matched the way I felt and shifted her bags on her shoulder.

"All right then, here's the deal. Meet me at my car at the end of the day as soon as you get out, and we'll zoom back to your place, 'kay?"

Samantha firmed up the remainder of our earlier plan.

"Yeah, will do. Thanks again," and this time I gave a real grin, "Sammy Blade."

Samantha chuckled once under her breath. "You just make sure you slice that lane wide open tonight, Razor." She grinned back at me.

"Hey, I'll slice, you dice," I joked back. We shared that smile just a bit longer, then both remembered we had to get to class. "I'll see you later, Sammy," I told her, still smiling.

"Yup," Samantha agreed, and after a quick nod at each other, we both took off for our lockers and homerooms.

It took me seconds to get everything settled in and to grab the texts and notebooks I'd need for the first four periods, and I opened the door to homeroom just moments before the bell rang.

Sister Carlos looked up from her desk. "It's so very nice of you to join us, Ms. Boyd, though it is a wee bit late," she said mildly, and she glanced up at the clock set on the back wall of the room, then back at me, emphasizing the point. "Are we feeling better today? We do still look a bit peaky. We'll not be passing the plague around school, will we?" she asked with a tolerant smile.

"Uh, no, Sister. I mean, yes, Sister. I feel better. I'm sure I'm not plague-ridden, not yet anyway, um, ma'am."

Instead of good cop-bad cop, we had sweet and sour nuns. I pictured a group of nuns, some covered in Chinese mustard and some in duck sauce, and smiled, then quickly swallowed it. I didn't want to get asked what I thought was so amusing—that would have been some explanation. There was absolutely no doubt in my mind that this day was just not going to improve tremendously.

"Do we have an absence note, Ms. Boyd?" Sister held her hand out expectantly.

Shit! No! Usually my mom left those on the counter, and she'd forgotten to do it, which was actually very unusual, and I'd forgotten to remind her. Actually, my mom had been sort of weird this morning, I hadn't even seen her. How often did that happen? And I think she was in the room with my dad. He didn't go to work? That was very strange. I hope he wasn't sick or something...

"Ms. Boyd?" asked Sister expectantly, "your note?"

I collected myself. "I'm sorry, Sister. I don't have it with me today."

"Make sure you have it tomorrow, then, Ms. Boyd, or you'll have to stay after for three afternoons next week. I understand your dance card this week has already been filled," Sister stated matter-of-factly.

How did she know already? How did the Sisters do that? I swear they had radio transmitters in their headgear! The antenna was probably in the band, and the beads were stations. The crucifix had to be a microphone, a direct line to God or to each other—whoever answered first, I guess, I thought wryly.

"Yes, Sister, I'll have it for you tomorrow." I was relieved. She had let me slide, and since she had returned her attention to her desk, I started to make my way to my seat. But just as I got there and put my books on the desk, the bell rang, signaling the beginning of first period.

"Nina, a moment, please?" Sister requested as we filed past her desk toward the door.

"Yes, Sister Carlos?" I turned to her from the doorway.

"Slice the lane, Razor!" Her crystal blue eyes twinkled like you imagine Santa's would as she smiled at me and gave me a thumbs-up.

"I'll do my very best, Sister," I answered honestly and smiled in return. I turned to leave but winced internally; there was nothing like pressure.

"That's all we ask for, Nina, your absolute very, very best," I heard her say as I walked out into the hallway to my first class of the day.

By history, I was trying to sneak some homework from English in, and by lunchtime, I sat with my little group busting my brain over quadratic equations, both from last night and for this night. Sister Attila was also my math teacher and, trust me, she had a few special words for me when class began, after we were all seated.

"Boyd, please stand," Sister requested, and I complied quickly. "Let's all welcome Boyd back today, shall we?" And she started to clap, indicating with a nod that the class should follow suit, which they did, but with no enthusiasm. They had to; the consequences would be dire if they didn't—this, what was happening to me, could be one of them. And it already had been. My ears reddened with embarrassment.

"And," Sister said, "let us also hope that Boyd performs better in tonight's swim meet than she did on Friday's exam, much better in fact, since if her grades are any indication of her performance, she should probably drown. But," she continued, and held up a finger, "at least

JD Glass

she's healthy—dumb, but healthy. I suppose then she could be thought of as stupid—pretty, but stupid. Which is probably how the term 'pretty stupid' was coined." Sister let the words echo in the classroom while I felt the warmth of my ears spread to the rest of my body.

Don't ask me how I felt, because I could never describe that combined anger and hopelessness, as well as silent pity, for all of us in that classroom, forced to suffer individually and collectively.

"Well, Boyd, you are not alone in being pretty stupid. You have plenty of company. Since I have reviewed your exams and saved the corrections for today," she spoke to the class at large, "I have a list of fellow idiots for you, Boyd." She looked at me again, then down at the papers on her desk. She began to go through them. "Bissel, Chin, Garcia," she read out, and as she called each one, the girls stood.

Thinking she was done with me, I went to sit, but...

"No, Boyd, keep standing. There are more idiots to keep you company," she said conversationally, and read on. "Marks, Pieta, and it certainly is a pity," she interrupted herself to peer at us, then went back to the exams.

The names kept coming, and forty minutes never lasted as long as they always seemed to in that classroom. There's absolutely no mystery as to why my group was so quiet and busy during each and every lunch—we were each and every one of us terrified.

The rest of my classes passed in a blur, between trying to get notes and homework from the day before, thinking about Kerry and the swim meet, hoping she'd understand, and just generally being uncomfortable in my seat. I think I was growing again, or rather, still. I wiggled and shifted, tapped and chewed on my pen, until Mr. Fender, the chemistry teacher and a kindly man who looked like everyone's favorite uncle, warned me about getting ink in my mouth.

"Ms. Boyd, blue Papermate ink is not on the list of basic foods for a very good reason, and should you insist on providing such capillary action to the tubule, forcing the fluid to rise, upon ingestion of said fluid, you will most certainly discover why," he lectured, and I took my pen out of my mouth. I examined my pen—it wasn't blue, it was black, but the point Mr. Fender had made was well taken, no pun intended. So I doodled instead.

End of day at 2:29 (okay, technically, two thirty, but those who rushed out were called members of the 2:29 club) didn't come soon enough, and the very moment the bell rang that announced incipient freedom, I dashed to and from my locker and hit the ground running, speeding down the corridor to the door and out to the parking lot.

A couple of girls called out, "Slice it, Razor!" and "Slice and Dice!" meaning they expected Samantha and me to bring in a couple of firsts and seconds, and I held out my hand in a thumbs-up and yelled back, "Thanks!" as I sped along.

Out the door, down the walkway, and up the hill, I ran the whole way to Samantha's car and there she was, leaning against it casually, cigarette in hand, and acting like she'd been there forever. She'd changed out of her uniform again.

"Been here long?" I asked her with a smile as she unlocked the door for me, and I threw my book bag in the back and jumped in.

"Nah, just a little bit," she answered as she got behind the wheel and flashed me a quick grin of her own. "Sister Theodocia let us out a little early, so I decided to slip into something a little more, um, comfortable."

"Lucky you," I told her enviously. "I have a lab partner who thinks two hundred percent error is acceptable and keeps trying to set the lab on fire. We never get out on time," I added darkly, more than a little annoyed. And it was true. This time, Danielle forgot to watch the Bunsen burner, and there was a dark spot on the ceiling—right over our desk. Dammit. I'd probably have to paint that next week.

Samantha laughed as I told her about it, and we settled into her car, closing the doors and adjusting our seat belts. "You're going to like being a senior, I think," she said, while tilting the side and rearview mirrors to her satisfaction. A few more microscopic alterations, and they were as close to perfect as she could get them. She nodded in satisfaction. Checking her seat belt for the final time, she turned to me and asked, "Ready?" She wore an evil smirk.

"Totally." I smirked back and firmly snapped my seat belt across my shoulders and hips.

She started the car and pulled out a tape from her pocket and slid it into the deck mounted in the dashboard. "Tally-ho, baby," she answered, gunning the engine. She turned the stereo on, and we peeled out of the lot, laying more rubber down on the much-abused tarmac. "Real Wild Child" broke sound barrier rules and neighborhood ordinances as the car flew forward. I briefly wondered how Samantha was able to keep herself in tires.

We sped down the hill to the exit, Samantha honking madly and scattering groups of students and teachers as they walked down. After they scrambled out of the way, some of them noticed whose car it was and who was in it, and they screamed "Go Blade! Slice and Dice!" and "Razor Blade, Slice and Dice!"

Samantha grinned madly, screaming "Yahooooo!" out the window, and we both waved and called out "Thanks!" to our fellow classmates. Still driving like madwomen, or rather, one madwoman and one madwoman's passenger with a cast-iron stomach, we passed the student bus stops, Samantha honking the horn like she was the Philharmonic Automotive Orchestra, to the same cheers and gestures.

Finally, we passed the last group of students, and Samantha looked over at me with a huge smile. "Having fun yet?" She eased back a bit, but just a tiny bit, on the gas.

I smiled back. "Hey, yeah! That was pretty cool. Thanks."

"*No problema.*" She grinned. "You wanna do it again?" Samantha flipped the turn signal as if she was going to turn around.

I grinned, too, and shook my head in the negative.

She laughed. "Just kidding. You are so going to love being a senior, Nina."

I quirked my lips a bit at that. "Guess so, I'll find out soon enough," and we drove down the local main strip, Hylan Boulevard, toward my house in a contented silence.

To be a senior, to graduate, to leave and never come back. To be of legal age and to have control over my own life, to be able to say yes or no as I chose and not be forced into doing things that I felt wrong about, like clapping at another student's misfortune or face even worse for the whole class. To not wake up every morning hearing how I should have never been born. To be able to drive, just drive away. Samantha didn't know just how much I was looking forward to that. Or maybe she did.

After a while of watching the local stores and homes pass by as colorful blurs, I turned to Samantha. "By the way, you do know where I live, right?" I grinned and lit two cigarettes while waiting for her reply.

"Um, I've got a general good idea. Light me one, too, by the way?" She waved her hand in the direction of my cigarette. "I know you're on

Richmond Avenue, not far from Eltingville train station." She grinned right back at me. "How about you just tell me where to turn when we're near it, okay? Cool enough?"

"Step ahead of you, chief," and I handed her a lit cig. "Yeah, cool enough," I agreed, and settled back in, both of us enjoying and singing along to the U2 tape Samantha popped into the deck.

As we neared my neighborhood, I pictured landmarks in my head that I could point out to Samantha so that she'd know where she was. Let's see, there was the Burger King, otherwise known as the "BK Lounge," the train station, Universe, shit! Kerry! She got out earlier than I did and was going to wait for me there, except that's not where I was going to be. An idea hit me. "Hey, Samantha, can I ask you a favor?"

"You mean, other than the one I'm already doing?" she drawled and glanced at me sidewise, then looked back at the road. "I'm just yanking your chain, by the way. I wanted to hang with you a bit."

"Um, yeah," I replied, absorbing that. Her statement had thrown me a bit off track, and I had to collect my words again. "I promised someone I was going to meet them at Universe, and I don't want them to wait for nothing. Do you mind if we stop there? I promise I'll only be, like, a minute."

"Isn't that the comic book place you told me about? Right by the train station?" she inquired as she focused on driving. The car had turned onto Richmond Avenue, and we were less than three minutes away, if that.

"Yeah, that's it. It'll be short."

"Okay, we've got a few minutes to spare," Samantha agreed. "Is that it?" She sighted down the block and pointed across the street.

Samantha glanced at me and I nodded. With luck that doesn't always happen when you're in a hurry, Samantha found and slid into a parking space right across the street from the store.

"I'll be right back."

I rounded the car and stood in the street, waiting for an opening in traffic to run across. One finally did and I dashed across, feeling my coat flapping out behind me. I hurried the few steps to the store, opened the door, and stepped in.

"Hey, Nina," Robbie greeted from behind the counter.

"Hey, Robbie, you see Kerry?"

Robbie flushed red to the roots of his hair. "Uh, yeah." He looked at me strangely. "She's in the back there, by the video—"

"Hopey girl!" Kerry rushed up to me and threw her arms around me excitedly. "I missed you!" she exclaimed and kissed my neck. I hugged her in return and kissed the top of her head.

"Hello to you too, missed you." My low tone was for her ears only.

"C'mere, come on," Kerry urged, disentangling herself from our embrace and grabbing my hand. She started walking into the back of the store, where the video games were in a narrow alcove.

"I've got to tell you something," I said, allowing myself to be led into the back and coming to stand in front of a row of machines. "I can't—"

"It can wait another second," Kerry told me, "but I can't." And with surprising strength, she pushed me into the narrow space between two of the arcade games and laid an enthusiastic kiss on my lips, which I returned.

A minute passed, another went by, and I broke off our kiss, breathless. "I hate to tell you this, but I can't stay," I told her. "I've got a swim meet tonight."

Kerry stared at me in wordless surprise.

"It's a big-deal event at Brooklyn College, and I have to be there. The team's counting on me, I'm anchoring the relay," I started to explain, "and I'm also doing my first—"

Kerry interrupted me. "Your school can wait another minute," she told me, and closed in on me for another kiss.

"I've got," I tried to speak between kisses, "to go."

"Okay, fine, you've been properly greeted, you can go now," Kerry informed me with a smile, releasing me and the lapels of my coat, which I had only just become aware that she'd been holding onto, and she reached for my hand.

I took it, and we emerged from between the machines, red-faced and rumpled. Just then I noticed a figure making a purchase at the counter. It was Samantha. Paper bag in hand, she turned and saw me standing there, hand in hand with Kerry, and we just stared at each other, the look on Samantha's face unreadable. "You ready?" she asked, with a look of polite interest toward Kerry.

"Who's that?" Kerry asked softly in my ear.

"This is my friend I've told you about." I stepped forward with Kerry to make introductions, "Samantha, my partner in the destruction of stupidity and also a captain of the swim team, and this…" I turned to Samantha, "is Kerry, the one I, um," I hesitated uncertainly, "the friend I was telling you about," I said. Okay, so I sounded a little retarded. I didn't know what else to say.

Samantha's face went from polite interest to absolutely blank. "Pleased, I'm sure," and she nodded a bit dismissively. She folded both hands over her purchase.

Kerry nodded back at Samantha, flicked her eyes past her to look through the glass door to the street, then back at Samantha. "Nice car," Kerry commented in an equal tone. Her expression was bland, and Samantha responded with a noncommittal shrug.

Whoa, okay. Back up. What the fuck was going on? It's not like I expected them to instantly become bosom buddies or anything, but this, this weirdness, was unexpected. I think I had just witnessed an instant, mutual loathing—how bizarre was that?

"We ready?" Samantha asked me, turning on her heel. "You coming?"

"Not with you, she's not," Kerry muttered in an angry undertone I hoped I was the only one who could hear. "Wait a second." Kerry grabbed Samantha's coat sleeve. "You taking Nina Cherry here for a ride?" she asked in a loud voice and challenging tone.

As Robbie choked and ducked under the counter and I stared at Kerry in shock, Samantha, who had turned back when Kerry's arm had reached out, stared at Kerry's hand on her sleeve until Kerry dropped it.

"Good," Samantha breathed out, and she leaned over and down, until her face was mere inches from Kerry's. "Now, her name is Nina," Samantha hissed at her. "Should you choose to call her any other, she has earned 'Razor.'"

I placed a hand on Samantha's arm. "Sam, Sammy, it's okay, she didn't mean anything by that." Well, all right, *I* knew what she meant, but I wasn't going to explain it to Samantha.

Samantha ignored me, her mouth a thin, tight line. Bright red spots stood out on her cheeks. "Should either of those not suit you or your," and she looked Kerry up and down, "uses," she said with a twist of her lips, "then I believe the proper form of address is Ms. Boyd. Are we clear?"

"Samantha, stop," I tried again. "We have to go."

Samantha just held her ground and Kerry's eyes until Kerry finally nodded. She looked positively furious. Her face was bright red, and her eyes were almost yellow with anger. I'd never seen her look like this, ever, and I'd never seen this side of Samantha, either. I wondered if there was something in the air. I was feeling a little snappish now, myself.

I gripped the arm I was holding. "Blade!" I spoke sharply, "save it for the water—let's go!"

Samantha shook her head and seemed to recover herself. "Jesus, yeah," she muttered and glanced around a second, then looked at me, a bit red-faced. "Sorry," she said to me, then looked at Kerry. "Pre-race anxiety," she explained, rather casually.

Kerry had the grace to accept that with a nod. "Fine," she replied curtly. "Now that you're done playing shark, can you give me a lift home in your…" she looked past Samantha to her car, then back, "*babe mobile*?" she sarcastically emphasized. "It's on the way to Nina's." And she stomped out of the store toward the car.

Glancing quickly at Samantha, I walked out after her, and Samantha followed me. We made our way through traffic, and the three of us stood around Samantha's car.

"I can't give you a ride home, um, Kerry," Samantha stumbled a bit over her name, "because I've already told my uncle where I was driving to and who I had in the car. I can drop you off at Nina's, though, okay?"

"That's fine."

Samantha opened the doors and we all piled in—me in the front, Kerry in the back.

Kerry pushed the book bags over and looked around her at the car as Samantha started it up and then leaned over me to place her purchase in the glove compartment. She closed it with a loud snap.

"Big backseat you've got." Kerry bounced on the seat a bit.

"Big enough," Samantha replied shortly. She gunned the motor and pulled out. We drove for a few blocks in silence until the block before I lived on.

"Just make the next left, then stop right on the corner, that's me," I pointed out for Samantha.

She nodded and did just that, pulling up to the side of the house. Samantha cut the motor, and I stepped out. So did Kerry.

"Nina, take a minute to change—it's cold!" Samantha called out from the window.

I nodded in agreement and walked to the front door with Kerry. I stopped as we reached the step and turned to speak to her. "Kerr, I'm really, really sorry about that, I had no—" Kerry placed her fingers on my lips to shush me, then replaced them with a gentle kiss which I returned. God, her lips were so soft, and it was so easy to just sink into them.

"I'm not mad at you for that, Hopey," Kerry said when we broke off. "I'm not mad at you at all. You know I understand being tense before a race. But…" and she took a breath and paused, "Samantha the Shark's a bitch."

I opened the door to the house and considered Kerry's thoughts and feelings before replying. I'd been shocked by the entire interchange between them, so I wasn't exactly sure what to say, do, or feel. On the one hand, Samantha had clearly been standing up for what she thought was an insult toward me, and to tell the truth, I was shocked that Kerry had said it in the first place—I'd thought that was, well, private, you know? It was one thing when she'd said it to me the day before, but it really sounded different when she said it in the store. I wasn't too sure whether or not I liked it. On the other hand, it seemed that the whole weird thing could have been avoided—it was like Samantha had wanted to, well, fight or something.

"Samantha usually, well, I've never seen her really do something like that," I spoke slowly, weighing my words, "unless…" Well, she was defending someone, I thought, but didn't say that. "I don't know," I said instead. "I guess, maybe, this is a tremendous meet for us, there's a lot riding on it, on her," I said. "I'm sure she didn't mean it." Okay, that sounded lame to me too, but what else was I supposed to say?

"Oh, she meant it all right, Nina," Kerry said darkly, "but don't worry about it. Go get your stuff and do whatever it is you do." And she kissed me again. "I'll see you later," Kerry told me and walked off. I watched her, then realized that Samantha had gotten out and come around the passenger side to lean against the car.

I wondered if she had seen the whole thing, and I hoped not, not so much because I was embarrassed or anything (well, maybe just a little—I've never been really big on PDAs—you know, Public Displays of Affection). It's just that it was, you know, personal—as in, none of anyone's business. Maybe the shrubs in the planter hid her view, and I was back a bit in the doorway.

Besides, if I was going to tell her and she was going to know, and eventually she would because that was right and fair, it had to be on my terms, when I could actually sit and talk with her and not have to worry about silly things like major swim meets or hostile interactions.

Kerry stopped a minute on her way and pointedly looked Samantha up and down, then walked on.

Shit. Oh yeah, that was going to make it better, I thought resignedly. I pretended not to see Samantha as I turned and went into the house. I dumped my books off by the door and ran up the stairs.

Changing my clothes in record time, I slid on a *Love and Rockets* tee and a pair of black jeans, then grabbed my boots and bag and ran back downstairs. I dashed off a quick note for my parents and siblings, telling them where I was and reminding them it was on the schedule I kept posted on the refrigerator.

I ran to the door, got out, locked it, and quickly made my way to Samantha's car. She left her leaning post against the fender and climbed in on her side as I crossed the sidewalk.

"Okay, we're good," I told her, tossing my bag in the back and shutting the door. Samantha waited, making sure I buckled my seat belt, then took off in a roar of rubber, gravel, and dust.

As we skidded down the block, Samantha popped another tape into the deck, and as we caught up to Kerry, Concrete Blonde's "The Beast" overflowed the windows. "Say good-bye to your," and her mouth twisted in distaste, "girlfriend," she told me as she skidded the car to a stop in front of Kerry, while words that said something to the effect of love being a killer you thought was a friend echoed down the block.

I know there was a message in the music, and while I probably had an idea of what it was, I just wasn't sure where it was directed. And if it was a warning, I didn't know who it was for.

I rolled down the window and leaned out.

"Nice choice of music," Kerry commented in Samantha's direction. "No fooling you, I guess."

"You didn't bother to try." Samantha had the same bored face and tone as before.

I turned back to look at her and she glanced at my face. I know I appeared a little confused; I had no idea what she was talking about. Well, maybe I did, but it didn't bear thinking about right then. For a little while, Samantha and I were still friends, and I wanted to keep it that way.

"Never mind, Razor," Samantha told me, her voice a touch warmer than frost. "Just say good-bye. Good-bye, Kerry," Samantha said flatly, "nice meeting you." She held both hands on the steering wheel and stared out the windshield, as if to say any more bored her and she might fall asleep.

"Likewise." Kerry smirked at her. "Thanks for the ride. I'll see you later," Kerry told me, bending down to look into my eyes.

"I'll call you when I get home."

Kerry reached for my face, softly stroked my cheek, and gently kissed my lips. "For luck."

"Great, just great," I heard Samantha mutter under her breath. "The whole team's gonna fuckin' drown."

If I'd been hoping Samantha hadn't noticed before, well, for sure she'd noticed now. I don't care how she stared out the window, I could feel her eyes on the back of my head like heat lamps trying to melt my skull as I kissed Kerry back. But really, fuck it. I was getting a kiss from a pretty girl—and if we were going to stay friends, Samantha would just have to deal, right?

"Okay, we've got to go. Bye," Samantha reminded us firmly, then gunned the motor.

"Thanks." I smiled softly at Kerry as we finally parted. I was touched by her concern. "Bye!" I waved to Kerry, and Samantha floored the pedal. The car lurched forward, and I slammed back against the seat.

"See you later!" I could hear Kerry call out behind the car, and at that, Samantha spun the tires. We were off, rocketing around the block, the only sound except the roar of the engine the next chorus of the song: love as leech and a vampire. The rest of it played on, and I carefully watched Samantha's face, her expression still as bored as it had been earlier, except for the tightness of her mouth. She hadn't said a word or kicked me out of the car—yet. I was waiting for the other shoe to drop, so to speak.

Finally, she reached over and turned the music down a bit and, with visible effort, relaxed her face into a calmer expression. She turned her head to face me. "Catch a nap, Razor, you could use it," and she gave me a small smile before returning her attention to the road.

I let out a breath I wasn't aware I'd been holding. She wasn't going to say anything, for now anyway. I guess she was focused on the meet and wanted me to be, too. Which is what we needed to be. "Thanks, then, I will."

I closed my eyes and did just that. I could deal with yelling, I could deal with outright disgust, or even some form of discussion, pro or con, but I wasn't prepared to deal with the silence. As I drifted off, I remember, despite my earlier bravado, thinking clearly, praying, I hope you don't hate me, Sammy Blade, and I thought I heard her answer, "I could never hate you, Nina." That would be nice, I thought, before I didn't know any more for a while.

What seemed like minutes later, Samantha was gently nudging my shoulder. "C'mon, Nina, we're here. Time for the Razor-Blade Slice and Dice."

I opened my eyes and looked around me, at the car, at the parking lot, gathering my wits and my bearings, and finally, up at Samantha, whose face in the quickly gathering twilight was pale, making her eyes a clear blue. Her expression was soft and open, and I just took in her eyes, the clarity of them, then shook my head. "Okay." I straightened out from my sleeping slump. "Let's get to it, then." I slapped my thigh.

"Yes, let's." Samantha grinned at me, and grabbing our equipment, we got out of the car and walked to the main entrance.

Samantha and I grinned at each other again, no longer simply Nina and Samantha, but Razor and Blade, and the familiar sense of anticipation and anxiety that I had before every meet curled in my stomach and grew until my nerves hummed like taut steel strings. I breathed in deeply and let the energy gather into my stomach, just building until I could focus it into a direction.

Our opponents were going to be tough, but we were going to be tougher. We were fierce, I was fierce, and while the main focus of all that competition was the other team, some of it was very personal. The coach would analyze each of our performances and shuffle our positions accordingly. Some would become heroes; they would earn names, awards, and pivotal positions. Others would be placed in less critical roles. Every meet, every race, was a test, a survival challenge to be faced, and it wasn't enough to merely survive. You had to excel.

We quickly climbed the stairs to the door and strode through. A few steps later, Samantha and I stood in an enormous lobby, with various side openings and disappearing cross hallways, and looked around. We were lost.

"Well, I don't suppose you know where to go?" Samantha faced me, one hand on her hip, the other on her bag.

I walked over to one of the bulletin boards and began to scan the pinned-up papers, searching for information or anything resembling a map. I would have settled for one of those you-are-here schematics. "Nope, no clue," I answered as I found nothing. "I'm trying to see if there's a map or guide somewhere."

Samantha came over to the board and stood next to me. "Good idea," she agreed, and placed a hand on my shoulder. I stiffened a bit at the awareness of her hand, of her proximity, that new awareness that I'd discovered earlier kicking back in. Perhaps Samantha had forgotten about all the stuff with me and Kerry. Or perhaps she hadn't but was being what she was, a good team captain, and didn't want to affect my performance. Of course, the possibility existed that she just didn't care, but I didn't hold out too much hope for that. I had the past events of the afternoon for proof on that one.

Samantha and I scanned the boards together.

"Find anything likely?" she asked, and I shook my head in the negative.

"Hey, Blade, Razor! Kitt sent me to get you guys!"

Samantha and I both turned our heads, and she dropped her hand. Standing in the intersection of one of the many hallways, Betta stood in swimsuit and gym pants, waving at us.

"Great," Samantha said, all business as she and I walked over.

"Glad to see you, Betta," I told her with a smile. "I sorta half thought we'd never find our way."

Betta moved excitedly, half walking, half running, ahead. "Yeah, Kitt told Coach you two would be late…the locker's this way." She pointed to the door, then opened it, and we all walked through.

White tile, tons of lockers, bathroom in the back, pool door to the front, diagonally opposite of where we came in. An aisle led to the pool door, with a long horizontal half mirror on it. Pretty standard locker room, except that it was empty.

"Okay, everyone's at the pool, Coach is doing the lineup for the heats, and I don't know what he's putting me in," Betta chattered, while taking her gym pants and sneakers off by the locker she had claimed. In record time, she clanged the locker shut and stood expectantly, ready to hit the water.

"We'll be out in a few," Samantha told her. "Go ahead if you want."

Betta trotted off to the door and grabbed the handle, then stopped. "You sure? You need help getting to the pool?"

"We'll get there just fine, I promise." Samantha smiled. "Go ahead,"

"Um, okay, yeah. Thanks, Blade! See ya in the water!" Betta flashed her a sunny smile and was off. The door whooshed shut behind her.

I found an empty locker not far from the mirror and the door and put my coat in it, then took my gym bag over to the "bathroom" area to change in one of the many stalls. No way was I going to change in front of Samantha and have her think I was looking at her the wrong way or something like that. Not that I would have, I never did, it's just not a me thing to do; but I was once told it's not enough to be good, you have to look good, too. I figured I might as well put that saying into action. I pulled my suit, cap, and goggles out of my bag and chucked off my boots, stripping quickly.

"Dude! What are you doing?" Samantha's voice floated over the door from the main room.

"The usual, you know? Taking care of business, talking to the monkeys!" I called back, stepping into my suit. "They all want to come and party after the meet—whattaya say?"

I heard Samantha laugh as I rolled my suit up and pulled the straps over my shoulders. I checked the fit around my butt—all the important stuff was covered.

"Tell 'em," Samantha called back, "tell 'em I said, 'shit, yeah,' but they gotta get their own ride!"

"I'll pass it on," I called back. I folded my clothes neatly and rolled my socks into my boots, then put it all into my bag. I stepped out of the bathroom, walked back to my locker, and put my stuff away.

Samantha was standing by the mirror, checking her swimsuit out, making sure everything was where it had to be. I stood next to her and did the same, adjusting the shoulders.

"You know," Samantha spoke quietly, "you and I have a lot more in common than you think."

I looked at our reflections and considered. Wearing black and aqua wave-striped racing suits, we had the same swimmer's shoulders and tapered hips. Almost the same red-brown hair color, though Samantha's had more brown than red and was longer than mine. We had the same eye color, but mine looked grayer at the moment. My chin had a little bit of a cleft that Samantha's didn't. She was what, three, maybe even five inches taller than me? That could change any day; then again, maybe it wouldn't.

Someone entered the locker room from the main side; I could hear their footsteps as they walked through. I checked myself out again, adjusting straps and bands.

"Turn around," I told Samantha, who was still standing next to me, doing the same thing. Well, might as well be normal about the whole thing, right? I mean, we were teammates.

Samantha presented her back to me, and brushing her hair aside, I checked her shoulder straps, straightening one that had twisted in a place she wouldn't have been able to reach. This was a little ritual we always went through before stepping out to the pool. Sort of like monkeys grooming.

"Thanks." Samantha nodded and turned around to me. "Turn." She twirled her finger, and I did, so she could check my back straps. She adjusted one and was straightening the other.

"Don't let me interrupt," came a sardonic voice, and Samantha let go so quickly, the tight elastic slapped across my back audibly.

"Ow, Blade, why'd you," I said, and I whirled around, "go and do that for?" My voice trailed off.

In flak jacket and army boots, wearing my pants and shirt from the morning, stood Kerry, wearing the most peculiar look—her face a bit red, and her mouth twisted into what I could only describe as a wry smile.

Samantha walked back into the aisle and busied herself at her locker.

I grabbed my cap and goggles off the bench and stepped toward Kerry, smiling, but a little nervous. I wasn't sure if she should be here, in the locker room, and really, this was extremely unexpected. "Hey, Kerry," I greeted her anyway, "this is, like, such a total surprise, dude! What are you doing here? How'd you get here?"

"I came," and she looked me up and down appreciatively, "to see you, and—" Something hit the ground with a loud crash, and we heard Samantha swear.

"Since my parents are still away," she paused, "I borrowed their car." She grinned at me, "*and* I brought you a surprise."

"Dude, you didn't have to do that, it's just a—"

"Say hello, surprise!" Kerry yelled to the back of the locker room, and I heard the door open.

"Hello, surprise!" yelled back into the room. It was Nicky.

Holy shit! She brought Nicky with her—cool! I hadn't had a chance to talk to him in days. And besides, nobody ever came to my meets or games. Usually my parents just dropped me off at the school gate, and I'd have to get a ride with either Coach Robbins, a teammate, or Sister Attila, and after, I'd get a ride back to school, then take the bus home. It would be great to finally have someone there. "Hi, Nicky!"

"Hi, Nina. I have to close the door now before people think I'm a pervert! I'm going to the stands, I'll save you a seat, Kerry!" he yelled back, and I suppose he closed the door, since I heard it creak.

I looked at Kerry and was about to say something, like, how cool it was or something, but then it hit me. Waitaminute, she borrowed her parents' car and brought Nicky with her? She was a sophomore, she didn't have a driver's license, and I was pretty sure she didn't even have a learners' permit. Shit. This was not good. This was a problem for her and for Nicky. And me—my parents were going to kill me if they found out, and God forbid if anything happened to either of them.

"Wow, I, uh, can't believe you did that," I said, but didn't get a chance to say anything else though, because with a loud slam, Samantha shut her locker and came stalking out, mouth a set line. She held her cap and goggles in one hand and handed me a ponytail holder with the other. I took it from her and stood between her and Kerry again, like the center point of some crazy triangle.

"Kerry, it was really nice of you to come out," Samantha said evenly. "You should go to the bleachers now, though. I believe that only students of the school and competitors using the facilities are allowed in the locker room."

"Thanks for the heads-up, Shark. I'll keep that in mind." Kerry grinned at her. "Okay, you guys have a good race, I'll see you out there, Nina." She raised her eyebrows at me, then stuck her hands in her pockets and sauntered off.

Samantha and I just stared at each other, me in shock, and she in, well, I don't know. Her face was still set, and very serious. "You and

I, we should talk later," Samantha said softly, and she stood still a bit longer, then put a smile on her face. "But for now, we gotta go Slice and Dice!" She clapped me on the shoulder. "You gonna slice, Razor?"

I forcibly placed all other thoughts and concerns aside. It was time to focus on the task at hand; it was sink-or-swim, do-or-die, "we-who-are-about-to-die-salute-you" time. Just like that, I was ready.

"You gonna dice 'em, Blade?" I asked in return, and grinning at each other madly, grimly, with the heat of competition pounding in both our heads, we put our hair up and walked out the door, ready to hit the water.

Chapter Nine:
Take On Me

The pool was huge. It was so huge, it had what seemed like twenty lanes, and it was double the usual competition length, which meant that the fifty, which is what I usually did, instead of being two laps would be one; a hundred, instead of being four laps, would be two; and so on. This was going to screw up the two hundred relay; we'd have to have each next person ready to go at either end of the lanes. In a word, this sucked.

I stood in a knot of girls in swimsuits and black caps (except for the captains, who had aqua blue ones that matched the wave-stripes on the suit) clustered about Coach Robbins, a nice guy with a mellow voice, slight paunch, and a large but neatly trimmed brown mustache, which was the only hair he had on his head besides his eyebrows. Kitt nodded hello at me, as did other girls on the team. Betta grinned excitedly at me and gave me a thumbs-up. Samantha focused her attention on Coach Robbins.

"Okay," he said, "here's the lineup," and he read out the list of events and what each of us would do.

We were short a couple of girls. I would do the freestyle fifty, the freestyle hundred, the backstroke fifty, the breaststroke fifty, and anchor both the two hundred and four hundred relays, with two medleys thrown in for good measure. Betta was excited and nervous. She would do all the fifties for the various strokes, and backstroke the two hundred relay, in my lane.

Oh, and the anchor is the last swimmer on the relay team—the stroke happens to be the freestyle. An anchor can make or break the scoring by salvaging a total loss, losing the lead, or nailing the lead to the ground. Hey, no pressure, right?

Kitt, master of the butterfly and breaststroke, would do all of the races of those particular strokes and anchor both the two hundred and four hundred, as well as perform in the medleys (these are races where an individual swimmer performed all the strokes in specific order, in case I didn't explain that before). Samantha would do the hundred, the two hundred, all the backstrokes and butterflies. She would also, with me and Kitt, anchor both relays. This was going to be a motherfuckin' hell bitch of a tough night.

Battle plans laid, Coach Robbins clapped his hands together. "Okay, warm up!" he told us all, and en masse, we jumped into the water, caps and goggles in hand.

I went in feet first, all the way down, making sure I was submerged, wanting to get the chill effect over with, and as my head went under, I was surprised—the water was actually warm. That almost never happened. Usually the water was at a temperature that kept you from outright freezing, but would raise your skin with a thousand million little bumps as soon as you stopped moving. This was nice, I thought as I surfaced.

I slung my goggles around my neck and dipped my cap into the water, filling it; then I emptied it again. A wet cap was a heck of a lot easier to put on your head than a dry one. I cast a wary eye over to the other side of the pool as I piled my hair on my head and stretched the cap out over it. The opposing team, in dark green and white suits and white caps, had come into the water. I sighted down the length of the pool. The end looked very far away.

As I focused on getting my hair into my cap, Betta came swimming over. "Help you with that?" She pointed to the cap.

"Yeah, thanks." I smiled and turned and crouched a bit so she could tuck the errant locks in. That done, I settled my goggles over my eyes to fit them, then pushed them back over the crown of my head, where they would rest until I needed them.

Satisfied and set, I offered to do the same for Betta and tucked in a few of the now–dark red strands that had escaped her cap. "Nervous?" I patted everything into place.

"Um, no, not really," she said, looking down at the water. She made little trails with her fingers. "Well, maybe a little, it's a really long pool." She gazed up at me with big eyes, then down the clearly marked length of the lanes.

"It is," I agreed, sighting down the lanes with her, "but it might make some things easier," I answered reflectively as an idea hit me.

"You think, Razor?" She searched my face with anxiety.

"Oh yeah, sure, in fact, I'm positive!" I answered with a grin, then explained further. "You don't have to do a flip turn, so it's just a straight-on run, don't have to worry about getting your turn straight. In fact," and I pointed, "see where the floor dips?" Not quite halfway down the length of the lane was the spot where the floor started to angle deeply, until it reached its maximum depth at the end of twenty feet or so, the end we'd be diving into, well, except for the "every other" on the two hundred relay, but that wasn't the point.

Betta nodded her head.

"That's where you'll make sure to start your sprint to the end. Go hard off the start, but because you're not going to get that kick from your turn or have your usual marker, make sure you go for maximum burn at that point, because you know you're just about halfway, unless of course," and I grinned at her, "someone's in front of you. Then burn, baby, burn, and just do your best."

Betta looked at me uncertainly.

"It's okay, Betta, honest. Just do the best you can, that's all."

She stared worriedly at the demarcation point.

"Hey, Betta? It's okay to be nervous," I told her and she stared up at me again, all worry, "really. Just don't think of it as being nervous."

"Huh?" she questioned, confused. Good; if she was confused, her brain would be too busy to be worried.

"Yeah, think of it like this. All being nervous really is, is your body and your brain building up all the energy you'll need to focus. That's why you feel shaky, it's all that energy running through you. So when you feel that kick in your gut and chest, take a breath and think, 'okay, I've got the energy I need to do what I have to do, all I have to do is channel it,' and then, do just that. Channel, focus."

"Really?" she asked incredulously, "just channel and focus it?"

"Really." I smiled at her. "Just channel and focus. You're not nervous, just building and releasing energy. It sounds a lot harder than it is to do—c'mere a sec, take a look around," and I clapped a hand to her shoulder and turned her to look at other members of the team.

"See there?" I pointed to Kitt, who was out of the water and alternately shaking her hands or her legs loosely. "She's got all that energy to focus, so she's putting it into loosening up, and see there?"

I pointed to another teammate, Mad Max, who as a junior was a classmate of mine and a major power on the team. She was windmilling her arms to loosen her shoulders and rolling her head. "She's using it too, preparing the body to respond, rehearsing it in her mind."

"What about Blade?" and Betta pointed to Samantha, who had crouched down at the lower end, submerged to her chin and concentrating down the length of the pool.

"She's building a strategy, how she'll approach the lane, where she'll alternately push, sprint, or just burn it out," I explained. "Everyone's nervous. You just have to use that as a tool to help you, that's all." I smiled reassuringly.

"So it's a perspective thing…"

"Exactly." I smiled. I knew she'd get it.

"Line up—laps!" called Coach Robbins, letting us know it was time to get out of the water so we could do a few warm-up laps and then sit and wait for our events.

I made my way to the wall to lift myself out and, once on the ground, turned and reached to give Betta a lift out.

She reached up and was on the ground beside me in a second. "Thanks, Razor." She smiled at me.

"Hey, no problem," and I started walking over to the deep end where the starting blocks were and the teams were lining up for laps.

"Razor?" Betta asked behind me.

"Yeah?" I answered, stopping so she could catch up with me.

"Thanks for everything, I'm okay now."

I turned around and smiled at her. "Glad to help."

"Slice the lane, Razor!" She grinned up at me and gave me a discreet thumbs-up.

"You show those fighting colors, Betta." I grinned back, then lightly ran the rest of the way to the starting block, Betta and a few other girls behind me.

I slipped my goggles back over my eyes and waited my turn, which would happen when the girl swimming back touched the wall under me, just like a normal relay. This avoided the collision of bodies, which could actually be dangerous, if you really think about it.

I got up on the block, perched my toes over the edge, and crouched down into a racing start, my hands almost below my feet. I focused on the lane in front of me and watched a swimmer come back my way. The moment she touched the wall I sprang, body stretched and flying over the water. I heard someone yell "Nina!" and then I skimmed the surface and was in, stroke, breath, stroke, breath, since this wasn't a sprint but a warm-up. The swimmer ahead of me went down for the flip and return, and I saw where the end of the lane was marked. The water eddied around me as she made her way back, and we each hugged to our right side of the lane. A few strokes later and I was there at the marker and set up for my flip, to return. I went over easily and kicked off the wall, gliding with strong kicks until I reached the surface. Stroke, breath, stroke, breath. I caught a glimpse of Betta closing in on the lane marker as I made my way back. Finally I was at the wall, and Kitt reached down to haul me out, her aqua cap dripping.

"We're only doing twos, not fours," she said, referring to the number of laps, "because of the length of the pool." We started walking over to the benches on the side. "And all the relays will be four hundreds—too dangerous to dive in over another swimmer at the other end. Relays will go off in two heats, instead of one."

I nodded in agreement at that. It made sense, but inside, I quailed a bit at the prospect. That was double what I was going to do, and it was a lot. Okay, I steeled myself. I'm in the pool for hours every practice. I can do this; it's no different, just more concentrated. Okay, I was okay, I could do this.

"The anchors the same for both?" I asked Kitt. I was unproven as an endurance swimmer and wouldn't have been surprised if Coach had wanted to switch me. We approached the benches and sat.

"Not in both, and lineups are gonna change for heats, and the rest of your events will remain the same. We're short-handed." Kitt smiled ruefully in apology—this was going to be hard on all of us. She continued, "We need at least four decisive wins and to secure that by capping it with a strong score in the relay. You're anchoring with Blade on butterfly, me on breast, and Mad Max on the back. We'll get center lane, and this lineup should help give us that decisive scoring." She flashed a quick grin at me, because we both knew that putting all your top swimmers on one team was either incredible arrogance or desperation. Missing that many teammates, and doubling up on events that much, it was both.

I took a deep breath and let it out slowly, feeling my lungs and diaphragm expand and letting the information sink in while Kitt continued. "On the second set, you've got Cricket on butterfly, Froggie on breast, and Betta on back, with Blade and me as the other two anchors. We're gonna try to sweep it."

I nodded thoughtfully at the new information. We were definitely desperate. First the strongest swimmers on one team to create a decisive lead, then having them split as anchors to attempt a sweep—first, second, and third place positions—to hold it. How many girls did the other team actually have, anyway? Well, I'd already known that it was going to be a rough night.

Kitt paused to let me process the information, then slapped me on the back. "Think you can do it?"

"Yeah, I can." I looked at her steadily with a confidence born of my certainty that I would do it or damn well die trying.

"Great, knew you could," Kitt said with another pat on the back, then stood. "I've got to talk with Blade and Mad Max."

"Hey, Kitt?" I called to her as she started to walk away.

"Yeah, Razor?" Kitt turned.

"I think I'm glad I ate my Wheaties."

Soon all the lineups, race-changing discussions, and other bureaucratic nonsense were done, and the team sat together on the bench, the other team on the other side of the pool, doing whatever it was they did.

"Okay, we're outmanned here, but we outgun them," Coach Robbins said. Sister Attila, who'd arrived some time earlier, stood next to him. "We've got stronger players, we've got bigger hearts, and we're determined," he continued. "We need a good showing in the individual races, but we need to really blow them away in points and time by the relay. You all know how the relays are going to work and how the lineups are set. Our last relay has Kitt, Blade, and Razor as anchors, with the rest of you spread out on the teams. Think of it as 'Operation Smooth Shave.'" He smiled broadly at his own pun.

It was a really bad joke. Kitt and Blade and I looked at each other, and none of us was particularly pleased. He got back thin smiles all around. "It's Razor-Blade-Kitt, get it?" he explained, seeming pleased, very pleased with himself.

No one said anything, except for a few, very forced, ha-has. Even Sister Attila looked toward the endless ceiling as if she were asking God why.

Silence continued to grow.

"Okay then, get in there and show 'em"—he gestured to the other side,—"what you can do. First race is up in five minutes, the fifty butterfly," Coach Robbins said and walked off, clipboard in hand, to the table behind the starting blocks where the other coach and the officials were.

Sister held up her hand in a "wait" gesture so we wouldn't disperse. "Before you get started," and she looked around at all of us, "remember this. If you hit the water with a clear head and get out of it knowing you've done the best you can," she looked at Kitt, then continued, "you've done a good job. If you hit the water with a clear heart and get out of it knowing you've done more than you thought you could," she paused, looked me dead in the eye, then at the rest of the group, "the best of your very best, you've done a great job, no matter how the timing or the points fall. I know you will all do a great job. I'll see you in the water." Sister nodded at us and made her way over to the stands.

At that, each girl wrapped up in her own private world, we made our way to the bench or the starting blocks, depending on what we were slated for.

With a sound like thunder, the first butterfly event went off, and the water churned with the strong kicking and pulling motions of the swimmers. I always loved to watch this event; the movements of the swimmers were incredible, dramatic. I myself was (and still am) terrible at this stroke, but boy, I admired those who did it, especially those who did it well.

I alternately sat on the bench or walked the length of the deck to each end with other members of the team, screaming encouragement at my teammates each and every time the starter gun went off—hugging, backslapping, and congratulating girls as they came out of the water.

Finally, what seemed like only seconds later, it was my first event, and with a final check of my shoulder strap, a snap of the leg, and a tug of my goggles over my eyes, I mounted the second block to stare down my lane, the lines below me wavering in the warm blue water. A swimmer in a green and white suit stood on either side of me.

There were twelve competitors for this event, so it would go off in two heats of six, and Blade was in the second. Girls with the top six times of both combined heats would compete in a third, final heat, determining first, second, and third places. This also meant it was possible to come in first in a heat and not even qualify for the third, if the other six competitors in the other heat all had better times than you. Still, the team would earn points by finishing order in both heats anyway, so it was never a total wash.

Actually, it was possible to have two heats, then a deciding third, with the majority of swimmers from one or another team. This point system also meant that a team could have consistent first-place finishes and still not win the meet, if the other team consistently scored second, third, and fourth. It was all about how the points fell and added in the end, although any individual could potentially outperform her entire team.

I focused my sight on the end. A straight-run fifty, no turn. I decided to do a dead-ahead sprint. I'd have at least a heat to sit out before a third final, and then a few events in between before my next few events. I could do this and not burn myself out for later. I was going to do this.

Now.

Later didn't matter.

Slice the lane.

"Swimmers—on the block!" an official cried out, his voice made mechanical through a bullhorn's amplification.

I curled my toes over the edge and bent my legs and arms, elbows slightly behind my ribs. Good entry was all about form and distance, how you came off the block. Sometimes a good entry could determine the whole race. Or so we were told, anyway.

"On your mark!"

I tensed my arms and legs, hung low over the block, and concentrated on a point about a dozen or so feet in front of me, directly centered, where I wanted to enter. Not that I could really jump that far, but it was always good to aim as if you could.

Bang!

The gun went off, and I imagined my body as a powerful spring uncoiling along its length as I stretched and leaped off, out and above the water.

I skimmed the surface and started moving. Breath, stroke, stroke, stroke, breath, stroke, stroke, stroke. There was no sound except the water rushing by my ears, my hands as they cut through the water. I could hear the sound my legs made.

My arms stretched, my legs moved, and the muscles that stretched over my hips and stomach strained in a gratifying way. I worked harder and felt the burn work its way through. What can I say? Pushing to the limit feels pretty damn good.

The drop-away point was ahead of me, and I dug within as deeply as I could. It wasn't about winning, it was about my best time. I had to at least beat my own best time.

The motion was mechanical and intense. I was in the water, focused on breath, focused on muscle. I reached the end wall and stood, gasping. As the water poured off my head, the sound came back on, destroying the peaceful calm of the water, and I could hear cheering from the stands.

"Great race!" greeted Mad Max as she reached down to haul me out, and I stood on deck, shaking and dripping.

I shoved the goggles off my eyes under my chin. "Thanks," I said, breathless, and we gave each other a brief hug, which Max followed up with a pat on the back. A couple of other girls came up to do the same.

We walked back over to the bench to grab a seat and found Kitt there, the world's largest towel draped over her shoulders while she waited for the next event. "Nice slice, Razor," she greeted as I sat down, "very nice race."

I sat down and Kitt looked over at me again. "Where's your towel?"

I was starting to shiver. "Oh fuck, I forgot it in the locker room," I said out loud, realizing what I had done.

"Here," she draped an end of her towel over me, "share mine."

I sat there, very grateful to not be freezing. "Thanks, Kitt."

She glanced at me. "No problem, Razor, no problem," and she focused her attention on the starting blocks. I followed her gaze and watched Samantha, Sammy Blade, take the center block and Betta take an outside one.

"We've had the Slice, it's time for the Dice," Kitt murmured, watching the swimmers take their marks. Kitt glanced over at me. "You finished in the top three, you know," she remarked, then returned to the race.

Wow. Not bad. But I didn't want to know where, which is why she didn't tell me. It would wreck my focus to know if I was first or second or third. Third, you just get disgusted. Second, you wonder why you didn't do good enough for first, and first, you worry you can't keep it up. Better to not know and just have your confidence built by the fact that you did well. As it turned out, my time qualified me for the third and final heat for the fifty free.

In the final heat for the fifty, off the block and in the water, as I passed the drop-off point or, actually, shallow point since all entrances were on the deep end, I came up for air and could hear people screaming "Slice and Dice! Slice and Dice!" and a new one—"Twin Blade!" I put my head back in the water and pulled harder. I slammed my arms into the wall, I was going so hard and so fast. It took me a second to understand that I was done, so I stood and saw Blade standing in her lane. I ducked under the lane divider, ignoring the girl in green, and Blade came over from her side. We hugged each other and patted each other on the back saying, "Great race, great race," and "that was motherfuckin' great," and other such terms that people use when they've given everything they've got and they're exhausted and up against the wall, and scared that they'll fail and relieved that they're all together, everyone has survived, no matter what the outcome.

The crowd was screaming and Mad Max came swimming over. She'd been in this heat too, and we were all hugging and cursing and slapping each other.

We stopped for a second and everything was silent as the bullhorn crackled and called out the finish times. The screams were louder than before. We had swept the heat. We hadn't won the race yet, but we had this event, motherfucker, we had it!

The rest of the meet until the relays passed in a blur, in the water, out of the water, sharing the towel with Kitt or Blade or both, watching the other events, arms and legs numb, chest tight from effort, eyes sore from the pressure of the goggles, and head burning hot from the latex swim cap.

In the first relay, Kitt and Blade, Mad Max, and me as a team, we nailed the fucker to the ground, baby, almost three body lengths ahead of the competition, fuckin' A, and while it wasn't a sweep, it was first and third, good points, very good points.

It seemed like seconds later that the second relay went off, and as I waited on the center block, alternately focused on the spot in front of me where I wanted to enter and Betta's cap as it came toward me in the backstroke, I crouched, ready to spring.

She was coming, she was two body lengths away, one, and I was ready, her hand reached for the wall, and I was stretched over her for a moment, her hand touched the wall, and I was off and going in, flying, and the water slapped me hard and cold this time when I hit.

My muscles ached and burned, and I was pulling steadily, pushing, but not too hard; there was another lap coming. Suddenly, my body became lighter than air, and I actually felt the water pulling me along, like I was almost hovering on top of it, and my work became effortless.

I had gotten caught in my opponent's slipstream and was being pulled in the drag, making my job easier. I'd have plenty left for the return lap. The midpoint came, and I started building to a sprint, found the marker for the return flip, and came off the wall with the strongest kick I had in me. I glided underwater for a precious few seconds, then broke the surface, pulling and kicking as if my life depended on it. I imagined the look on Blade's face, or Kitt's, if we didn't do well. I actually heard Sister's words, telling us what a great job was.

I gasped for air and heard the crowd yelling, "Sweep! Sweep!" and then nothing mattered but the swimming. I kept pulling, kicking, my heart almost bursting, my lungs burning, and the water hissing past my ears as I sliced through.

My hand hit the wall, followed by my shoulder, and I brought myself up just before I smashed my head too. It was a good idea to keep it safe in case I wanted to actually use it for something later.

I hung on to the ridge around the wall by my fingertips, gasping and choking, so numb I couldn't even understand what I saw or heard. The crowd must have been on its feet from the sound, and I watched Blade come in, then Kitt, then the other team, and waiting until everyone was finished, then ignoring the girls in their lanes, Blade and Kitt swam over to my lane, and we hugged and kissed and slapped each other, wordless, except for the occasional "Good," or "Fuckin' great race," and we were not Kitt, or Blade, or Razor, but Fran, Samantha, and Nina, hanging onto the ropes and the wall and each other, breathless and exhausted from effort, hope, and fear.

Silence reigned again as the bullhorn crackled and a voice read out the final times—we heard we had swept the relay, and again we were whooping and yelling and pounding each other. Kitt grabbed my head, kissed the crown, and knuckled it, then did the same to Blade. We looked at each other and dunked her.

Silence stretched, then stretched some more as the judges tallied the points and discussed them. We waited in that quiet, just staring up at the table, waiting to know what had happened, who had won, which school team had the honor of defending a first-place position for the rest of the season.

Finally, the points were read, and as their meaning became clear, pandemonium ensued, as the whole team jumped in the water—we had won! Our school now had a second year of aggressive early first-place positioning to defend, giving us a great shot at regional—East Coast—finals at the end of the season.

Coach Robbins came running over to the edge to congratulate us, just as happy as we were. "Great job, girls! Great job!" and he put a hand down to haul Kitt out. She held it a moment, looked sidewise at me and at Blade, then with a kick off the wall, *plunk*! Coach was in the water.

He went under, then came up a few feet away, spitting out a stream of water like a fountain and pretending to be a ballet dancer, or an overgrown cherub, and we all laughed with him, clowning around some more.

See? It was all okay, we didn't hurt him. He was the swim team coach, after all; it was fine if he got wet. This time, anyway.

Sister came walking over to the edge of the deck and stood, watching us all with that evaluating expression she sometimes wore. Finally, we all quieted down and gave her our attention. "Great race, girls, great race," and she smiled a very rarely seen smile at us. "I knew, I truly knew," and she glanced at each of us, one by one, "that you would all do a great job, and you all have." She smiled again. "More than the school, more than I, and more than Coach Robbins," she nodded at him where he'd gone under and come up again, "you should—all of you," and she gave us each another glance, "be proud of yourselves. I will see all of you of tomorrow," and with a final nod, Sister turned and strode away from the pool.

That seemed to wrap it all up, and in twos and threes we got out of the pool and walked back to the locker room, but not me, not right away. The stands had already emptied, and I knew that Kerry and Nicky would be waiting for me, either by the locker room or at the main door.

I stopped at the bench, took the damn swim cap off my head and sat—I needed a little space to think. I rubbed my hair out a bit and reflected. I didn't want to join all the locker-room chat, didn't want to have to wait for an empty shower, wash, dry, and change in front of everyone. This had been a long day, an exiting one, true, in many ways, but really, really long. I just wanted to sit there a little while and let my head drain, let the adrenaline run out of my system until my mind was as clear as the water in the pool I had just struggled and fought in, and I knew what to do next.

Lost in my thoughts, I didn't notice Samantha sit down next to me until she threw a towel and an arm over my shoulders. She had gone into the locker room, taken her cap off, and come back out, not bothering to change out of her swimsuit. "You okay?" Her voice was soft, full of concern.

I snuggled gratefully into the terry cloth and the warmth of her arm; I hadn't even realized I'd been shivering until that second. I enjoyed the warmth a little longer and, jamming both elbows on my knees, made a resting platform out of my hands and buried my face in them for a bit, took a deep breath, then rested my chin on them.

"Yeah, just tired," I exhaled, staring moodily out over the water, its surface quiet and smooth now that the do-or-die competition was over. Samantha's hand was still on my back, and I could feel its heat burning through the towel. Well, at least that spot would be dry, I thought.

"Yeah, me too," Samantha returned. "Big day, huh?"

"Mmm-hmm."

Samantha rubbed my shoulder for a couple of warm seconds and stood to face me. "C'mon, let's get out of here and grab a butt."

"Sounds like a plan." I stood, stretching, holding the towel out behind me to loosen my back and shoulders.

We started walking to the door that would lead to the locker room.

"Hey, share that thing, it's cold!" Samantha requested with a laugh and, chagrined, I handed her a corner, which she promptly draped over her back. It wasn't as big a towel as Kitt's, though, so Samantha put a hand around my shoulder, and I put an arm around her waist as we approached the door.

I put a hand out to push it open, when it snapped wide and we were brought up short by Kitt, showered and dressed in a white sweatshirt with the team logo on it and a pair of blue jeans and sneakers. The only hint that she'd been in the water at all was her hair, still wet from the shower.

I don't really know why, you think swimmers would be paranoid about ear infections and stuff, especially since our school competitive season covers the deadest, coldest part of winter, but no one really ever dried her hair. Yeah, maybe sometimes, if after a Saturday morning practice someone had to be somewhere, you might see her actually bother to bring in a hair dryer, but not very often. Weird, I know, but there you have it.

We looked at each other, Samantha and I arm and arm under the towel, Kitt fully dressed.

"You guys okay for the ride home?" Kitt asked. "I'm closer to you, Nina. Sammy, would that be easier for you?"

"Um, actually, I've got a ride," I told her, and I felt Samantha's fingers tighten on my shoulder, "so I'm good. But thanks, Fran, really." Hey, the meet was over, we had another two days before our next practice; we were just ourselves now, not competitive swimmers.

"Yeah, all clear here, Fran, it's good," Samantha added.

"Cool, cool," she nodded. An awkward silence grew.

"Hey, great racing today," I told Fran. "I love watching your form in the 'fly, wish I could do it."

"Wish I could do what you guys do, so it's all even." She laughed good-naturedly and clapped us each on a shoulder, the awkwardness past. "Great job today. All right then, I'm off. Have a great night," and she turned to go and we finally entered the locker room. Samantha dropped her hand from my shoulder, and I handed her back her towel.

"Double-check the locker before you leave, 'kay?" Fran the Champ turned and asked, then made her way through the rows of empty lockers and was gone.

I went over to my temporary storage space and pulled my bag out. Yep, there was my towel, right on top. Well, at least it would be a comfortable shower since I had a dry as opposed to damp towel, and pulling out shampoo and soap, I made my way over to "shower lane," just wanting to get it over with. Soon I'd have to face Kerry and Nicky, and I wasn't happy about it, at all.

Hanging my towel off the showerhead and just behind it so it wouldn't get soaked, I turned the faucets and adjusted the temperature of the spray. There. Not too warm, definitely not cold.

Fun and games was one thing, I reflected further, but I wasn't really thrilled at the thought of an unlicensed driver in a car that wasn't theirs taking me or Nicky anywhere, even if it was Kerry. Rebellion could be cool, but not when it involved possible danger to my brother or anyone else.

Drenched again, I peeled off my suit and hung it on a hook under the shower. Maybe I could drive. I had a permit, and if I got stopped I could just claim extreme circumstances, I mulled as I shampooed my hair.

Not that I could actually drive. I wasn't allowed to, and I only had my permit because I'd saved some money and gone down to the Department of Motor Vehicles one day after school instead of the comic book store. I'd had Samantha's old book and studied that, took the test, and passed. That line took forever, even though the test didn't.

So I had my piece of paper and a good general knowledge of the rules of the road. Gas on the right, brake on the left. How hard could it be? This could work. I was a little nervous. I would have to follow Samantha to the bridge at least, but it wouldn't be too hard. I hoped.

Lost in thought, my head covered in soapy lather, I yelped in surprise when I received a sharp poke to the ribs. "Hey, quit hogging all the hot water," Samantha joked as she stepped into shower lane, under the head next to mine. She hung her towel up and behind the showerhead.

As her body twisted slightly with the lift of her arm, the muscles rippled across her arm and back. Her deltoids were large and really prominent, like all swimmers', but the rest of the muscle definition was smaller, lined and refined, every rib was clearly marked, and a band of muscle lifted across them. I could make out every bit of the structure, like a dancer's, like a work of art. Her body was beautiful, and I wished then and now that I could look like that.

She brought her arm down and I turned away. I'm not looking, I'm not looking, I thought. Of course, that's when I got soap in my eye. Ouch. Nasty stinging soap. God was punishing me, and I wasn't even having bad thoughts.

"Argh!" I bellowed, desperately wiping and rinsing my eyes, and in a flash Samantha was next to me.

"Hey, you okay? What happened? You get burned or something?" Samantha patted my shoulders and back to see if I'd hurt anything.

"No," I spluttered through the spray, "just some soap"—I swallowed some and spit—ick!—"in my eye." Finally, the irritation gone, and clear-sighted, I looked up.

Bad idea, bad, bad, very big bad idea.

Soaking wet, her hair streaming down her back, Samantha stood before me as naked as the day she was born. If I said she was beautiful before, I lied. She was breathtaking. Her eyes, now a calm and deep blue, held mine, and I felt my pulse pounding in my neck, realizing, as if I'd never thought of it before, that I had always felt that way—how every single one of her smiles was like the sun breaking through the clouds for me, and her tears broke my heart; how we always found a reason to sit next to one another; how much I wanted her shoulder against mine every time we joked, or her hand on my waist as she leaned over my back to grab something that was out of my reach when we were doing detention or whatever silly thing.

I also realized that it wasn't too much purple Hi-C and clear liquors that had made me feel the way I had at the beach—it was Samantha—it was me.

I watched the color of Samantha's eyes deepen, and now they were like a night ocean under the moon, and they were closer to me than they'd been before.

I had a funny revelation: I actually liked detention because Samantha and I spent time together; that we would have, should have spent more time together this summer, except her life had blown up in a horrible and tragic way and she needed the time, so I became close with Kerry and now…Kerry. I was fucking stupid.

Suddenly I realized that I was staring, that I was just as naked, and I blindly reached for the taps to shut the water off, my face steaming hot.

"I'm done." I grabbed my towel and threw it over my head to hide the blush I could feel burning a path up my cheeks. "I'll see you in a few," and wrapping myself in the towel, I rushed off to my locker and my clothes.

Stupid, Nina, fucking stupid, I told myself over and over as I shoved myself into my underwear and bra. Just motherfuckin' stupid. Maybe my father was right after all; I was too stupid to fucking live, I thought bitterly as I jammed my feet into my boots.

I packed my gear and sat on the bench. Great. Fuckin' great. I had a situation here and one waiting for me the second I opened the door to the main hallway.

Samantha came up out of the showers, and I faced the long end of the bench, away from her so she could dress privately. "Sam?" I asked as I heard her start to jam things into her bag, "would you mind if I followed you to the bridge from the parking lot? I'm not really sure of how to get back to the Island from here."

Samantha closed the locker and dropped her bag on the bench, good indications that she was dressed. I stood and turned around, and she was shaking her head. "You're not driving," she said incredulously. "I'm driving you."

She hefted her bag over her shoulder and I slung mine. We did a quick check of the locker room as we made our way to the exit, making sure no one and nothing had been left behind.

"Nah, Sam, Kerry's here. She's got my brother with her, and she doesn't have a permit—I do. I can't let her drive my brother like that." We kept walking and, finally, there was the door. Samantha put her hand out and leaned on it, holding it closed so I couldn't open it. I turned to face her.

"I'll take Nicky, too," she offered decisively. "She can drive herself. Those are her own consequences for doing something so fuckin' stupid." Samantha's face was severe.

"I can't do that, Sam. She's my, well, she's"—I didn't want to say it, not now; I wasn't sure anyway and it was too weird—"she's my friend, and I can't leave her like that."

Samantha huffed and looked at the ground, then back at me. She was definitely mad. "I don't like your," and her lip curled in anger, "girlfriend."

Ooh, that came out nasty and cold, and I got angry in return. I could feel my eyes glint back at hers. "Then *we*," and I paused for emphasis, "have a problem," and I swung open the door and stepped out. I was so damn angry I almost couldn't think, and I didn't know how to explain it to Samantha, anyway.

Of course it was a better idea, safer all around, to go with Samantha. But let's just see here a minute. I had just made, no, Kerr and I had just, um, shared this big, momentous, incredible, first-time, life-altering thing the night before.

Telling her to go fuck off after all of that, after she'd taken the risk of borrowing her parents' car and driving to see me at my meet, didn't seem like the right thing to do, did it? It didn't to me. Even if it was dumb. And wrong. And just stupid. And even if we hadn't "done the deed," so to speak, what kind of a friend would I be to let someone else just go blindly into trouble like that? Especially if, wrongheaded or not, she had done it for me. At the very least, I could take some responsibility for the situation and try to make it a little better. Besides, Nicky and Kerry were both younger than me, even if it was only by a little bit. I was older—it was my responsibility.

I took a few steps into the corridor, fuming, letting myself breathe it all out. Samantha came out behind me. "Nina, that's not what I meant to say, I just think—"

Sister Attila on one side, Nicky and Kerry on the other, were bearing down on us. Nicky, holding Kerry's hand, came running over. "That was great! You guys are incredible! I didn't know you could swim like that!" he enthused as he arrived and gave me a one-armed hug, which I returned enthusiastically. Kerry joined in on the other side, and I gave them each a kiss on the cheek.

"Thanks, guys," I told them, untangling myself from the tangle of arms, "it's a very good team. Oh, by the way," and I turned to include Samantha, "this is Samantha Cray," I said to my brother, "otherwise known as Blade."

"Dude!" Nicky exclaimed, and put his hand out, "you put the ice in dice, man! You were awesome out there!"

"Thanks, just part of being on a good team—we carry each other." Samantha smiled at Nicky and shook his hand.

Nicky smiled back, then remembered something. "Oh, this is…" he started to introduce Kerry.

"They've met," I told him flatly and just then, Sister arrived.

"Boyd, Cray, ending the day the way we started it, I see?" Sister asked with a smile, then turned to get a good look at Nicky and Kerry. "You must be her younger brother Nicholas. I can see it in your face."

Nicky blushed and dropped Kerry's hand.

Don't ask how Sister knew that, other than the obvious fact that Nicky and I look very much alike. Nuns know everything. Nuns have files and archives. Nuns read everything. Nuns ask everything and extrapolate arcane knowledge of the universe and what you really did during lunch and summer break. Accept that, and life is easier, much, much easier. Scarier, yes, but still easier. Besides, even if they don't know everything, they're hooked up at the source—they have a direct connection to God, remember?

"Yes, Sister, I am," he stammered. "Pleased to meet you."

"Pleased to meet you as well, Nicholas. I do hope that you're as proud of your sister as we all are," and she glanced at me, still smiling, "and that you follow her example both in school and in sport?" The smile she had for Nicky could only be described as kindly.

Samantha and I looked at each other in surprise, and my jaw almost hit the ground. Proud? Of me? The last words Sister had had for me personally were about being stupid and drowning, and that was not too long ago. Where was Attila and what had they done to her? A spaceship was hovering over the campus somewhere, I just knew it.

Nicky's face turned almost purple. "I try, Sister," and he glanced at his sneakers, "but she's so very good at everything!" He gazed back at her earnestly.

My face flamed and my ears burned. That most certainly wasn't true, and I wished he hadn't said it. I knew better than anyone else how stupid I really was, and if I forgot it, I had my father and Sister Attila to remind me. Every single day.

Sister chuckled. "Well, dear boy, it's all in the trying, isn't it, girls?" and she angled her chin at me and Samantha to confirm.

"Yes, Sister," we both nodded in agreement, still mildly numb from this new facet of Sister Attila we had never seen before—ever. I mean that.

"And you're not her little sister Nanny, are you," stated Sister, visually measuring Kerry. "A friend of Mr. Boyd's or a fan of our Razor?"

Kerry blushed and ducked her head. "Um, a little bit of both, actually," she answered from under her hair.

"I see," Sister said, as she slowly surveyed Kerry head to toe. To tell you the truth, she probably did see. All things aside, she was one very, very sharp person—which is probably how she became a math teacher in the first place. The other possibility that remained was that she read minds—and that was never to be discounted as an option. Forget that at your own risk.

She looked at us all for a moment, then turned to Samantha.

"As a team captain, you'll be taking Razor here home, yes?" she asked in a tone that implied this was an order and not merely a request for information. Sister turned back to Kerry and Nicky. "Since neither one of you is of legal age or Ms. Boyd's legal guardian, and this is a school event," she paused to let her words sink in, "I can't allow her to go home with anyone but a parent or a school representative, someone who can be legally responsible. I'm sure you understand that, don't you?" Sister kept smiling. I had to wonder if Sister had been listening at the door to Samantha and me earlier, then dismissed the thought; she'd been down the hallway at the time.

Actually, I found out later from Nicky that Sister had been sitting near them during the race, and some logical deduction of my own says she probably heard them talking about Kerry's "borrowing" the car.

Nicky's eyes widened in surprise, but Kerry wore a bland expression. "Oh, no problem, Sister," she said, very politely. "We were going to let Nina drive because she has her permit, but Nicky has his license." Kerry shot me a quick look. "So we'll just catch up with her and Captain Shark at home," she finished with a smile of her own that showed all of her teeth, and reached for Nicky's hand again.

Now you're probably wondering why that didn't bother me, Nicky and Kerry holding hands, I mean, and to be honest, I didn't think anything of it. Hugging and holding hands and stuff wasn't unusual among my group of friends. Why would I think anything about a friend holding another's hand, anyway?

"I thought it was Blade?" Nicky questioned Kerry in an undertone, but she elbowed him into silence.

I glanced over at Nicky. License? I mouthed silently from the corner of my mouth.

He blushed and stared at the floor. "Dad took me a few weeks ago," he whispered to his sneakers. "I've got my card."

"Oh. Okay."

Well, that was news. Nobody had told me about that—why hadn't Nicky told me? Waitaminute, why hadn't my father asked me or taken me? What the fuck was that all about?

Sister had been watching us in her usual observant silence, and when she spoke again, it jolted me out of that train of thought, and I forgot it until later, much later.

"Is everyone out of the locker room, Ms. Cray, Ms. Boyd?"

"Oh, yes, Sister, it's all clear."

"Yes, Sister," I confirmed.

"Fine, then. Ladies, gentleman," she nodded to us all, "have a good night. Ms. Cray, Ms. Boyd," she addressed Samantha and me directly, "I'll see the two of you tomorrow," and she turned and started down the hallway.

"Have a good night, Sister," and "Very nice to meet you," we all variously called out.

The four of us just stood there awkwardly, then I turned to Nicky. "You have your fuckin' driver's license?"

Nicky blushed again. "Uh, yeah, Dad's been teaching me Saturday mornings, when you're at practice. It was supposed to be a surprise thing, so I could go out and, you know, do stuff with you and other, um, things." The red of his cheeks reached his ears as he stared down at his sneakers.

I was furious. Nicky was my younger brother, not my older brother. I couldn't drive but he could? What the fuck was that? I was speechless with indignation.

"Hey, Nina, that's how we got here," Kerry volunteered, and I favored her with a dark look. She could have, should have just told me that before.

Samantha, silent this whole time, readjusted her bag on her shoulder. "Well, let's get going, shall we?" she asked nonchalantly, and she began to walk down the corridor, in the same direction that the good Sister had.

I stared wordlessly at Kerry and Nicky as they stood holding hands. I was still silent, still angry. I felt trapped, confused, and even bewildered. "Do Mom and Dad know where you are?" I was finally able to focus enough for a logical question to Nicky.

"Yeah, they know I was coming to your meet, and that I'm out with Kerry."

I searched his face closely. He was sincere. "They didn't give you a hard time?" It was weird that they wouldn't, since my dad wasn't her biggest fan.

"No, why would they?"

No, why would they? I asked myself. It was just me. The problem, the burden, the freak of nature too stupid to fucking live. "Fine," I shortly returned, "let's go," and I started walking in the direction Samantha had gone, Kerry and Nicky following me.

When we finally got outside to the parking lot, there were only about a dozen or so cars in it. Samantha was already waiting by hers; Nicky and Kerry had parked just one row over. I could see the metallic gold Cadillac that was Kerry's parents' glinting dully in the talllights that lit the asphalt.

A black Lincoln with the headlights on faced Samantha's car. Sister. Making sure we all got out and home in the right way.

I made my way to Samantha's car, and Kerry and Nicky went over to Kerry's. I stood by the passenger door.

"You coming?" Kerry called from the gold monster, where Nicky had already slid into the driver's seat.

I glanced at Samantha across the hood of the car. She stared levelly back, then opened the door and got in. She reached over to unlock my door, then started the engine.

"No, I really have to go with Samantha," I called in answer to Kerry. "I'll see you guys back at the house." I opened the door and tossed my bag in the back, sat down, and slammed the door closed to avoid further conversation across the parking lot.

Since Sister was watching in her car, Samantha didn't tear out, but she did start moving as soon as my butt was in the seat. Through the window I could see Nicky pull out of the lot, and as we exited, I saw Sister's car finally leave as well.

I put on my seat belt and dug into my coat for my cigarettes. As far as I was concerned, I'd fuckin' earned it after the day I'd had. I pulled one out, thought about it, then pulled out another and lit them both. I handed one to Samantha. Okay, she was mad, I was mad, but we were still friends for now.

"Thanks." She took it with a small smile and dragged deeply.

"No problem," I answered with a small smile of my own. Our eyes caught and held, then I broke the contact as I turned and took a long pull on my smoke, cracking the window a bit to let the air flow, and I watched the streets go by. We rode in relative silence until we got about halfway over the Verrazano Bridge.

"I'm sorry, Nina. I didn't mean that the way it came out. I just—"

"It's fine, Sam," I interrupted, still looking out the window, "don't worry about it."

"Nina, I…" Samantha trailed off as we came to the toll plaza, and I released my seat belt and fished inside my pocket for some cash. "Here." I leaned over her and handed it out the window. "I owe you at least for that," I explained, when I sat back down.

"You didn't have to do that," Samantha said quietly as we pulled through the toll booth. "I'd have had to pay for it anyway, you know."

"Yeah, well, you're driving me home and all that. Save it for gas or something." I stared out the window again.

The silence continued as we got closer and closer to my home. I felt like I was wrapped in a dark fog, and I knew I should feel different, if not better, than I did. The day before had been beautiful in ways I hadn't imagined it could be; this day we'd won our qualifying meet of the season, against our toughest opponent, and I'd performed rather well, if I do say so myself. Sister had actually complimented me in front of me, to another person, and Nicky had his license. This was a good thing. These were all good things, really, so why was I so miserable?

Samantha reached a hand over and fumbled with the music console, flipping back and forth until she found what she wanted. I didn't really pay too much attention; I just let the scenery keep passing. We would arrive at my house in another ten minutes or so. Samantha shut the music off again, and I tossed the dead cigarette out the window.

About three blocks from the house, Samantha pulled over and parked the car. She cut the motor and turned to face me. "Nina," she said softly, "we have to talk." Her voice was so low, so concerned, so filled with unnamable feeling that my own emotions rose up, threatening to overflow.

I faced her in turn, eyes full and tears held in check. "Samantha, I'm sorry," I said. "I just, I wanted to…" In the faint light that shone in from the street, Samantha's face was again pale and her eyes—I couldn't tell what color they were, so full of unexpressed thought, of intensity as they were. I tried again. "Sam, I…" and I stopped again, unable to speak, and I could feel the tears start to flow down my face as I just looked at her, intense and wordless.

"Hey, it's okay," Samantha soothed, and came a bit closer. "Come here, it's okay," and she opened her arms in invitation. Without a moment's doubt or hesitation, I buried my head on her shoulder, her arms closed around me, and everything I felt and wondered and feared just poured out in a flood of tears. All the while Samantha comforted me and whispered, "It's okay, I've got you, you're okay."

I cried because my father called Kerry a dyke, and because I knew deep down inside that Kerry didn't really care about me, no matter how intense what we had shared had been.

I cried because Samantha had, when her father died and I had held her in just this way for days, during the wakes and the funeral—there had been nothing else I could do.

I cried because Nicky had lied to me, and my father thought I was a waste of living flesh.

I cried because those guys that had chased me and Kerry scared me deeply and because Joey really cared about me and I would never care for him the way he wanted me to.

I cried because right then and there I felt safe and warm and loved in the circle of Samantha's arms and words, and Samantha would leave when she graduated in June, and I wished I could go with her.

Eventually, I stopped crying, and as I quieted down, I listened to the sound of Samantha's heart beating under my ear and felt her fingers run soothingly through my hair as she rested her head on mine.

God, I always hated crying.

"Let's have that talk now, okay?" Samantha murmured into my hair, and I straightened up a bit, digging into a pocket for a tissue so I could wipe my face.

"I'm sorry about that." I pointed to Samantha's damp shirt.

Samantha glanced down at the spot, then looked back at me. "Don't be," she insisted, and reached for my hand. "Don't ever apologize for feeling or for sharing with me." She squeezed my hand, and I returned the pressure.

She stared down at our hands while she let out a breath. "Okay," she said slowly, "first things first," and she looked up at me.

"I'm sorry, but I don't like your girlfriend," Samantha stated very clearly and steadily.

I started to respond, but she held up a hand to forestall me. "Now, that doesn't mean that I don't like the fact that you have one." Her lips tightened, then she took a breath and let it out heavily before she continued, "Or that I don't like you for that reason," she said very seriously. "That would be a little hypocritical of me, anyway."

My eyebrows raised in the famous "huh?" expression. Excuse me—did she say what I thought she had? Yeah, yeah, I know, you were all waiting for that, right? Should have seen it coming and all. Sorry. I had no clue.

Samantha smiled ruefully down at the seat. "I've had one or two of my own. I don't think you would've liked them much, either," and her eyes met mine again in a smile.

My brain reeled. Wow. Samantha dated girls. Whoa there. How long had that been going on? Who had she dated? Someone in school or out of it? Was she dating someone now? Why hadn't she told me before? And again, who was it? But suddenly, I knew.

"Fran," I said aloud. It all made sense. There was always such weird tension between them, a semihostile barrier that made no sense. They were schoolmates on the same team, co-captains; they were supposed to be friends.

"Kitt," Samantha corrected softly. "She really is Kitt most of the time." Samantha's smile twisted on her face, and her eyes tightened with what could have only been anger or pain.

"You're right," I told her with a grin, trying to lighten the mood, "she's terrible for you."

"Don't I know it," sighed Samantha, then smiled at me again, the tightness gone. "I really, really know it."

"When?" I asked, and I took my hand back to gesture.

"Spring after you joined the swim team, actually." Samantha grinned bashfully.

"That's when it started?" I was really curious to know all about this previously unknown facet of my friend, schoolmate, and teammate.

"Nope. When it ended." Samantha was very matter-of-fact. "You and I started hanging out, polishing trophies and banisters, doing the occasional math marathon," she grinned at me, "and Kitt said I wasn't focused enough on swimming, on my potential champion performance, and that I was spending way too much time on detention. So I told her not to worry so much about me, and that, as they say, was that."

"Wow," I breathed, and looked down at my hands. "I'm sorry." I meant that sincerely—breaking up with someone, whether you want to or not, is never easy.

"It hurt surprisingly little, actually," Samantha told me, smiling again, "because it wasn't really healthy, and it wasn't anything truly real. We have different views on what's important. For Fran," she paused to correct herself, "Kitt, it's swimming. That's everything to her, there's no room for anything or anyone else, really. For me, it's…" She trailed off, reflecting, looking down at nothing.

I hunched down a bit and lightly reached to raise her face, so I could see her eyes again.

"What is it?" I asked her gently. "What's everything for you?" I laid my hand on her shoulder. "You can tell me, I swear it's okay."

Samantha's hand came up to cover mine and her eyes searched my face, trying to read me, and that was fine with me. I was wide-open, hiding nothing. Anything she had to say, I would hear, and gladly. I'd share it with her, help her achieve it if I could, just be there if I couldn't. I tried to say that with my eyes, hoped she could see that, could read that.

"You don't know?" she asked, still searching. She took my hand in both of hers and dropped her gaze again, just watching my hand in hers. "Since my dad died," she started in a low voice, "I…I've had to do a lot, make a lot of decisions, and I learned some really important things, and one is—you can never, ever, get yesterday back. My dad, he"—and her voice caught—"he loved me, and I loved him so much. I still do…"

She stopped and I reached to brush the hair off her face, wanting to comfort her. I gently put it behind her ear, then laid my hand over both of ours on the seat.

"I learned," Samantha continued, her voice now slightly hoarse from unshed tears, "that the most important thing, the most important thing in the world, Nina, is the people in our lives—our friends, our families—and to let them know how we feel, not just in words, but in deeds. 'Actions speak louder than words,' as they tell us all the time," and Samantha looked up to give me a little grin.

"So this summer," and this time as she spoke, Samantha looked at me directly, "I had to take some actions. I wasn't sure how I felt about," she hesitated, "things, and I had to take a break, get myself together, know if what I was feeling was real or just based on grief, not just a desperate reaching out, instead of a real, um, affection. Every time you called, I listened to your messages over and over."

I felt bad—maybe I should have just gone over and visited or something, ignored the instinct that told me she needed time to heal. "Samantha, I'm so sorry that I didn't—" but she hushed me with a quick shake of her head in the negative.

Her hand strayed up over her chest to play with the miniature blade that was her namesake. "I've worn this every day since you gave it to me," Samantha said gently, a soft smile on her lips, "and no...I couldn't see you, especially after, um, after that party."

She held my hands between her own, holding them tightly. "God, Nina, everything about you is so fucking real. Everyone promising, swearing, 'I'm here for you' and all that, and you," she shook her head in wonderment, "you don't say those things, you just do them. You showed up at every wake, you held my hand at the funeral, let me cry if I needed, or just sat there silently, and..." and Samantha smiled at me again, "you even remembered my birthday."

"It wasn't too hard to do, Sammy." I smiled back. I guess maybe I didn't understand. Didn't everyone do stuff like that for their friends? It really wasn't a big deal.

Her hands held mine tighter. "I just needed to be clear," she looked down at our hands, "about what and why, that it wasn't just grief mixed with friendship, that it would be welcome, or at least, okay, especially after..." she freed one of her hands to grasp the charm dangling from her neck, "after this, because it's so very important, so damned special, just fucking—God!" she exclaimed softly, "everything to me. Do you understand?" She looked at me intently.

I gazed back into her eyes and an alarm bell softly pinged in my brain. Jesus Christ. My heart hammered, and I felt cold and hot at the same time. What I felt for Kerry I could define now, a mix of affection and attraction, and I truly enjoyed her company, especially when we weren't running for our lives or breaking laws. But what I felt for Samantha was entirely different, like knowing her somehow was the little piece that made me whole, but that little piece was larger than everything else, more important than the rest in its own way. Not knowing Samantha was unimaginable, the thought of her not being in my life, somehow or other, unbearable. I didn't care who or what was everything to her, as long as we remained friends. "I'm not sure...I think I do."

Samantha leaned in closer. "The most important thing to me," she whispered, "everything to me," and her face was so close to mine we breathed the same air, "is you, Nina."

Her lips were so close to mine, and it was easy, so very easy to turn so slightly and touch them with my own. In the moment I had for rational thought before I was completely unaware, I felt like I remembered this, that we had done this thousands of times before, and it was never enough, and then, quite literally, the world, the car, everything, sound, sight, my mind, my body, disappeared, and I was floating like a warm and happy little bubble in a darkness that was for the first time in my life soothing and not frightening. In that darkness I gradually became aware of a sound, a low, rhythmic, and steady sound, and as my awareness gradually came back, I realized that I was listening to a heartbeat that seemed to come from around us.

I was home.

There was no need for rationalizations, logical explanations, or daring little experiments, no fear either, just the awareness that this was right, just so very right somehow, an affirmation, a sealing of something deep and real and true, so deep that it's a matter of the soul, leaving the body behind. We recognized, we remembered each other somehow, and it woke something within me that had been sleeping all this time. I knew because I felt, clearly, how truly, how deeply, Samantha felt.

Eventually, awareness of the world filtered back in, and I was conscious first of the gentleness of Samantha's mouth on mine, then of the awareness that it was Samantha. Our kiss ended gently, reluctantly, and I leaned back a bit to look at Samantha with new eyes and new awareness. The simple, gentle kiss we had just shared had shaken me to the core, more than anything else I'd ever experienced, including the last few days. I was very unprepared for that—I'd been overwhelmed again.

"Samantha," I said softly, "I don't…I didn't know before, and now…" I sighed and looked down at our still joined hands. My mind was swirling, nothing made sense, everything was out of place, and the only thing that seemed solid and still was Samantha, but that was confusing, too. I looked back at Samantha and shrugged, letting my confusion show on my face.

"Nina, it's all right," Samantha answered my mute question. "You're not ready for this yet and," she paused and smiled ruefully to herself, "neither am I, really."

I nodded slightly and absorbed what she had said. I was still dazed from what she had said just before and by what had just happened. "I'm sorry, Sam," I whispered, and squeezed her hand, trying to tell her with my skin, through the intensity of touch, how I felt.

"Don't be," Samantha said, and returned the squeeze. "We have the rest of our lives to work this out." She kissed my hand, then put it down and released it with a little pat. "I better get you home." She smiled, then put on her seat belt and started the motor.

"Yeah," I sighed, "good idea." I shifted in my seat and put on my own seat belt.

We pulled out of the space and were off, arriving at the corner of my block seconds later. Samantha pulled into an available space and let the engine idle.

Removing my seat belt, I reached over the seat behind me and hauled my bag over it, settling it on the seat. "Sam," I touched her shoulder, "thanks."

Samantha looked back at me with big shining eyes. "You're always welcome," she said softly, and gave me a lopsided grin. We just watched each other and I couldn't bear it anymore—the look on her face that told me so strongly she was trying so hard not to cry.

Impulsively, I leaned over and put my arms around her, pulling her into a tight embrace. "Thank you for everything, Sam, Samantha, Sammy Blade," I whispered fiercely. "Thank you for your friendship and your wonderful, noble heart. Thank you just for being," I told her as I held her close.

Samantha returned my hug with honest strength and intensity. "No, Nina, thank you, for just being," she whispered intently in return. "Remember, always, always, I will be right here for you, just like you've been for me, no matter what happens, no matter where you are, no matter where I am. Always, Nina, always."

We held each other a little longer, sealing our pledge. Then finally, as if we were physically spent, we released each other.

"Have a good night, Sam." I smiled at her as I looped my bag over my shoulder and opened the door.

"Have a good night, Nina." She smiled back at me, and I closed the door. I made my way to the front door.

"Hey, Nina?" Samantha called from her car. I stopped and turned.

"Yeah?"

"I'll take you driving Saturday, after detention, okay?"

"Cool! Thanks, Sam!" I smiled and waved. "Good night!"

Samantha watched as I got to the door, and when I opened it, I turned to wave at her to let her know I was okay. She waved back, then gunned the motor, pulling out in not quite as spectacular a show as she could, but with enough flair to impress any of the neighbors that might be watching, and hey, in a neighborhood like mine, someone usually did.

Chapter Ten:
Bloodletting

I stepped into the house and put my bag on the floor while Ringo trotted up to greet me. After I scratched his head and ears, I took my coat off and hung it behind the door. "Hello!" I called into the house. "I'm home! We won!"

No one answered. That was really strange. I walked to the stairs and looked up—no lights on up there. I walked back through the living room, back to the kitchen, passing the dining table on the way. No note on the table, nothing on the fridge, nothing on the stove, either. Nobody had had dinner, it seemed. How bizarre.

I opened the door to the fridge and got out some milk, setting it aside on the counter. I rooted around a bit, looking for something to eat. I collected items. Okay, eggs, frozen broccoli, cheese. This would be decent enough. I poured myself a glass of milk and got out the tools I needed to make my supper.

Everything together, it struck me—I hadn't called Joey in a few days; he was probably a crazy man by now. Well, I had to talk with him anyway. I finally remembered that I was still annoyed with him over the whole gossip with Robbie. This weird thing we had between us had gone on for too long and had gone too far, and it had to end; I couldn't handle another human being.

Okay—there was no time like the present. I grabbed the phone and dialed, then held it between my cheek and shoulder while it rang, so I could make myself dinner.

"Hello?" someone finally answered.

"Hi, this is Nina Boyd. May I speak with Joey, please?" Joey had younger brothers and sisters, and I couldn't tell any of their voices apart, except for the youngest one, who still had a baby voice.

"Sure, Nina, no problem," one of his siblings answered, then dropped the phone. "Joey!" I could hear them yell, "it's Nina!"

"I've got it!" Joey called out. "Hey, Nina? How you doing?"

"Hey, Joey. Doing fine. Just got in from my meet. What's up with you?"

"You know, the usual stuff. I really missed you, I'm glad you called," he said, and we heard a little giggle on the line.

"Wait a sec," he told me, and I heard him put the phone away from his mouth.

"Hang it up over there!" he called out, and the giggle was louder.

"I hear you! Hang it up, dammit!" He brought his mouth back to the phone. "Did you hear the click?"

"No," I answered, amused. I had to go through the same thing too, with my younger sister, "no click yet."

"Just a sec." He sighed heavily, and I heard him put the phone down this time. "I'm coming to get you, and when I do…"

A shriek and a few giggles came back into the phone, followed by the sound of a hasty hang-up. Joey was back on the phone two seconds later.

"They hang up yet?" he asked with slight annoyance, not that I blamed him.

"Yeah, they're gone." I laughed. "They're probably going to play with your stereo now."

Okay, now was the time. I took a deep breath and steeled myself. I didn't want to hurt him, he really wasn't a bad person, but I wasn't comfortable with some things he seemed to think were okay.

Not to mention the fact that I think I was dating or something one of my best friends and had discovered an interest from another—but that really wasn't the point right now. We didn't belong together, and I knew it, and I didn't want to let this drag out either. That would just make it worse in the end, I knew that much.

"Joey, I have to…I need…" I paused to get this right. My words wouldn't come out right. "Joey, I can't date you anymore." There, I'd said it. I let out my breath.

Silence.

"What?" Joey was incredulous.

"We can't go out anymore." I clarified, "We can still hang out and be—"

"You're not doing this because of the Jack and Kerry thing, are you?"

I'd been going to discuss the gossip thing and the forcibly carrying me at the train station, as well as his grabbing my arm, but his question stopped me cold. What Jack and Kerry thing? What did I miss this time? My brain was pinging again, but this time the alarm was neither soft nor gentle. I had a full five-alarm alert blazing in there. "What are you talking about? What Jack and Kerry thing?"

"Kerry and Jack, they…" he paused. "Kerry didn't tell you?"

I didn't answer. I let the silence fill until he spoke again. His words had my full attention, and I suspected that blazing red alert in my brain might soon become a call to arms.

"Well, it's all okay now, at least I think it is," he said. "Are you sure Kerry didn't tell you already? You guys are always talking about stuff." He said the last a little resentfully.

"I'm sure," I told him flatly. "What happened?"

"I just want you to know that I would never do anything like that, and if that's why you're breaking up with me then don't, because I really love you and respect you," he rushed out, but this time I interrupted.

"What. Happened?" I asked again, enunciating each word. "Tell me or don't tell me, Joey, but don't fuck around, okay? The point?" That was probably harsher than it should have been, but I was getting irritated and not just a little scared. I knew, I just knew, that not only was I not going to like this, but it was going to affect me somehow. I just wanted to get it over with.

"Okay, okay," Joey attempted to calm me. "Here it is…" and I could hear him inhale in preparation.

"After you guys went to CBGB's on Sunday, do you remember?"

Yeah, like I was ever going to forget that Sunday. What a fuckin' day that had been, probably the most memorable of my life next to the day that followed it. Not that I was going to mention that to Joey.

"Yeah?" I answered, omitting the other stuff. "What about it?"

"Well, Kerry called Jack, you know? And he, like, went over to, like, visit, and her parents weren't home?" He paused.

Yeah, yeah, I know. Cut to the chase, boy, I thought impatiently. "Uh-huh," I answered instead, and flipped my eggs-cheese-broccoli combo in the pan so it wouldn't burn. I was starving. Again. Big surprise, I know, but hey, I was growing!

JD GLASS

Joey took another breath, then started again. "So, Kerry was going to break up with him, and he didn't want that, so they got into this really big argument and…"

Okay, I'll cut to the chase for you. I can't stand the way he delivered the story, and the story went like this.

Apparently, during the aborted breakup attempt and argument, things got a little crazy and then suddenly things turned, um, very friendly. Anyhow, one way or another—Joey wasn't very clear as to whether this was during the argument, after, or because of it—"and then it just sort of happened, before it could be stopped, Jack told me," Joey finished, "so if that's why you're breaking up with me, you just can't, because that's not me, and besides, Jack's really sorry about the whole thing."

I was stunned. On the one hand, one friend of mine was either a rapist or an idiot, a victim of circumstance, as it were, and I could empathize with that. On the other hand, the friend that I was close to, the one I'd actually been intimate with, was either a liar or a victim.

This was way too fucking much, just too fucking much for one day. I was going to eat my fucking dinner, do my fucking homework, and just go to bed. I didn't even care where everyone was. This was enough. Game over. I was taking my ball and going home. I was starting to realize why so many adult "role models" drank—I needed a drink myself.

"Nina?" Joey inquired. I'd been silent this whole time.

"Yeah, Joey? Aw, shit!" I'd forgotten the omelet I'd been making for myself, and it kindly reminded me of its existence by starting to smolder. I shut off the burner and removed the pan, still cradling the phone between my head and shoulder. I found an empty plate and dumped the sorry mess I'd created into it. Well, at least it was only a little brown. I'd drink a lot of milk to kill the burnt taste.

"So, are we okay now?"

I threw the pan into the sink with a crash I was sure he could hear over the phone. "No, we're not okay the way you think," I answered with controlled anger. "I can't date you anymore. My reasons have nothing to do with Kerry and or Jack. They can fuck themselves or each other, I don't fuckin' care." I was finally able to hold the phone with a hand instead of my shoulder and, plate in hand, made my way to the table.

"I was sick yesterday, I'm taking shit at home, shit at school, I had a fuckin' meet from hell today, I've got fuckin' exams to take, I'm supposed to be trying to get into the fuckin' service academies, my grades are suffering, I've got no fuckin' time to spare to date, and you were so damn worried about what Kerry and I talk about and how I feel about the Kerry-Jack stuff you just told me, that you were too fuckin' afraid to call me and ask me—kinda like you told people we're getting married next summer or some shit, and you didn't even bother to ask me about that, either!" I exploded and Joey got hit with the burst. I set my plate down on the table with a thud.

Joey was silent for a bit. "Nina, sweetheart…" he started, then stopped. What could he say?

"I don't want to hurt your feelings, Joey, but I can't, I just can't right now, and I don't know when," if ever, I mentally added, then continued, "and this has nothing to do with what you just told me."

He sighed heavily. "Are you sure?" he asked me. "I love you so much," and his voice was so sad, I felt like the most horrible person on earth. But he wanted my love, not my sympathy, and I had the one, but not the other. It wouldn't help either of us.

"I'm sorry, Joey, I'm sure."

"Can I…can I call you sometime?" he asked in a choked voice. Yes, it's true, I was a first-class bitch. But it would have been crueler to pretend something that just wasn't true. I still tell myself that.

"Yeah, of course," I said softly. "I do care about you. I want us to still be friends, really." I meant that sincerely. He wasn't a bad guy, he just wasn't for me, and I wished he could understand that in a way that didn't hurt.

"Okay." He sighed again. "I'll let you go now. Good night, Nina."

"Good night, Joey. I'm sorry."

"Yeah, me too," he replied softly, "me too," and we both hung up.

After I put the phone back on the cradle, I found my books and started to do my homework while I ate my well-done dinner, and by the time I was finished with both, still no one was home.

Okay, I was going to bed. This had been the longest day in creation, and I had definitely had it—and there was still the rest of the week to get through yet. I left a little note on the table. "We won!" I wrote in extra-large letters with a smiley face. I passed the cable clock on my way to the stairs—it was nine o'clock.

I thought Nicky would have been back with Kerry already, but maybe they had gone to hang out at Universe. Unusual for a school night, yes, but it seemed the rules for Nicky were different than the rules for me. Whatever. I didn't know where my parents were, but maybe they had gone to a parent-teacher night for Nanny. I left it at that—I was going to bed.

I got to my room and undressed in the dark, throwing my stuff in a neat little pile into the basket that I shoved back under my bed. Sometimes, okay, most of the time, I like to sleep in the buff, it's just more comfortable, and that's what I was doing this night. The cool cotton sheets were soothing on my skin, especially after a meet like this one had been.

I lay on my side, just thinking. What had happened to Kerry on Sunday with Jack? Was she okay? Was she fucked up about it? She seemed okay, she hadn't said word one about anything on Monday. Damn, then there was the flip side of that: was Jack or Joey lying? Was Kerry? I shied away from that. Tremendous pain was involved if I went that route, and I didn't want to start doubting Kerry or being suspicious. Joey or Jack, or even both of them, was potentially lying, and I was Kerry's friend before I was a friend to either of them, literally and chronologically.

Okay, well, at least I'd managed to end it with Joey, a minimal amount of bloodshed involved. I winced inwardly thinking about that. I hated hurting people, but I knew it was the right thing—for both of us.

And then, finally, there was Samantha—beautiful and real, and intense. I loved that about her, the honesty, her realness. I spent a bit remembering that feeling of true homecoming that I'd had for those brief shining seconds. I had a friend, a real friend, and that was a good thing to have in life. I'd learned something, at least. I smiled to myself.

I had a sudden thought: I was going to have to talk with my parents, though, and soon. I'd tell them about me, how I was feeling, all the stuff that was going on. They'd help me make sense of it all. After all, I was their child, the "product of their love," as they always said. They'd be okay. They'd always said that we could tell them anything, anything at all, no matter what it was, and that they loved us. Okay, so they were tough on us, and sometimes they went a little nuts and even slapped us around, but it would be okay. I would tell them, maybe tomorrow, maybe Friday. I'd find the time. That settled in my head, I finally fell asleep.

It seemed as though only seconds had passed before I heard Nanny speaking to me in a loud whisper. "And then they took me ice skating, and then me and Mom and Dad had dinner with Nicky and his new girlfriend!"

I rolled over and cracked an eye open. Light was streaming in from the hallway, but otherwise, it was definitely still night. Which meant it was still time to sleep. "That's nice, Nanny," I mumbled, "I'm glad you had fun," and I turned back over, covering my head with my pillow. I returned to the land of Nod. It seemed like only another few seconds before I heard someone calling my name.

"Nina. Nina Jameson Boyd, your father and I want to talk with you."

It was my mother, and her voice was very serious, serious enough to use my entire given name. I rolled over and opened my eyes. Oh my God, I thought, they know, and I panicked, then let it go. How could they know anything? I hardly knew for myself yet, and besides, they were my parents; they'd love me. It's not as if I was a drug addict or a criminal or something.

"I'm coming," I called out in a stage whisper, and reaching under my pillow for a T-shirt and shorts, I pulled them on and swung my legs out of bed.

As I tried to quietly leave the room, Nanny picked her head up. "What did you do now?" She sounded sleepy.

"Nothing." I racked my brain just in case there was something. "Nothing I can think of. Don't worry about it," I tried to reassure her. "Go back to sleep."

"'Kay," Nanny yawned back at me, then settled down.

I made my way down the hallway, the only light coming from the TV in front of their bed, and as I stepped into the room, my mom and dad were both sitting up, my dad under the blankets on his side, my mom on the edge of hers.

That was weird, I thought. My dad had a book in his hands, but it didn't seem like there was that much light to read by. Whatever. I dismissed it.

"Hi, Mom. Hi, Dad." I yawned. "What's up?" I was sleepy, but my guts were shaking and that didn't make any sense to me at all. It's okay, I told my guts. They're my parents, they love me.

"What's this…" my mom said, then paused and started again, "what's this we're hearing about that you might be bisexual or gay or…" She let it hang.

Relief washed over me like a bucket of ice-cold water. Stupid gut. Parents know everything. I didn't have to figure out how to talk with them after all; they were going to open a dialogue with me. How great was that? But my insides wouldn't stop shaking.

"Oh, wow, I'm so glad you know," I said. "I didn't know how I was going to—"

"So it's true?" my mom interrupted, shock writ large on her face. I started to nod in confirmation when my father's book flew across the room, hitting the bridge of my nose, and then my mom was on me like a flash, the combined force of her hand and the rings on them sending me backward onto a long, low dresser. I smashed my back on its edge, sending electric shocks through my stomach and up and down my arms and legs, then fell to the ground.

Oh…my face…hurt. I raised a shaking hand that still tingled to my nose to feel it and found that it was so tender, I could hardly touch it. My lip felt wet, and I looked at the floor and couldn't help but wonder, why am I drooling? The gem on one of my mother's rings had caught on my lip, and I was bleeding to beat the band.

I was definitely in shock. I'd never expected this from my parents, I mean, not really. My dad, well, he said stuff, sure, but he always qualified it, like he didn't mean it, at least, not that way, I thought. I thought wrong.

Something was sticking in my throat, and I couldn't breathe. I coughed and blood sprayed out. My nose was bleeding; it was fuckin' broken, I realized, and I was swallowing the blood coming down on the inside.

I looked up to see my mom standing there, legs splayed and fists curled, staring at me with an expression on her face I'd never seen before. "Mom?" I choked out, spitting out more blood.

She rushed over and was on me like the Furies, slapping and punching and kicking. I curled into a ball to protect my head and bleeding face, and she pulled my hair to expose it, raking her nails across my cheek. I curled tighter. "Don't you ever," she spat out between blows and kicks, "call me that again!"

My mother. Who told me that she had waited her whole life to meet me, her first child, had loved me before I was born, and reminded all three of us that we were blood of her blood and bone of her bone. My mother who called me "morning songbird," or "morning bird," or some variation of that every day, because she said I'd started every day of my life singing, even before I could talk, that even when I'd hurt myself or was sad or scared as a little one, I wouldn't cry, but sang instead, and still did. My mother, Mom, Mommy, the first name children ever know for God, for love. Gone.

"Everything we've done for you," she cried, "all the sacrifices we've made," she kicked my back and ribs, "the ballet and the schooling," she sobbed, "all for nothing." With both fists she pounded on my hands, which were covering my head, and my forehead bounced on the wood floor. I could hardly hold my arms up anymore, I ached everywhere so badly.

"The bright child, the golden child, the best of the best, and all that talent, that brain, that brilliant mind, wasted, wasted, wasted!" she screamed and emphasized each "wasted" by grabbing my hair and dropping my head on the floor. I had no energy left to even try to prevent it anymore.

Finally, an aching, bloody, eternity later, she stopped. I lay on the floor, just simply breathing, swallowing blood, and I figured that was a good sign. If I could still breathe and still bleed, then I was still alive. Then again, I hurt so much, maybe that wasn't such a good thing.

Cautiously, I wiggled my fingers and toes. Still attached, still working. That was a good start, if I was going to be a member of the land of the living.

I heard my mother's footsteps retreat, and using my arms to help me, I forced myself to sit up and look at her, my mother. I set my face in the blankest expression I could muster and, never taking my eyes off her, slowly, painfully, I got to my feet and stood on my own.

"I had an interesting call from our neighbor Kathy, late last night," she started, then stopped. Right then and there, I knew that whatever came out now would be a lie or, at least, partly one.

The same neighbor who had ratted me and my friend out for smoking, Kathy was, like—no, she actually was the village troublemaker. If there was a truth and then an exaggeration, Kathy would take the truth, the exaggeration, and her imagination to create a plausible, but false, tale. For example, the smoking thing? My buddy and I were lighting cigarettes and then watching what happened when we stuck a liquid soap bottle filled halfway with water to the filter and made it "inhale." We wanted to see if the water changed color. Kathy told my parents that *I* was inhaling and shoving the cigarettes up my friend's nose—no joke. Of course, no one believed our side of it. Who believes kids, anyway?

But no one ever called Kathy on that or anything else, because at least once a year, whether she had to or not, she told the truth, and even her lies had truthful elements, so you were never really sure which would come out of her mouth: the truth or her truth. But she and my mother were good friends, so it wouldn't do any good to contradict anything the "wonderful friend" Kathy said. They were so close, her and my mom I mean, that we had to call Kathy "Aunt Kathy." Get the picture?

She'd gotten us, meaning Nicky and Nanny and I, into trouble many times before, and only once had it been an unvarnished truth.

"Nanny overheard a conversation you were having with a friend about being a bisex, or a gay or a...a les..." she almost gagged but forced the word out finally, "a lezzie, and she's afraid of you, that you might do something to her one night. So she told Kathy because she didn't know who else to tell out of fear that if you found out she told us, you might kill her or something."

"What? Are you crazy?" I asked in disbelief. "How can you possibly believe that? I would never, ever, *ever* do *anything* to hurt Nanny. I love her!" I was beyond shock.

"I spoke with Nanny when we went to dinner tonight, and she told your father and me very clearly that she *is* afraid of you."

Oh my God, Nanny was afraid of me? Why didn't she just talk to me, ask me? Maybe my mother misunderstood, maybe Nanny was afraid for me, or maybe she was afraid of the way I liked to dress. Why didn't she talk to me? We'd never had problems like that before, even if we did squabble from time to time. She asked me everything, and I shared everything I could with her.

She was my baby sister. I had been the first one, before grandparents or aunts and uncles or family friends even, to hold her when my parents brought her home. They, meaning my parents and the baby, had walked in the door the whole family had crowded around, laughing and smiling, and had asked that I be put in this big plush armchair in the baby's room. And while everyone asked to hold the baby, my mother shook her head no and smiled, carrying the little blanket bundle over to the chair I'd been placed in.

"Nina," my mother smiled at me, her big beautiful smile, "this is your baby sister, Nancy," and she put her in arms I hadn't realized I'd already stretched out.

"Nanny," I repeated as best I could, and I looked down at the tiny little face and the delicate lashes over apple-bright cheeks. "Nanny," I said again, liking the way it sounded, easier than Nancy. She smelled nice.

"Here, Nina." My father came over and crouched next to me, handing me a small baby bottle filled with what I thought was water, and with him guiding my hand, I helped and witnessed Nanny's first meal at home.

"Come here, Nicky." My mother reached for my brother, who had hidden under the crib. "Come meet your little sister Nancy, help Nina feed her." And before I knew it, Nicky's hand was next to mine, and it was just the two of us, my father letting us do this on our own.

"Nanny," Nicky said softly, and gently reached to touch the little half-moons of the baby's eyebrows with a tentative finger.

"Oh no, don't..." someone started to say, but my mother shushed them. "It's okay, Nicky, it's your little sister."

Nicky gently smoothed the tiny little brow in peace, then looked up at our father. "Boy?" he asked hopefully, and everyone laughed.

"A little girl." My father smiled at him. "A beautiful baby girl."

"Brother," Nicky said firmly. "Boy."

"That's right," our mother came over and said, "you're a big boy and a big brother now, just like Nina is your big sister. Nina, you're not just a big sister anymore, you're the oldest now."

My eyes widened, and I looked up at my mother, wondering what she meant.

"You have to love and protect and care for your little brother and baby sister because they're smaller and younger than you. They are blood of your blood and bone of your bone," and my mother gently stroked my arm to illustrate, "and you're my big girl, okay?" she explained gently, and I nodded solemnly. This was a big thing, and I wasn't really sure what it meant, but if Mommy asked, I would do it, because I loved Mommy and Daddy and Nicky and baby Nanny, who was tiny and couldn't take care of herself.

Someone reached to take the baby from me, saying something about their turn or something, but I put the bottle down and, scowling fiercely, used both my arms to hug the little sleeper and hunched my body over her. "My Nanny," I said, forcing myself deeper into the chair and away from the hands that weren't mine or Nicky's or Mommy's and Daddy's. Protect the baby. I would, no matter what that meant.

How could anyone, especially my family, my parents, Nanny, possibly think I could even remotely dream of hurting my baby sister, blood of my blood, bone of my bone, even this many years later? My Nanny.

But then, I reflected, the one time Kathy had gotten us in trouble for something true, it had been Nanny who told her, and Nanny herself was also known to stretch the truth on occasion. Kathy had probably seen Kerry and me or something, or maybe just had a suspicion, then had buttonholed Nanny in the last few days with a few gossipy questions. This was not only possible, this was actually probable.

A thin little wisp of anger curled in my stomach and went straight to my heart, killing some of my affection for my baby sister. Fuck her. I would avoid her then, if she was so fucking afraid. But it hurt, all the same.

"And your father," my mother indicated him where he sat, silent this whole time, just watching, "tells me that Nicky and Kerry spoke with him at dinner."

What? They didn't come to my meet; they all went to dinner, to talk about me? What the fuck?

"Nicky told your father that Kerry told him, that on Sunday you, that you, tried to force yourself on that poor girl," she stated, her voice shaking.

I glared at my father, who was watching me with a tight, smug little smile.

"Are you people completely fucking insane? Hello? It's me—your," and I twisted my mouth a little, "daughter? I would never do a thing like that. You raised me, you should fucking know me better! I'm the same person I was last week, the person who would never, ever willingly hurt another, and especially never do a thing like that!"

I caught my breath in anger at the injustice of it, then went on. "Besides, I talked to Joey tonight. I was home by nine on Sunday, Jack was there at nine thirty, and Joey says that Jack and Kerry, the girl that Dad," and I looked at him directly, "always calls a 'dyke,'" I spat that word out and let it hang in the air, "did it that night with Jack, so go fuckin' ask him, ask both of them, before you're so damned quick to believe someone else before you believe me." And I stopped, wordless, shocked at the shots that were coming in from all sides.

My mother's face was surprised by my revelation, my father's had gone blank. Apparently, this was news to them. Well and good, then. It had been news to me, too.

My brain jumped back into gear and then into overtime. "And another thing…if that was true, why in the world would she have come over and stayed last night? Why would she and Nicky come to my meet? Did you even stop to think about that?" I stood there, dripping scarlet drops on the floor, just breathing in and out. "I can't believe you people."

There was silence as my mother looked abashed. She sat back down on her edge of the bed and glanced over at my father to see what he would say, but he refused to meet her eyes. Instead, he glared at me with such vehemence, and with such anger, that I knew, deep within, that Nicky had never said that to my father. My father had lied, had taken Kathy's story and added a lie to it to further egg my mother on, to make her angry enough to hate me, her beloved child, and I would think, no matter what happened, that it was my mother's fault. I would blame her, be hurt by her, not by him.

It was a great plan, except he'd forgotten one very important thing: I wasn't as stupid as he loved to say I was every morning of my misbegotten life. I curled my lip at him, glaring back just as strongly.

"You lose," he spat out, "you lose if you do this."

I just stared at him, waiting.

"You can't do this," he continued, his voice full of anger and solemnity.

"I didn't do anything wrong."

"Forget Annapolis. Forget West Point. Forget ROTC and Harvard, Princeton, or Yale. You wanted Princeton, right? For engineering math and science? Who's going to pay for it if you don't have that scholarship? We're not. We're not paying anything—" my father said, but my mother put a hand on his arm to shush him.

Any blood that wasn't falling from my face fell down to my feet. Oh my God, that was true. I couldn't go into the service and become an officer, couldn't become a pilot, couldn't become an engineer, couldn't become an astronaut. Over something really stupid and insignificant. My body shook so badly now I thought my guts would fall on the floor.

My mother looked at me. "It's very simple, Nina. You do this our way, and we'll take care of it. We'll work it out, no matter what we need to do. You don't want to join the military, you don't want to be an officer anymore, fine, that's not a life for everyone and you don't have to do it, even though you've been preparing your whole life for this, and why we sent you to your high school. You don't have to say you're, a, a bi, um, a whatever, to get out of it. You don't want to be in the armed forces, we understand."

She was very serious and solemn, and waited to see my reaction before she continued, and I'll be honest, I'd started to rock side to side a bit in agitation and agony. This was my life we were talking about, after all. "Do it your way, Nina, persist in this, and we will not support you. I will not support any monstrosity in my home."

My legs in a slight horse stance, I now stood stock-still and stared intently. "I'm not doing anything wrong," I said in a low tone to my mother directly. "He…" and I gestured in my father's direction to my mother. I would have said more, but my mother held up her hand for my silence and I complied, listening hard.

"The law says we have to provide for you until you are of age, which is eighteen. If you decide to live here until that time, we will provide you with food and shelter, but nothing else, until you are no longer our legal obligation, which your father and I have decided will be when you graduate, if you graduate, from high school, instead of your actual eighteenth birthday." Considering my birthday was in winter, that was a good thing, I thought grimly.

My mother continued, "We will not sign transfer papers or write you notes or sign anything with your name on it. If you decide to go to a different school anyway, you will not live here. If you do not want to live here, we will not pay for you to live anywhere else. Should you decide not to live here, we will have you declared a runaway and a criminal, and you'll be taken to a home for juvenile delinquents, where you'll be treated like an animal—"

My father interjected at this point, "You'll have a new uniform, three squares a day, and continue your," he sneered, "education, and then you'll learn, you'll really learn. How to sleep with your eyes open, where to walk, where to look or not look, so you don't get gang-raped by a bunch of thugs." His face had the dim shine of animated wax in the light from the TV that was still on. "That'll fix you, fix you good, too." He seemed almost pleased. "I bet," he paused a moment, a strange expression on his face, "you'll beg—"

"Roger," my mother turned to him and said sharply, "that's enough!" She turned back to me and placed her hands in her lap, composing herself before she continued, and continue she did. "You will have to take care of your tuition, your uniforms, your sports and all of your other expenses, including your transportation and all of your exam and application fees, yourself. You will still have household responsibilities, to pay for your room and board, and you will still follow all of our rules. You have no rights, except to eat and sleep here. You have no phone privileges. You may read your books. You may, of course, use the washer and dryer. Also, if you quit any of your school activities, you will no longer be welcome in this home. You must continue to do it all, without our support.

"Once you graduate, you may continue to live here, but you will have to pay rent. We will not support you in any way. You are not our child."

My mother stared at me and I stared right back, wordless and now numb. So far, I had understood. I was still to make dinner, do dishes, do the laundry, somehow pay for school, study for school, take care of all my extracurricular obligations as well, or be homeless. Gee, what a bargain.

"If you persist in this path, Nina, and you are able to do this, finish high school, go to college, take care of yourself financially, if you can do all these things and not become a depraved sex- and drug-addicted alcoholic monster, I will still not love you. I will respect you, but I will not love you and I will not help you."

The rocking and shaking finally stopped, and I just stared. Something, and I don't know what it was really, grew within me. It had the power, the strength of anger, but it was different somehow. It was cold and hard. Like ice. Like stone. I had a vision of ancient glaciers carving through mountains. Slow, inexorable, and inevitable. Unstoppable. Was I the mountain or the glacier?

"Do this our way, Nina, and it's all there for you. We will take care of everything, and you will spare yourself tremendous hardship. You will be our beloved child, our brightest star, our child who goes to Princeton or Harvard or Yale or any other place you choose. We will find a way to send you. You will have our love, our assistance and support."

I couldn't believe what I was hearing. They were going to pretend that none of this had ever happened, these words had not been said, that it wasn't my own blood running down the back of my throat and spotting the floor, if I lied, if I said that it was all a mistake, a misunderstanding. It would be easy, too, just a few words, and then I'd just have to live with myself for the rest of my life.

I could, possibly, do like people I read about, just hide it and be a liar with those whom it was most important to be honest. These were big stakes here, and I had no way, no knowledge of how to really take care of myself. They were backing me into a corner, and it would be almost impossible, actually, being underage, undereducated, to survive, never mind succeed, considering the very constricting requirements, narrow definitions, and permissions of what I needed to do to "pass" their test.

But, I realized, I had a higher standard to live by, my conscience, and I had another surge of insight: the glaciers were inexorable, unstoppable, merciless. But the glaciers were gone and the mountains, no matter how carved or scarred, remained, still mountains.

"How can you ask me to do that?" I asked them, "how can you respect me, if I just say, sure, no problem, whatever you say? How can I respect you if you actually do that? That's hypocritical, it's not truth, not real!" I tried to desperately explain. "How can we ever believe each other again? How will you know if you love me or just a make-believe or incomplete picture of me, or me of you guys?"

"Just do it our way, Nina," my mother ordered.

My eyes narrowed as I spoke to both of them. "You," I said very distinctly, "are asking me to lie." Suddenly, it was very clear, and I was possessed of an almost unearthly calm. Mountain or glacier.

I took a breath, steadied my stance, then glared at each of them in turn, first my father, expressionless except for the smoldering anger in his eyes that told me how much he hated me, and then my mother, whose eyes begged me to pretend this all away. I held her gaze with mine. "I am not," I paused for emphasis, "a liar, and it's wrong of you to try to force me to be one."

Quick as a rocket, my mother flew off the bed, but this time, I was ready. Oh, she hit me all right. The slam across my face knocked my head back and hit my poor nose again so hard I cried out but swallowed it down quickly enough. The rest of my body remained solidly planted.

Blood poured again now, out of my nose, from my lips, and at least one cut on my face. It poured down my shirt, but I stood and did not falter or fall, watching my mother, legs wide and fists at my side. I watched her, and I suddenly realized I was looking down. I was taller than she was, by almost a head, maybe more, since my legs were splayed. I took comfort from that fact in a small obscure way, and I realized my mother must have noticed how much taller than she I was, too. She took a step back.

"Do it our way, Nina, and we will give you the world. Do it yours and"—she shrugged—"you'll earn my respect, but that will be all you get. I will not love you, support you, or help you. I will, however, respect you."

My eyes still narrowed, I squared my shoulders and stood up as straight as I could, back held proudly. I wiped some blood off my mouth and chin and flicked it away. It landed on the corner of my parents' bed, and I watched my mother's eyes follow it and rest there, before they came back to me.

I stood even prouder and looked down at her straight in the eye. "You're just going to have to respect me, then," I told her calmly and clearly and, executing a perfect right face, strode from their room without another word. Get thee behind me, Satan, I thought. The world on a silver platter was not enough to trade for my soul.

I was a rock.

I didn't even stop in the bathroom to wash off. I didn't want to give them the satisfaction of hearing the water run, knowing that I was cleaning up the mess they had made. I just went straight to bed and went to sleep, vowing through my tightly gritted teeth that I would make this work somehow. I wouldn't let them break me; I could do this and not become lost, not lose my integrity. I wouldn't let them win, mold and make me into an unreal person.

Then I remembered it was November, and I would be seventeen in February. I was sixteen years old, and my life was destroyed, by the people who'd given it to me in the first place.

Chapter Eleven:
Bad Reputation

Just before my eyes popped open in the early-morning darkness, I thought, oh thank God, it was only a dream. That is, until I heard my father's steps thumping down toward the end of the hallway.

"Lowlife fuckin' piece of shit, can't wait till you get out," he cursed, and his footsteps paused by my door. "Get out, bitch, get out," he stage-whispered at the door, then slammed into the bathroom with such a loud bang that Nanny actually woke.

"Nina, what did you do now?" she asked me, her voice both sleepy and exasperated.

"Nothing, Nanny," I told her honestly, "nothing but tell the truth. Go back to sleep."

"Must've been some truth," she muttered, and I heard her roll back over.

"You don't know the half of it."

I stayed awake and I remembered—I was mad at Nanny, I was done with Joey, I was beyond belief at my father's machinations, and forget about "Aunt Kathy." I hated her anyway. I had to talk to Nicky.

I remembered I was bereft—my mother didn't love me anymore, because the simple little fact that I might actually be gay outweighed every other quality and facet I had; this little thing carried enough weight to wipe her heart clear of me.

I was alone.

It was a bizarre feeling, lying in that bed, still living there but knowing I wasn't a part of the family anymore, not in any real sense. I was a stranger to them all now, yet still one among their number.

I had to think, I had to plan, I had to figure out what I was going to do. I was old enough to drop out, leave, and get a job doing something, but that wouldn't be living, really, and a GED had never been on my horizon. I had to think about it now, though; there was a good chance it would be a part of my future.

I needed to raise cash and fast, too. Tuition wasn't fully paid for the whole year yet; swim team fees had to be met; I was supposed to get new uniforms, if I was staying at my school. I needed money to get to school, too, and lunch and stuff like that.

Okay, I would go through a normal day and start making some inquiries at lunch and after school about transferring if I had to, if it was possible, but I'd still need money for later. And I remembered I still had some cash left from the weekend and my emergency stash behind the washing machine—that's where I put my money, so it wouldn't get "borrowed" by my siblings, especially Nanny, who seemed to live by the philosophy "what's mine is mine and what's yours is mine." Aside from that, though, I also had a small joint account with my grandmother that was supposed to be for college, and once a month, I'd take the money from behind the washing machine and put it in the bank. I'd be using that soon, too, I guessed.

My father finished his morning ritual, and once I heard the door close to his bedroom, I decided to get moving. My plan so far was to leave after he did. Because the school opened very early, I could sit in homeroom and do some thinking there. Also, I didn't want to see anyone that morning, either in the house or on the way to school, so I could avoid that if I was early enough.

I sat up and swung my legs over the edge and was brought short by pain, blinding pain, in my head, my back, my neck, everywhere. Nausea hit me like a fist to the gut, and dizziness slapped my head around. I bit my lip to stop from vomiting and tasted blood. I'd opened the cuts on my mouth again.

I forced myself to stand up and fumbled my way across the room in the dark. I felt for my uniform in the closet, and finding it with my fingers, I grabbed it, wincing and inhaling sharply at the pain that lanced across my ribs when I raised my arm.

I stumbled but quickly recovered, then went to the dresser by the door and, feeling around, found underwear and socks. I was good to go. I steadied myself a moment against the waves of nausea and the sloping floor, then quietly made my way out of the room, to the bathroom.

I heard my father go downstairs. Everyone else was still asleep; I was the only one he ever woke up anyway. I quietly shut and locked that door behind me before I turned on the light, and I was sorry when I did. Not only did the brightness hurt my eyes, but I caught a glimpse of myself in the mirror that ran the length of the sink and accompanying counter.

Shit. I looked like shit. My T-shirt, which had been white, had been drenched down the front in blood and slime, was spattered everywhere with fat drops of dried blood, and one sleeve was totally ensanguined and had dried brown, stiff, and wrinkled. That must have been where I'd hidden my face when I was on the floor. My shorts had blood on them, the hem of one leg was stained halfway up. I must have sat in a puddle of the red goo. Well, at least I didn't piss myself, I thought, and tried to smile, but that was painful, and that's when I actually looked at my face for the first time.

Oh my God, my lips were crusted black and so swollen; I saw at least three major splits and one jagged tear along the corner, where a ring had caught. I tried to push the little flap of skin back over the wound, but there was too much crusted blood there to let that happen. I inspected my teeth—still there, and they were also black and brown with blood.

I raised my eyes to the rest of my face, and the view didn't really get much better—my cheek was a definite light blue and swollen from the impact with—well, what did I call her now? Mom was out. Mrs. Boyd? Ma'am? The person who bore but now hates me?—that woman's hand, and there were scratches near my eyes. Two lines ran down my cheek, where her rings had caught my skin, and the lines were still open, pink and puffy. I reached for the peroxide, catching myself with pain again, then saw the other side.

I had a light purplish-blue circle under my left eye, which itself was slightly swollen, and a cloudy dark blue band across the bridge of my nose. I gingerly touched it—ouch! I wouldn't do that again anytime soon. I turned my head gently from side to side. My ears were both full of dried blood, and it had gotten matted in the hair right above them. I was never going to get that out. Carefully, I placed peroxide where I could, then rinsed my mouth out with it.

I examined myself again and considered. I slid the mirror and dug around, not sure what I was searching for until I found it: hair scissors and a hair buzzer. If I did this fast, I could be done before the noise woke anyone up. There was so much blood dried in there from cuts on my scalp, and I clipped the matted hair as close to the skin as I could.

JD GLASS

When I couldn't cut anymore, I used the buzzers, and I had to go up about an inch, inch and a half. The buzz lines on the sides of my head were now level to a single finger width above my eyebrows. I inspected my handiwork, then evened it out on both sides, but it still looked a little weird. The strands that come down in front of the ears were just, well, not right. If only I could just get rid of that, get a nice clean line.

I spied my father's razor, which my mom and I were forbidden to use on our legs.

Fuck him. He thought he knew what was fuckin' punk? He knew shit. Liar.

I put a little soap and water on each side and carefully, very carefully, shaved the "sideburns" or whatever they're called. I shaved until there was a straight, neat line, right above the ear.

There. It was even and it was done. I cleaned everything off and put all the tools away, wiped the hair off the counter, and flushed it. Stripping off my stained and destroyed clothes, and believe me, the undressing process was slow, as every motion produced pain, I finally maneuvered into the shower, and another wave of dizziness washed over me.

I leaned against the tile wall to regain my equilibrium, then finally got down to business. I had bruises everywhere, dark, livid, eggplant purple and cornflower blue, some mottled blue and purple, like speckled eggs. No, on further inspection, they didn't look like speckled eggs; they looked like brains.

Damn! I remembered I was supposed to have gym that day, fuck. Sweatpants for me. I was going to swear up and down that I'd forgotten my shorts. No, amend that, sweatshirt, too—my arms were also covered in scratches and bruises.

Aw fuck, I wore a skirt, too. Okay, I was going to wear pants into school and change when I got there. If I wore opaque white stockings and tucked my legs under my desk all day, no one would see them. I'd wear my blazer or a sweater all day, too. And as for my face, well, I didn't have a true Mohawk, a thin strip down the center. I had a wide band that came down to my temples. The rest of my hair was really long, so I'd just keep bent over my books and suck on some ice cubes, hold a Coke can to my face, bring the swelling down. Problem solved.

Done washing and brushing and attempting to hide or correct the just-got-mugged-by-mom-n-dad-'cuz-they-hate-me look, I slipped on my underwear and socks.

I spared a glance at my destroyed clothes and made a quick decision: I folded them neatly, with the blood on top, and left them on the counter. Let Mrs. Whoever she was to me now explain that to Nicky and Nanny; I'm sure she'd be able to think of something. Satisfied, I ran as quietly as I could down the stairs, uniform in hand.

Down in the basement, I got some clothes and reached behind the machine for the box I kept my money in. Finally, I snagged and pulled it out. It was an old metal Band-Aid box with a flip-top lid, and effective, may I add, in holding all my adolescent earnings.

Dressed, a couple of bucks in hand, I went back up to the main floor to get my gym bag and my school bag. I passed the dining table where I had left my note the night before; it was still there. God, my head hurt. On impulse, I snatched it up and tore it in two, then went to throw it away in the kitchen, where I saw my schedules on the refrigerator, my classes and teachers, practices and meets, all listed. There were pictures of all three of us from the annual school picture-taking fest. No, wait, there were only pictures of Nanny and Nicky.

A hunch made me look into the newly bagged garbage pail. My picture was there. I pulled it out and stared at with shaking fingertips, tracing the edges of what my face used to look like.

Suddenly, I was angry, just so damn infuriated, I tore the schedules and my picture up and threw them on the floor. I stared down at them, wondering if fire was going to come out of my nostrils. I turned around, and in the dining room, I spied the certificates and trophies I'd earned over the years on a shelf. In one instant I swept them all out into one arm, marched back into the kitchen, dumped them in the garbage, picked the papers up, put them there too, then put my picture on top.

Fine. Throw me out, hate me, God damn it, but don't dare fucking use my accomplishments to show off. Those were mine. I sweated for them, worked and suffered for them. Me, the piece-of-shit bitch. The same monster lowlife they hated had earned every single one of those fucking shiny things they were so proud of. It was a package deal, baby. Love what I can do, better love me, too, or kiss the whole fucker good-bye.

I heard footsteps sound across the floor upstairs as my mother walked across her room to the door and opened it, then continued down the hall. "Nicky, honey, time to get up," I heard her call into his room.

I was disgusted and nauseated. I spat on the pile and left, slamming the door behind me, not caring for once who heard or woke. The air was very cold, and my breath came out in little gray clouds.

The walk to the train station was a carousel of pain—the ache in my head, the dizziness, and most especially the nausea forcing me to stop every block or so—but eventually I got there, climbing the steps and everything to the platform.

It was empty so I wandered around a bit, and I noticed that under the platform itself, and behind it, lay tons of cans and beer bottles—it was really messy under there. They all had a five-cent deposit on them. Okay, then, as of tomorrow, I'd bring another bag with me, and I'd climb under the platform and pick up the bottles and cans. I could keep them in my gym bag, then take them over after school to the local grocery store and redeem them. That would be some money, anyway—better than nothing.

What if I had to get an apartment? Who would rent a place to a kid who'd gotten kicked out of their parents' home? They'd probably think I was a criminal or something. And what if the landlord went through my stuff or something?

I had to keep going to my school. It was the only place that had a 92 percent scholarship rate for its graduates. That's why I was going there in the first place, and okay, if I didn't take the ROTC one or an academy appointment, there had to be other scholarships, right? I'd just have to suck it up at "home," or whatever it was, the place I was permitted to sleep and breathe, and get myself a scholarship.

The first part of my plan for the day went well enough. I got into the rather empty school building and changed, then just sat quietly in homeroom, going over my homework, studying. It was hard to pay attention, though, because I felt so nauseous, and my body just ached everywhere.

I know Sister Carlos eventually asked me about my absence note, but I don't remember what I told her. In fact, I don't really remember too much about my classes that day, because at some point, I do remember being walked by someone to the principal's office—I can't for the life of me remember what class it was, could have been English, it might even have been math (but I hope not, that would have been humiliating in front of Sister Attila)—and being led into the nurse's room.

The very next thing I do remember, though, is feeling an ache in my head and sides that was related somehow to the bitter taste in my mouth. I was lying down on my side, and for some reason I kept thinking that I had to get up to walk the dog, Ringo was waiting for me. I could hear him whining, whimpering at my door. Damn, this pillow was hard. Small, too.

If Ringo would only let me sleep a few more minutes, I'd be okay, I'd stop feeling so sick. Please, Ringo, just give me a few more minutes, I promise, I'll walk you; I just feel like such shit, Ringo, please. And I'm so cold, just a few minutes to get warm, to feel better, but the sound just wouldn't stop, and it felt like I was floating in electric blue water, like being dipped in peppermint, but the water was made of a piercing high note, and I could breathe in it if only I tried. All I had to do was try, but I was scared because I didn't think peppermint would feel good in my lungs, and I couldn't find the surface.

It occurred to me that my eyes didn't burn, so maybe this wouldn't burn my lungs either, and I was about to breathe in when I wondered, what if I change my mind? What if I want to get out of the water? But even though I was floating, I couldn't see the surface, I couldn't find it, and no matter how I moved, I couldn't float up where I thought the surface was supposed to be, I couldn't get to the air. I'd be stuck there, in that electric blue water that felt like air and stung like peppermint, and no one would know where I was.

It struck me then that my father wouldn't find me, and that made me grimly happy in a small way, relieved even, but then I realized, neither would my mother or Nicky or Nanny, even though I was sort of mad at her. But Mom didn't love me anymore, and I had to tell Nicky and Nanny that it was okay, that I was okay and I loved them, Mom too, and Dad, even though he was cranky. But I started to move and I knew there was a city at the bottom somewhere, and I didn't want to go, but I was falling, not down, but in somehow, through the water, and it was beautiful; and I knew if Samantha was there I'd stay, but Blade wasn't in the water with me, there was nobody there, why was I alone in the water?

Suddenly, I realized that if I moved any farther I'd never get back to the surface, wherever that was, and I could see the beautiful lights now, below my feet, but I couldn't see my feet so maybe it was in front of me and that was weird, and I knew that I had to share that beauty with someone. I knew with a very certain surety that Samantha would recognize those lights and want to see them, too, and Nicky, he would love it there, I knew he would. I had to go back and find them, had to bring them with me because they'd understand it. I had to get out of there, but I'd come back with people who would understand and appreciate the beauty of it.

There was a voice, and it was talking. No, it was yelling. It was me. I was telling myself to get up, Nina, get up, wake up, open your eyes, and I didn't know why I was yelling at myself, when my eyes were already open. "See, it doesn't sting your eyes," I told my silly voice, "and we can breathe, too," and I started to take a deep breath to demonstrate, but before I did a thought struck me. "Nobody cries here, you know," I said, and I thought, that was good, because I was never ever going to do that again, anyway. I was going to the beautiful place with all the lights. I could see them all now, and they were like clouds or bubbles, and they were people; they were coming to meet me, to share their beauty and their warmth with me. I could tell because I wasn't cold anymore.

Nicky would find me someday, so would Samantha, and I'd greet them when they got there, and I told them so. I was going to go wait for them and make beautiful things while I waited, and we'd all laugh about it later, because it was funny, delightful, because it felt good. I laughed in pure joy and moved forward to join the dance that was starting, no, it was ongoing, it was. There was a place for me, waiting all this time, there, a hand stretched out for mine, and I knew who it was, my friend, my dear beloved friend, my family, I was so glad, so very glad...

Now the sound was back, no, it had been there all along, and my voice was screaming at me to get up, get up, get up. "Okay, Ringo, I'm coming, I'm coming."

There was a gentle hand on my back, but it hurt where it touched, and my ribs and head ached as I opened my eyes and puked my guts up into the pail a hand held in front of my face.

"Okay, now, steady there. You'll be all right, you'll be all right..." a sister's voice soothed and she gently patted my back.

I flinched away from the touch and, finally, the gagging and outpouring stopped. The sister handed me a napkin and a paper cup with water, and I looked up to receive them, right into Sister Attila's eyes. "Thank you," I rasped out, tired, aching, and grateful.

"You're most welcome, Nina," Sister answered gently, and I took the napkin and the water, wiped my face, and drank. The water was soothingly cool as it went down my tight and hot throat. There was blood on the tissue, and as I sighted along the green leatherette chaise

I'd been lying on (you know the kind—flat, hard, rounded, one end raised about twenty degrees), I saw blood on the little pillow someone had put there for my head. "Home Sweet Home," someone had stitched in butter yellow on the blue silk, and now it was red. My nose or mouth must have started bleeding again. I was embarrassed.

I threw both the cup and the tissue into the basket, and Sister Attila removed it, then watched me as I struggled to sit up straight. I couldn't. The pain was too intense in my ribs and head but, mercifully, the nausea and dizziness were gone.

I leaned my head back against the wall. Okay, so it was math class that I'd lost track of. I eyed Sister warily while she watched me. I'd tried so hard to never show the slightest sign of weakness in her class, dammit, and that was gone now. I was sure I'd hear about this in class to no end. I could just imagine it. "Boyd, think you can stay awake this time? Perhaps you're reacting to your last exam? That would make me ill, too, I'm sure. Nauseous, even," but she said not a word for a bit, just watched me, analyzed me.

Finally, she spoke. "Are you okay, Boyd?"

Well, let's see, I was broke, homeless, disowned and disavowed, beaten and bloody, had just embarrassed myself by bleeding and puking in front of her, I think I had just spoken to God and S/He was blue water and peppermints. Did I forget something?

Oh yeah, I was gay. Grounds for excommunication, execution in older times. And the girl I was dating or whatever you want to call it (fucking just didn't really seem appropriate for me) had either been the victim of my father and Jack and Joey's lies and machinations or was the, with a capital THE, biggest bitch in the world. And my nose was broken. And maybe a few ribs. And I think I had a concussion. Does that sound okay to you? Nah, me either. I didn't say any of that, though. Concussed I might be, crazy, never.

I tried to nod, then decided against it. "Yes, Sister, thank you," I said instead. The queasiness came back, making me blink.

"Would you care to tell me what happened?"

Automatically, I went to shake my head to the negative. Mistake, big bad mistake. I swayed from my position against the wall, and Sister came over to help me (do life's little humiliations ever cease? No!).

"Never mind, Nina, just lie here a bit," she ordered softly, putting the little pillow back in place for me with a little tissue over it, so I wouldn't have to lie in my own blood again. "I'm going to see if the principal, Sister Clarence, has gotten in touch with your mother."

"Please, don't call my mother," I said as she left the little room, and I don't know if she heard me or not. I closed my eyes, and seconds later both sisters had come into the room. I sat up as best I could on my own, so I could pay proper attention. They stood before me.

"I've spoken with your mother, Nina." Sister Clarence spoke first. Her expression was very serious and she didn't seem pleased. I could only wonder what my mother had said. "It seems that there's no one available to pick you up, and even were we to send you home in a car, there's no one there to watch you…" She let that hang in the air, her expression concerned and puzzled as well. I'd been sent home from school before when I'd been sick, and that had never been a problem, and Sister Clarence knew that. As the principal, she'd been the one to send me home.

Sister Attila's brow furrowed in concentration as well. "She can't just stay here till the end of day, and we can't put her on the bus at that time…hmm…" She spoke softly and stroked her chin in thought. She turned to Sister Clarence. "Clarence, I have an idea. If you'll excuse us, Boyd." She nodded at me, and they stepped out, closing the door behind them.

I couldn't really hear what they said, but I knew whatever they were discussing, it would put the needs of the school first—couldn't have improprieties, I knew. But I was starting to feel sick and sleepy again, so I wasn't going to worry about it more. I put my head down. The next thing I knew, Sister Clarence was helping me sit up and put my coat on. I couldn't really focus; her words were swimming in and out, and I couldn't see very clearly. Something was on my left eye, weighing it down, making the lids heavy. A bar or something was in front of it.

"Okay, Nina, the seniors get out early today…" I lost the rest of that statement as I stood, "walk you down—"

"No, Sister, I'm fine," I protested. "I can walk, really, I'm okay." I didn't understand her, really. The seniors were going to escort me down the hill? Was this an exit party? In that case I didn't want company.

In the end, Sister Clarence walked me out of the school and to the main door, where a black car stood waiting. Sister had carried my book bag and gym bag, someone took them from her and placed them in the trunk, while someone else opened the back door and let me in. I put my head down right away. I had no energy left for anything else, and my head was painful and heavy.

"Keep her with you, keep an eye on her until you can get in touch with her parents at home. Then see what they want to do." I heard Sister Attila's voice faintly through the window. I heard Sister Clarence add something, but I couldn't hear what it was. The roar in my head was too loud; then very clearly, I heard, "I'll do whatever is necessary, Sister."

It was Samantha, I was in Samantha's car, and suddenly I could fill in the blanks to what Sister Clarence had been trying to tell me. The seniors got out early today; they were sending me home with Samantha until someone could take me home, so that way there'd be someone to keep an eye on me. I didn't think I needed anyone's eye on me, though; I thought I just needed a nap. And maybe a new life. Could I get a do-over?

Samantha got in and the door closed with a thump that jarred my whole body and made my teeth bounce. I must have made a sound, because Samantha softly apologized as we pulled out. "I'm sorry, Nina, I didn't mean to hurt you."

"Samantha, Sammy," I singsonged from my perch on the car door. "I'm A-OK, you can just drop me off at the train, I'll be fine."

"Okay, later. I think I'll do what Sister Clarence asked first, though, if that's all right by you, okay?" she asked me, and I could hear the smile in her voice. That made me feel good, and I closed my eyes again.

The next thing I knew, I heard the trunk opening and closing, and a few moments later, the back door was opening. "Must be one hell of a flu you've got there, Razor," Samantha was saying as the door swung wide. "I knew you should've gotten some rest last night. You gave it all in the pool last night, I—" she broke off with a gasp, "guess," she finished softly, staring.

I'd finally sat up, and Samantha could really see for herself what I looked like. I suppose the nuns had just told her I was sick, so she wouldn't worry unnecessarily.

My head throbbed as I looked back at her through my right eye. The left just didn't want to work for some reason; it wouldn't open more than a crack. "I caught the flu with my head," I tried to joke and smile, but smiling hurt my face.

"You sure did," she tried to joke back. "C'mon, let's go inside, okay?" Samantha urged gently, and she smiled at me, but her eyes looked large and frightened. And even with the smile, the corners of her mouth were tight, like I'd seen them get before when she was angry, and I was now much more familiar with what she looked like that way.

"Are you mad at me?" I asked her cautiously, because I wasn't sure anymore, not of her, not of anyone, and I was better off finding out sooner rather than later. "I'm sorry Sister made you drive me," I apologized as I struggled out of the car. Samantha caught me around the shoulders and walked me up the flagstones to the steps that led to her front door.

"I volunteered, Nina," she informed me softly as she opened the door and guided me in. I noticed my book and gym bags were right by the door as we walked in; she must have brought them in for me, I thought vaguely as she guided me past one room, through another, and up some stairs.

"Here, lie down," she ordered gently, and I did. I have some fuzzy recollections of Samantha helping me get changed, helping me get my shoes off, stuff like that. I remember I was very reluctant to lift my arms because of the pain, and Samantha gasped when she saw my ribs.

A soft, clean white T-shirt floated down over my head and arms, covering my torso, and as I lay down, Samantha asked me in a whisper, "Who did this, Nina. What happened?"

My eyes were closing as my head touched the pillow. "It's okay, Samantha, it's not a big deal," I tried to tell her, "it was just, you know, a disagreement." It's not that I was trying to blow Samantha off; it was just that I was feeling sick again, and I didn't want to go into the whole thing right now. That hurt much more than just my body to think about.

Samantha tried again, "Oh Nina, your beautiful hair…what about your parents? Do they know?" She ran a soft fingertip along the exposed skin above and in front of my ear. "Have you told them? Did anyone call the cops?"

That got me, and I tried to laugh bitterly but failed; the sharp pains across my ribs prevented me. "Yeah, they know, they know all about it, and they don't care," I told her. I was drifting again, and I could feel fresh breezes make their way across my face, like a perfect summer's day. A thought struck me, and I spoke aloud without realizing it. "My mom, she doesn't hit like a girl."

"Baby, that's just not possible," Samantha whispered, still stroking the one part of my body that didn't make me grit my teeth. I could hear the shock in her voice, and a trace of the anger I was starting to recognize. "Sleep, Nina. I'm right here, rest a bit, okay?" I felt her lips softly touch the bare skin I'd shaved that morning.

Someone was calling my name, and there was a dance I was supposed to be part of. I had to get there, the call was irresistible, and I didn't have too much energy to stay to talk. My eyes were closed, but I saw stars and bright fields and clear blue water. In the middle of the field stood a huge stone, big enough to climb, big enough to comfortably hold six people, a dog, and a picnic, and I knew that it would be a perfect place to watch the stars from.

It was striated, weathered, and worn, and I could tell that it had been dumped there a long time ago, after the earth had cooled then warmed again. The weather came and went, but still that stone remained, cracked and unlovely, yes, but still looking at the stars.

"I'm a rock, Samantha," I said dreamily, and I smiled.

Chapter Twelve:
A Sort of Homecoming

Someone was crying—not sobbing hysterically, but the kind of crying you do when you're helpless and there's nothing left to be done and tears are useless, but you can't stop them. It wasn't me, I knew. I wasn't doing that anymore.

I felt a soothing, cool pressure on my face, and I realized I was lying on my side. I still hurt all over, but there was a clarity to the pain, not the disorienting twisting and half awareness that I'd had before.

I raised a hand to my face and encountered a cool, damp washcloth over my head and left eye, so I gently removed it and opened them—both of them. The left one was still sore, but at least there was light, and it was good.

The first thing I noticed was the light streaming in through the blinds covering the windows about ten feet away. The walls were a light yellow, and the rug across the floor was a tawny beige. About three feet from the foot of the bed was the door that led out to a hallway; if I tilted my head a bit, I could see stairs that went down. To the right of the door was a desk, with a pile of books and a few small pennants, and on the wall was, of all things, a *Love and Rockets* poster, and next to that, a Led Zeppelin one—you know the one, with the angels being cast out of heaven? I looked at the pennants on the desk again; they were from school.

Samantha, I realized, I was in Samantha's room and I still heard soft crying, and it was above my head somehow. No, it was a little off to my right and behind me. I stretched my neck in that direction, and against the wall, all curled up in a wicker chair, blue-denimed knees to her chest and arms wrapped around them, head buried, was Samantha. It was Samantha crying, and somehow that hurt me more than anything.

"Samantha?" I tried, but my voice was so faint I could hardly hear it myself. Uck. My mouth and throat felt like I'd been sucking on sand. I had a faint image of cool electric blue and peppermint. I could use that now, I thought wryly.

I shifted onto my elbow and, reaching a hand out, placed it on Samantha's arm. "Don't cry, Samantha, please," I asked her. "It's okay." My throat was still raw, and I could still taste blood in the back of my mouth, but at least I was now audible, and I knew that because Samantha raised her head to look at me. Of course, it could have been my hand on her arm, but I like to think that she could hear me.

Samantha had wiped her face on her sleeve, but I could still tell she'd been crying because it made her eyes luminous. She unfolded herself and came over to kneel at the edge of the bed. She caught my hand up in hers and pressed it to her face. Her skin was so very soft and warm under my hand, and I was again struck with that feeling of familiarity, of home.

Samantha kissed my palm, then just held my hand tightly between her own. "How are you feeling?" she asked me very softly, concern etched in every corner of her face as her eyes inspected mine.

"Better," I answered, "much, much better." I sat up farther, my hand still held between Samantha's, and I carefully swung my legs over the edge of the bed, patting the space on the right next to me in invitation. Samantha needed no further urging and came up on the bed, maneuvering cautiously, until her back leaned against the wall.

She held her arms out for me, and I went into them willingly, trying to find a way to rest my bruised cheek on her shoulder without it hurting so much. I finally found a spot, with my forehead against her neck, and brought my knees up a bit as Samantha created a warm wall against my back with her legs.

Samantha brought both arms around me and rested both hands on my shoulder, which seemed to be the only place that didn't hurt, and I laced my arms around her waist. She rested her head against the wall, while I felt her body rise and fall in time with her breath. I rested comfortably like that for a while, then Samantha kissed the top of my head. "You don't have to go back there."

I took a deep breath, considering. "Yes, I do," I said resignedly. "I really, truly do." I let the breath out.

"Why, Nina? Why in the world would you have to, would you want to?" Samantha's voice was confused, exasperated, and I disentangled myself from our embrace and moved over a bit so I could speak with her directly, face-to-face.

Samantha was all concentration and focus as she looked back at me.

"I can't let them win," I told her simply, "I just can't. Besides, they'll have me sent to jail."

"What?" she asked incredulously. "What do you mean?"

I took a deep breath, mentally girded myself to relive the late-night events, and launched into a semiedited version of the story. I left out as much of the physical stuff as possible, and my father's speech as well, although Samantha did ask me to explain what had happened to my face specifically, and my back and ribs. She had helped me to change, after all, and had seen some nasty-looking contusions along my torso.

I also left out the insights I'd had about the mountains—they just didn't seem appropriate, somehow. "And so, if I can do that, I'll earn their respect. That's what I have left," I finished, "theirs, grudgingly, and my own, intact."

Samantha was absolutely livid. Her face was stark white with rage, and instead of the tight, thin line I was getting used to her mouth becoming in anger, she was practically snarling. Her eyes snapped with crystal fire, so light they were almost colorless, and she'd clutched the edge of the bed with such strength that the tendons in her hand stood out in sharp relief.

"You, after all that," she paused, "have to earn their respect? Your whole life on the line, you keep your integrity intact, and you have to earn their respect? Their respect," and she said the word with contempt, "should mean nothing. They don't deserve you, not your love, not your respect, not your care or your time, Nina.

"They're going to make your life hell for nothing, Nina, and it's going to be almost impossible for you to make it. Stay here with me. I'll talk with my uncle. It won't be a problem."

I shook my head no. "Legally, they're responsible for me, and if they can make up shit to have me jailed, what do you think they'll say about you? Or your uncle? They can say he's harboring a criminal, a minor. They can accuse him of kidnapping…"

It was starting to hit me. They really could do that—just call the cops, say I'd stolen something, or, holy shit, I'd forgotten—what if my father hadn't lied? He was a manipulator, true, but he wasn't really a liar, except when he wanted me to be one, apparently.

What if Kerry had really said that? Oh my God, if I wanted to leave, I would really have to be homeless, a street person, so no one could find me, and how long could I live like that? Even if I sold everything I had, it wouldn't be enough. I'd have to run and keep running, because I'd be thrown in jail for one thing or another. And God forbid I broke the law; then I'd be everything they'd said I was. My blood ran cold, so cold I started to shake.

"Nina, what is it? You've gone absolutely white. What's going on? Should I call the doctor?" Samantha lunged forward and caught my shoulders, and I was shaking so hard, I could only stare at her in utter horror. Because I couldn't lie, because it was wrong to do that, I was going to jail, or I was going to die, or both.

"No, no doctor, that's not it," I finally managed. "It's just, they can really do this. They can really, truly, do this." My voice strangled.

Samantha stroked my hair to calm me down, and I admit, it helped, a lot. I felt my heart return to a somewhat normal pace, and warmth flowed from her fingertips down my head.

"Do what, Nina? What can they do, huh?" She gathered me into her embrace again, and I held on to her as if she were the only thing between me and the void. In some ways, she was. Cuddled up again, and safe for a little while, I told Samantha the whole thing this time, including my father's accusation that had supposedly come from Kerry, and his threats and visions for my future in juvenile hall.

I felt Samantha stiffen in anger next to me, and her breathing, though forceful, was very even and controlled. She held me tighter, almost crushing me. "Sam," I protested, "that hurts."

"God, I'm sorry," she apologized immediately, and loosed her hold a bit. "Better?"

"Much, thanks," I answered and sighed. I was all out of words, all out of feelings, and it seemed like I was out of options, as well.

Why had I told the truth, anyway? Was it really such a big deal? I had a whole world of possibilities open to explore and, since I wasn't locked into being an officer in the army or the navy anymore, everything to look forward to.

All I had to do was agree about one little thing, such a minor aspect of an entire personality. But it wasn't such a little thing, was it? I mean, look at what had happened. Sure, I'd been physically disciplined before, but never like this. Ironically enough, I'd been disciplined severely as a child for once telling some sort of stupid little lie that children tell, because I had wanted to please my parents, and this time, it had been for honesty, for a truth that didn't please them.

And I couldn't understand it, either. Up until a few months ago, the beginning of summer actually, my parents had both always been tolerant. They'd never said anything about gay people, except that everyone was different, amen. Until my dad had changed, I mean. What was up with that, anyway?

What if I just went back to them, told them I'd been temporarily confused? They'd love me, they'd care for me, my parents, I mean, if I just went along. But I couldn't. I'd know the truth, and I'd never really trust them again, if they were happy to live with a lie. And I couldn't live with them knowing that they loved me under false pretenses, that they really, deep at the heart of it, thought I was flawed, less than human.

Funny, I didn't feel flawed. I didn't think anything was really wrong with me—not before, and not now. Maybe a little stupid sometimes, but not flawed.

No. It became crystal clear to my mind. They were wrong, because if they weren't, then everything they'd told me and taught me before was a lie. No, it dawned on me, they were hypocrites, which was even worse, because it meant they pretended to live up to ideals and principles, just mouthed them, didn't really mean them or practice them.

But I did, and that's why they were so mad, because I showed them their values were false, and mine were the genuine article, the real deal. I was—what was I? I was authentic! That's it! Authentic! But the knowledge was a cold and lonely thing, knowing what the future held, and I shared those thoughts with Samantha.

"I've always known that," she said, with a slight smile that came through in her voice, and she kissed the top of my head. "That's the very thing that I, um," she faltered, "admire about you."

My heart smiled at that. I'd heard what she said and what she meant.

"I don't see why we can't work something out, why you can't stay here," Samantha said softly, still gently stroking my hair. "There has to be some way to make it work, legally, I mean."

I pulled back a bit to look her in the eye, directly. "Samantha, legally I'm chattel, possessions, goods, and as long as they don't kill me or do anything outrageous, like permanently maim me, they can do whatever the hell they want," I told her. "They'd have to voluntarily give up their rights to me, and that's not going to happen." My mouth twisted in a bitter smile. "That," I said, "would make them look bad. They want to punish me, break me, not look bad to the neighbors." I thought of "Aunt Kathy" bitterly.

"Believe me when I tell you," Samantha said fervently, "they look pretty bad already."

I smiled, carefully because my mouth hurt, but still a smile, grateful for the support. But I sobered quickly enough. It would have been lovely, perfect even, if I could just quit worrying about my parents and stay with Samantha. That was even more tempting, but I knew it couldn't happen. I had to live the life handed to me, just as Samantha had to live hers, and I knew I had to face this on my own, to know for myself whether or not I could be broken. I was scared and angry, but I was determined, too, to overcome, in my own way.

I'd just have to be the "family's" living reminder of what honor and integrity really are, set an example for Nicky and Nanny so that one day, when they needed to stand up for something, they'd know how. "You know, Sam," I said thoughtfully, "I'm really going to just have to suck it up and tough it out until I can leave. They hold all the cards. The only thing they don't control is my mind."

Samantha was not at all happy with my decision and was vehement in her responses. "God, Nina, they could have killed you!" she practically yelled, pacing the confines of the room. "There has to be another way!" She ran her hands through her hair and just stared at me, considering. "I don't suppose you're going to decide to just go with it, with them, and just suck it up that way?" She watched me carefully, obviously waiting for a response.

I rubbed my face, then dropped my hands into my lap. I just looked down to collect my thoughts, then back at Samantha. "Who am I?"

"What do you mean?" Samantha said, her expression puzzled. My question had thrown her off.

"I mean," I said slowly, "who am I? Am I Nina? Razor? Kerry calls me," and I smiled at myself in self-derision, "Hopey. Am I a student? An athlete? A musician? A faggot? Stupid? Crazy? Smart? You see, there's a lot of names and words out there, and I've got this stupid idea that maybe one word just isn't enough, that there's this me that exists, an identity sort of, that doesn't have a name. It's just, well, me," I started earnestly. Oh, this was coming out all wrong, but Samantha just nodded at me to continue.

"I'm not saying that I believe or not in a soul or something like that," I said. "It's just that before I had a name given to me, by my parents, school, friends, the world," and I smiled a bit, because I knew most of the names the world held for me weren't complimentary, "there was, there is, this me, this self, and that self wants to be, just be, and if I deny it, then, somehow, it's like I'm being unfaithful to it or disloyal, or, or…" I searched for the words to describe how I felt, what I meant, and I hardly knew truly what I was saying, just that I really meant it.

"Samantha, if I have to lie about something fundamental about myself, to the people who are most important to me, then it's like I'm killing something, something important. It's like I'll never be real again. It would be the same if I had to pretend I didn't care about music, or my family, or…" and I paused, stunned by the enormity of the realization, "or you," I finished softly.

And that's what denying meant, I realized. It meant that I could never really feel, never really love, never know if I was loved or if all the words of love, affection, and loyalty were true or not, because I'd always know that mine were false because I wasn't giving of myself totally. I couldn't in return expect or even hope for that same totality, and it meant I'd have no true connections, because mine weren't complete—at least not with those I wanted to be connected. Who cares about strangers, right? Right.

Samantha's expression during my little speech was one of interest, until I reached the last part. Her eyes opened wide and she hugged me again. "I wouldn't want you to not feel that," she said softly, "and I really don't want you to lie either."

I returned the hug and simply rested my head on her shoulder. Hey, I was taller than I thought! My eyes were level with her ear, well, sort of.

For the rest of the afternoon until Samantha took me home (she lent me a pair of jeans and a sweatshirt; it was weird hanging out in my underwear and her T-shirt, and I wasn't going to sleep any more), we talked, cuddled, and talked some more, going over solutions, avenues of probability, that sort of thing.

At one point I did ask her, "Does your uncle know? Did your dad? About, you know," I hesitated, this was still new territory, "you, and all that?"

By this time, we were sitting on the floor, backs up against the bed, just chilling (and I know, I know, me and floors, what can I say? It's just a thing with me and my friends, I guess. Maybe I'm just trying to be "grounded"), talking, whatever, and Samantha laughed at my question.

"Actually, yeah," she said with a smile. "My dad told me, before I was going to tell him, that he didn't care who I brought home when I decided when and who I was ready to date, just so long as he or she," and she stressed the words, "was a decent person."

"Really?" I asked dryly, and Samantha grinned a bit more.

"Actually, he said, 'that there Fran, she likes you now, right?' and I just stared at him in shock because I wasn't even sure." Samantha chuckled.

"So? What did you do?" This was interesting. I mean, I'd never really heard of anyone having a cool parent or parents before, at least when it comes to this sort of thing, ya know?

"I, um, I mumbled something about not being sure of that, and my dad just laughed, clapped me on the shoulder, and said some things were universal and don't worry about it, actually." She grinned up at me.

"That's a cool thing, truly." I had met her late father at a few of our meets. He had been a kindly sort of man, very salt-of-the-earth type, and I could just hear him saying that. "And what about your uncle?"

Samantha blushed. "Um, he asked me if my father and I had had the talk, you know?" she looked at me, cheeks glowing, "and I said, uh, yeah, but it probably wasn't what he thought it was. So he said he figured my father would have covered it, and he was pretty sure that he could handle anything I had to ask, because he figured I wouldn't really need to worry about the, um, birth control thing." Samantha flushed a deeper shade of red. "And that he didn't know if he could give me any truly helpful advice, because I probably knew more about women than he did, but at least he might be able to help me out in tricky situations, because he liked to think that because he was a little older, he might be a little wiser, that sort of thing."

I laughed, because it was funny, and because it was probably true, and after a moment or two, Samantha laughed with me. My face didn't hurt so much anymore, and I was starting to experience freedom of movement again. I stretched experimentally, to get some of the kinks and the soreness out.

The sun was going down. It was definitely time to go home and comply with the new world order. I wasn't 100 percent sure of what my next moves would be, but I knew one thing for sure: I was at least going to graduate from my high school and not any other, no matter what I had to do, as long as I didn't compromise my own ethics.

Samantha drove me home, and on the way we made plans. I was going to skip swim practice until Saturday, then after practice and detention, she was going to teach me how to drive; that would be a start on the road to independence. One thing we both managed to agree on: knowledge was power, and the school I was going to would give me the best education I could get, pretty much anywhere. Throwing that away was out of the question, and Samantha wasn't thrilled with the idea of my crawling around the train tracks, but she could at least see where it would be helpful, in my quest for funds, anyway.

I'd also decided that the very next morning, I would go into Sister Clarence's office, explain that there was a financial difficulty, and that I would be paying my own tuition. Maybe she'd be able to work something out with me, and I shared that thought with Samantha as well as we approached my street.

"Hey, now when we polish banisters together, I'll be the one on detention, and you'll be actually working," she teased.

"Hey, yeah, maybe I'll never have to do detentions again!" I grinned back. We'd been lucky that day, since we'd had detention given to us the day before by Sister Attila, but very obviously, circumstances outside of her control had excused us from that. We probably wouldn't be quite as lucky the next day, but, hey, stranger things could happen, right?

I was feeling fine, like everything would be okay, until we pulled into my block. Then my stomach kicked me with a double dose of anger and fear, and I can honestly tell you, it was the anger that got stronger, until the fear went back into its corner to hide.

We pulled onto the corner and I released my seat belt as Samantha parked the car. "You gonna be okay?" she asked with concern. "You can come stay with me, at least for a few days, you know, if you don't want to stay longer," she reminded me, placing a hand on my shoulder.

I sighed and nodded affirmatively. "I'll keep that in mind, in case they get crazy, okay? If something happens, maybe they won't have a strong case for the cops if they beat me up two days in a row, and then, well, that's a whole 'nother story."

"Are you sure? I think we might have a case now," she said softly. "Nina, you don't know what you look like. I don't want to see you hurt further." She ran a gentle hand along the side of my head that was now skin and short fuzz. "I'm scared for you," she whispered intently. I don't think she meant me to hear that.

I caught her hand up and kissed the palm, holding it between mine. "Sammy, I'm scared, too. But I have to try. I have to face them, at least once. If I don't, I'll just let fear win. I'll be running away, and then I'll be running away forever. I can't live like that. Believe me," and my eyes pleaded with intensity for her understanding, "if anything happens, I'll call you right away, I promise."

"What if something happens and you can't run, Nina?" Samantha asked with real worry. "What if you can't call?"

I hadn't thought of that possibility, and now I knew why. "It won't happen again, Sam, not like that. I won't let it." I smiled grimly. "I let it this time, because I felt I owed my parents respect, and that they wouldn't do such things. Believe me, I will not," I paused for emphasis, "let myself be touched like that again. I swear."

Samantha looked very uncertain and said as much. "How can you be sure?"

Her face was the very definition of doubt and concern, and I wanted to reassure her that I meant it. I'd suffer the parental units' shit if I had to, but I would never allow them to harm me again. "Samantha, remember your freshman year?"

"Yeah?" she drawled out and cocked an eyebrow at me.

"Do you remember what was required besides Latin?" I hinted, trying to jog her memory. Freshman year was a year no one could ever forget, though I'm sure plenty of therapists are out there making an entire living from those trying. And yes, Latin was among one of the many required subjects for all freshmen, because it would "help us with our English and other language studies," and dammit—the nuns were right—again. Sigh. Oh, wait, can "nun" and "dammit" coexist in the same sentence? Too late, oh well.

"We had Latin, Afro-Asian studies, oh!" Samantha brightened up suddenly as the realization hit her. "Everyone had to take judo/self-defense with what's her name, from that federation!" Samantha nodded her head, "Yeah!" and grinned.

Yeah is right. Like I said way back before, all freshmen had to take judo/self-defense; it didn't matter whether the student was a jock or not, and no excuses about asthma. The thought was that every woman should know how to defend herself (never mind the fact that the uniform made us a target), and our class was taught by the woman who took judo and women in martial arts to the Olympics. (You can look her up if you're into that sort of thing—just search under "judo" and "Olympic history"—you'll find her).

She taught us how to drop, roll, throw, take a punch, and use our size to our advantage—she was incredible! And she also taught us that if we knew how to defend ourselves, we'd never feel helpless, no matter what happened. You know what? She was right.

But the grin faded from Samantha's face. "Are you sure you're going to be able to take that on?" she asked me seriously. "That's a lot of responsibility…" She trailed off, obviously watching my reactions, waiting for my reply.

I nodded firmly in agreement. "Yeah, if I'm pushed to defend myself, I'm ready to be responsible for the outcome," I said very solemnly. That was something they had impressed upon us from the start, that once we'd tried all other options and physicality was the only avenue open, then possibly someone could and would get hurt, and there was no telling to what depth the injury might go.

This was a very serious thing, and I did not then and do not now take violence lightly. In fact, I'm a lover, not a fighter, but if my life was at stake…I took a deep breath. I was scared, but prepared. Samantha seemed a little reassured, but not much.

The little voice in my head interrupted my concentration, and the fear came out of its corner to reassert itself. It could happen again, really, couldn't it? What if I was sleeping? I shared a room with Nanny;

my dad could just open the door—undo the lock. It wasn't hard. I'd done it myself, plenty of times. They could, possibly, just come into the room, do whatever they wanted. And it wasn't like I could stay awake all day and all night. I had to recover from the meet, from the beating, from being ill, and I had to be able to do all of my activities.

My mind raced for solutions because I wasn't going to let fear rule me, or Samantha, either. An idea came to mind, and I squeezed her hand again. "Samantha, listen. If I'm not in school for whatever reason tomorrow, and you can't get in touch with me here, then…" I took a breath then let it out, "tell whoever you think you need to tell whatever you think they need to know, and call the cops, 'cause in that case, I'm in real trouble."

Samantha nodded and returned the pressure on my hand. "Okay, if I don't see you before homeroom starts, I'll call you first, then, honestly, Nina? I'm gonna call my uncle and the cops. Cort knows a thing or two about a thing or two, and," she paused and smiled darkly, "he's pretty big, too."

Great. I was a touch relieved; at least someone would know there was a body to go look for. Why lie? I was scared. I didn't want to go back there. Like I said before, I'd been disciplined, sure, but never a wholesale knockdown like that before, never anything that had left me both bruised and bleeding. Not to mention broken.

My face was starting to ache again, and my head was pounding in time with it. I wasn't sure if I was mentally or physically able to withstand another onslaught like the night before, and despite my words to the contrary, I didn't really know what self-defense meant.

"Samantha, if you need to do that, go right ahead. Do what you have to do." I released Samantha's hand, grabbed my stuff from the backseat, hauled it over, and put my hand on the latch. "But I don't think it'll be necessary." I smiled as reassuringly as I could, which wasn't much, because the corner of my mouth was scabbing up. Nasty, nasty feeling. Definitely on the bad list. Oh yeah, I have a list—several, in fact: the good list, the bad list, the hit list, and the shit list. Everything has its place, ya know.

"Thank you, for helping me out today," I told her softly. "I will always appreciate this."

Samantha caught my hand in hers again and kissed it. "I will always be there for you," she swore, and we gave each other one last long hug before I got out of the car and trudged to the door.

I didn't even look back because if I did, I was afraid my resolve to see this through one way or another would break, and I couldn't bear the look in Samantha's eyes. I could feel her watching me.

You want to know what happened next, right? You're probably thinking, hey, she dumped that Kerry chick on her ass and had it out with everyone, then everything settled back down to something resembling normal, because Nina decided she couldn't live without Samantha, and the deities intervened, and they lived together forever and ever, amen, and they got wonderful jobs in some wonderful company and bought a house that they live in and have hot monkey sex when they're not busy being heroes and saving the world from evildoers.

No. Wrong.

Although I like the hot-monkey-sex part. And the deities (such as they are) remain uninvolved. And heroes are people like Gandhi and Martin Luther King, or even Joan of Arc, and people who are everyday people trying to be better, make it all better, no radiated spiders giving anyone special powers or swords to be swung, Joan notwithstanding, of course. But—and this is important—she burned at the stake rather than deny her own truth. That's a powerful thing, truth. Now *that's* punk.

And heroes are those, big and small, who strive every day just to live, to be themselves and make the world a little better just by being around. You know these people. They're friends. Teachers. Doctors. Lawyers. The nice lady at the insurance company who goes out of her way to help you out, even though you don't know her mother is sick, her kids are driving her mad, and she just discovered her division is being outsourced. And the guy at work who tells the boss he didn't appreciate a bigoted joke that was made. These things only seem small, but they aren't—they require goodness of heart and bravery—and the effects of these actions ripple outward. These are the people that are heroes, and if you really think about it, you might be one too.

That night, after a silent dinner (which I made, by the way) and a few hours of homework and guitar playing, deep in the dark of the night when everyone was asleep, I got dragged out of bed by the hair compliments of my former incubator and thrown on the floor again, though this time it was in the hallway and under the bright light that hurt my not-fully-awakened eyes. She and the sperm donor pulled my hair and shook me around, trying to rub my face into the top steps because I hadn't completed some household chore.

Quite honestly, I don't even know what it was—I was still out of it—but when macho man lifted me by my shirt and threw me against the wall right by the top of the steps, I was suddenly aware of something. I had both arms up having blocked a punch coming for my face and had just stopped my foot from smashing the source of my origin—namely, his balls. The cotton of his pajama bottoms was warm on my bare foot, and I could just feel the weight of his pride. Yuck, actually.

I was horrified, my father, Daddy, I'd almost hit Daddy. God, Daddy, and we all froze in shock. My father's face was bewildered, my mother's scared, and I was terrified at this capacity I had discovered within myself.

They both kept screaming at me about their disappointment. They were disappointed with me? They were the disappointment because they lied. Love was conditional, acceptance was something done at a distance, removed from the immediate environment, and brutality was evil, unless they practiced it. They wanted me to be just like them. It was enough to make me weep.

And despite everything, they were my parents, and I loved them. I couldn't stop that, couldn't help it. Daddy, who had taught me to swim and to fish, how to ride a bicycle, who used to just swing me up in the air and put me on his shoulders so I could see the parade or the fireworks or touch the leaves from the trees and who had given me my first microscope and chemistry sets, had played with me, laughed when my little Bunsen burner set the table on fire or I'd exploded something—again. Daddy, with his strong arms and warm hugs, who said we'd never be too big for him to cuddle. I'd almost hit him, and I hadn't meant to—how could I hit Daddy?

I was furious with them, furious with myself, and I realized I grieved, too, because I couldn't understand how it had all come to this, screaming and flailing in the hallway in the middle of the night, a family of strangers.

I lowered my leg to the ground and stood up straight against the wall at the top of the stairs, arms and fists in a defensive posture, as tears of rage and frustration poured out of my eyes. I could feel the rush of blood in my head and neck, could taste it in my mouth, and I realized another cut had broken open again.

"I'm sorry, I'm so sorry, Daddy. Don't make me do this," I begged my father, my voice thick and harsh. "I don't want to do this, I don't.

You're my father, I don't want this," I cried, while the tears flowed hot and fat down my face, and I hated that, because I couldn't stop them, because I hated doing it, and grief and fury combined are too powerful a force to be halted.

Nanny came out of our room; the commotion had woken her up. "I hate you, Nina. You're ruining this family!" she screamed at me from our doorway.

My mother said nothing, just watched me and my father with frightened eyes, and I turned to look at Nanny. "That's not—" true, I had started to say, but my father's left hand caught my face, and my shoulders spun as my head snapped to the side. I caught myself before I went headfirst down the stairs entirely, one foot on the landing, one down the first stair.

I heard the door to Nicky's room open, and I turned my head. I thought I saw his face as my mother screamed, "Roger! Don't!" but too late, he swung again.

Faster than it takes to tell, my right arm was up and blocking, and I grabbed the wrist and twisted, bringing it down and behind him, while I threw the left side of my body up and in, my shoulder crashing into his sternum, the momentum carrying us into the opposite wall, away from the stairs. I quickly shifted weight from one shoulder to the other, my right hand still holding the twisted wrist, my thumb digging into the pressure point and drew my left arm back.

"Nina, don't!" Nicky whispered from the door, and my fist came to a full-force stop less than a centimeter before his nose.

The angle we were at had his face level with mine, and I looked into his eyes forever. I refused to take my gaze off the man who had just tried to send me flying down a flight of steps.

"Stay out of this, Nicky," I told him from the corner of my mouth where the blood ran freely again. "Macho man, beating on girls," I hissed into this stranger, my father's face, contorted in surprise and anger, with an expression in his eyes I'd never seen before, not more than five inches from my eyes. "Touch me like that again, old man, and I will fucking kill you," I growled. "I will be only too fuckin' happy to stab you in your goddamned fuckin' sleep." My blood spattered a little onto his face. Blood of my blood. I hated that too, hated that he was half of who I was.

"Who's gonna fuckin' stop me, you little piece of shit bitch?" he hissed back. He tried to move, but I jammed my shoulder harder into his. He grunted when he hit the wall again.

"I will," I told him very evenly. I released him and took a step back, nodding my head up and down as if I suddenly had a clue.

Free, El Testostero rubbed his pained wrist, while my eyes swept the hallway.

Nanny was crying, "I hate you, Nina, I hate you," in the doorway of our room, but Nicky had come out to stand next to our mother as she stood and stared at me; I read sorrow on her face.

My father just glared up at me, wishing me incinerated and gone with his gaze.

I stood up straight, while Nanny closed the door to our room. "Try that again, and see what happens. I'm not just some defenseless little girl," I told him. "You made sure of that." I walked past my mother to my bedroom door. "Oh, by the way?" I said conversationally, as I put my hand on the doorknob—I noticed it had been practically destroyed in the unlocking—before I turned to look at them both. They hadn't moved from their positions at all, except for their eyes, which were following me. "If I don't show up at school tomorrow or any other day? It doesn't matter if you call or not. If there's no contact with me directly, the cops will come here." I opened the door and started to make my way in.

"Cops'll come and get you, bitch, and then you'll go to fuckin' juvie hall where you belong," my father threatened.

The door was wide-open and in the light that flooded in to the room from the hallway, I could see Nanny sit up in her bed. I stopped and turned around in the entrance. "Look at me, look at my fucking face," I said with strength. "See this?" and I lifted up my shirt, so they could see the dark splotches on my ribs. I heard Nanny gasp as she saw them, and Nicky winced and turned his head. I didn't blame him. "You tell them what you want, and I'll show them the truth. I've got evidence on my side—what have you got?" I challenged, lifting my chin.

"I've got Kerry, you twisted little shit," my father spat out in angry triumph.

My mother gasped and went pale as I dropped my shirt and took a step forward, hands knotted at my sides. "You've got nothing," I hissed back, "nothing. You forget, I have friends, too, and they tell a different story," I reminded him. "And I'm sure there are plenty of people who can vouch for my character, my honor. Who's going to vouch for a man," and my mouth twisted with disdain, "who allows or causes his own flesh-and-blood child to be harmed like this?" I spread my arms to indicate my body, "or would rather see his child beaten and raped than possibly be gay? What honor do you have?" I asked him contemptuously. "And all because you're afraid of what the *neighbors*," I emphasized the word with heavy sarcasm, "might say."

"You little…" he started and took a step toward me.

"Now wait a moment," I cautioned him. "I can't really tell what I'm capable of doing in self-defense. I'm feeling a little edgy, a little crazy now." I started to bounce, just a little on the balls of my feet, and it was true. I was feeling a little out of control, and energy was curling in my stomach the way it did before a game or a swim meet.

I was trying to handle it, but the force was bouncing wildly in my chest and arms and legs, like a caged tiger leaping at the bars of its cage and smashing its head over and over again against my heart, pushing to the breaking point so it could burst free.

"You know, those judo classes, they just ingrain themselves in you somehow, just like you said they would." I had a responsibility for the outcome, I told myself over and over; warn your opponent, warn your opponent.

He stopped in his tracks and just watched me.

"Here's the deal," I said, pausing to look at him and then my mother. "I will follow your rules, I will comply with your ridiculous demands. However, I will not change who I am or lie to please you or anyone else. You *will* respect me. Touch me again, and I swear you better make sure you kill me, hide the body, and tell everyone you sent me to boarding school in South America, because I have people ready to call the cops on both of you. That'll look great." I smiled grimly. "You'll get arrested for child abuse. You can explain that at the next PTA or block association meeting."

My mother's face went blank, and she looked at me in a way she never had before. Well, I guess it was just a week of firsts, all around. She was actually taking my measure.

I turned back into the doorway. "And one more thing." I paused and turned again. "No, wait. Two more. First, Dad," and I laced the word with heavy sarcasm, "I think you lied. I think at most maybe Nicky said something about how Kerry and I get along, or maybe something along the lines of how you've picked the wrong Boyd she'd be more likely interested in, and you just twisted it up."

His face was angry still, but his mouth became a thin flat line—
and I knew then, for sure, not just that gut surety from the night before
but with his own face as proof—that he had stretched a truth for his
own purposes. That was the only time he had that expression.

"And the second thing? I don't know if you were right or not,
father of mine, about Kerry being a dyke." Oh hell, that was for her to
say, not me; I wasn't in the business of outing people. "But I can tell
you this with absolute certainty: I am. You'll have to deal." I paused
again, making sure I pinned him with my gaze. "You shouldn't be so
fucking jealous."

And while my mother's mouth dropped open in shock, she turned
to stare at him. Asshole. As if I couldn't tell that he didn't know what
bothered him more: that my mom was heartbroken because of her
perceived amputation from me, or because he thought the girl I might
be dating was hot too. Now he knew that I knew, too. I went into my
room and slammed the door.

Nanny said not a word to me, and I finally got the sleep that I had
earned, without further word or interruption from anyone—for a few
days.

The next night, Nicky had been given a new room—the entire
basement, complete with a lock on the door and its own entrance,
because a "man needed his privacy." And Nanny inherited his old
room—which already had a lock on it.

For the first time in my life, not counting the year I spent in a
crib, I had a room to myself, but I had no lock. The doorknob had to be
replaced, and I was no longer allowed to lock my door. Whatever.

I took all the money I had and divided it into piles of not much—
diddly divided by squat, in effect—one for school now, one for college,
one for the nebulous "future" when I'd have to pay rent, and I did go
talk with Sister Clarence about my tuition.

We worked out a deal, Sister Clarence and I, and yes, all that
experience I'd already had polishing and dusting came in very handy.
My tuition was reduced, though I did pay Sister some money every
month that I'd earned collecting cans, and though my gym bag smelled
like a brewery, not a word was said about swim fees to me for that year
or the next.

My uniforms, well, they looked ratty enough until a neighbor said
something to my mother, and my parents actually purchased new ones

for me—didn't want to look bad, you know.

I finally talked to Jack one day when he waited for me by the train station after school. I had sort of dropped off the face of the planet, what with school stuff, chores, and my odd jobs, and I rarely had a chance to use the phone. No one knew what was going on, and Joey, Kerry, and Jack just assumed it was because of the story Joey had told me.

Anyhow, that's how I found out the whole Jack-Kerry-Joey thing was a lie—figures. Kerry and Joey sent Jack to talk with me because they figured he was the one I'd be least likely to be mad at. Anyhow, it so happened that Joey and Jack had ended up making out that night after we'd gone to the city together, and while Jack did go to Kerry's that night—and not only am I still unclear on what happened, I don't care—Joey came up with that story to reinforce their machismo or some such stupidity, and they both figured Kerry would go along with it to protect all of their collective images, since they went to the same high school. And by the way? She did. What fuckin' bullshit. I've no respect for that.

Oh yeah, and Nicky and Nanny cornered me one day to tell me that they admired what I had done, but they wouldn't let what happened to me happen to them. "I'll lie, I'll tell them whatever they want to hear. I'm just gonna use them, get the money for school, and then I'm so fucking far out of here, they won't even be able to imagine me," Nicky swore, and Nanny nodded with him in agreement. They felt bad for me, and they felt our parents weren't being fair or right at all, and I had their silent support, but there would be no real help from that quarter.

I have to admit, I was shocked, disappointed even, by Nicky's reaction. I hadn't really expected anything different from Nanny. I guess I can't really blame them, though. I didn't want them to go through that either; I'd just hoped that it would be easier for them to do their own thing if they knew my parents had practiced parental indignation on me first, ya know? Oh well. So much for trying to lead by example.

And Nicky told me he had mentioned to my father he wasn't the Boyd Kerry would want when my father had teased him on their way to the men's room during dinner—see? I knew it, I just knew it!

Nicky was sorry for all the trouble his remark had caused. He'd told me he'd had no idea that our parental units would react that way—and it was stupid, anyway. "You know, how, like, the units always tell us we can talk to them about anything?" Nicky asked. "You think they knew what they were saying?"

I considered the question seriously. "Naw, Nicky, when they told us we could talk with them about anything," I grinned, "they meant we could talk about drugs, not sex."

Nicky laughed and smiled at me. "Yeah, well, maybe I'll just save all those questions for you. You've probably got a better handle on it anyway."

I blushed and chuckled with him. It felt good to share a laugh with my brother, to find the humor in everything that had happened and smile anyway.

Afterward, Nicky sobered in tone and expression. "Uh, Nina, um, are you, ah, going out with Kerry?" he asked me softly, looking me directly in the eye.

I just stared at him, not knowing what to say. Kerry and I, well, we had hung out, even made out a few times since things had gone down, but things were different, very different, and not just because of the sex thing, which we hadn't really done again—close to it maybe, but not really, just some make-out sessions that got a little outrageous, resulting in extra workouts and guitar practice for me. At least I was starting to improve as a guitarist.

Kerry ran hot and cold with me, playing the come-here-go-away game, and I, knowing she had been willing to play a part in Jack and Joey's story, wasn't very trusting, just occasionally hormonal, I guess. It was weird. We'd have these moments where it seemed like we couldn't wait to get away from each other, or at least, it seemed that we both felt like that, and other times, we were all over each other. But that weirdness would come back into play again, where we were so damned awkward with each other that we'd either say good-bye or start making out again.

And that wasn't really comfortable either, the making out or the hanging out. Every time I closed my eyes in Kerry's arms, trying to regain some of the feeling that we had shared, a memory of warmth pulled me away from the moment, and I would find myself thinking of Samantha and the clear blue of her eyes, or the way she smiled, or how her entire face showed the intensity of what she was thinking or feeling.

Were we dating, Kerry and I, I mean? In the world the way I understood it, you generally were dating people you made out with, and on the other hand, you actually went *out* with people you were dating, and except for occasional trips to the Village, we didn't really do anything else.

It wasn't like I had time to hang out or anything, anyway. I was now working part-time at Universe when I wasn't in school or practicing or studying, and I knew Nicky and Kerry had been hanging out together a lot since I wasn't around. I sighed. Might as well bite the bullet and answer the question. I looked at my hands again and took a deep breath.

"I guess, we're, ah, sort of seeing each other, I guess, I mean, we're not—" I stopped suddenly, understanding dawning on me as I watched Nicky's face. He liked Kerry, I could see it, and he was asking me for permission to ask her out. But this wasn't just a friend asking me, it was my brother, and I could never be jealous of my brother.

Besides, I didn't own Kerry, just as she didn't own me. I had no right to allow or deny anyone their own personal feelings or growth, and I suspected that maybe Kerry wanted to explore herself more. Nicky and I were so alike; we were like male and female bookends. Maybe Kerry wanted to comparison shop—or kiss.

"Go for it, Nicky," I grabbed his hand and told him. "If you really, really like her, ask her. It won't make me mad." I put my other hand on his shoulder. "It's okay. We don't own each other, me and Kerry, I mean," I explained to him, "and I wouldn't ever want to come between someone and what's in their heart." I smiled at him, and I meant it.

It was weird, but I was totally okay with the whole concept. I mean, Nicky was a good guy, and if he wanted to date Kerry, and she wanted to date him, well, it would be a good thing, for Kerry anyway. I had my reservations about whether or not it would be okay for Nicky, but I kept that to myself for the moment. I'd handle that issue in my own way, later.

"I, uh, didn't want to step on your toes or anything like that," Nicky said. "I just, well, I guess I was wondering if it's, like, a serious thing between you or if you both see other people."

And that's how Nicky and I ended up dating the same girl at the same time, for a little while anyway. After he asked her out, about a week or so later we were all out together at the movie theater (and no, this time we weren't going to see *The Rocky Horror Picture Show,* and yes, I had a date who was meeting me there—a friend, really, well, sort of—but that's not important right now, so don't worry about it). I took

Kerry to one side by the concession stand and told her bluntly, "Break his heart, and I'll break your face."

Kerry stared up at me in surprise. "Getting really butch, huh? I heard about what you did on the bus," she answered archly, and reached up to play with the collar of my jacket.

With the weather getting warmer and all, I'd stopped wearing my checked coat and starting wearing an old leather jacket, sort of an old-fashioned bikers' jacket that I'd picked up at a Salvation Army sale. Since I couldn't really get detentions anymore, and I'd stopped caring anyway, I wore it all the time, even with my uniform. I'd also started carrying a knife, but let's not get into that either.

One particular day about a week before, I'd decided to take the bus home instead of walking to the train, and I was sitting in the back, smoking illegally out the window on the crowded bus filled with students from schools all over Staten Island, which meant that there were more than a few rival schools all together on one public transportation unit—sort of like the United Nations, but without the fancy clothes or the funding.

Voices were loud and raucous as usual, and I ignored most of them until I heard a nasty tone and words float above the usual hubbub. "Look at this Hill kid—what a faggot, with that uniform and all those stupid books. All that red hair—you must be a flaming faggot, aren't you, froshie?" a girl's voice sneered out. "What are you reading, a million and one ways to be a geeky dyke?"

I threw my cigarette out the window, and without truly thinking about it, I was out of my seat and leaving my books behind. I stomped over to the source of that nasty, annoying voice. Right before the rear doors of the bus, I stood behind a girl with dark hair, sprayed way too high, who didn't see me between the crowd around us and her struggle to take a book away from the freshman she was torturing—who just so happened to be Betta.

I tapped the nasty on the shoulder. "Hey, why don't you stop now you've had your fun?" I asked her politely as she turned around, book in hand.

Betta looked up at me with big eyes, and I nodded at her with a little grin to let her know it was all going to be okay.

The chick before me had hair that was higher in the front than it had seemed from the back, and in pop-fashion cropped denim jacket and raccoon-eyed mascara, she glared at me.

"And what are you gonna do about it, dyke?" she sneered back at me, and poked my shoulder.

"Well, first I'm going to ask you to give her back her book," I said blandly, nodding in Betta's direction.

We all lurched a bit as the bus pulled into a stop.

"Don't listen to the dyke, Gina," someone called out; and Gina, I guess that's who she was, started to laugh. "Oh, that's rich. You're gonna ask me to give her book back," she drawled. "What if I just…" and she swung at me.

Oh, no way, man. You don't swing at me, and you especially don't swing at my face. There was a new fucking world order going on here, and I do not—ever—take kindly to bullies. I blocked and caught her wrist in my hand, using it to twist her around. "Oh no, honey. You give her the book back," I growled in her ear, "and you apologize." I waited while Gina stood silent. "Now!" I hissed at her, and gave her wrist a slight tug to emphasize our positions, in case I hadn't been clear before. "I'm not a freshman you can fuck around with."

Gina craned her neck over her shoulder to glance at me. "Geez, you Hill girls have no sense of humor. I was just joking with the little twerp."

I let her go and she handed the book back to Betta.

"Sorry. I was just messing with you," she told Betta, who took the book back and quickly tucked it securely into her book bag.

"It's cool," Betta said shortly, and looked down at her bag as I nodded my head.

"Cool," I said, and turned to ease back to my seat.

Catcalls went back and forth across the bus. "She got you, Gina. Yeah, Gee, prissy little schoolgirl showed you, girl," and so forth, so of course, you know, she couldn't just let it go.

"You and me, we're not done yet," Gina said to my back, and she grabbed my shoulder, spinning me around for an openhanded smack.

Didn't we just go through this? Sometimes people just don't get it. I ducked again, but this time, I brought my shoulder into her sternum, grabbed her shoulders, and shoved her the two feet over to the exit, down the three steps to the door. "Grow the fuck up," I told her as she leaned her back against the doors, breathing heavily and spitting fire.

She lunged back up at me again, but that's when the doors opened so I did the only logical thing: I shoved her through them. She fell backward onto the grass lining the bus stop, right on her ass.

Someone handed me a book bag, and I threw it at her chest.

She caught it and glared up at me. The doors to the bus closed in her face as she stood. "Fuck you!" she screamed at me.

I smiled my biggest and brightest, then waved to her through the glass with my best beauty-pageant imitation as we pulled away. I turned and climbed back up the steps through utter silence. Everyone suddenly seemed to have found interesting things to look at either on the floor or out the windows.

"You okay?" I asked Betta as I passed her.

"Yeah, thanks, Razor," she answered, her face almost as red as her hair, and she gave me a small grin and a thumbs-up.

"No problem," I answered with a small quirk of my mouth. My plan was to get back to my seat, bury myself in a book, and not come out of it until we hit my bus stop by Universe, where I was working that afternoon.

"I'm going to call your principal," a snotty voice piped up behind me, just as I reached my seat.

I'd heard that before. In fact, there probably wasn't a student at the school who hadn't, and believe me, people did—call the school, I mean—telling the principal we'd been smoking, or rolling our skirts up, or wearing our sweaters without the blazers.

I turned around and found the source of the voice, another pop-crop denimed raccoon-eyed girl, and I looked her up and down. "You be sure you do that." Funny—wasn't she the girl who had handed me Gina's books? I turned back to my seat and sat down. A thought struck me, and I leaned forward in the girl's direction. "Oh, by the way? It's Boyd. That's Bee. Oh. Wye. Dee. Make sure you spell it right when you call Sister Clarence, you know, the principal?" I told her conversationally, then settled back in to get in a good read.

That's the story that Kerry had heard; it must have made the rounds. I suppose it wasn't every day that a Hill girl got into something resembling a fight. And by the way? If the girl did call the school, I never heard a thing about it.

"So, you've decided you're gonna be a fuckin' hero?" Kerry drawled.

Her fingertips glanced along my neck, but I shrugged myself away from her. She was out with my brother, not me, and I wasn't going to play that game. "Whatever, Kerry," I answered, irritated. "Look. I don't care what you do to me. Don't hurt my brother, I fuckin' mean it." I was dead serious, looking her straight in the eye.

She stared right back, then dropped her gaze. "I get you, Nina, I get you," she said softly to the floor, and then looked back up at me. We watched each other, then she glided into my zone and placed her palm against my chest.

Gently, I took her hand and moved it, and we slowly shuffled forward in the line for popcorn and soda (extra salt and butter-flavored oil substance with a Coca-Cola for me, thanks. Accept no substitutes).

"I'm not Nicky," I reminded her softly, looking down into those cat green eyes, "and you're out with him tonight." A decision formed in my head, and I put Kerry's hand down. I actually backed up a step or, at least, as far as I could without banging into the person behind me. "I'm going to make this easy on you, babe," I said seriously, and Kerry turned again to look at my eyes. "You're out with Nicky, not me. Let's just put a hold on this whole thing, okay? You figure out what you want, and then we'll talk about it, okay? I think you've got a little too much to deal with."

Kerry arched an eyebrow at me. "Jealous?" she smirked, and reached a hand up to my collar again.

I deflected it in irritation. I was starting to get annoyed, I can't really explain why. But I did seriously check myself for a moment—was I jealous? "No," I answered flatly and honestly. "I'm not that kind of person. I just don't want your confusion to become my confusion."

We were finally at the front of the line and waiting for the next "customer service representative."

"You're dumping me?" Kerry asked me with surprise and anger in her voice.

I squirmed a bit uncomfortably. This wasn't really the way I'd planned for the conversation to go, and I definitely did not want to have it in the crowded concession area.

"Dude," I said, "we weren't, you know, it's just—"

"*Next!*" bellowed the voice of the next friendly and capable counter person, and I was saved from having to answer as Kerry went to place her order.

It was my turn seconds later, down at the other end of the counter, and when I was done, I turned to make my way to the door of the theater. Kerry took a few seconds longer with her order, and I politely waited for her.

"We'll talk more about this, after the movie," Kerry said, peering at me over the huge box of popcorn she had precariously balanced on top of two humongo sodas.

"There's not a lot to talk about, Maggie, and especially not tonight," I replied, deliberately using that nickname. I don't know what made me do that. "We can talk about this some other time." I turned to grab the door to the auditorium with my free hand when I heard someone call my name.

"Hey, Nina! Glad I found you!"

I turned back and found a pair of smiling brown eyes shining in my direction. Wavy honey blond hair now came past her shoulders, which were covered in a varsity jacket, navy blue wool body and white leather arms, complete with swim insignia and the "C" for captain on the left breast and "Kitt" in script across the left.

"Hey, Fran." I smiled back.

You didn't think I was going to ask Samantha, did you? Actually, I had wanted to, but she had to go interview at some college, and besides, remember the last time Samantha and Kerry met? I wanted to leave the theater in good repair when the movie was done.

Besides, Fran was cool. Something had snapped back to normal between Fran and Samantha, and sometimes we all hung out together after Samantha gave me driving lessons. In fact, Fran actually let me drive her car sometimes, since she did live only a few minutes away, and it was fun getting to know her outside of the pool.

Kerry turned to see who it was as well and gave me an angry but amused look. "Another shark, Nina. Seems like you've got a bit of a bite yourself," she murmured in an undertone as Fran strode over.

"Hey," Fran greeted and gave me a quick hug, which I returned one-handed, "y'all got seats?"

"Yeah, my brother Nicky's saving them for us. He's in the auditorium." I waved in Kerry's direction. "This is Kerry, a friend of mine. She's Nicky's date."

"Nice to meet you, Kerry. I'm Kitt." I arched an eyebrow, and she shrugged. "But you can call me Fran." The glance Kerry shot me was one of pure venom, which she quickly changed into a smile as she looked back at Fran. "I'm sure I'm pleased. Nice jacket." There was that silence I'd learned to recognize, then Kerry opened her mouth again. "You going to let Nina wear it sometime?"

Ooh, was it just me, or did I feel the temperature drop? Okay, well, time to watch the movie, right? Right. I reached for the door again. "Okay, well, let's go find Nicky and get our seats," and I held the door as Kerry and Fran filed past me.

But I heard Fran respond in an undertone to Kerry as I walked behind them. "Nina doesn't need mine, 'cause she's earned one of her own, complete with her own letter *C* and everything," and at that, Kerry hurried in front of Fran to find Nicky and our seats.

Fran glanced back at me and grinned, and I grinned in return.

"Really?" I mouthed at her.

"Really," she affirmed with a nod and a smile as I caught up to her. "It's supposed to be a surprise, a gift from the team at the award dinner next Friday. You did know you're slated to be captain, along with Mad Max, didn't you? The team voted the week you were out, uh…" She paused, uncertain. I'd told Fran nothing about what had happened between my parents and me, and I didn't know what, if anything, Samantha might have said, but I do know that a lot of those bruises were visible for days, if not weeks, like my hair. "…sick, and both Coach Robbins and Sister approved the vote. Even Mad Max voted for you," she added, her smile standing out as the lights started to dim.

I felt the grin on my own face widen. I had nothing to say, just, well, wow.

"C'mon, Razor. Let's go sit and watch the movie. One of those for me?" She indicated the two sodas I had in a tray, over which I'd balanced the not-large-enough-to-feed-a-continent-but-large-enough-for-a-family-of-four popcorn.

"Oh yeah, take one," I offered distractedly. Wow. I was going to be a team captain. The team got me a jacket. Just, well, wow, again.

"Don't let anyone know it's not a surprise, though," Fran cautioned me. I was still in a daze. Team captain with Mad Max. Wow.

Fran ended up leading me to our seats, and as we settled down in the semidarkness, I lost myself in thought over all that had happened during the past several weeks, the changes in my life, in my family, such as it was. I didn't really know what the future would bring, but I felt free and light somehow. I was still on my own, but I knew that some way I'd find a way through. I had friends, I had what was in my head, I had me. Hey, I was going to be a team captain, after all.

CHAPTER THIRTEEN:
UNDER THE MILKY WAY TONIGHT

S o, what else do you want to know? This is the stuff that's running through my head while I wait to go onstage for the band's and my chance to sweat it all out and see what'll happen, while Trace runs her hands up and down my body.

I got my driver's license, and on the first shot, too, thankyouverymuch, and I went to both my junior and senior proms with Jimmy Dolings. I even went to Joey's senior prom, along with Kerry and Jack. I couldn't turn Joey down when he asked, and it wasn't too bad, and no, Kerry and I did not end up making out or anything.

I cried like hell when I got home after Samantha and Fran's graduation in the beginning of June, though I smiled and clapped louder than anyone there, happy for them both.

Samantha was supposed to go away on a trip to Europe with her uncle, and we were going to hang out when she got back in the middle of July—in fact, we were going to meet up at the annual beach party— but after receiving a few postcards, I didn't hear from her. The number had been disconnected when I called, and when I drove by her house, I saw a large for-sale sign on the lawn in front of an obviously empty house. I still have those postcards somewhere.

I dogged out the "living conditions" set for me at "home" during my senior year and took my SAT, with pretty good results if I do say so myself, and even though I was working full time, overtime, all the time, I made myself free to go to the "Everyone's Birthday in July" party.

I walked down to the water before the sun went completely down and just looked out over the endless expanse, thinking about the first time I'd been there, and how different it was, I was, how much had changed, how Samantha wasn't with me this time, but the ocean still was.

"She called, you know," Nicky said softly behind me, and I turned to face him, salt spray still on my face. I said nothing, just waited for him to catch up with me, then I faced the water again. Nicky put an arm around my shoulders, and I slid one around his waist. I leaned my head on his shoulder—Nicky had finally caught up with me in height. Amazing how insightful he'd grown, too.

"Samantha?"

"Yeah, about two, maybe three weeks after she graduated," he affirmed in just as soft a tone. "Dad answered the phone, asked who wanted to speak to you, because you were working. He told her you were dead and never to call his house again. He hung up before I could pick up on another line." His voice was quietly bitter.

A moment passed.

"I'm so sorry, Nee," Nicky whispered, and his arm squeezed around me, "I should have told you then—I know she meant a lot to you—I just couldn't stand to see them go after you like that again."

I knew he meant my parents and I squeezed back wordlessly; there was nothing to say. He was right—it would have started a huge fight for me with my parents, because I would have been furious.

It's funny. It had taken me a while to figure out that Samantha had planned on asking me out that night after our big meet. No wonder she'd been so flipped out about Kerry. But now, I didn't even know where Samantha was going to school; we'd been going to discuss it—that and other things, like our maybe actually dating each other—when she got back. Had I known she'd tried to get in touch with me, I don't know what I would have done, but I would have done something, and maybe, just maybe, we'd be standing in that water together. My mind spun with the pain of lost potential, and in a blank shock, I let the sun sting my eyes as it sank behind the waves.

I still miss Samantha sometimes, but I've learned not to think about her too much. It's a very strange ache the thought of her brings me, and when I do think of her, it's with a very full and warm heart.

Kerry and I finally drifted completely apart over time. My music took me in one direction, and her wildness and predilection for trouble took her in another. Like I mentioned quite a while ago, I don't do drugs and, knock wood, never will.

Surprisingly (okay, actually, not at all), she and Nicky didn't really last past that first date, and though she and I saw each other on and off, things were never the same. The fact that she'd been willing to participate in the kind of lie she and the boys had concocted really rubbed me raw, even though I'd been willing enough to let bygones be bygones so Joey would have a date for the prom, and besides, what I'd told her was true: I didn't want her confusion to become mine.

But still, we knew a lot of the same people, and I had news of her from time to time—not that it was anything ever really newsworthy, just the usual garbage. She was dating someone new, dumped a boy for a girl, a girl for a boy, cheating, drunk, or crazy.

Fran, on the other hand, I'd run into a few months ago at a club I was filling in at as a DJ. Of course, one of the first things I'd asked was if she ever spoke with Samantha, and Fran told me that the last she'd heard from Sammy Blade was a letter a few years ago. A rumor had been going around that I was dead, and as far as she knew, Samantha had stayed in Europe to study botany or alchemy or history, but she, Fran, was in her last year of law school at Columbia—and could she buy me a drink? I accepted, and beyond that, let's just say we hang out sometimes.

Yeah, I learned to really play guitar. It's a lesbian requirement or something, but I have to say for the record, I did it before it was fashionable.

College? Me? Well, it's a long, sad story. Suffice it to say, I did get an academic scholarship to NYU (and before y'all start comparing me to someone else, let me stop you now), but I couldn't take it. I couldn't afford to go to school and pay rent, and with a couple of "fuck-you" moves thrown in by my ever-loving parents, I lost that opportunity. 'Sokay, I ended up at a local college. I haven't finished yet, 'cuz I finally moved out and have to be my own version of a grown-up—pay rent and stuff—but someday I'll get there.

Right now, I'm a musician in a band, waiting to test the waters and enjoying my life, the occasional angst notwithstanding.

Trace's hands work magic on my shoulders, and her lips stir my blood as she presses them against my neck. Suddenly, I'm struck with a sense of familiarity, of presence, and it disturbs me. I sit up straight, removing myself from Trace's embrace.

"'Smatter, baby? You okay?" Trace asks in throaty concern, her hands reaching to pull me back into her.

I run my hand distractedly through my hair, making it stand up higher. "Yeah, I'm fine," I tell her, and smile as reassuringly as I can.

"Pre-performance anxiety. I'm just gonna get some air." I stand up, make my way through the press of bodies to the door, and step outside.

It's a cool night for April, but I stand outside anyway and let the breath of the city brush over my face, alive and vibrant as always. I breathe in that energy as deeply as I can, and I look up at the night sky, right there on the Bowery, and let my breath out slowly. Just above the reddish black skyline, because for some reason that's what the sky looks like at night sometimes in Manhattan, I can make out a few stars. I make a wordless prayer to the universe, not really knowing what I'm praying for or who I'm praying to, just please, please, please, this time, please.

Enough communing with the cosmos. It'll soon be time to hit the stage.

I'll tell you something. In rock and roll, no one really cares about anyone but themselves, and by that I mean unless you're friends with another band, you don't usually stay to watch them play, unless they're going on before you and you have to wait.

We're the last act on the bill tonight, and believe me when I tell you that it's no small feat to have a big crowd on the worst night during the worst time slot of the week—and have the two bands that precede us stay to watch and rock along, and baby? It's magic—we're magic.

We run through our set, and the crowd gets wilder and wilder. By the end, when we've finished all of our material, they still want more, and we repeat the set—to enthusiastic cheers.

It's incredible, the feeling of communion with the music, with each other, with the audience. No words exist to describe it—the overflowing, humbling, beautiful feeling, the power and the passion, the certain knowledge of the immanent, the ineffable, the divine, channeled and flowing through you to the band, to the audience and back again, a complete circle, part of the dance, part of the whole.

The applause is very sweet when we're finally allowed to stop, and there's much backslapping and congratulating as we disassemble our equipment and make our way down from the stage.

We're offered another gig by the sound guy, who's none other than Ronnie the Bouncer Boy from all that time ago with Kerry, only now he has a long-in-front crew cut, and his beard is trimmed in a military style. I don't ask if he remembers me; it's enough that I do, and the memory makes me smile.

I quietly pack my guitar and equipment, and Nicky comes rushing over.

"My God, you guys are fantastic! I always knew you were good, but wow!" He hugs me and lifts me off the ground.

"Thanks, bro, thanks," I laugh as he spins me around, "Nicky, you can put me down now before I—yelp!"

Nicky slings me over his shoulder and starts to bounce me up and down. "Hey, I'm your little brother and it's Nico, remember? Be nice!" he teases as he bounces.

He's right, everyone's been calling him "Nico," as in "nee-ko," for a while now and I promise myself for the umpteenth time that I'll remember it, but right now I'm going to puke, I swear, and the feeling from the stage is rapidly decreasing as the nausea increases. "Nico, I'm going to puke very nicely and neatly down the back of your shirt if you don't stop soon," I manage to gasp out between jolts.

"Sorry, sis," Nicky, um, Nico, says, not at all repentant as he puts me down. He gestures to straighten my clothes out and down, and I playfully smack his hands away.

"No, no, you've done enough, thanks. I'm going to go get something to drink. Watch my guitar, okay?" I ask him, and I hear him agree as I walk away.

My head's buzzing, and I need to get clear, get a grip, get some focus. I'm also parched—a two-hour performance is exhausting, believe me.

I nod polite thanks to the people who come up to compliment the band and make my way over to the bar, which is now rather empty. Most people are still up front, by the stage. I get the bartender's attention. "Water?" I ask, and he nods.

Trace comes up to me out of nowhere, grabs my head, and plants a solid smooch on my lips. "That was great, baby, just great!" she breathes, and kisses me again.

Oh, those lips are baby soft, but I'm tired and fuzzy, and the kiss I return is sincere, but just as tired. "Thanks, Trace, really. I'm just going to get something wet. I'll be back by the stage in a minute, okay?"

Trace studies my face with concern in her own, then smiles. "No problem, Nina, no problem. Sit here a moment, get your drink, I'm gonna hang with Nico and the rest of the band, and I'll see you in a few." She kisses my cheek again and strolls away, and I turn back to the bar.

The bartender finally comes back over with my glass of water, and I sip it in silence, head blank and muzzy from the show. Again I'm struck by that sense of, I don't know what, something, but I shake my head and dismiss it. Probably a result of stage anxiety and postshow blues, I tell myself.

Someone comes and sits next to me, but I ignore them, focusing alternately on my water glass and the wall in front of me, without really looking at either. Out of the corner of my eye, I see an arm raise to signal the bartender. He nods in acknowledgment, then goes back to whatever he was doing, drying dishes or something.

Finally, he slides a beer over, money hits the bar, and the person leaves. I don't care—I'm just going to finish this water, then get my ass back to my guitar. I toss my head back and the water down. I can feel its coolness radiating through my body, and it's a welcome feeling. I hold the smooth glass in my hand longer, enjoying its texture, then set it back down on the bar, and as I do so, something catches my eye.

It isn't money on the counter like I'd originally thought—it's a coiled jewelry chain, with a shiny and worn miniature sword attached to it. I stare at it dumbfounded while my head roars with the sound of the surf in storm. I reach down with a tentative hand to touch it and suddenly someone's behind me, so close I can almost feel the heat radiating from their body. I feel them lean over me, whisper in my ear.

"I don't like your girlfriend," says a voice I can't believe I'm hearing.

I gently, unbelievingly, close my fingers around that shiny little piece of silver, sit up straight, and carefully push my seat back. "She's not my girlfriend," I answer with a steadiness I don't feel. I put both hands against the edge of the bar to balance myself as I stand up.

This will be a hell of a dream to share with my roommates tomorrow; I think to myself, I must be losing it. I've never read anywhere that this is a part of the post-performance reaction. And if this is a joke? It isn't fucking funny.

I make myself turn around, to face who or what's behind me, and my heart hammers in my chest like it had before the show, but with a shakiness that hadn't been there earlier.

I raise my head and look straight into eyes that are the blue of the water under moonlight and a smile like the sun breaking through the clouds on a stormy day.

I open my arms wide and am enfolded next to a heart that thuds against mine. "Welcome home," I choke out as tears come to my eyes for the first time in years. "Welcome home."

About the Author

JD Glass lives in the city of her choice and birth, New York, with her beloved partner. When she's not writing, she's the lead singer/guitarist in Life Underwater, which also keeps her pretty darn busy. JD spent three years writing the semimonthly *Vintage News*, a journal about all sorts of neat collectible guitars, basses, and other fretted string instruments, and also wrote *Water, Water Everywhere*, an illustrated text and guide about water in the human body, for the famous Children's Museum Water Exhibit. When not creating something (she swears she's way too busy to ever be bored), she sleeps. Right. Oh, and she's what Dilbert would call "a sexy engineer." She is hard at work on the forthcoming sequel, *Punk and Zen*.

Look for information at www.boldstrokesbooks.com.

Books Available From Bold Strokes Books

Wild Abandon by Ronica Black. From their first tumultuous meeting, Dr. Chandler Brogan and Officer Sarah Monroe are drawn together by their common obsessions—sex, speed, and danger. (1-933110-35-X)

Turn Back Time by Radclyffe. Pearce Rifkin and Wynter Thompson have nothing in common but a shared passion for surgery. They clash at every opportunity, especially when matters of the heart are suddenly at stake. (1-933110-34-1)

Chance by Grace Lennox. At twenty-six, Chance Delaney decides her life isn't working so she swaps it for a different one. What follows is the sexy, funny, touching story of two women who, in finding themselves, also find one another. (1-933110-31-7)

The Exile and the Sorcerer by Jane Fletcher. First in the Lyremouth Chronicles. Tevi, wounded and adrift, arrives in the courtyard of a shy young sorcerer. Together they face monsters, magic, and the challenge of loving despite their differences. (1-933110-32-5)

A Matter of Trust by Radclyffe. JT Sloan is a cybersleuth who doesn't like attachments. Michael Lassiter is leaving her husband, and she needs Sloan's expertise to safeguard her company. It should just be business—but it turns into much more. (1-933110-33-3)

Sweet Creek by Lee Lynch. A celebration of the enduring nature of love, friendship, and community in the quirky, heart-warming lesbian community of Waterfall Falls. (1-933110-29-5)

The Devil Inside by Ali Vali. Derby Cain Casey, head of a New Orleans crime organization, runs the family business with guts and grit, and no one crosses her. No one, that is, until Emma Verde claims her heart and turns her world upside down. (1-933110-30-9)

Grave Silence by Rose Beecham. Detective Jude Devine's investigation of a series of ritual murders is complicated by her torrid affair with the golden girl of Southwestern forensic pathology, Dr. Mercy Westmoreland. (1-933110-25-2)

Honor Reclaimed by Radclyffe. In the aftermath of 9/11, Secret Service Agent Cameron Roberts and Blair Powell close ranks with a trusted few to find the would-be assassins who nearly claimed Blair's life. (1-933110-18-X)

Honor Bound by Radclyffe. Secret Service Agent Cameron Roberts and Blair Powell face political intrigue, a clandestine threat to Blair's safety, and the seemingly irreconcilable personal differences that force them ever farther apart. (1-933110-20-1)

Protector of the Realm: Supreme Constellations Book One by Gun Brooke. A space adventure filled with suspense and a daring intergalactic romance featuring Commodore Rae Jacelon and the stunning, but decidedly lethal, Kellen O'Dal. (1-933110-26-0)

Innocent Hearts by Radclyffe. In a wild and unforgiving land, two women learn about love, passion, and the wonders of the heart. (1-933110-21-X)

The Temple at Landfall by Jane Fletcher. An imprinter, one of Celaeno's most revered servants of the Goddess, is also a prisoner to the faith—until a Ranger frees her by claiming her heart. The Celaeno series. (1-933110-27-9)

Force of Nature by Kim Baldwin. From tornados to forest fires, the forces of nature conspire to bring Gable McCoy and Erin Richards close to danger, and closer to each other. (1-933110-23-6)

In Too Deep by Ronica Black. Undercover homicide cop Erin McKenzie tracks a femme fatale who just might be a real killer...with love and danger hot on her heels. (1-933110-17-1)

Stolen Moments: *Erotic Interludes 2* by Stacia Seaman and Radclyffe, eds. Love on the run, in the office, in the shadows...Fast, furious, and almost too hot to handle. (1-933110-16-3)

Course of Action by Gun Brooke. Actress Carolyn Black desperately wants the starring role in an upcoming film produced by Annelie Peterson. Just how far will she go for the dream part of a lifetime? (1-933110-22-8)

Rangers at Roadsend by Jane Fletcher. Sergeant Chip Coppelli has learned to spot trouble coming, and that is exactly what she sees in her new recruit, Katryn Nagata. The Celaeno series. (1-933110-28-7)

Justice Served by Radclyffe. Lieutenant Rebecca Frye and her lover, Dr. Catherine Rawlings, embark on a deadly game of hide-and-seek with an underworld kingpin who traffics in human souls. (1-933110-15-5)

Distant Shores, Silent Thunder by Radclyffe. Dr. Tory King—along with the women who love her—is forced to examine the boundaries of love, friendship, and the ties that transcend time. (1-933110-08-2)

Hunter's Pursuit by Kim Baldwin. A raging blizzard, a mountain hideaway, and a killer-for-hire set a scene for disaster—or desire—when Katarzyna Demetrious rescues a beautiful stranger. (1-933110-09-0)

The Walls of Westernfort by Jane Fletcher. All Temple Guard Natasha Ionadis wants is to serve the Goddess—until she falls in love with one of the rebels she is sworn to destroy. The Celaeno series. (1-933110-24-4)

Change Of Pace: *Erotic Interludes* by Radclyffe. Twenty-five hot-wired encounters guaranteed to spark more than just your imagination. Erotica as you've always dreamed of it. (1-933110-07-4)

Honor Guards by Radclyffe. In a wild flight for their lives, the president's daughter and those who are sworn to protect her wage a desperate struggle for survival. (1-933110-01-5)

Fated Love by Radclyffe. Amidst the chaos and drama of a busy emergency room, two women must contend not only with the fragile nature of life, but also with the irresistible forces of fate. (1-933110-05-8)

Justice in the Shadows by Radclyffe. In a shadow world of secrets and lies, Detective Sergeant Rebecca Frye and her lover, Dr. Catherine Rawlings, join forces in the elusive search for justice. (1-933110-03-1)

shadowland by Radclyffe. In a world on the far edge of desire, two women are drawn together by power, passion, and dark pleasures. An erotic romance. (1-933110-11-2)

Love's Masquerade by Radclyffe. Plunged into the indistinguishable realms of fiction, fantasy, and hidden desires, Auden Frost is forced to question all she believes about the nature of love. (1-933110-14-7)

Love & Honor by Radclyffe. The president's daughter and her lover are faced with difficult choices as they battle a tangled web of Washington intrigue for...love and honor. (1-933110-10-4)

Beyond the Breakwater by Radclyffe. One Provincetown summer, three women learn the true meaning of love, friendship, and family. (1-933110-06-6)

Tomorrow's Promise by Radclyffe. One timeless summer, two very different women discover the power of passion to heal and the promise of hope that only love can bestow. (1-933110-12-0)

Love's Tender Warriors by Radclyffe. Two women who have accepted loneliness as a way of life learn that love is worth fighting for and a battle they cannot afford to lose. (1-933110-02-3)

Love's Melody Lost by Radclyffe. A secretive artist with a haunted past and a young woman escaping a life that has proved to be a lie find their destinies entwined. (1-933110-00-7)

Safe Harbor by Radclyffe. A mysterious newcomer, a reclusive doctor, and a troubled gay teenager learn about love, friendship, and trust during one tumultuous summer in Provincetown. (1-933110-13-9)

Above All, Honor by Radclyffe. Secret Service Agent Cameron Roberts fights her desire for the one woman she can't have—Blair Powell, the daughter of the president of the United States. (1-933110-04-X)